Katie Mettner wears the title of 'the only person to lose her leg after falling down the bunny hill' and loves decorating her prosthetic leg to fit the season. She lives in Northern Wisconsin with her own happily-ever-after and spends the day writing romantic stories with her sweet puppy by her side. Katie has an addiction to coffee and dachshunds and a lessening aversion to Pinterest—now that she's quit trying to make the things she pins.

USA Today bestselling author **Kacy Cross** writes romance novels starring swoonworthy heroes and smart heroines. She lives in Texas, where she's seen bobcats and beavers near her house but sadly not one cowboy. She's raising two mini-ninjas alongside the love of her life, who cooks while she writes, which is her definition of a true hero. Come for the romance, stay for the happily-ever-after. She promises her books 'will make you laugh, cry and swoon—cross my heart.'

GW00702153

HOLIDAY UNDER WRAPS

KATIE METTNER

BODYGUARD RANCHER

KACY CROSS

MILLS & BOON

First Published in Great Britain 2024
by Mills & Boon, an imprint of HarperCollins*Publishers* Ltd
1 London Bridge Street, London, SE1 9GF

www.harpercollins.co.uk

HarperCollins*Publishers*
Macken House, 39/40 Mayor Street Upper,
Dublin 1, D01 C9W8, Ireland

Holiday Under Wraps © 2024 Katie Mettner
Bodyguard Rancher © 2024 Kacy Cross

ISBN: 978-0-263-32259-0

1224

This book contains FSC™ certified paper and other controlled sources to ensure responsible forest management.

For more information visit: www.harpercollins.co.uk/green

Printed and Bound in the UK using 100% Renewable Electricity at CPI Group (UK) Ltd, Croydon, CR0 4YY

HOLIDAY UNDER WRAPS

KATIE METTNER

For the 'Jameses' of the world. It takes someone
special to do what you do. Thank you.

For the supply chain managers.
You truly are unsung heroes.

Chapter One

"Hey, there, Lilah," a voice said.

She smiled as she turned to him. "Luca. Where have you been?"

"Reloading our water and campfire supply. Did you find anything?"

"Sea glass," Delilah said, holding her hand out to show him a broken piece of pottery. It was worn smooth from tumbling around in the lake for years.

"Your favorite," he said, taking her hand and pulling her into a dance pose as he rocked her back and forth on the sand. "What will you do with all that sea glass, Lilah?"

"I don't know," she whispered, gazing into his eyes. "Maybe I'll make art from it to always remember the summer we turned twenty-eight."

"I hope you won't need the sea glass to remember." Luca lowered his magical lips to hers and kissed her like a man in love. While they had never said the words, they didn't need to. Their bodies did the talking. "I hope to be by your side the summer we turn sixty-eight." He spun her around in a wide arc until they toppled to the sand, where they stayed, laughing as Lake Superior lapped over them and the sun shone down to dry them.

"Luca, you're the kind of guy my daddy would have wanted me to bring home. I know it."

"You think so? I thought your daddy was strict about everything, including his little girl dating."

"Oh, he'd hate that I left the church and went to war, but he'd have loved you."

"Since he's been dead for twenty years, I guess I'll have to take your word for it."

"I've been thinking, Luca."

"Uh-oh. It's never good when a woman opens with that line."

Delilah rolled up onto her arm to look him in the eye. "You won't think it's good, but I made a phone call yesterday while picking up groceries."

"Who did you call?" His words dripped with defensive dread.

"The VA hospital in Minneapolis. It turns out they have a program there that helps veterans with PTSD."

"I don't need a shrink!" His growled exclamation should have made her pull back, but she was past that fear. Delilah knew he'd never hurt her, but he might hurt himself. She couldn't let that happen.

"It's not just a shrink, Luca. It's talking to other people in your situation and developing ways to channel your anxiety so you can live in the world as it is now."

"My PTSD isn't any worse than yours, Lilah." His words were soft this time, and he caressed her face as though she would drop the conversation and fall into bed with him. In the past, she might have, but with his episodes escalating, she couldn't put off the hard stuff any longer.

"But it is, Luca, and it's okay to admit that. We had different experiences that did different things to our minds.

I can't wake up to find you in the middle of Lake Superior again. Not when I know there are people who can help you."

"Will you go, too?"

"If you want me to," she agreed, even though it was a lie. "I'll do anything if it means you get help before it's too late."

"How long do I have to be there?"

"I can't answer that question, Luca. That's up to you and the doctors to decide, but from what I understand, it's usually one to three months."

He gathered handfuls of the warm September sand as he stared at the cloudless Wisconsin sky. "I don't want our time here to end, Lilah. When I'm here, I can forget what happened over there. When I'm holding you, I can forget about the men who—"

What was that music? It was familiar, and Delilah Hartman was supposed to remember what to do when she heard it. Her eyes popped open and she grabbed her glasses, slipping them on to stare at the phone screen.

You've been found.

Technically, that's not what the screen said, but she knew that's what it meant. Her gaze flicked to the time at the top of the phone. It was 2:37 a.m. Not a great time of day to tuck tail and run, but she didn't know if she had five minutes or five hours until someone started breaking down her door, so she couldn't worry about anything other than getting out undetected.

She slid out from under the covers and stayed low below the level of the windows. Her go bag was packed and easily accessible, something she made sure of every night before bed. Her only decision was how to exit the apartment. It was the start of December, cold, and the recent snow was going to make footprints easy to follow. She could walk out the front door as though everything was fine and it was any other early Wednesday morning, climb in her car and drive away, or opt for escape via the balcony. She'd rented this apartment for the balcony. Beyond it was a forest as far as the eye could see, giving her a place to disappear as soon as she made the tree line. This escape would be the eighth in six years. It was a habit she didn't like, and as she tied on a pair of boots, slid into her winter gear and slung the go bag around her shoulders, the truth settled low in her gut. She couldn't do this alone any longer, but the only man who could help her lived somewhere in the middle of northern Minnesota. The one thing she knew for sure was that she wasn't a Christmas present he'd be happy about unwrapping.

Then again, maybe he would be.

Delilah wondered how Lucas would feel about her popping back into his life unexpectedly after disappearing six years ago. He was probably angry that she'd dropped him off at the VA Medical Center and never returned. That wasn't by choice. If he wasn't angry with her, that would quickly change if she brought a passel of bad guys along with her, so she had to be thoughtful about her approach. None of that mattered if she didn't successfully escape from 679 North Bradley Street in one piece.

Her fingers found the scar on her chin and traced it while she rechecked the app. They had just broken the code and accessed her information, so there was no way they'd be here this quickly. She had time to walk down the stairs, get in her car and drive away. She'd abandon the car at the airport and hop on a plane. When she did, Lavena Hanson would cease to exist. The same way all those other names had over the years. Whether she liked it or not, it was time to be Delilah Hartman again if she ever wanted to live a normal life. Not that she could even define what a normal life was anymore. Normal ended the day she signed up for the army. What a lousy life decision that turned out to be. Not that she had many options. After her father died, her mother struggled to make ends meet, much less pay for college. Enlisting was a way to get her education paid for and come out with real-world work experience. Delilah couldn't argue with that. She'd gotten the necessary experience, but she couldn't use it if she wanted to stay alive. Not exactly what she'd had in mind as a fresh-faced army recruit.

Crouched low, she snuck out of the bedroom into the sparse main room of the apartment. The one-bedroom upper had been the perfect place for her when she'd found it nearly five months ago, but she knew better than to do anything but live in it like a hotel room. A stopover on the road of life. She'd been disappointed the first time she'd had to leave a place she'd made her home and promised herself she'd steer clear of using that word again. She patted the fridge on her way by, which held her only decorations for the holidays. Magnets in the shape of Christmas ornaments covered the front of it in holiday cheer. They'd remain there now for someone else to enjoy.

Delilah had her hand on the doorknob when she heard a commotion in the hallway. "Hey, man, you don't belong here," came her neighbor's muffled voice through the front door. She peered through the peephole, and her insides congealed with fear at the scene in the hallway. There was a man dressed in black with a gun, and behind him was the man who fueled her nightmares. He'd come again, and by the looks of the knife in his hand, he meant business this time.

She heard the *pop-pop* and was running for the balcony before she even registered that her neighbor had just been shot. *Don't die. Don't die.* She hummed to herself as she silently cut the screen and slithered down the rope tied to the balcony post for this very purpose. She hit the ground quietly, flipped her night vision goggles down, a throwback to her military days, and searched the grounds for signs of life.

Movement to her left caught her eye. The dude was in black head to toe but had his back to her as he faced the front of the building. Slowly, she turned her head to the right and saw another guy dressed the same at the opposite end of the building. Unfortunately, they were wearing night vision goggles, too, which meant she wasn't undetectable. She pulled her pistol from her holster and steeled herself. She had to make a run for it, but she had to do it right if she didn't want to be caught in the crossfire. She also didn't want more innocent people to die here tonight. Her bullets had to find their marks for multiple reasons, the least of which was this snow was going to make it easy to track her. Shooting on the run was always hard, but she had no choice. A part of her brain registered that this was the first time they'd sent more than two guys. Maybe that meant something, maybe it didn't, but she didn't have time to dwell on it if she wanted to stay alive. Her concentration could be nowhere but on getting to the trees.

A deep, steadying breath in and she ran, her movement catching their attention, as expected. The guy to her left turned first, and the pop of her gun had him on the ground before he got off a round. Unfortunately, the guy on her right heard the shot and swung his gun in an arc toward her. By the time his buddy hit the ground, she was already firing. Dude number two crumpled, and she turned tail, slid through the trees and ran like the hounds of hell were on her heels.

DEATH. NOT AN easy word to wrap a person's head around, especially when no one can escape it. At the same time, very few people live like they know that. Lucas Porter wasn't one of those people. He had intimate knowledge of how swiftly death came and held no illusions that he had any control over it. Lucas agreed with the idea that when it's your time, it's your time, but he didn't agree with the old saying that someone *cheated* death. No. No one ever *cheats* death. It simply wasn't their day to die. He'd seen it on the battlefield so many times. Days when three men rode side by side, an IED exploded and two died, but one was unscathed just inches away. That soldier didn't cheat death. He had something left to do before death took him. And it took everyone.

Lucas saw death enough times that he made the conscious decision to live every day like he was dying. He wasn't afraid of death, knowing it was inevitable, so he also made every effort not to leave anything unresolved in life. Unresolved situations only hurt the living, and Lucas never wanted to put that on anyone's shoulders. He carried some of those situations and feelings that could never be resolved as anyone does, but those memories were motivation not to create more.

He could accept those unresolved situations as casualties of the war he had been forced to fight. He went into the army thinking he could make a career, make a difference, right some wrongs—how wrong he'd been. He was sold a pack of lies, shipped off to a foreign land and given no choice but to fight for his life by taking someone else's way too many times. He understood it had to be done to protect his country, but he didn't have to like how it had to be done.

"Time to work, Haven," Lucas said, unsnapping the dog's seat belt from the SUV. "Get dressed." The German shepherd patiently waited while Lucas slipped the military-style harness over his head, fastened the buckles and then double-checked the patches to make sure they were easy to read. Six words stared back at him. PTSD Service Dog. Do Not Distract.

That was Haven's job. When they were at Secure One, the dog didn't need his harness to announce why he was there. He was an extension of Lucas, and everyone knew why. When on assignment, not a soul on the team cared about the real reason Haven stood beside Lucas. They knew he would defend any team member. Haven may have been the runt of the litter, but dressed in a black harness with his ears at attention, Lucas hadn't met anyone who would take him on.

Was he ashamed of having PTSD? No. He knew it wasn't his fault that he had it, but that didn't mean he liked announcing to the world why Haven was always with him. Despite the acceptance of PTSD throughout the country, it still carried a stigma that was difficult to see on public faces when they read the patches. He couldn't count the times he'd been told to "get over it," "just forget about it, you're home now," "just think happy thoughts" and "it will go away with time." Lucas wished even one of those things were true, but they weren't and it had taken a lot of therapy for him to trust in his coping mechanisms.

Truthfully, PTSD was a shared experience at Secure One, which Lucas had come to appreciate quickly. The team was great at pulling someone back who was falling too deeply into the past. Haven was trained to key in on Lucas and keep him steady, but he never ignored signs of anxiety from any team member. If they needed help returning to the present or decompressing from an assignment, Haven was there for them. He felt lucky that he could contribute to the team by sharing his dog that way.

"Today, you're all mine, buddy," he told the dog as he checked the SUV and glanced around the area, a habit he had picked up on the base that now came in handy working for Secure One. "If what Cal said is true, I'll need you to keep me steady."

A deep breath in and a walk up the sidewalk gave him time to focus on the perimeter of the past instead of the center of it. He reminded himself that he didn't have to think about his time over there, only the time he'd spent with Delilah on the beach six years ago. Determined to keep his breathing steady, he opened the double door and entered the funeral home. The plush carpet deadened the sound of his footsteps, as though even his footfalls were too loud for the dead.

Silence pervaded the funeral home, other than a piano rendition of "Silent Night" flowing through the speakers. Apparently, you couldn't escape Christmas music anywhere this time of year. A glance to his left revealed a small tree decorated with white lights, gold ribbon and a gold star. It was simple and understated, but felt like it belonged in the space where it sat. Recognition of the hope and peace of the season, even in a place where there was likely little of either to be found for families of lost loved ones.

He'd been told to ask for James, but first, he'd have to find a living soul in the building. Haven whined and stepped on Lucas's foot twice, a sign that his anxiety was building. He stopped and inhaled a breath, counted to three and let it out. Then he held his breath for the count of three, inhaled to the count of three and then held his breath to the count of three. He'd been taught several breathing techniques in therapy, but box breathing was the one that helped him the most. It distracted his mind and his body from the situation that was causing the anxiety. Technically, it was called the triple fours, but he'd modified it using a three count, something he'd been accustomed to using in the service and could do without thinking.

"Are you Lucas Porter?"

Lucas turned to a man dressed in a dark gray suit. His shirt was white, bright and starched, with a dark burgundy tie resting against his chest. He wore a name tag that said Edwards, Roberts and Thomas Funeral Home. James.

"I am," he answered, shaking the outstretched hand. "Nice to meet you, James."

"I'm sorry that it's under these circumstances."

Lucas suspected James said that a lot in his line of work. The man was shorter than Lucas's six feet, had a head full of blond curly hair and a baby face that was at odds with what he saw and did in a place like this.

"Me, too. It's been a long time since I've heard the name Delilah Hartman." That was a lie, for James's sake. Lucas heard that name every night in his dreams and thought of it every time he looked at Haven. "Is this situation common for you?"

"You mean having decedents arrive in the mail?" James asked, motioning him into a small room. At the front was a granite altar the size of a podium where an urn sat next to a spray of flowers. "More common than you might think. With the rise of cremation and the ability to send remains through the mail, we're often the go-between for families who live across the country to get a loved one home to a family plot."

"That makes sense, I guess," Lucas said, awkwardly shifting from foot to foot. "Not that I ever thought about it. We have a much different system in the military."

James patted his shoulder. "From what I understand, Delilah was no longer active military?"

"As of six years ago, she had been discharged. What happened after that, I can't say. I haven't seen or heard from her. That's why I was so surprised to get this call."

"I'm sure you were. I wish we could have softened the blow, but sometimes, there is no easy way to break the news to someone."

How well Lucas knew the truth of that statement. Too many times, he'd had to be the one to break the news to someone on the base that their buddy, girlfriend or boyfriend was not coming back.

"I understand that on a level that would probably surprise you."

James's gaze landed on Haven for a moment before he spoke. "Truthfully, not much surprises me anymore, Lucas. Did you serve with Delilah?"

"Indirectly," Lucas answered, inhaling a breath and holding it for the count of three. "Is that her?" He motioned at the small altar where the urn sat. There was a laser-etched American flag on the front, the only indication that the person inside had once served her country on foreign soil.

"Yes. The box next to it is also for you. It came sealed and has remained sealed to maintain privacy."

"Do you know how she died?"

"I'm sorry, we don't. It all arrived in the mail with a note to ensure you got the items and Delilah's urn. We're still working to get a death certificate. The whole thing has also surprised us, but we'll try to sort it out. In the meantime, take as much time as you need. The room is yours for the day. Did you bring anyone with you?"

"Just Haven," Lucas answered, staring at the box by the altar.

"Then please, stay until you feel comfortable driving again. Would you or Haven like some water? We also have coffee and pastries."

"We're okay for now. Thank you, though."

"You betcha," James said with that classic Minnesota

twang. "If you have questions, I'll be around. Don't think you're bothering me by asking them."

"Yes, sir," Lucas said with a nod. Haven stepped down on his foot until Lucas shook his head. "Sorry. That urn is throwing me. Can we turn it so the flag isn't facing out?"

James patted Lucas's shoulder and walked to the altar, turning the urn until only the brushed steel faced them. "I'll be right outside this door." He showed Lucas where, and after he nodded, James walked through it and closed it behind him.

"Delilah, what happened?" he whispered, dropping Haven's lead and walking to the altar. He rested his hands on the cold granite and hung his head, the memories of the summer they spent together rolling through his mind and his heart. Those days had been some of the best and worst days of his life. While he hadn't talked to Delilah in years, he thought about that summer they spent together every one of the last 2,190 days apart.

Haven budged his leg with his nose, and Lucas snapped back to the room, eyeing the dog for a moment before he nodded and picked up the box. It was small and weighed almost nothing, which surprised him, though maybe it shouldn't. Delilah was never about material things. She was always about experiences. Probably because her job in the army focused on things. Things people needed and it was her job to get, and things that other people wanted and would do anything to obtain at any cost.

"Something feels smudgy about this, Haven," he whispered to the dog as he stared at the box. "Delilah was a veteran and would have been treated and buried as such, even if she had no one else."

Voicing what his brain had been saying freed him. He split open the tape on the box and moved aside the packing paper. At the bottom was an envelope that said Luca. She had always called him that, and he allowed it, but only from her. He recognized the slanting *L* immediately as her handwriting, so he gingerly lifted it from the box. Under it, taped to the bottom, was her army Distinguished Service Medal—the only possession she ever cared about in life and wanted to be buried with in death.

Chapter Two

Lucas pulled the medal from the box, tucked it into his shirt pocket and then slipped his finger under the lip of the envelope. He hesitated when he grasped the note inside. Hell, he did more than hesitate. His fingers shook, knowing that one of those situations he thought could never be resolved was about to be. He opened the note and stared at the handwriting scrawled across the page.

Hey, there,

Those two words brought everything back. Every touch. Every fear. Every moment they spent together seared his already muddled mind. The hope that the letter wasn't from her had ended when he read the greeting. That was their greeting. He always sang the words whenever he approached her from behind so she didn't get scared. He shook his head to clear it and forced himself to keep reading.

Don't show anyone this, Luca. I'm not dead, but I am in trouble, and you're the only one who can help me now. I saw in the papers that you're working for Secure One. They sound like great company to keep and just the kind of company I'm going to need if you don't

*want this note to be my last will and testament. Since
I couldn't find their address, I had to hope the funeral
home could reach you. I'm sending my medal along so
you know it's really me. It's the only possession I care
about other than the one I left with you long ago. I need
it back now, or someone will make sure those ashes in
that urn aren't fake. I'll explain everything when you
catch up with me. I'm on island time now, but you can
call me at the number printed below. When you come,
come alone. Don't tell anyone. Don't use the internet
to search for me. They have eyes everywhere. Mele
Kalikimaka. Lilah*

Lucas lowered the paper to the table and stared at the urn.
What was going on? Was this a joke? He read the note over
and over until Haven whined and butted his thigh with his
nose. It broke his concentration, and he glanced down at the
dog, who put a paw on his leg. A sign that his anxiety was
too high. Lucas did another round of breathing to calm his
mind. When he finished, he reread the note, this time with
the trained eye of a security expert, not as a man who had
once cared deeply about this woman. Hell, as a man who
still cared about this woman.

I'm on island time now. Mele Kalikimaka.

Why was she wishing him Merry Christmas in Hawaiian? The penny dropped, shooting Lucas to his feet. "Boy,
it's time to go."

He grabbed Haven's lead after folding the note and tucking it into his wallet until he could return to Secure One.
He was never more grateful that he'd be back on base in

less than an hour, but first, he had to get out of there without raising any suspicion.

An idea came to him, and he pulled the medal from his pocket, rubbing his thumb across the gold eagle. Delilah always said after everything she did over there, the least they could do was give her a medal or two. She was kidding, of course, until she was notified that she'd be getting this one. The service had been short, but he remembered every second of it as though it were yesterday. He'd never been prouder of a human being than he was of her that day. Little did he know how quickly life would change right after.

Making a fist around the medal, he held it like a lifeline. A part of him couldn't deny that it was for the simple reason that, for the first time in too many years, he could feel Lilah in the present instead of the past. For now, he would play the part of a grieving friend, and while he knew too much about military funerals, he didn't know much about civilian ones. He stuck his head around the door and noticed James sitting at a table, working on a laptop.

The man lifted his head as though his tingly funeral senses told him someone was in need. "Everything okay?" James asked, standing and walking to the door.

"As okay as they can be when you lose a friend and fellow soldier." Lucas held out his palm. "She sent along her Distinguished Service Medal. It was the only thing she ever wanted buried with her."

"Was there a note indicating where she'd like to be buried?" James asked as they walked back into the room to face the urn. The urn Lucas now knew was, thankfully, not holding what was left of his friend.

"No, there was nothing else in the box. I know where Delilah would like to be spread, though. Am I allowed to take the urn?"

"Not yet," James answered immediately. "We're still try-ing to sort this out, so I can't turn it over to you until we have a death certificate in hand."

Lucas nodded solemnly, though he felt terrible that the funeral home was spending time and resources on a futile endeavor. Maybe he could fix that much, at least. "If you keep the urn, I'll move things up through the chain of com-mand at Secure One and the military. Just sit tight and don't do any more work on it until I get back to you. There's no reason for you to dump a lot of time into it when I can get the answers much quicker and easier."

"Are you sure?" James seemed uncomfortable now, and Lucas wondered if he saw right through his words. "We're generally able to get all the information we need, but we're hitting a brick wall." So, he was uncomfortable because it looked unprofessional, not because he suspected Lucas was playing him.

"Likely because of who she was and what she did for the government. I can't say more than that, but I'm confident you understand what I'm saying." A curt nod from James was all he needed before he continued. "I appreciate the time you've put into this and for reaching out to us at Secure One. I'll find the answers you need and get back to you."

That was the truth. Lucas would get answers, hopefully, from Lilah herself.

"We're happy to help or facilitate anything we can, once we know where to start," James said, walking along as Lucas moved toward the door with Haven following him dutifully. "Here's my card." He pulled a business card from his pocket and handed it to Lucas. "When you know some-thing, please call. We'll go from there. Again, I'm sorry for your loss and that things are complicated."

"No need to apologize. Not when you did the hard work

of tracking me down so my friend's wishes could be followed. I appreciate all your help. I'll contact you as soon as I know something."

With a final handshake, Lucas left Edwards, Roberts and Thomas Funeral Home and helped Haven into the SUV. As he pulled away from the curb, he glanced at the dog, who had settled on the seat, content that his handler was steady again. "Looks like we're going island hopping, buddy." Laughter filled the cab as he shook his head. "Too bad I'm going to need a parka instead of a bathing suit."

LUCAS WALKED INTO the cafeteria hoping to locate his boss. Whenever they weren't on assignment, the core team gathered for lunch to chat and plan for the afternoon. Today, he was both grateful and terrified that they were all there.

"Secure one, Lima," he said, releasing Haven from the lead.

"Secure two, Charlie," Cal answered, standing immediately and walking to him as a hush fell over the room. "Was it true?"

"No." The word expressed a heaviness he felt through his entire body. His feet felt like lead weights that tethered him to the ground. "It's a mess, though."

Cal held up a finger to him and turned his head. "Sadie, could you feed Haven for Lucas?"

"Oh, you know I will! Come on, boy," she called from the kitchen, giving him a whistle. "Time for lunch!"

Haven bounced on his front paws while he stared at his handler, awaiting a command. Lucas couldn't help but laugh before he pointed to the kitchen. "Rest time!"

The dog skittered off to get his lunch while Cal led him to the table to sit. Eric, Roman, Efren and Mack sat finishing their lunch. The same lunch magically appeared before

Lucas as soon as he was settled. He pushed the plate away, his appetite long gone after the events at the funeral home. "Hey," he said, glancing around the table at the brotherhood he'd come to rely on over the last eighteen months. "I don't know where to start to sort out this mess."

"We're good at sorting out messes," Mina said, walking into the room with her noticeable baby bump. She was five months pregnant with a baby girl, and everyone at Secure One had pink fever. "Break it down for us." She sat next to her husband, Roman, who kissed her cheek as she got out her computer, something that rarely left her hands.

Lucas reached into his shirt pocket and pulled out Delilah's medal, lowering it to the table. It earned him four deeply inhaled breaths from the guys who had served in the army and knew it wasn't a medal just anyone received. "That medal is the only possession my friend Delilah ever wanted to be buried with her."

"This is the friend the funeral home called about?" Efren asked, eyeing the medal. "Not just anyone gets the Distinguished Service Medal."

"Yes, Delilah Hartman. We served on the same base. She was a security tech and supply chain manager. Since I was an ordnance officer, we interacted frequently. She earned that medal the hard way."

"Munitions," Roman said. "That's dangerous stuff."

"It is, but I was more on the IT side of the weapons systems. Since Lilah was also techie, we often helped each other with glitches in the field. As you know, the bases were well connected, but the tech was always at the mercy of what was flying overhead."

"Which made both of your jobs harder over there."

"It did on the satellite base. Oddly enough, our main base was in Germany, but we never ran into each other until we got on the smaller base. We had only been on that base for a month when it fell." Lucas cleared his throat and shook his head, trying to force the memories of that day down and away so he could focus on Delilah. Haven nudged his side, telling him he was back and ready to work. Lucas stroked his head several times as the dog put his paws on his lap. "We haven't seen each other in six years."

"Then, out of the blue, you get notice that she's dead and wants you to bury her?" Eric asked. "That's the military's job for veterans."

"It is," Lucas said with a nod. "That's why I was immediately suspicious. A box was sent with her remains. When I opened it, the medal was inside. I was with her when she got it, so I knew it was real. On top of the medal was a note."

"Read it," Cal said.

They all stared at him as he pulled the note from his wallet. He noticed his hand shook as he opened it. Was he afraid that, somehow, the words had changed, and she was dead? Truthfully? Yes.

"'Don't show anyone this, Luca. I'm not dead, but I am in trouble, and you're the only one who can help me.'" Lucas read the first line, and their brows all went up. "No one else ever called me Luca. I know she wrote this." Their nods told him they understood, so he finished reading the note to them.

Mina was already typing. "A 904 area code? Jacksonville doesn't make sense unless she's on Sanibel or Key West?"

Lucas shook his head and set the note down on the table. "It's not a phone number. Try 46.8135 north and 90.6913 west."

Mina typed and then glanced up at him. "Madeline Island?"

"Yep," Lucas agreed, his hand straying to Haven's head

again. "After we were healed and discharged from the army, we met up unexpectedly in Duluth one night. We decided to camp on the island for the summer."

"'I'm on island time now,'" Roman repeated. "Smart."

"She knew if I got the letter, I would understand that she just transposed the numbers in the coordinates to confuse anyone else."

"What percentage of you believes she's really in trouble?" Cal asked.

Lucas reached for the medal, picked it up and ran his finger across the eagle again. "Every fiber of my being. I haven't heard from her in six years, and suddenly, out of the blue, she's sending me her ashes. No. For whatever reason, she's desperate. The way she mentions Secure One tells me that much."

"Let's talk about the elephant in the room," Efren said. "What do you have of hers that she wants back? It can't be the medal."

Lucas's fist closed around the metal eagle. "Oh, she'll want this back, but whatever she thinks I have, I don't have."

"I don't understand," Eric said, leaning forward on the table.

"I don't, either." Lucas's growl was enough for Haven to press his nose into his side again until he did his breathing while the team waited. They all understood how difficult it was when their service life crossed into their present life. "I don't have anything left from our time together. Listen, that summer we spent on Madeline Island was rough. We were both dealing with what happened on the base and its fallout. I'd been in a rehab facility for my back for almost two months and hadn't addressed anything that had happened to me, emotionally or physically. All these years later, I can admit that the PTSD was spiraling out of control, but she was the only one who could see it. Delilah dropped me off at the VA hospital in Minneapolis that September when we left the island. She promised to return the next day, but she never showed her face again. When I left the hospital almost three months later and started the training program with Haven, I tried to find her. By all accounts, Delilah Hartman had disappeared into thin air."

"We all know you have to go to her now," Mina said, typing on her computer. "Madeline Island is rather chilly in December, though. How long ago was this note written?"

"She's there," Lucas said with conviction. "Delilah will stay on the island for as long as it takes me to find her, or until someone else finds her first. The box that her 'remains' came in," he said, using air quotes, "was dated less than a week ago from Minneapolis. That means she mailed them and went to the island."

"If she made it to the island," Roman said. Mina elbowed him, and he huffed. "Someone had to say it."

"No, you're right," Lucas agreed, shaking his head with frustration. "If she mailed the box from that far out, which I'm sure she did on purpose to confuse anyone looking for her, then she wasn't on the island yet. I still have to try. The fact that she reached out to me all these years later tells me she's desperate for whatever she thinks I have. Whether I have it or not is irrelevant. She needs help. That's something we can provide her, right?"

Cal was the first to stand up from the table. "No one left behind. This search and rescue will take some coordinating, though."

Efren stood and headed for the door. "Meet me in the conference room in ten minutes."

"Where are you going?" Cal asked, and Efren stopped in the doorway.

"If we're going to undertake a search and rescue, you'll need my future wife. Tango, out."

When Lucas turned back to the group, they were all grinning as they gathered their things. For the first time all day, he felt like he might be able to save the woman he hadn't stopped thinking about for six long years. If nothing else, bringing her back to Secure One and helping her out of this dilemma might be his one-way ticket to getting her out of his system. That, or finding her, only to lose her again, would make his soul bleed forever.

Chapter Three

Delilah crouched low in the darkness, praying the falling snow would hide her as she crossed the open expanse of the lake. She had lucked out. It was two weeks before Christmas and northern Wisconsin was in a deep freeze. That meant Lake Superior between Bayfield and Madeline Island was frozen, which didn't happen every year. The freeze allowed her to snowshoe to the island from the mainland under the shadows of darkness. She just had to be careful about where she stepped since there could be open spots she couldn't see in the dark.

She glanced down at her new white winter gear. Everything was new, from her snowsuit to her snowshoes to her backpack. Knowing she had no trackers on her didn't mean she was safe. It just meant it would take them longer to find her. And they would find her. Hopefully, it would take them even longer this far out from civilization.

Her choices were few, though. If the funeral home found Luca and gave him her "remains," she had to be on the island as promised. Were there better places to meet up with the man she'd abandoned without so much as a word? Yes, but Madeline Island would be a safe zone for Luca and his emotions. At least, she prayed it still would be. It had been enough years that she could no longer assume she knew anything about the man. She knew if he didn't show, she would have to initiate a more direct approach with him, putting both of them in undue danger.

Faking your death and sending an urn of fake ashes was dramatic, but Secure One was so off-the-grid that she couldn't find it. Considering all she needed was a computer for an hour and she could find anything, that spoke to the lengths Secure One went to remain incognito. Their business phone number was easy to find, but the address, not so much. They'd been in the news multiple times over the last few years, and Delilah had followed those cases, completely unaware that Luca was working for them. She was watching a news report on how Secure One had rescued two kidnapping victims from the Mafia, and when the news team panned out during a live report, Luca walked behind them. She had watched the clip at least two dozen times, trying to convince herself it wasn't him and trying to convince herself it was. Over the years, Delilah had kept track of him, but the last information she had put him as a guard for a state senator.

That was then, a time when she believed she'd finally outsmarted the people after her. But that time was over. Delilah glanced behind her, satisfied that the snow covered her tracks across the lake, even if it covered her head to toe, too. She had to get to base camp, set up her tent and get the stove going so she could dry out. After some tense moments searching for a way onto the island with thick enough ice to support her, Delilah finally stepped on shore. She'd made it. Before her stretched a winter wonderland that didn't hold the promise of snowball fights and cups of hot cocoa. It held the promise of death if Luca didn't find her.

He had seven days before she'd have to return to civilization or freeze to death. She didn't like either of those options, so she prayed Luca was willing to stick his neck out to find her despite breaking his trust years ago. She had to hope that his curiosity wouldn't let her down. He had always been a curious soul, and she had to play on that personality trait if she had any hope of convincing him to help. She just hoped popping back up in his life out of the blue would override the anger and disappointment he surely felt about how things ended between them. Once they were face-to-face again, she could explain why she ran.

A shudder went through Delilah, and it wasn't from the cold. It was from the memory that invaded her mind. She had dropped Luca at the hospital, her heart heavy as she pulled into the parking lot of her long-term-stay hotel. Barely out of the car, she was attacked by two men—one with a knife—and only managed to escape thanks to some kind older man who shouted out his window when he heard the commotion. She'd been running ever since. She had reached the finish line, though. To say she was exhausted was an understatement. Nothing was left in the tank, and she feared what would come if she didn't get the only possible thing they could want.

Concentrate on the now, not the tomorrow.

Those were his words. He would recite them whenever she tried to talk about the future with him that summer on this island. Now, they were a reminder to take things one step at a time. Getting hung up on what could happen tomorrow manifested itself frequently and unexpectedly, but Delilah chalked that up to her PTSD. She had lied to Luca the day she told him she didn't qualify for treatment at the VA. She had simply convinced herself Luca needed help more than her. How wrong she'd been.

Those thoughts had to go back into the box she kept them in if she hoped to survive alone in the wilderness.

She rolled her shoulders and stayed low as she approached the campground in case someone else was winter camping, too. She doubted it. As Christmas approached, most people were with their families inside a loving home filled with the scent of pine trees and cinnamon. She wasn't like most people. Never had been. All she wanted now was a place to rest—if not her tired mind, at least her exhausted body. Ironically, when she got the travel stove fired up to warm the tent, the scent of pine trees would be in the air. She would be thankful for that, too.

Campsite 61 came into sight, and she slowed as the memories rolled through her one after the other. Delilah lowered her pack to the ground at the ghostly sound of Luca laughing. Luca crying. Luca screaming in terror. The loudest of those ghostly sounds were of Luca loving her unlike anyone else ever had.

She lifted her face to send a message into the atmosphere. "Find me, Luca. I need you more than I ever have before."

When she lowered her head, she was sure of one thing: the countdown started now.

A WHISPER OF cold air swirled through Lucas, and he shuddered. It had been five days since Delilah mailed that urn, and he was running out of time to find her. If he missed her on the island tonight, he wouldn't give up. Those two words weren't in his vocabulary. Never give up, never give in. Those were the words he lived by. There had been plenty of times he could have given up, but there was an unseen force that kept him going. Death had walked alongside him, but he was still on this earth for a reason, whether he knew why yet or not. As he stared at the snowy tundra below, he was acutely aware of how unusual it was for the lake to be frozen this early in the season, so he couldn't help but wonder if this was the reason. If *Delilah* was the reason.

"You sure you want to do this alone, son?" Cal's words came over the headset he wore in the chopper as they flew toward their destination in Bayfield, Wisconsin. "I've been a ghost before. I can do it again."

"As much as I appreciate it, Cal, this bird is our ticket off that island, so I need you behind the controls. Delilah's note said to come alone. If I show up on the island and she gets a whiff that I'm not, she'll bolt. Besides, I don't know what I'm walking into. The less collateral damage, the better."

"That's the thing, kid," Roman said from where he sat next to Cal. "We'd be there to prevent the collateral damage. Think long and hard about this, Lucas. Having an unseen lookout may be the only reason you both walk out alive. You don't know why someone is after her, so for all you know, you're walking into a trap."

Lucas bit his lip as he considered what Roman had said. In the end, they were both right. It wasn't exactly smart to walk into the situation alone, but he also couldn't scare Lilah away.

"If we'd had more time to plan the mission, that would have helped," Cal said, as though driving home the point. "You barely let Selina call her contact at The Cliff Badgers Search and Rescue team to find the best way to get Haven to the island. I don't like leaping without looking."

"I know," Lucas said between clenched teeth as he stroked Haven's head. The dog sat beside him with one paw on his lap to keep him grounded. They'd worked together for so long now that Lucas never had to give the dog a command for help with anxiety. Haven knew it was coming long before he did. "I don't like it, either, but it's cold and she's probably been out there for days. If we wait too long, she'll dip and we'll be back to square one. We had to move on it and move on it in the dark."

Lucas waited, but neither of the men in the chopper said another word. Was he nervous about going out onto that island alone? Yes. But he was more nervous about seeing Lilah. He'd buried her so deep that he was afraid seeing her would dig up all those emotions he never wanted to see the light of day again. Did that make him a coward? Probably, but the truth was true, as his mom used to say.

"Let me ask you a question," he said, waiting for Cal to nod. "What would you do if you were me? Be honest."

"When I was your age, exactly what you're doing now," Cal admitted with a chuckle. "Since then, I've learned the importance of tactical strategy. I learned that strategy by almost dying more times than I want to admit."

"And he means that literally," Roman added. "I was there for several of them."

Cal reached over and punched his brother playfully while laughing. Roman and Cal were foster brothers who grew up together and joined the army. When they got injured on a mission and left the service, Cal went into private security while Roman went into the FBI. Now they were working together again, and Lucas trusted the two of them explicitly. The thought made his chest rise with surprise momentarily before he spoke.

"Are you guys familiar with the island?" Lucas asked, and they both made the so-so hand motion. "That's a no. Here's what you don't understand, guys. The island is much bigger and denser than it looks on a map. Lilah won't be near a paved road, so if you aren't standing next to me, you're impotent in an emergency. The forest is dense, which means the snow will hamper us even more. I know I need your help, but tactically, I'll be better off with you providing air support."

Lucas's mind entered planning mode. He ran through his intimate knowledge of the island, the best place to approach and all the ways he could stay hidden while doing it.

"It's impossible to be stealthy while offering air support," Cal finally said.

"That's fine, as long as you don't start this whirlybird until after I've met up with Delilah. I'll explain that I'm alone, but you're our ride out of there."

"You wear an earpiece and keep it on at all times?"

"All times?" Lucas shook his head. "No, I'll have to mute it when I approach her. I don't know what this is about, and until I do, I won't expose you guys to something that you can't deny to the authorities."

"You think it's that serious?"

"I don't know what to think," Lucas admitted. "I haven't seen her in six years, but the Delilah I used to know had never been dramatic a day in her life. She was calm, cool and calculated, so if she's scared and scattered, I'm terrified."

"Understood," Roman said.

"What's your plan?" Lucas asked, knowing they needed to be all on the same page.

"Don't you worry about what we're going to do, son," Roman answered. "Worry about what you have to do." He held up an earpiece for Lucas to see. "We'll all have one, and we can talk to each other." He held up his hand. "Yes, you can mute it so we can't hear you and Delilah talking."

"The rest of the time," Cal butted in, "mute is off so we can communicate. Understood?"

"Heard, understood and acknowledged," he said with a nod.

"Good, then let's get you out there to find this woman. My curiosity is piqued. I'm dying to know the story."

"Can we not use the phrase 'dying to know' for the next few hours?" Lucas asked, glancing out the chopper's window at the blackness below.

"Heard, understood and acknowledged," Cal said with a chuckle before he headed for solid ground.

Chapter Four

Lucas glanced at the sky as he and Haven stepped onto the island. The moon was starting to peek out from behind the clouds, which meant the temperature was about to drop again. He used hand motions to tell Haven to follow him into a wall of trees. When Lucas took the job with the senator as a security guard, he'd taught Haven hand signs he could use when situations didn't allow speech. The dog, a former K-9 in the army, had taken to the training immediately. Lucas had been grateful he'd already taught him the signs, so when he applied for the Secure One job, he could prove the dog wouldn't be a liability in a tense situation.

He paused for a moment and checked Haven over. The walk to the island had been less difficult than expected since the wind had blown them a path relatively free of snow. He'd come prepared with a sled at the recommendation of Selina's friend Kai, but it hadn't been necessary, so he abandoned it on shore for someone else to use. Now that they were on land, moving around would get more complicated. He straightened Haven's coat, checked his boots to ensure they were secure and did the same with his gear, including stowing his snowshoes on his pack. The shoes would only inhibit his ability to move quickly and efficiently through the forest and brush. If he was lucky, a path would already be made once he reached the campground.

Lucas clipped a short lead on Haven and quietly motioned him forward. They had purposely approached the island at an angle closest to the campground when he noticed a whisper of smoke through the trees as he stood on the shore. He had no doubt that the long-lost Delilah Hartman was awaiting his arrival. His mantra as he traversed the lake had been simple: *Stay neutral. Learn the facts. Act accordingly.* Something told him it would be a harder mantra to stick to once he was face-to-face with Lilah again.

"Secure one, Lima," he said into the earpiece.

"Secure two, Charlie," Cal said in his ear to tell him to go ahead and speak freely. If he ever heard a different greeting, it was an immediate signal that their teammate was in trouble.

"On the island, about half a klick from the campsite."

"Smoke in the air at your target. Proceed with caution."

"I noted that from shore. It's in the right vicinity for site 61. Will make contact in under five."

"The bird will be in the air in a few," Cal said, and Lucas could hear him flipping switches as they spoke. "I'll be waiting at the extraction point. You can hear us even if we can't hear you."

"You've got twenty minutes to convince her to leave with us, kid. Get it done," Roman said.

"Roger that," Lucas answered and then muted the microphone.

Did it annoy him that they always called him kid and son? It did initially, but now he saw it for what it was. Team members had to earn their stripes at Secure One. Until he did, he was a kid to them, but they never said it in a derogatory way. It came from a place of protection and teaching.

Lucas had made sure to pay attention and learn those lessons well. If someone shared their knowledge with him, it only made sense to listen and learn so he could implement it when the time was right.

The time was finally right. He had no question in his mind as he silently approached the edge of the campground through the snow. Undoubtedly, Lilah was aware someone was nearby. That was who she was, but he couldn't worry about that as he approached. All he could do was continue to move forward, hoping she believed he'd come for her.

One last obstacle to overcome was the steep bank they had to climb. Lucas glanced at it and then at Haven, wondering if the dog could even make it, but the eye movement must have been enough because Haven plowed his way forward, forcing Lucas to follow as he held the lead. They were on top of the bank in just a few seconds. He was surprised how much easier it had been to scale that bank than it used to be. Whether that was due to the snow or the fact he took care of himself now was hard to say, but he was glad he was back on even ground.

Lucas stood in the tree line and took in campsite 61. A canvas cowboy range tent was set up with a stovepipe through the center, explaining the smoke's origin. The tent could belong to anyone. He eyed the area around it, noting a large wood berm built next to the tent the way they used to build their sandbag bunkers in the army. Lilah was here somewhere.

He had no choice but to announce his presence and wait. He unhooked Haven from the lead and pulled his Glock out from under his coat. After crouching into the shooter position, he flicked on his earpiece. "Found her campsite. I'm about to call out to her. Going dark for a few."

"Ten-four," Cal said. "Loop us back in as soon as you find her."

"Ten-four," he whispered, then put his microphone on mute.

Lucas cleared his throat and prayed his voice didn't sound like a scared twelve-year-old when he spoke. "Hey, there, Lilah." His words were firm but laced with the nervousness that filled him.

He'd been scared while running missions overseas, but hoping that Lilah was in that tent while worried she wasn't terrified him more than any of those missions had. He waited, the air crackling with tension, hope and fear. Had he missed her? Had it taken too long to get the message to him? Maybe she left information in the tent to tell him where to go next. Did he dare look? No, that didn't make sense. There was still smoke drifting from the stovepipe, which meant the fire was recent.

His gaze darted around the area, while his mind took him back to the time he had spent with Lilah here. It had been her suggestion to spend the summer on the island. After the base fell, they both ended up at the Minneapolis VA to heal, but never ran into each other. It was an unexpected meeting in a bar in Duluth that had reconnected them. That night, they'd shared a hotel room, not platonically, so he was all in when she suggested taking a summer to find themselves again before worrying about school or a job. They both had money; there was no problem in that respect, but they were both quick to realize they had no one but each other.

Lilah's parents were both dead by the time she was eighteen and Lucas never had parents to speak of. Sure, his mom was around, but she was too busy getting high to worry about what her kid was doing. By age eight, he was in foster care, so it made sense for him to join the service when he graduated. He had been led to believe it was his golden ticket in life after enduring a crappy childhood. Little did he know it would be a ticket to a house of horrors far worse than any childhood nightmare.

They'd brought only what they could carry onto the island, knowing there was access to everything else already there. That included access to nature therapy to help heal their fractured minds. Lucas glanced down at Haven and sighed. Nature therapy may have been enough for Lilah, but not for him. Still, all he could remember about his time at campsite 61 were the good memories—the memories of her touching him, loving him and protecting him from himself.

"Hey, there, Lilah," he said again, a bit louder, hoping she just hadn't heard him the first time. He doubted that was the case. Maybe she wasn't on the islan—

"Are you alone, Luca?"

The question came from his left, and he recognized the voice immediately. He fought back the wave of equal parts nostalgia and desire to focus on his pounding heart. *Stay neutral. Learn the facts. Act accordingly.* He ran the motto through his head before he answered.

"Other than my dog, yes." He had a decision to make. Keep his gun out in case she was being controlled by someone out to hurt them or put it away so he didn't scare her. "Are you alone?"

"I've never been more alone, Luca."

At the sound of her voice, he slipped his Glock into his coat pocket and stepped out of the woods with his hands up. "You're not alone, Lilah. You called, so I came."

And then, before his eyes appeared an apparition of his past. Delilah was dressed in white from head to toe. Even with most of her face covered, he knew it was her. The eyes never lied, and the gray ones hiding behind those prism lenses told him more than her words ever could. She had seen things over the last six years that haunted her and terrified her in equal measure.

Lilah pulled the balaclava down and sent him back to that summer under the Wisconsin sun. Life was complicated but simple. Love was in the air, and for the first time, Lucas was sure he'd found his family. He could still feel the softness of her skin under his hands as he ran them down her ribs to rest on her hips. Then she'd plaster her lips on his and carry him to another place where everything was simple. The only thing he needed back then was her.

Lucas hadn't agreed to get treatment for himself. He'd agreed to go for her so they could live the life they'd planned that summer. Once his treatment was over, they'd get a little apartment in Duluth and find work. They'd put down roots, learn about each other, build a life together, whatever that may look like as the months and years passed. He'd held on to that idea for the first month he was at the VA, hoping and praying that she hadn't visited because she was busy setting up their life. How naive he had been.

"I don't want you to leave," Lucas said, holding her hand at the entrance to registration.

"I don't want to leave, but you need to be here, Lucas. You must find a way to live with the horrors you saw over there. I don't want you to be a statistic. I want you in my life for years, okay?"

He trailed a finger down her cheek and tucked a piece of hair behind her ear. "You promise you'll visit?"

"As much as they'll let me," she whispered, lifting herself on her tiptoes to kiss him. "In between those times, I'll find us a place and prepare it for your homecoming. I know we can do this if we do it together, Luca."

"Together," he whispered.

Haven dug his nose into his thigh, leaned against him and rumbled a low growl as a reminder to return to the present. Lucas took a breath, his gloved hand stroking Haven's head as he gazed at the woman he'd been sure was lost to him forever.

"Delilah Hartman, long time no see." Lucas forced the words from his lips. His mind was having difficulty accepting that the woman who stood before him was the same woman he had shared so much with on this island.

He wanted to demand to know why she'd abandoned him. He also wanted to hug her and never let her go. She took a step toward him, and that was when he saw it. A scar ran from under the balaclava's edge to the side of her lip and another one across her chin and down her neck. The intensity of the situation was written on her face. The black bags under her eyes said she wasn't sleeping, and the fear in those globes of dusky gray told him she was scared, tired and unsure about everything. Everything but him.

"Luca. You came."

"Of course, I came. You fell off the face of the earth six years ago, and when you pop back up in my life, it's in an urn full of God knows what? I had to come."

"Sand."

"Sand?"

"That's what's in the urn. I'm sorry for the dramatics. I could find a phone number for Secure One, but no address."

"I'm just glad it wasn't you, Lilah." He took his glove off and traced the scar across her chin. "Help me understand. You dropped me off at the hospital and disappeared from my life. I waited for you for months, but you never returned. When I got out, there wasn't a trace of you. If you wanted to break things off, you should have at least said it to my face. I imagined all kinds of horrible things that may have happened to you."

"I know, I know." Her words were filled with desperation. "None of this was supposed to happen. I didn't want to break things off, but that choice was taken from me. You'll know everything soon, but we don't have much time. We have to get off the island. How did you get here?"

"I snowshoed from the mainland. How did you get here?"

"The same way. If we're going to get back before daylight, we have to go now."

She dashed into the tent, and when he pulled the side back, she was putting out the fire in the small travel stove. Once that was out, she grabbed her pack and flipped it over her shoulders.

"What's the dog's name?" she asked when leaving the tent.

"Haven." The dog immediately stood at attention next to his handler. "We went into a training program together when I left the VA hospital. He's a retired army K-9 turned trained PTSD dog. Haven is what allows me to function normally in the world we live in. He won't slow us down," he added, sure that was why she asked.

"That wasn't my concern," she assured him, holding her hand out for Haven to sniff. "If we're traveling together, he has to know I'm a friend and not a foe."

"Are you a friend, though?" he asked, the bitterness loud and clear in his words. "Or am I merely a matter of convenience for you?"

"No, Luca," she said, turning and stepping up to him so he had no choice but to meet her gaze. "I know you're hurt and you don't understand what happened. That's on me. I'll explain everything, but you're not a matter of convenience. You're the person I've been protecting all this time. I hoped it wouldn't come to this, but here we are, so first we must get somewhere safe, and then I can help you understand."

"I just don't know if I can trust you, Lilah."

"That's fair," she agreed with a nod of her head, but Lucas noticed her shoulders slump with shame. He instantly felt horrible. "I'll tell you how you can trust me." She pointed to the scars on her face and chin. "These are some of my visible scars from the last six years. There are more that damn near killed me, but they didn't—for one reason. I refused to die. If I did, they were going to come after you. Every scar on my body is a mark on the tally board of trust, Luca."

"How many scars are there?" His question was filled with anguish this time. The idea of her being tormented to protect him was too much to bear.

"We need to get out of here, Luca," Lilah whispered.

She wasn't going to answer him, leaving him with a decision. Do as she said and get them to safety so she could fill in the picture or press her here where danger lurked around any tree. Lucas held up his finger and flicked the mute button off his earpiece. "I need to let the team know we're on the move."

"Team? You said you came alone."

"I did, but two of the best army special ops police are in a chopper on the mainland. We were afraid to land on the island and draw attention, so I shoed in. We'll shoe back out and catch a ride to Secure One with Cal and Roman. You can trust them. I wouldn't be here if it weren't for them."

With her nod, he hit the button and spoke. "Secure one, Lima."

"Secure two, Charlie. Did you find her?"

"Affirmative," he answered, his gaze pinned to hers by an unseen force. "We're loading up and heading to you."

"ETA?" Roman asked.

Lucas did some calculating, considering that he would have to go at Lilah's pace and she was exhausted. "Haven will slow us down, so plan for seventy-five minutes."

"Ten-four. I'll have the blades going," Cal answered.

"Lima out," he said before clicking the mute button again.

"Haven will slow us down?" Lilah asked with her brow in the air. "You don't have to spare my feelings by lying to your team, Luca. I'm fully aware I'm a hot mess, but I want to get off this island alive, so set the pace. I'll keep up."

He should have known she would see right through his excuse, but being with Lilah again activated his protective side. There had never been a time since he first laid eyes on her that he didn't want to protect her. He would have died if it meant she lived, and he nearly did, but he forced his mind away from those thoughts. Concentrating on the past would do him no favors when trying to navigate the wildness of Lake Superior in the dark.

"We can't return to Secure One, Luca. We have to find the—"

The first pop confused him until a tree to his right exploded. Before he could react, Lilah grabbed his backpack and hauled him behind the wood berm, Haven hot on his heels. He dropped his pack and swung his automatic rifle to his shoulder, returning fire.

"What the hell have you gotten yourself involved in, Lilah?" His question was yelled over his shoulder as he tried to take out an unseen enemy. The question was rhetorical, but he swore he heard her say, "A living hell," right before the next barrage of bullets rained down.

Chapter Five

"They shouldn't be here already!" Delilah yelled as he ducked behind the wood. "I came in clean!"

"Someone forgot to tell them that!" he yelled as more wood exploded around them.

Luca had come for her, but Lilah couldn't help but think he'd brought some unwanted guests. Not that it was his fault. He couldn't have known that her every move was tracked by an unknown enemy. A bullet dug into the log fortress she'd built for this very reason. Haven pushed her back toward the woods, his experience with combat obvious as he protected her from harm. She was glad Lucas had Haven now.

There were a lot of cases of PTSD after the war. Hell, she had her own to deal with, but Luca's was by far the worst she'd ever seen. They had only been on the base a month when it came to an unexpected, barbaric end. She'd been protected from some of the horrors he'd seen, so she could only imagine what he'd witnessed before they jumped on that last Black Hawk out of hell.

Lilah noticed him touch his earpiece before he yelled. "Under fire! Need extraction! Need extraction!"

While he waited, he sent a few more bullets over the top

of the wood berm. If they didn't end this soon, even her wooden fortress wouldn't be enough to protect them.

"Negative," Lucas yelled just as more gunfire filled the air. He tucked his gun around the wood's edge and sent some bullets into the darkness. All Lilah could do was sit idly by and pray one of them would find their target. Her handgun would do no good in this firefight. "We're due east of Basswood Island. The airport is miles away!"

Lucas turned and addressed her as bullets slammed into the wood protecting them, throwing splinters into the air. "Who are these guys?" She saw him take notice of Haven, who had positioned his body to block her lower half.

"I wish I knew!"

Her words had barely died off when the report of gunfire ended. Lucas took his chance. He flipped his night vision goggles down, stood and sprayed the woods with bullets. He dropped down again and turned to her. "Two down," he said, and she wasn't sure if he was addressing her or the team in the chopper. "It seems like they'd send more than two guys." His gaze darted to her, and she shrugged.

"Hard to know," she whispered, in case others were out there. "I've always only been approached by two, but the last time there were four. This island is a bit of a needle in a haystack for two guys, so starting with the campground makes the most sense."

Lucas nodded and then spoke, but not to her. "The sat phone should have sent my coordinates." He stood cautiously, his gun aimed at the woods, as he scanned the area with his night vision goggles. "Still just the two," he said, talking to his team again. "Ope!" His rifle cracked once, and Lilah noticed a shudder go through him before he spoke. "Target down. Both targets are down." He nodded as he stood, searching the forest beyond the berm. "I don't see much choice. Yes, we can make it there in twenty minutes if we don't encounter more friends along the way." Lucas ducked back down and flipped his goggles up. "We have to move," he said to her. "Cal is bringing the chopper in to pick us up, but he can't risk landing on the ice. He'll get close, drop the basket and we'll have to climb in."

Knowing she had to help any way she could, she slung her pack off for a moment and dug in a side pocket, pulling out a handgun. "Don't ask me where I got it. Just tell me what to do."

Luca handed her a pair of night vision goggles. "Put these on and stay on your toes. The extraction point is two klicks west. We should be able to cover that in twenty minutes."

"As long as there aren't more guys waiting for us," she said, slinging her pack back on her shoulders.

"The only way out is forward," Luca said with half a lip tilt. "Haven, fall in," he said, and the dog stood and went to his handler.

"Side by side?" she asked, and he nodded once. "What about those two?" She motioned toward the forest.

"They started it?" he asked, and she heard all those same emotions in his voice that she'd heard when they were on the island so long ago. Disgust. Anger. Pain. Terror. Haven noticed, too, because he butted him with his nose three times. Luca stroked his head while he breathed in and out before he nodded. "Let's hope they're the last of it. We need to move. Cal is coming in over Big Bay for extraction."

"Ten-four," Lilah said but then held up her hand for him to pause. "Let's avoid the stairs. They could be waiting to ambush us there."

"Everything else is pretty craggy, Lilah," he said, grabbing her suit as she fixed her balaclava.

"Lucky for you, I already planned a route. You better let your team know it will only take us six minutes to get there."

"Six minutes?" he asked, dropping his hands. "That's impossible."

"Not if you trust me, Luca," she said, flipping her goggles down. "Follow me?"

Lilah stepped around the berm and prayed they were still alone and that he would trust her enough to get them to safety. Within a few steps, she heard them following and picked up her pace, jinking and jiving through the woods on a path she had memorized the first day she was here. It was one of several escape routes she had mastered because no matter what Luca thought, she would walk through fire to protect him.

"So far, so good," Luca said from behind her. "How much farther?"

"Two minutes," she answered, surprised by how easily Haven kept up with them as they ran. "I hear the chopper."

"They'll be waiting," he assured her as they ran, their heads on a swivel, waiting for a sneak attack that could end this reunion much quicker than she wanted.

As soon as the white ribbon came into sight, she threw her arm out as a sign to slow. "I marked this because the rocks here can have ice under the snow. You have to go slow, but you're also exposed, so stay vigilant."

Since she was the reason they were in this position to start with, she took the first step into the open so that Luca could follow safely in her footsteps. Funny. Up until now, they'd been equals in every way. Today, she could no longer say that about her relationship with Lucas Porter. While she'd been running for her life, he was building one. Suddenly, the wasted years without him weighed heavily on her shoulders. This situation was hers by default but not her fault. She just had to stay alive long enough to get that flash drive back from Luca and, hopefully, end this chess match for good.

Lucas and Haven met her on the ice, where she crouched low and waited. "Thirty seconds out," Luca whispered, and she nodded. "Roman will drop a basket big enough for all of us. Pile in and grab hold. Cal will take off while Roman lifts us on board."

"Ten-four," she said, fighting back the racking shudders that went through her. The scene felt too much like the last time they had to jump on a chopper and pray they made it inside before a bullet took them out. "Be careful," she whispered. "Your back."

"Is fine," he answered in her ear.

"It can't be like last time, Luca. It can't be," she said, the tone going higher with each word. "It can't be."

"Focus on three," he whispered into her ear. "Breathe in for three, hold it for three, breathe out for three. If you do that, you'll make it. I promise."

"You did always like the number three," she said with a lip tilt before she did what he'd instructed. The fact was, it did calm her and let her focus on what needed to be done to stay alive. "Maybe they only sent in the two guys."

The thumping of the chopper blades drowned out her voice, and in seconds, it came into view. She followed Luca out into the open, praying they had time to get on board before anyone else could reach them. She wanted to believe only two guys were on the island, but she wasn't that naive. The two he took out were just their scout team, but the gunfire and chopper would now draw them like a moth to a flame.

"Go, go!" Luca yelled, pointing at the basket as it came down from the chopper. Lucas helped her in before hoisting

Haven into it. The first bullet whizzed past her ear just as Luca somersaulted into the wire basket. He motioned with his arm over his head for Roman to go but quickly dropped it as more bullets came their way. "Stay down!" he yelled, covering Haven with his body while Roman returned fire.

They were going to ride this basket until they were clear of the gunfire, so all she could do was hang on for dear life and pray.

"THAT ONE GAINED purchase, eh?" Selina asked as she dropped a bullet into a pan next to him on the table. "Didn't anyone ever teach you to duck?"

Lucas meant to laugh, but it came out as a groan. "Must have been sick that day. Better me than Haven, though," he said, hissing when she stuck him with a needle and filled him with more Novocain.

"You're lucky you had that pack on your back or you'd be in a hospital. Maybe even a morgue."

"Trust me, I wish things had gone differently. We're lucky to have walked away with only minor injuries."

"Patch him up good, babe," Efren said, walking into the med bay. "They're not staying."

"They have to stay long enough for me to pump him full of antibiotics and make sure this doesn't end up infected."

"Better talk to the boss about that. He says this is a pit stop to change tires and fuel up before they hit the track again."

Lucas glanced between them. "Cal wants us out?"

"He's waiting in the conference room to discuss it, but from what Delilah has said, if she's here, no one is safe."

"I haven't even had a chance to talk to her," Lucas said between gritted teeth as Selina started suturing the wound.

The ride back to Secure One had been short but tense.

Lilah spent the ride holding pressure to his wound while all he wanted to do was hold her. Once they arrived at Secure One, Mina had whisked Lilah off while Selina tended to his leg. Thankfully, his pack had diverted the bullet and it lodged in the flesh of his thigh rather than his back or his head. In a few days, he'd be fine, but Lilah wouldn't be if Cal couldn't offer her protection.

Selina smoothed a clear bandage across the small wound, then snapped off her gloves. "That plastic coating is Tegaderm. You can shower with the stitches as long as the Tegaderm is in place. I'll give you some extra to take, but it's meant to stay on until it loosens itself. I used dissolvable stitches, so you don't have to worry about removal. They'll disappear on their own. Keep them dry."

"Thanks, Selina." He tried to stand, but she forced him back to the stretcher.

"Not so fast," she said, spinning her stool around. "You need antibiotics. If I can't give them to you via intravenous, then you'll have to take pills. We can't risk an infection. Especially if you won't be around for me to keep an eye on it."

Selina was their head medic on the team, but she was also an operative. In her prior life, she'd been a Chicago cop and search and rescue medic, so she understood the situations they often found themselves in when a case took a turn.

"Fine, give me the bottle." He held his hand out. "I need to get down to the conference room."

"I'll let them know you're on your way," Efren said before he kissed Selina on the cheek and left the room. It was only a few months ago that Selina spent her days snipping at Efren for every little thing. It turned out that forcing them together to save their own lives changed their relationship for the better. He could only be so lucky. Then again, the Delilah he picked up off that island wasn't the same Delilah he knew six years ago. She was different. Sadder. Untrusting. Harder.

"What's going on here, Lucas?" Selina asked, grabbing an empty bottle from her cabinet and counting pills from a different bottle.

"I wish I could answer that," he admitted. He climbed off the gurney, pulled up his pants and tested his leg. It was tender, but he'd had worse injuries in the field. "That's why I have to get down to the conference room. If Cal isn't going to let us stay here, I'll have to figure something else out."

"If Cal isn't going to let you stay here, then that woman is in serious trouble."

"And me by default."

"I also know that Cal isn't going to abandon you. He'll have a plan, so stay calm and listen to what he'll lay out. Twice a day for a week," she said, shaking the bottle before she handed it to him. "More a precaution than a certainty, but try."

"Got it, doc," he said, pocketing the bottle.

"Do you want me to keep Haven for you?" Selina asked, walking him and the dog to the door.

"Yes, but no. I don't want to put him in danger, but—"

"But you're going to need him," she finished, taking his hand to stop the patting to the count of three on Haven's head. "Before you leave, get his bulletproof vest. I know it's heavy, but it's smart to have the Kevlar on him in this situation."

"I agree. I should have done it when we went out there, but I wasn't expecting a full-blown war within minutes of arriving."

"I don't know anyone who would, Lucas. You got this. We're here for you, so if anything happens, you call in and we cover your back. In any way we need to, right?"

Lucas rubbed his hand down over his cargo pants, now torn from the bullet. "I feel terrible that Secure One has gotten hit with this after what happened with you and Vaccaro. I can't lose this job."

"Listen," Selina said, grasping his shoulder. It offered him a moment of solidarity in a situation he couldn't control. "You might be the newest member of Secure One, but you have saved all of our butts multiple times since joining the team. Cal knows that, and so does everyone else who will be around that table. Whatever is going on has nothing to do with you and everything to do with you, but not by your creation."

"Truer than you know," he agreed with a nod. "I'm afraid this will come to a fast end when I tell Delilah I have nothing left from our time together. Then she'll disappear from my life forever, and I don't want that to happen. She may not be the Delilah I knew six years ago, but it's easy to see that's because of what she's lived through since we parted ways. If we force her out, I'm afraid she'll end up in an urn, for real this time."

"Then stand up and be the person she needs to help her out of this situation. We're here for backup, but we know you can do this."

"I'm glad someone has confidence in me. I barely got her off that island alive."

"But you did," she said with a wink. "You know what to do. You just have to remember how to do it."

Lucas stroked Haven's head three times and then met her gaze. "That's the problem. If I remember how to do it, I also remember everything else. Everything they taught me how to forget."

Selina leaned back on the wall and crossed her ankles.

"Then the question you have to ask yourself is, if you don't help her, can you live with the consequences?"

That question had been sitting hard in his gut since they'd climbed aboard the chopper. He could give her what she came for if he had it and leave her to sort it out. But if he did that, would he be able to live with himself when she met an enemy she couldn't evade? The unequivocal answer to that was no. Knowing that he could have helped her but was too much of a coward would be worse than taking a stroll down memory lane. At least at the end of the walk, there was a chance for a happy ending.

Lucas kissed Selina on the cheek with a thank-you and left the med bay to rediscover his past.

Chapter Six

"I think this should fit," Mina said, handing Delilah a pair of black cargo pants. "They were mine before this." She patted her pregnant belly. "If they fit, I have several more pairs. You'll also need some of these." She handed her a stack of black T-shirts and sweatshirts.

"Black seems to be a theme here," Delilah said as she sat on the bed to pull on the pants.

"Makes it easy to match your clothes in the morning," Mina said with a wink before she handed her a pair of boots, also black. "Once we know the mission plan, we'll hook you up with the outerwear you need."

Delilah nodded but was only half-focused on the woman before her. The other half was focused on the man who had gone straight to the med bay to have a bullet dug out of his thigh.

"He's fine," Mina said, and Delilah glanced up. "Lucas. Selina messaged me she's already got the bullet out and the wound sutured."

"Luca took that bullet because of me. That's messed up."

"You weren't the one out there shooting up the island. Remember that."

"True, but I was the one who made a decision years ago that put him in danger. That was never my intention."

"I'm sure Lucas knows that, but you can tell him when we get to the conference room. Are you ready?"

Mina held the door for her, and then they walked down a hallway that could only be described as a fortress made of wood grain and steel. The log exterior made a person believe you were walking into a cozy log cabin, but instead, the interior housed high-tech security equipment and, from what she could gather, some rather deadly security techs.

The flight back from the island had been strained and nerve-racking. Cal was a master pilot, though, and managed to get them out of harm's way quickly. The problem? He made the point that whoever was after her now knew his chopper. Eventually, they'd show up at his door looking for her. That was not her goal. Her only goal was to get what she needed from Luca and go before anyone else got hurt. After he took a bullet on the way into the chopper, all she could do was hold pressure on it for the short ride back to Secure One. She hadn't seen him since. Delilah was desperate to tell him everything so he could promise to take care of her, but the chopper was not the time or the place. Instead, that time and place would be in front of people she didn't know.

Talking to Luca alone was preferable, but she also understood the complexities of the situation and that the team had to know the specifics. At least the specifics that she knew, which weren't many. She had suspicions, but that's all they were. She had no choice but to air her dirty laundry in front of all. Her steps faltered when she glanced up and noticed Luca walking toward them, Haven by his side. "You're walking," she said when they neared.

"Of course," he said with a smile. "It was just a flesh wound. I suffered worse injuries on the base."

"I know, but that doesn't make me feel better. If you'd lost Haven or gotten hurt worse because of me, I couldn't go on."

"Good thing that didn't happen then. Now it's time we sort out who is after you and why."

"We?"

"We," he said, squeezing her hand. "Secure One isn't just a company. It's a family, and we take care of our own."

"I'm not one of you, though. My situation isn't your responsibility beyond giving me what I need."

"The moment you involved me in this, you became one of us. That's how it works, so there's no sense arguing with anyone here."

"Sounds like you already tried," Lilah said, holding his gaze. His brown eyes were just as bottomless as they had always been, but now they held a touch of something she couldn't name. Pain? Distrust? Or was it something else entirely?

Luca tipped his head in agreement. "They're already involved, so we may as well let them help us, right?"

With her nod, he motioned her forward into the conference room. There was a large whiteboard at the front of the room and a festively decorated Christmas tree in the corner that belied the reason they were here. A large wooden conference table sat to the left of the whiteboard with at least a dozen chairs around it. Filling those chairs were a few familiar faces and many unfamiliar ones, but they were all smiling as she walked in behind Luca and Haven.

"Welcome to Secure One, Delilah," Cal said. "I'm sure you're nervous after the situation on the island, but we're here to help, so don't feel bad about it. When one of ours is under attack, we all fight back."

"And make no mistake," Roman said, facing her. "You're one of us now."

"See?" Luca whispered in her ear, sending a shiver down her spine.

She might be one of them now, but in a few minutes, they would learn that what she brought to the table would take them back to the life they'd tried to leave behind.

"As some of you know, this is my friend Delilah Hartman. We were stationed together nine years ago in Germany before we were moved to a satellite base."

"What base?" Mack asked, taking notes on a pad.

"I wish we could tell you," Delilah said, biting her lower lip momentarily. "Unfortunately, we can't."

"You can't tell us the base you were on?" Efren asked to clarify. "What's the big secret?"

"The base," Lucas answered with a shrug. "It was classified. That's why you never heard about its fall. It was never in the news and was that way by design. I know you're all ex-military, so you'll understand that we still can't disclose the location."

Heads nodded around the table before Cal spoke. "Seems a moot point if the base no longer exists. We can work around it. Go on."

"Right, well, when we were discharged nearly eight years ago, we both had some recovering to do from injuries we sustained getting off the base. My back was broken in several places." He glanced at Lilah, who nodded. "Lilah suffered a TBI that left her with double vision, among other issues with her eyes." Everyone nodded, so he cleared his throat and went on. "When we were free of the hospitals, we ran into each other unexpectedly in Duluth. We decided we'd spend the summer on Madeline Island. The base fell in an unexpected and traumatic manner, but we had no time to decompress. We thought nature therapy might help as we considered our futures."

"It became obvious quickly," Delilah said, picking up

the story, "that Luca—I'm sorry—Lucas started spiraling further and further into his episodes of PTSD. I knew we would never be able to have the life we wanted unless he got treatment as quickly as possible. While I witnessed atrocities on the base that day, they didn't hold a candle to what Lucas saw and did. I knew he would need a better way to deal with it before rejoining society."

"What Lilah's not saying is she saved my life several times that summer. She pulled me out of Lake Superior more than once," Lucas said, his spine stiff. Haven leaned into his leg, keeping him grounded in the room.

"Trust us," Mack said. "We've all been there. We understand the hard fight required to accept what we did when we had no other choice."

"It was one of those situations where I knew I needed help but didn't know how to ask for it," Lucas admitted. "Thankfully, Lilah realized it and got me into the VA hospital."

"While he was undergoing treatment, I planned to set up our new life in Duluth. That's when everything fell apart." She paused and shook her head as her gaze dropped to the floor. "I don't know how to explain what's happened since then."

"Just start at the beginning," Lucas said. "If we don't understand the beginning, we can't make this end."

"He's right," Cal agreed. "Feel free to use the whiteboard. Sometimes it helps to write things down chronologically for you and us."

Lilah walked to the board while Lucas took a seat next to Cal. He was just as anxious as the rest of them to find out what had kept her from him all these years. From the little she'd said and the scars she had, it wasn't simply because she didn't want to be with him. She had been fighting her own war these past six years. When she stepped away from the board, she had written and underlined several names.

"To start, you need to know my background," Lilah explained, pointing at the board. "I began as a supply chain manager for the army. Eventually, that morphed into cybersecurity, which is where I earned my keep. So, as a cybersecurity expert, it was my job to protect the base and to follow the intel on ops occurring off the base."

"Wait, you're a cybersecurity expert?" Cal asked, a brow raised.

"Well, I was six years ago. I may be a little rusty after being in hiding, but I've tried to keep my skills current. My commanding officer, Major Burris, knew I was also a supply chain manager. He ordered me to document historical antiquities found within the rubble and brought to the base by the locals or nervous curators. The agreement was, once the antiquity, artifact or artwork was documented, I shipped it to a museum here in the States for safekeeping."

"Were you still doing that when the base fell?" Mina asked, typing on her computer.

"I was, but over the time I was there, I backed up all the antiquity information and shipping schedules to a flash drive," Lilah explained. "When I returned stateside, I learned that Major Burris was being investigated for war crimes. Something felt off, not that I could tell you what it was other than this feeling that I needed to protect myself."

"I think we all understand that feeling," Cal said. "We all did sketchy stuff on the orders of our commanding officers."

"Then you'll understand why I told no one I had the flash drive. I didn't want anyone to know until Major Burris's case had been sorted out. I worried that I may need it to prove my innocence."

"Rightly so," Roman said. "We all know bad things roll downhill."

Lilah pointed at him with a nod. "Exactly what I was afraid of, so I was happy to keep it under my hat and go on with my life. At least until I was either called to the stand or it no longer mattered."

"How many antiquities are we talking about here? A dozen?" Efren asked from his end of the table.

"Oh, times itself and then quadruple that, at least."

"Seriously?" Mina asked. "There were that many curators worried about their collection?"

"Considering how long the war had gone on, yeah. Think about what happened in World War II with priceless artwork. Mind you, they weren't bringing one or two things, either. They brought large collections of items they didn't want to fall into the wrong hands. Keeping track of it all and organizing the shipping schedule on these items was a full-time job that I was trying to do on the side."

"Did you get the Distinguished Service Medal for your work with the antiquities?" Eric asked. "That medal is only given to soldiers who do duty to the government under great responsibility."

"That defines what Lilah did over there." Lucas's voice held respect and adoration when he spoke. "If it hadn't been for her, no one would have gotten off that base alive."

"The medal wasn't for saving the antiquities but for saving lives?" Roman asked to clarify.

"No," Lilah answered. "The medal was for what happened when the base fell. I can't say more than that, but if you're implying that the antiquities cataloging wasn't on the up-and-up, you're wrong."

Roman held his hands up in front of him. "Not what I was

implying. We're just trying to get a feel for what's happening right now, considering the situation on the island tonight."

"That's fair," she said with a tip of her head.

"From the news articles, Major Burris never went to trial," Mina said, her fingers stopping on the keyboard as she read the screen before her.

"I found that same information three years ago," Delilah agreed, stepping forward. "That's when I expected everything to die down so I could get my life back."

"That's not what happened?" Cal asked.

Lilah shook her head. "No, if anything, it got worse."

"What happened after you dropped me off at the hospital?" Lucas asked, his impatience loud and clear in the room. "You said someone attacked you?"

"Several someones. After I dropped you in Minneapolis, I went to a long-term-stay hotel. I planned to stay for a week so that I could visit you. I was barely out of my car when two men attacked me. I managed to get away when someone yelled out their window about the commotion, but not before they did this," she explained, motioning at her chin. "With my face bleeding and sliced open to the bone, I tore out of the city. The men who attacked me were trying to abduct me by knifepoint. I had originally thought it was a random attack until one of them said I should stop fighting and go with them because they'd keep coming until I gave up my information."

"Gave up your information?" Mina asked with a raised brow. "You were their information?"

"That's the vibe," she agreed, crossing her arms over her chest. "At first, I thought they knew I downloaded information before the base fell."

"Probably a time stamp in the code," Mina agreed.

"Right, that's what I thought, but then I realized that

wasn't true. My flash drive has information that isn't down-loaded. I transferred the information for each item to the flash drive before I put it through to shipping, so there was no way for them to know I made a backup."

"Which brings me back to the fact that at some point you were feeling sketchy about that whole side of the operation," Roman said.

Her shrug said more than her words. "As someone who works in the cyber world, I was protecting myself."

"Okay, so if that's the case, and there was no way for them to know you made that copy, then they wanted you because you had the information in here?" Cal asked, tapping his temple.

"That's been my working theory thus far," she agreed.

"I still don't understand what I have to do with this," Lucas said, standing and walking to where she stood by the board. "I haven't seen or heard from you since that day at the VA. I have nothing left from our time together. What is it that you think I have?"

"The flash drive. I tucked it in your army bag for safe-keeping."

Chapter Seven

Lucas took a step back as a shudder ran through him. "What now?"

Lilah refused to make eye contact with him when she spoke. "When we stopped at the storage facility in Superior before we left for the VA, I stuck the flash drive inside the bag so I didn't lose it. Since the storage unit was in both of our names, and I was going to set up house in Duluth, I had easy access to it should I need it while you were in the hospital."

"Why didn't you put it with your things?" Lucas asked, his teeth clenched tightly to keep from yelling. "You knew better than to ever touch that bag."

"I don't think that matters six years later, son," Cal said, trying to diffuse the situation. "What matters is now we know what Delilah needs."

"It does matter," Lucas answered, spinning on his heel. "I haven't opened that bag in seven years. It's a Pandora's box that would have grave consequences for me and all of you. It means reliving everything I've tried to forget. It means nightmares, flashbacks and losing the parts of me that I've found since that time."

"No," Delilah said, stepping up until they were chest-to-chest. "We aren't going to open the bag. The flash drive is in the outside pocket. I didn't open the bag, Luca. That's your history. I respect that. It was an afterthought on the way out. I had planned to move it as soon as I got back to set up the house. Somehow, we need to get to Superior and get the bag without being traced."

"No, we don't," Lucas said, gazing into her eyes. They were still terrified, but he noticed the same heat that was always there between them. Smoke tendrils that curled across her pupils to tease him into submission. "When I started working here, I moved everything in that storage unit to one just outside of town."

"Name?" Mina asked, already typing on her computer.

"Sal's Storage," Lucas answered without taking his eyes off Delilah. "Unit 57."

"That's twelve miles northwest of our location," she answered. "Corner unit with two doors."

Lucas heard them talking and making plans around him, but he couldn't drag his attention away from the woman who held him tightly in her aura. There had been an electric draw between them since the day they met on the base most unexpectedly.

The collision rattled his teeth. The cart in front of him had stopped dead in the middle of the road, and he'd had no time to react. When he looked up, a woman was on the ground next to the cart. Lucas jumped out, running to the woman staring at the blue sky, blinking every few seconds.

"Are you okay?" Lucas asked, checking her over for injuries. "I didn't have time to react, much less stop."

The woman blinked twice more, drawing his eye to hers. They were the most unusual shade of gray but beautifully framed by her heart-shaped face. Her strawberry blond hair was shoulder-length and topped with an army cap. She let out a puff of air, and he couldn't help but smile at the way her Cupid's bow lips puckered as she tried to form words.

"I'm fine," she finally managed to say. "Just stunned. Help me up."

"Maybe we should call for help first? Make sure you don't have anything wrong with your head or neck?"

"I don't," she promised, pushing herself to a sitting position. "Just got the wind knocked out of me when we collided."

"I'm Lucas," he said, sticking his hand out to help her. "Glad you're okay."

"Thanks," she said, taking his hand until she was upright. She seemed hesitant to drop it, so he didn't let her. He held it loosely while they stood on the old tarmac. "I don't know what happened, but it just came to a grinding halt and tossed me out."

Lucas released her hand and crouched to look under the cart. "Looks like you blew the drivetrain. That will bring things to a halt quickly. Let me push this one out of the way, and then I'll take you back in mine."

"That would be great," she said, starting toward her cart. "I'm Delilah, by the way."

"Hey, there, Delilah," he said with a wink. "I bet you've never heard that before."

"Oh, no," she agreed, helping him push the busted cart off to the side. "Only once or ten thousand."

His laughter filled the air, and he brushed off his hands. "Fair, but I've always loved the name. Just never knew anyone with it before."

"Well, now you do," she said, climbing into the passenger side of his cart. "Would you drop me off at the cafeteria? I was going to grab lunch, but I guess the cart *decided I needed more exercise. Too many hours sitting at the computer."*

"The cafeteria it is," he agreed. "I was headed there myself." He wasn't, but it was lunchtime, and he would take any chance to share lunch with a beautiful woman. His mama didn't raise no fool. Besides, Delilah intrigued him, and he knew nothing about her other than her name. "I haven't seen you around the base before."

"Just got here a few days ago," she answered with a shrug. "Pulled me in from a unit in Duluth stationed in Germany due to my skill set."

"No kidding?" he asked, nearly swerving off the road. "Duluth, Minnesota?"

"You betcha," she said with a cheesy grin.

"Small world. I'm out of Superior, Wisconsin."

"The good old Twin Ports. Looks like we have something in common, Lucas..."

"Ammunition Warrant Officer Lucas Porter," he said to finish the sentence. "What's your skill set? Must be big if they pulled you in for it."

"Looks like we have quite a bit in common. I'm a cyber warfare officer," she answered, with a flick of her eyes toward him. "Intel on ops. Maybe I shouldn't be telling you this stuff."

"You're fine. I work in munitions. My team plans those operations, and we provide the ammunition support. Looks like we go together like peanut butter and jelly."

Her laughter filled the cart, and Lucas couldn't help but chuckle, too. The way she tossed her head to the side, allowing the sunshine to kiss her cheeks with freckles, was too adorable not to notice. There was nothing about Delilah he didn't like, but he knew better than to start an on-

base relationship. That was an excellent way to get your heart broken—

"Luca?"

The name hit him and he snapped back to the present, realizing the room had gone silent. He turned toward the table where everyone sat expectantly. "Sorry, I got lost in thought for a moment there. What was the question?"

"In a nutshell?" Cal asked, and Lucas nodded. "How do you want to proceed?"

"Alone," he answered, and with one last look at Delilah, he walked out the door.

"I'LL GO TALK to him," Cal said as he stood.

Delilah held up her hand. "Give him a few minutes to settle down. I knew he wouldn't react well to this, but unfortunately, contacting him was my only choice."

"What's the big deal about his army duffel bag?" Charlotte, Secure One's public liaison and Mack's girlfriend, asked. "Everyone around this table has one."

"True, but for Luca, it holds the reminders of what happened that day on the base," Delilah explained. "All of his medals went into it, too, because those remind him of what he didn't do instead of what he did do."

"Medals?" Cal asked in surprise. "We had no idea he had medals."

"That doesn't surprise me," Delilah said. "He doesn't tell anyone. He refused to do anything more than have them mailed to him. He never even opened the boxes, just stuffed each one in the bag and walked away. I can't remember them all, but one is the Purple Heart and the last one he got while I was with him was the Distinguished Service Cross."

Efren whistled low before he spoke. "That's not something you hear every day. I had no idea he was so decorated."

"Well—" she motioned at the door "—Luca likes it that way. That duffel bag is a time capsule that'll never be opened if he has anything to say about it. I tried to bring it with us to the VA hospital so that they could go through it with him, but he refused, adamantly so. Selfishly, I'm glad he's moved it with him over the years rather than dump it. I could never return to that part of the state to get the flash drive. I banked on the hope that, while he hated everything the bag represented, he would never get rid of it."

"I don't care what he says," Mina interrupted. "He's not doing this alone."

"She's right," Roman said. "The smart move would be for a team of us to retrieve the bag."

Delilah laughed loudly, and they all turned to stare at her. "Sorry," she said, momentarily putting her hand over her mouth. "But trust me. That will never happen. You saw his reaction to the idea that I even touched the bag to put the flash drive in the pocket. There's no way he'll let anyone else pick it up."

"You're saying Lucas is possessive of something he wants nothing to do with?" Marlise, who was Secure One's Client Coordinator and Cal's wife, often broke things down in a way that made it easy for everyone to understand.

"Everyone carries their ghosts differently, I guess. Mine are wrapped up in the medal I sent him, and it's the only thing I carry from that time. If you knew the things he did that day, it would be easy to understand why he is the way he is. Right now, none of that matters. Top priority is convincing him to go with me to get that flash drive. I need to get out of here before all of you pay the price."

"I couldn't agree more," Cal said with a nod. "We'll prepare a plan to help you get to the storage unit and then find somewhere safe for you to go while we figure out who is after you. That somewhere will not be here."

"Understood," Delilah said with a nod. "Believe me when I say I never intended for any of this to happen or to drag all of you into this. I only wanted to get the drive and disappear again."

Mina's laughter filled the room as she shook her head. "You honestly thought you could contact Lucas the way you did and expect him to be like, 'Here's your flash drive. Bye,' as though the last six years hadn't happened?"

"You must understand that I was desperate," she said imploringly. "I didn't mean for any of this to happen or to drag Lucas back through his past. That's the last thing I wanted to do, but I was out of options."

Mina stood and walked around the table. "You have to stop apologizing, Delilah," she said, taking her elbow. "You're here now, which means you're one of us."

"We're called Secure One for a reason," Cal said from where he sat. "We are one under this roof, which means we are one for all and all for one. Right now, we are all for you, so this is what will happen. You'll help Lucas find the headspace he needs to be in while we make a plan. When he's ready, we'll be ready."

Mina walked Delilah to the door and leaned into her ear. "The only way out of this is through it, so start at the most important place. The beginning."

As Delilah walked out the conference room door, she couldn't help but think that was why they were in this spot to begin with.

Chapter Eight

Lucas sat in the dark kitchen with his head in his hands. His rhythmic breathing was second nature as Haven kept his paws on his leg and his muzzle under his handler's chin. If putting eyes on Lilah again wasn't enough of a shock, what she told him in that room pushed him past his breaking point.

"Luca," she said from the doorway, but he didn't look up. "I'm sorry. This was never supposed to happen. When I put the flash drive in the bag, it was for a week, not six years."

"It's the fact that you put it in there at all, Delilah. You knew how I felt about that bag."

"You need to get a grip, Luca," she said, and he snapped his head around to make eye contact. "Seriously. In the years since the war you've made yourself a new life here and found a brotherhood again. Yet, you continue to act like that bag is going to stand up and gun you down. I see all the work you've done to overcome everything that happened that day, and I respect the hell out of that, but you're not done. You can't have your life back until you open that bag and face the items inside."

"That's never going to happen."

"What are you so afraid of?" she asked, frustration loud

and clear in her tone. "The memories? The idea that you saved lives and were commended for that?"

"I also took lives, Lilah. A whole lot of them."

"True, but they were trying to take yours and a whole lot of other Americans' lives."

"So that makes it right?"

"Luca, we both know there is nothing about war that is right to anyone with a decent moral compass. That doesn't mean we're given a choice. If you hadn't stepped up to be the hero that day—"

"Don't," he hissed from between his teeth. "Don't use that word."

"This is what I'm talking about," she said with a shake of her head. "Maybe you don't feel like one, but to me, you are. To the people you saved on that base that day, you are one. That doesn't mean you're flying through the sky with a cape. It means you stepped up when no one else would or could. That's what makes someone commendable. I understand that you're still mad all these years after you were put in that position, but it must be an awfully heavy load to carry every day."

"You don't know anything about it, Lilah."

"But I do. You always seem to forget I was also there. I live with the nightmares and the terror, too. My trauma may be different than yours, but that doesn't mean it's not there. None of this has been easy for me, either. The last thing I wanted was to be on the run for my life for six years, but here we are, aren't we? If I could go back and do things differently, I would, but I can't, so can we make a plan to get the drive? Without it, I'm a dead woman walking."

"Who are these people after you?" he asked, finally turning to face her again. If she wanted to read him the riot act about his choices in life, he could do the same. "You can't expect me to believe you have no idea who they are if this has gone on for six years."

"I honestly don't, Lucas. All I know is it has something to do with the antiquity cataloging."

"You swore you were only keeping the flash drive until Burris's trial."

"That was my plan, but again, I never returned to Superior for the flash drive. I was already on the run when the investigation ended without charges. I know you don't want to face that bag again, but it's time, don't you think?"

"You're not giving me a choice, are you, Lilah? You're just waltzing in with the demand that I do."

"There are no demands here, Luca," she said with a shake of her head. "Cal and Roman offered to go get the drive and leave the bag untouched. You're the one who said you were going alone."

"I don't want anyone around that bag but me."

"Do you keep that bag in the storage unit because you're afraid to face it or because you're afraid to live?"

He gazed at her in confusion for a moment. "What does that mean?"

"Every day that you keep that bag 'alive,'" she said, using air quotes, "is another day you can keep living in the past. From what I've seen about this place and its people, you could have a successful and fulfilling future if the past wasn't hanging around your neck like a dead albatross."

Lucas whistled while he shook his head. "Boy, you think you know a lot, don't you?"

"That's not what I think at all. The thing is, I know you, Luca. You can pretend that I don't or that the years we've been apart mean I can't possibly understand who you are now, but that's all it is—pretending. I know who you are to your core," she whispered, tapping her finger on his chest.

Lucas grabbed her finger and held it tightly. He tried to tell himself it was because she was annoying him, but the truth was, he wanted to touch her. He wanted to feel her warmth again after all these years. He wanted her to see how much he'd changed and the improvements he'd made in his life.

She can't do that if you don't show her those things. You're behaving the same way you did six years ago. Be the man she needs right now.

The thought halted his count of three, and he pulled in one breath and held it. The voice was right. He wasn't showing Delilah that he'd changed since she left. If anything, he was proving to her that he hadn't moved anywhere or learned anything about himself since they were last together. The very idea stiffened his spine. He stood, holding his hand out.

"Can I trust you, Delilah Hartman?" What he didn't ask was if he could trust her not to break his heart.

"You can, Luca. I know how much I hurt you by disappearing from your life, but know that was the last thing I wanted to happen. The choice was run and protect you, or stay and risk them trying to get to me through you. I couldn't let that happen."

"Then let's do what we've always done best."

Lilah lifted a brow, and it brought a smile to his lips. "The one thing we did best probably shouldn't be done right now, Luca."

This time, he couldn't help but laugh when he chucked her gently under the chin. "Let me rephrase that. The second thing we did best."

"Work together?"

"That," he agreed, taking her hand. "We were always a great team. Maybe that was practice for what was to come."

"For the time when it would be imperative to know each other's strengths and weaknesses?"

"And that time is now," he finished. "Let's find out what the team has planned, get that flash drive and win your life back."

Delilah leaned into him, resting her head on his shoulder. "Thank you, Luca. I hate that I've stirred all of this up for you again."

"No," he whispered, holding her gaze for a beat. "Thank you for reminding me that I'm standing in front of the person who changed my life six years ago and the person I wanted to change my life for back then. I have changed, and now it's time to prove it."

"And I'm standing in front of the person who changed my life six years ago and the person I was protecting all this time. I don't regret losing out on those years because you were safe, but I'm glad we have this time together, even if it's fraught with danger."

"Me, too, even if it looks different than the life we planned." He led her toward the door. "Haven, forward," he called to the dog. Once they got to the doorway, he paused. "I will still do everything in my power to protect you, Lilah. That means whatever needs to be done, I'll do."

"There's the Luca I knew was in there," she said, dropping one lid down in a wink.

THE DARKNESS SWALLOWED them as they slid from the van parked southwest of the storage units. They hadn't picked up a tail as far as they could tell, and Lucas had been in constant contact with the other two cars that held Secure One teams running diversions. She and Lucas planned to slide in, get the flash drive, head back to the van and drive to a small motel an hour away from the Canadian border.

Once they had the flash drive, they couldn't go back to headquarters, but Mina sent a laptop and equipment for Delilah to communicate with her once the flash drive was in their possession.

Delilah glanced over at Lucas, who was gauging the distance they had to walk without cover. Trees surrounded the storage facility on three sides, leaving the only unprotected side at the driveway approach.

"My unit is in the back corner. If we stay in the trees until we're opposite it, the only time we'll be exposed is the time it takes to unlock the door."

"All of this cloak and dagger stuff might be a bit much, Luca," she whispered as they walked, Haven glued to his handler's side, step for step. This time, the dog was wearing his bulletproof vest, too. "Lately, it has taken them four or five days to find me."

"Maybe, but that was before the island. Now they know who you're with, so I'm not taking any chances."

"Fair enough," Delilah said, but she still thought it was unnecessary. It would take that team on the island a long time to regroup and relocate her. They hadn't been at Secure One longer than three hours before the team had a plan and implemented it.

Another hundred yards farther, and Lucas pulled her to a stop. "The unit is right there," he said, pointing at the metal building in front of them. Not surprisingly, strings of Christmas lights hung from the eaves of the metal buildings. It offered a little light in the darkness, and it slowed her pounding heart. "As soon as I open the side walk-through door, you get inside. I'm not going to mess with the roll-up door. That leaves us too visible."

"Why don't I just wait here?" she asked, leaning into his

ear to speak now that he had her spooked. "The flash drive is in the outside pocket—"

"I can't prevent a sneak attack if you're in the woods and I'm not. We're a team and we stay together."

"Ten-four," she whispered with a smile he couldn't see. They were a team. It hadn't taken much to remind him of that.

Lucas gestured to Haven and slid out of the woods like a ghost. It was easy to see his time at Secure One had taught him new skills that she suspected took a lot of practice. Especially since he took Haven with him everywhere. He had the door open by the time she reached him, and he practically shoved her through the small opening, followed her in with Haven and closed the door with barely a click.

Lucas flicked a flashlight on and shone it around the space. One glance was all she needed to see that the only thing in the storage unit was the bag. Rather than comment on it, she glanced up at him.

"The side pocket," she said as Lucas knelt over the bag. She noticed him hesitate with his hand over the pocket. She crouched and put her hand on his shoulder. "You got this," she whispered. "Baby steps."

He nodded as he breathed in and waited, then blew it out and reached for the pocket just as the first bullet slammed into the metal unit.

"Dammit!" Lucas hissed, grabbing her and shoving her behind him as another bullet hit the side door. It was a steel door but wouldn't hold bullets back for long. They were trapped in a tin box and had no way out except through the steel curtain roll-up door, which was padlocked from the outside.

"Stay down," Lucas yelled, and she could tell he was running their options through his head. They didn't have many other than praying the steel door held. "Get down on your belly and get to the back of the unit. It's protected by the opposite one! When they hit that rolling door, it will give quickly. I'll get one chance to end them before they end us."

Delilah was pulling Haven down by her when the shooting stopped. "Now," Lucas hissed, moving with her to the back of the unit until a sound stopped them in their tracks.

"Secure one, Charlie," Cal called through the door.

"Secure two, Lima!" Lucas answered, scrambling to the side door and throwing it open. "Cal! Are you alone?"

"Not a chance," Roman said, stepping out of the woods.

"I thought we were screwed six ways to Sunday until you called out. You guys being here wasn't part of the plan."

"It always was, son," Cal said while they checked the pulses on the four guys on the ground. "We didn't want you to argue about us coming along for the ride. If you didn't need us, you never had to know we were here."

"I probably would have argued, but I'm sure glad you're here."

"Four this time," Delilah said, stepping around Lucas. "They're upping the ante."

"All carrying ARs," Cal said as he got to the final guy. "Got a live one." He grabbed a pair of restraints and cuffed him.

"These three have gone on to the great hellscape beyond," Roman answered. "No IDs. No anything other than their weapons."

"Did you find the drive?" Cal asked, standing up to address Lucas.

"I was just reaching for the bag when they started shooting. They had to be hot on our heels by no more than minutes. How did they find us so quickly?" Lucas turned to her. "What did you bring from your last place?"

"Nothing," she swore, holding up her hands. "I bought everything new before I went to the island, including undergarments."

"I don't understand it," Lucas said. "They're tracking you somehow. Your glasses?"

She shook her head. "I buy new ones every time I move, and always from a different online provider."

"What are we going to do with these guys?" Roman asked, interrupting Lucas's train of thought.

"Well, we can't exactly hide this," Cal motioned around the area with his hands. "Shall we claim it was a shoot-out at Christmas corral?" Lucas grunted with laughter, something he didn't think he was capable of at the moment. His laughter brought a smile to Cal's lips, too. "I'll call the cops, and we'll say we were working security when we heard the ruckus."

"How are you going to explain the bullet holes in them?" Roman asked with a smirk.

"We've got a live one here. Since he's unconscious, we blame it on him. He can sort it out when he's awake, alert and oriented."

"I just want to know who they are and what they want with me!" Delilah exclaimed, frustration evident in her voice.

Lucas ran to her and put his arm around her shoulder while Haven moved in and propped his snout under her elbow. "It's okay. We'll figure this out," he promised, helping her over to where Cal and Roman stood. "Same plan?"

Cal nodded. "Take the van to the motel while we handle this situation. Once you're there safely, call in. Mack and Efren report that these were the only guys in the area, so your walk to the van is clear. Lucas, grab your bag."

"We only need the flash drive," he said, headed toward the doorway, but Cal grabbed his arm.

"The cops will be crawling around here in about an hour. Take the whole bag, or it will become evidence. What else is in the unit that's tied to your name?"

Delilah noticed Lucas's spine stiffen as he considered Cal's words. "Nothing. The only thing in it is the bag. I rented the unit online under a different name and a PO Box."

Cal nodded once as he glanced around the units. "It looks like Sal invested in Christmas lights instead of security cameras, so that helps. Get the bag and get out. We'll take care of everything else."

The door was open, so Delilah watched Lucas stare at the bag for a full thirty seconds before he slowly bent over and picked it up. When he stood, the expression on his face was unlike any she'd seen before. It was determination mixed with something else. Pride? Hatred? Pain? Maybe all of the above. As he strode toward her, the look intensified until he took her hand.

"We'll be in touch once we're safe. Give us three hours. I want to be sure we don't pick up a tail."

"I've got GPS on the van, so we'll keep a close eye on it. I would send a follow team, but I don't want to make your identity obvious."

"I've got this," Lucas assured his boss. "Hopefully, we can get a few hours head start before the next team is sent out."

"There will be a next team," Delilah added, glancing at Cal and Roman. "Watch yourselves."

"Haven, forward," Lucas ordered, and the dog lined up beside his leg. "Lima, out," he said as they entered the tree line.

Delilah jogged through the woods next to Lucas, but they

never spoke. As he held the bag tightly, it was like watching him be reborn. The bag used to be the enemy, but now, he was ready to make peace with it.

Then he glanced at her, and the look in his eyes said that was the furthest thing from the truth.

Chapter Nine

"The dome light is disabled. Climb in while I get Haven situated," Lucas whispered to Delilah once he cleared the van of interlopers. While she settled in the front, Lucas slid open the side door and lowered the sizeable duffel bag to the floor. He struggled to unclench his fist of its prize. It wasn't that the bag was physically heavy, but emotionally, it weighed more than he could carry. This time, he hadn't been given a choice. He had to carry the weight for her. If what she said was true, she'd been fighting this war alone for the last six years. She needed a team to back her up now.

He hooked Haven into his seat, slammed the door and jumped in the driver's side. "Buckle up."

Delilah slid her seat belt over her chest while he started the van. "Did you find the flash drive?"

"Didn't look," he answered, straightening his seat belt. "It's hidden in the bag right now. We'll leave it until we get to the motel. If we get into an altercation on the road, I'd rather it wasn't on your person."

"They won't find us that fast," she said, turning in her seat to look at the bag.

"That's what you said about the guys we just took out." Lucas was ready to put the van in Drive when something Cal said sent a zap of fear through his gut. "GPS."

Delilah's look was curious. "What about it? Cal said he was tracking the van. That can only help us if we encounter more resistance."

"What did you bring from Secure One?" he asked, leaving the van in Park and turning to her.

After glancing down at herself, she met his gaze. "Just the clothes Mina gave me and the issued equipment Cal insisted I take, like the handgun and cuffs. Mina gave me a new lip gloss and a few toiletries. The only other thing I have is my identification, which is fake, and my medal."

Disgust slithered through Lucas's belly at the thought running through his mind. "Do you keep the medal with you all the time, or do you normally leave it in a safety deposit box?"

She shook her head immediately. "It's always with me, since I'm never in the same place very long."

Lucas swallowed back the bile in his throat and held out his hand. "Can I see it?"

"Why?" she asked, digging inside her jacket pocket for a moment before she pulled it out. "It hasn't changed since you gave it back to me."

Once it was in his hand, he ran his fingers over the medal, looking for bumps or outcroppings. "That's what has been bugging me, Lilah," he explained, holding up the medal. "You carried this everywhere and they kept finding you. You sent it to me, and I showed up on the island with extra visitors. You have it in your pocket tonight and they're on us in minutes. They're using the medal to track you."

"Impossible," she whispered with a shake of her head. "There's no way there's a tracker small enough to put in that medal. Not to mention, I've had it for six years. The battery would never last."

"Nothing is impossible if it's the military tracking you.

You'd be surprised by the tech they have that no one knows about, including solar-powered trackers."

"You can't prove it, though." She motioned at the medal in his hand. "And we don't have time to take it apart."

"Don't need to, as long as it doesn't go with us."

He climbed out of the van and dug a hole with his multi-tool deep enough to lay the medal in and cover it up. He took a picture with the Secure One phone and sent it to Cal with a message before he climbed back into the van. She stared at him with her lips pulled in a thin line.

"I'm sorry, Lilah, but we can't take it with us. Just in case. I sent the information to Cal to get the medal and move it somewhere." He pulled the lever into Drive and left the curb, knowing there were still over two hours to go in this long night. "He'll keep watch on it. If another group of armed guys shows up at the location, it's a good bet the medal is to blame."

"That doesn't make sense, though, Luca," she said, leaning back in the seat with her arms crossed. "Why would the military want to track me? I've been discharged free and clear for years."

"Let me ask you. Who else knows about these antiquities being in the States?"

"Now? I don't know. Back then, only my boss, his boss and the museum curators."

"Which tells me it was a top-secret operation at the time. That means you are one of the few people with the information in your head."

"I'm probably the only one with it in my head, but my boss and his bosses have access to that information, too," she said, throwing up her hands. "I had to transmit the information daily to the person in charge of the shipments."

"I could be dead wrong about everything," he said to appease her, but he was convinced the medal was to blame. "It's just a better-safe-than-sorry situation. If we don't have the medal with us, and the guys find us again, then we know it wasn't the medal."

"All I know is, I'm exhausted," she said, staring out the back window as though she expected headlights to pop up and mow them down. "I've been running for so many years, all over the country. It isn't conducive to having any quality of life." She turned around in the seat and slumped down into her coat.

Lucas reached over and turned up the heat. "I wish I hadn't been so angry with you and had tried harder to find you when I got out," he whispered, squeezing her shoulder. "When the information didn't come easily, I gave up. It was easier to convince myself that you didn't want me to find you, and it was better to let you go, than it was to fight against the memories of us."

"It wasn't easy staying off the internet," she admitted with a tip of her head. "It required burner phones, lots of fake identifications and some pretty shady living situations."

"But no matter what you did, they kept coming for you?"

"They always found me. Sometimes it was weeks or months, and one time it was a year, but whoever they are, they're great at keeping me unbalanced and unhinged."

"You aren't unhinged," he corrected her as he steered the van down the two-lane highway. "You're scared and confused. After being attacked like that, it had to be difficult to trust anyone."

"I didn't trust anyone. In hindsight, I should have trusted you, Luca."

Lucas heard the slur to her words, and he turned the radio up as Frank Sinatra crooned about having a merry little Christmas. He glanced away from the road for a split second to see her sinking into sleep, comforted by the warmth of the van and the company of another person after so many years alone. They were both exhausted, so he'd let her sleep while they found their way to safety—at least for a little while—and then he'd sit her down and get the real story. The guys they'd come across screamed military to him, and that scared him more than anything else would. If the government wanted her, they'd have her. Lucas could do nothing to stop it.

LILAH WOKE WITH a start to realize the van had stopped moving. She glanced at the old blue building in front of her and then to her left, where Lucas sat in the driver's seat, grasping the steering wheel with an iron grip.

"We made it," she said, stretching in the seat. "I didn't mean to fall asleep. You should have woken me so I could keep watch."

"It wasn't a problem, Lilah," he said, his gaze firmly planted on the building beyond the windshield. "The drive was uneventful and I had some thinking to do, anyway. I need to go check in. The second I close the door, move to the driver's seat and keep the van running. If anyone approaches you, get out of here."

"I can't just leave you!" she exclaimed, turning in her seat.

"You can and you will. The van is being tracked in the control room, and we'll catch up with you."

"What about Haven?"

"He's coming with me, of course. If everything is safe, we'll return to the van once I clear the room. Ten-four?"

"Heard and acknowledged," she agreed, waiting for him to unhook Haven from his seat belt. After he checked all sides of the van, he climbed out, and Haven hopped over the console and out of the van to follow his handler.

The moment the locks engaged, fear drove Lilah to climb into the driver's seat and put her hands on the wheel. She had to stay on her toes and shut out the memories of the last time she was in a place like this with Luca. It had been a beautiful summer day, and they'd been driving up the north shore along Lake Superior. Their destination had been Thunder Bay, but they had no schedule to follow or place to be. They'd come across this little town, well, you couldn't call it a town as much as a place you passed through on the road to somewhere else. Luca had seen the blue brick building and steered the car into the parking lot—

The locks disengaged and Lilah jumped. Her attention captured by the memories, she totally missed Luca returning to the van. She was lucky no one else approached her while she was daydreaming. "All clear," he said, grabbing their bags from the back. He helped her out of the van before he propelled her into the small room. He closed the door, threw the lock, drew the curtains and dropped the bags on the floor. "I need to let the team know we made it."

"You said they were tracking the van. Aren't they already aware?"

Rather than answer her, he pushed past her and grabbed a gear bag, unzipping it and pulling out computer equipment. She left him for a moment to use the bathroom. The shower beckoned her, so she stripped from her dusty clothes and stepped under the warm spray. She forced the memories of a long-ago time in a place like this where she and Luca had shared the shower—had shared everything—and focused on the present. She couldn't help but wonder if what Luca thought about the medal was true. In hindsight, it was the only thing she always had with her when she moved from place to place. The sticking point for her was, if someone was tracking her with the medal, that could only mean one thing. They had to be military. She couldn't think of any reason why the military would track her or accost her. They didn't even know the flash drive existed.

But you exist.

The thought jarred her, and she dropped the soap bar on the floor. She stooped to pick it up and thought back to the day she'd found the secret file on the server. There was no identifying information as to who had put it there, but there was also no way anyone knew she had a copy. She'd covered her digital trail over there to avoid being picked up by the enemy, who were always looking for a way to start a cyberwar. There was no way anyone could know she'd seen that file, right?

A cold shudder went through her even as she stood under the hot water. None of this made sense. She was distracted and jumpy, which made her feel out of control and scattered. It didn't help that she was continually trapped in small spaces with the man she'd loved for years, all while knowing she could never have him. Not as long as she was being hunted. There was no way she would be the one to remind him of the things he tried to forget.

It's too late for that.

Slamming the water off, Lilah huffed at that voice. She was starting to hate it, mainly because it was always right. It was too late to protect Luca from the memories of that time. As she dried herself, part of her wondered if that was such a bad thing. He'd told her he learned how to work around the memories of what happened to him, not that he'd dealt with them head-on. She was well aware through personal experience that confronting them wasn't going to make them go away, but not being afraid of how each memory ended, because she already knew what was coming, did make it easier to let them roll over her and fall away rather than roll over her and drown her.

Lilah tucked the towel under her armpit and glanced at herself in the minuscule mirror over the sink. "That may not be the case for Luca, and you know that. The things he saw and did are incomprehensible to most people."

With a tip of her shoulder, she gathered her clothes off the floor. Maybe that was why he learned to work around them rather than face them. Talking about those things, admitting to what he did that day to ensure his fellow soldiers got off that base, might make everything worse.

When she opened the door, Lucas had finished with the devices he'd laid out on the small desk against the bathroom wall. "Are there clean clothes in any of those bags, or should I put these back on?"

He spun as though he hadn't heard her come out but came to an abrupt halt when he saw her wrapped in only a towel. He cleared his throat before he spoke. "Enjoy your shower?"

"I did, but don't worry, I left you plenty of hot water."

"I'm not worried about the hot water. I am worried about you. You're hurt," he said, stepping forward and tracing a large bruise on her shoulder.

She glanced down at his finger on her skin. He left a trail of deep yearning that burned her skin with every inch. She deserved the pain of the bruise and to withstand his touch, knowing his hands would never be on her as a lover.

"It's fine. I must have hurt it on the island and didn't realize it. What did Secure One say?"

Luca shook his head as though the question snapped him back to reality. "The cops bought their story and took over the scene, but not before Cal snapped pictures of the guys' faces. Mina was able to use facial recognition to identify them. They're all ex-military."

Lilah's heart sank as she sucked in air. "Dammit. I've been telling myself there's no way they could be military. This doesn't make any sense, Luca."

"They aren't military. They're ex-military, but that raises the question of who they're working for now."

"Good point," Lilah agreed, sinking to the bed in the center of the room. "I'm no closer to figuring this out now than I was six years ago."

"You haven't had time to figure it out," he said, kneeling beside her. "You've been too busy trying to stay alive, right?"

"Which would have been easier if I knew who was after me and why," she admitted to the man who was much too close for her liking. All she had to do was turn her head, and she could have her lips on his. She resisted by staring straight ahead at the door.

"We'll get to the bottom of this so you can have your life back," Lucas promised. "Mina is working on things now and will keep us posted."

"What life?" she asked with a shake of her head. "I have no life, Luca. I haven't since the day I left you and ran headlong into the night. The cut on my chin turned the car into a crime scene, so I had hoped by abandoning it, they would think Delilah Hartman had died a tragic death. How wrong I'd been. Getting to the bottom of this means I'm free, but I'm thirty-four years old and have no idea how to live a normal life."

They sat in silence, their gazes locked together, and Lilah wondered if he was thinking about the last time they were together in a place like this. She couldn't force her mind away from those memories, even as they heated her cheeks and sent waves of sensation through her belly, then lower to the place she had shared with no one since she lost him. Back then, Luca had been a fast and furious lover. It was rare that they took their time, even if they tried. The heat built too quickly and drove them to touch, taste and tease each other as fast as they could until the explosive end.

"Do you remember the last time we were in this motel?" Luca's question pulled her out of her daydreams and back to reality.

"I haven't stopped thinking about it since I opened my eyes in the van. It feels like we were in a motel like this just yesterday with fewer, or maybe different, worries."

"Not a different motel. If it were daylight, you'd realize this is the same motel, on the same road, just not the same room."

"You mean, this is—"

"Yes," he answered, dropping his knee to the floor. "Mina picked it. I had no idea it was the same place until I realized it could be the only place."

Lilah's fingers traced his five o'clock shadow, and the rasp against her skin reminded her how he felt against her as they made love. "If you're uncomfortable, we can keep driving."

"I'm not uncomfortable," he promised, his hand capturing hers against his cheek. "At least not in the memory department. In the 'being trapped in a motel with an almost naked woman who I know can blow my mind the moment I put my lips on hers' department, I'm uncomfortable."

Instinctively, she tightened her grip around the towel. "I'm sorry. Let me get dressed so we can focus."

"You think we'll be able to focus just because you put clothes on, or do you think no matter what we do, being here together is a walk down memory lane we need to take?"

"Are you saying what I think you're saying?"

He tipped his head in agreement. "Once and done. Get it out of our system so we can focus on the case without this constant pull between us."

He was dead wrong if he thought falling into bed with him once would stop that pull between them. Lilah wasn't sure years of falling into bed with him would stop that pull, but she had to ask herself if she wanted to be with him one more time or if she wanted to remember who they were together before all of this happened.

Her decision made, she stood and walked into the bathroom, the memory of the days those brown eyes were hers too much to bear.

Chapter Ten

Lucas watched Lilah close the bathroom door to shut him out. He knew it was a risk to suggest they make love again, but he was scared. He was scared that the connection between them was stronger than ever and the only way for him to know for sure was to be with her in the most elemental way. If the connection was just as strong as it was six years ago, he had to rethink how he'd been living. Delilah's reappearance was going to put a crimp in his ability to live in the land of denial he'd so firmly planted himself in at that hospital when she never showed again.

He stood and glanced at Haven, who lay on a makeshift bed of blankets in the corner. The dog kept his eyes on him but didn't approach, which meant he didn't think his handler needed him. Yet. That time could come, but for now, Lucas raised his hand and knocked on the bathroom door. "Lilah? Come out and talk to me. You don't even have any clothes in there."

Her heavy sigh from the other side of the door made him smile. She always hated it when he used logic to thwart her emotions. She told him it took her out of the moment and forced her to think instead of feel. That's what he needed her to do right now. Think. Research. React. Participate. She couldn't do that if there was a constant wall between them.

The doorknob turned, and the door swung open. She held his gaze as she walked out and motioned at the bags. "Which one is mine? I'll get dressed."

"Sit," he said instead, motioning at the bed. "If we don't clear the air between us, working together as a team will be impossible." What he didn't say was working with her was tasking his emotions, and clearing the air wouldn't help that, but it would, hopefully, help her. Once she was sitting, he pulled the blanket up and wrapped it around her shoulders, then he sat next to her. "You're walking on eggshells around me. That can't continue."

"I'm trying not to upset you," she whispered, her eyes on the floor until he tipped her chin to face him.

"Stop doing that," he ordered, and her gaze snapped to his. "I'm not emotionally labile the way I was the last time we were together. I don't snap the way I used to. I've learned how to manage my emotions in a way that doesn't hurt anyone, including myself."

"I'm glad," she said with a smile. "I could tell how different you were the moment you showed up on the island. That's not why I'm being cautious."

"I don't understand then, Lilah. Explain it to me."

He watched her tighten the blanket around her chest and drop her gaze again. He let her, for now, in case it was the only way she could talk about what she was going through. "I need help, and I can't—"

"Make me angry, or I might stop helping you?" He'd interrupted her in hopes of taking her by surprise. She could say whatever she wanted and he wouldn't know if he could believe it. If he told the truth, there would be no way she could hide her reaction from him. The fact that she hadn't looked up and continued to stare at the floor told him he was right. He tipped her chin up again and cocked a smile across his lips. "You're stuck with me, kid."

"I don't want you to feel obligated, Luca," she said in a whisper. "I can take the flash drive and go. Then I'm no longer your problem."

"Not exactly true," he said, that smile faltering. "We're connected now. Whoever is after you knows that. Besides, you've been my problem for many years, so now that you're back, I can't let you walk out the door while you're in danger."

"I've been your problem?"

His stomach roiled at the question. If he answered it honestly, he would hurt her. If he lied, he hurt himself. Gazing into her eyes, he decided this one time, he could take the pain. "As I told you, I looked for you over the years, Lilah. I went from a man in love, to a man who was hurt, to a man who was worried, to a man who was numb."

"I wanted to contact you, Luca, so badly—"

"But you couldn't, or you'd put me at risk, too."

"Truthfully, I couldn't be sure of that, but I had to assume that if you were connected to me in any way, you'd be in danger. I didn't want you to live the way I had to live. Going from town to town, seedy apartment to seedy apartment. Low-wage job to day work here and there. Spending time in the forests surviving on fish and rabbits as I moved across the countryside."

"That doesn't sound like any kind of life."

"It wasn't, but I had to keep moving or risk being captured again. If you're right about the medal, they must laugh at my stupidity whenever they come after me."

"No," he said, taking her hand between his. "You knew you were being tracked, but you didn't know how, so there was no reason for you to suspect it was the medal."

"I was so careful with everything else, Luca. If I hadn't let my pride overrule my common sense, I would have put the medal in a safety deposit box and walked away. The thought never crossed my mind."

"Was it pride that made you hold on to that medal?" She didn't answer, so he pushed her a bit. "Was it, Lilah? Or was it something else?"

"That ceremony was the last time you told me you were proud of me before I dropped you at that hospital and abandoned you!" she exclaimed, tears shimmering in her eyes. "I abandoned you. For that, you should never forgive me, Lucas Porter."

"Wrong," he insisted, wiping away a stray tear that fell lazily down her cheek. "You didn't abandon me. You left me somewhere safe with every intention of returning, right?" Her nod was enough for him. "You couldn't control what happened after that to either one of us, so you have to stop carrying guilt about it. Was I upset and angry in the beginning? Yes. Have I been angry at you all of these years? No. I locked away every emotion I didn't need to live in the outside world into a box. That box was locked tight until I got called to a funeral home to collect the ashes of the woman I thought I'd love forever. That's when the box broke open again."

"I wish so many things, Luca," she whispered. "The biggest thing I wish is that I could have spared you all of that pain. That I could have gotten you a message somehow or someway, but I couldn't risk it."

"Because you didn't want me to get hurt, right?" he asked, thumbing away another tear. Her tears always broke his heart, and tonight was no different because, once again, she was crying over him.

"Yes, of course. I couldn't risk that my message would

lead them to you and they'd hurt you to get to me. Can you ever forgive me, Luca? I mean, truly forgive me for all of this."

"There's nothing to forgive, Lilah. That's what you aren't grasping. You didn't start this. But what you did after it began, you did out of love. I know that, sometimes, doing something out of love is the hardest thing of all." Like pretending for the rest of his life that he no longer needed this woman to feel alive. "Carrying around anger about it only wastes energy we could be using to find the guys after you and end it so you can live again. Right here, right now, you have to let the guilt go. You've carried it too long and for no reason. The biggest thing they taught me at the VA was to let go of anything that didn't serve to improve your life. This guilt and shame you're carrying doesn't improve your life. It keeps you from staying present and being my partner as we try to navigate who's after you and why. Do you understand what I'm trying to say?"

Lilah never answered him with words. She purposefully leaned forward until their lips connected. A bright light exploded behind his eyes, and he dragged her to him. The sensation of her lips on his had been a memory for so long. Her body, soft and warm under his hands, moved against him in familiar ways as his tongue probed her lips to take the kiss back to days gone by. The moment he slipped his tongue between those sweet lips, he knew she hadn't put their past behind her, either.

"Lilah." The word fell from his lips as he kissed his way down her neck toward the towel that had slipped, teasing him with the imagery of her sweet body. "You're so beautiful."

She jerked, grasped the towel and tried to push him away

all in one movement. It was more knee-jerk than intentional, so he held her still. "We can't do this," she finally gasped.

"Feels to me like we should," he answered, holding her gaze so she knew he was fully engaged with her. "We're explosive together, Lilah, and we don't want that explosion to happen at the wrong time and put us at risk. We're safe here tonight. After that, I can't promise anything."

She pushed herself off his lap and grabbed a bag off the floor. "That's where you're wrong. We aren't safe here. Those guys could surround this place as we sit here letting our hormones run away with our common sense. You're a security guy. You know I'm right. That," she said, motioning at the bed she'd just leaped from, "will never happen again." The slamming of the bathroom door punctuated her sentence, leaving him to do nothing but stare after her and wonder where he had gone wrong.

THE KEYBOARD CLACKED as Lilah finished sending her message to Mina. She wanted to know if they could track the men at the storage unit to any particular employer or if they were more of a thugs-for-hire situation. Knowing they were ex-military explained their ability to penetrate her defenses without fail, but that didn't explain who they worked for or what they wanted. She had to know who was giving the orders if she was ever going to solve this problem and move on with her life.

A quick flick of her gaze to Luca told her that may never be possible. At least not fully moving on. Having her lips on his was as explosive as it ever was until she remembered she wasn't the same woman he had made love to in this motel the last time. She wanted him to remember her body the way it was then rather than see her body now. There was nothing beautiful about her anymore—body, mind or spirit.

Unfortunately, she had hurt him by reacting the way she did without explanation. That couldn't be helped. What he didn't know was helping him move on with his life. She could only make him understand that with deeds and not words. Luca had a future, a promising future where he could help others. She didn't. She lived in the moment, knowing any moment could be her last.

He'd been standing by the window for the last hour, peering through a crack in the curtain. He had his gun out and at his side with his spine ramrod straight, or as straight as it would go since he broke it trying to defend the base all those years ago. He never talked about how he had broken multiple vertebrae in his back that day or how lucky he was that it never impinged the spinal cord. They were able to stabilize his spine, and with six months of physical therapy, he could now do most things again. It appeared he had a new health regimen that kept him in far better shape than when she left him at the VA, too. She didn't need him to tell her that lifting weights was part of his workout routine. She liked that he cared for himself and knew he mattered to others who depended on him. That hadn't been the case for the longest time.

She pushed herself up from the desk chair and walked closer to him, still keeping a healthy distance so she didn't throw herself at him again. "We should get the flash drive while we wait."

Luca turned from the window and stuck his gun into the holster at his back. "I'll grab it for you." His steps were stilted, but he reached the bag and stuck his hand into the pocket, feeling around. "It's not here."

"What?" Her heart started racing, and she ran to him, grabbed the strap and tossed it on the bed. She didn't care if he liked it or not. If her bargaining chip was gone, she was as good as dead. She didn't know much, but she did know that. Whoever this was, they weren't hunting her for funsies. She stuck her hand into the pocket and felt around, her pent-up breath releasing when her finger entered the bag's main compartment. "There's a hole," she said, looking up at Lucas, watching her closely with his hands in fists. "It had to have fallen into the main compartment."

"There shouldn't be a hole in it. It's been untouched for years."

"Luca, you've had it in an unprotected storage unit surrounded by woods. Chances are a mouse found its way in. You should probably brace yourself for what's inside, both from the memories and the fact that some of it may now be in a mouse's nest."

She stepped away and let him be the one to unhook the strap and open the bag. It opened at the top, so he had to remove each item to get to the bottom. Soon, the bed was covered in his fatigues, dress uniform, medals and boots. He pulled a wooden box out that fell open when he set it on the bed. Inside were letters, the envelopes dirty and wrinkled.

"Letters?" she asked, glancing up at him. She knew better than to reach for them. There was little Lucas was territorial of other than the contents of this bag.

"From my mom," he agreed, running a finger across the top of one. "She died when I was at the training facility with Haven."

"Did you go to her funeral?"

"The hospice center called and told me it was time to come say my final goodbyes. The school packed up Haven and sent a trainer with me for the two-hour trip to Rochester. I was with her when she took her final breath. She asked me to wear my dress uniform to her funeral, but that was a final wish I couldn't grant."

She grasped his elbow, hoping it would keep him grounded in the room with her. "I'm sure it mattered more to her that you were there with her at the end, Luca. I'm proud of you for going to her when she needed you."

"Our relationship had always been strained," he agreed, staring at the letters. "I was always surprised when a letter would arrive from her. She could have sent an email, but she went to the trouble of writing a letter and mailing it every time."

"A mother's love is like that," Lilah said, gently rubbing his shoulder. "She wanted you to know she cared."

"Some might say a day late and a dollar short, but I tried not to look at it like that," he said, closing the box with a click. "She did her best with what she had, and that wasn't much of anything. Mom was who she was, but by the time I went into the service, she was clean again and had found stable work and an apartment."

"Then the dementia struck."

"And it struck hard," he agreed with a nod. "Mom was barely fifty-five when she died, but I always knew the years of drug abuse would come back to haunt her."

"I'm glad you got to make amends with her, or at the very least, you were together when she took her last breath as you were when you took your first."

His lips turned up in a smile, and he glanced at her for the first time since she'd pushed him away. "Now, that is truly a Delilah Hartman statement. You always had a way of summing everything up in the neatest bow."

"I don't know if that's a compliment or a knock."

"A compliment. I always appreciated your ability to eliminate all the noise so I could hear the truth." Rather than continue speaking, he eyed her as though he were challenging her to do the same now, but she couldn't. Wouldn't. Not when their lives were on the line. Once she knew he was safe, she could leave him to live the life he'd built without her. A life he had worked hard for and didn't need her screwing up more than she already had.

"I don't see any evidence of a mouse yet. Or my flash drive," she said, returning them to the business at hand.

"There's not much left in here." He pulled out his army-issued winter coat, and a black rectangle fell to the floor.

Delilah scooped it up and held it to her chest with an exhale. "We got it." She held her hand out, revealing a high-tech drive. "Now we just have to hope the information on it isn't corrupt."

"What are the numbers for?" he asked, pointing at the buttons on the outside of the flash drive.

"A passcode to open it. This drive encrypts the information as you transfer it to keep the information secure."

"Do you remember the passcode?" Lucas asked as she walked past him toward the computer.

"Of course. I used a number I could never forget." She typed in a sequence and pulled the cover off the top of it. "Your birthday."

Chapter Eleven

Lucas's gaze roved over the bed that now held his old life. The uniforms. The boots. The medals. All the things he wanted to forget but couldn't. They stared back at him in judgment. They weren't judging him, though. Only a human could pass judgment, and he was excellent at being his own judge and jury. He couldn't help but wonder if his judgment of himself had been too harsh. Truthfully, he'd played judge, jury and executioner for so long he wasn't sure how to stop.

You can't have your life back until you open that bag and face the items inside. What are you so afraid of?

The words she'd said floated through his mind. He'd done what he had always believed was the impossible. He'd opened the bag and was again face-to-face with his past. That meant only the last question remained. What was he afraid of and why? When and why did he give this bag the power over him? He wasn't even wearing these clothes or boots when the base fell. Those items were cut off him and destroyed at the hospital in Germany.

The bag was on the floor, and he picked it up, sticking his hand into the pocket to pull out his discharge papers. He read them, his unconscious mind forcing him into the triangle breathing as he did so. He read every word, letting them pulse boldly in his head before shrinking back to normal. Each word released a little bit of hold the bag had on him. Each paragraph he finished snapped a bind that had tied him to it for years. When he finished, he slid them back into the envelope, ready to put them back in the bag. Something stopped him. Instead, he slipped them into the side pocket of his cargo pants and lifted the medals from the bed.

They had arrived in the mail each time he refused to go to the ceremony, and went directly into the bag. He never even opened the boxes to look at the medals. What was the point? Pieces of metal and ribbon didn't change what he did to earn them. Earn them. How ridiculous did that sound? It was a way to pretty up the fact that he had killed for them. Bled for them. Hurt for them. He didn't want to be remembered for any of that.

It means you stepped up when no one else would or could. That's what makes someone commendable.

All of the therapy he'd gone through hadn't had the same effect that hearing her words in his head had. He allowed them to be there and change his perspective. He earned the medals for things he did that were good, not the things he did that were bad. Yes, people had died, but had he done nothing, everyone would have died. They'd lost people on the base, and he caused deaths on the enemy side doing what he did, and chances were some civilians, too, who were caught up in the fight that wasn't theirs. That didn't make it his fault.

"This is Warrant Officer Lucas Porter!" he yelled into the microphone. "The base is under attack! We need air support! Air support!" Another round of gunfire tore through the station, and he dropped to the ground, his heart beating wildly in his chest. He looked left and right, knowing he was alone but hoping and praying he wasn't. Being

alone meant being the one to make the decisions. Life and death decisions.

A firm headbutt to his thigh brought him back to the motel room. Haven was budging him, a whine low in his throat as he looked up at him with worried eyes. "I'm okay, boy," he promised, stroking his head until the dog sat back on his haunches. Haven didn't relax, but he didn't force him into the comfort position, either.

Lucas's gaze strayed to the bed again, and he lifted the fatigues, his fingers working at the Velcro on a patch that said PORTER until he could pull it off. The sound was soft but felt like ripping a bandage off an old wound. Sometimes, removing the bandage revealed a healed wound. He reached for the next patch, pulling that one off, too. Lucas held the patches in his hand, closed his eyes and did a mental search of his body for wounds. They were there. Some were healed. Some were closed over but still oozing. That told him he was getting somewhere. Slow as the healing was, he *was* healing.

The patches went into his pocket and the fatigues, dress blues and shoes were tucked into the bag. Before he put the medals away, he opened each box and ran his fingers over the object inside. "Earned for saving lives, not taking them," he uttered with each medal.

The one point they drove home at the VA in therapy was that he had to do the hard work if he wanted to be free of the guilt that plagued him. Would his mind ever heal from the horrific things he saw and participated in? No. Those scars would always remain, but if he could stop carrying some of the guilt and shame about them, his life would be better by default. He'd feel better physically and emotionally. Life still wouldn't be Skittles and rainbows, but it would be manageable again. He'd genuinely believed he'd done that, but seeing this bag again told him in no uncertain terms that he hadn't done anything at all.

His gaze strayed to the woman sitting at the desk, her concentration on the screen in front of her. She made him want to forget the guilt and shame he carried from those years long ago. Her honesty and openness about her struggles with PTSD made him feel less shame for having it, too. Her beliefs that he saved countless lives, including hers, made him want to set the guilt on a shelf somewhere and stop carrying it around in such a destructive way. There would always be triggers he'd have to work around. Those triggers were frequent and out of his control, and the reason he had Haven by his side. He had worked hard to protect himself and others by working with Haven, but now he understood the truth. He hadn't done the most demanding job of all. With his gaze pinned on Lilah's beautiful hair, he wondered if the episodes might be less frequent and less crushing each time they happened if he found a way to free himself of the shame and guilt. For the first time, he wanted to try.

Once the medals were back in the bag, he closed it and clicked the handle through the loops. The bag felt lighter when he carried it to the door and set it aside. Not just because he'd taken items out but because he did the hard work of taking back some of his power from it.

"You forgot the coat," Lilah said, and his head snapped up to meet her gaze. She was turned halfway in the chair and pointed at the bed with the field jacket spread across the end.

"I was thinking about keeping it out," he said, walking over to where she sat by the computer. "It was a new issue to me in Germany, but I never wore it but a couple of times. I noticed snowflakes earlier, and let's face it, that coat is warmer than anything we have with us. Seems smart to keep it handy, just in case."

"As long as you think you can," she said, her gaze pinned on him again.

As much as he wanted to talk to her about his feelings, he bit back the words on his tongue. They needed to concentrate on staying alive. "We have bigger problems on our hands right now, Lilah. Were you able to access the flash drive?"

After glancing at him, she turned back to the computer and clicked on the mouse pad. "I was. I've been familiarizing myself with it all again."

"These are the files that I was working on at the time of the attack," she explained, running the mouse down the screen, and he counted twelve files. She clicked the first one open. "I don't even know if these got shipped. As you can see," she explained, pointing out the different pieces of information on the screen, "I had just hit Send to get central shipping the routing information when the first missile hit." She closed her eyes with her breath held tightly in her chest. It had always been that way for her. Thinking about the first minutes of the attack. The confusion. The terror. All the things that go through your mind when you think you're about to die.

He gently massaged her back while Haven rested his chin on her lap. "Open your eyes. You're not there anymore. You're with me again. I'll keep you safe."

Lilah opened her eyes and turned to meet his gaze. "Just like you did that day, Luca. I hate having to put you through that again. I hate that my presence here has put you in danger, but I can't change it, can I?"

"Nope," he said with a chuckle. "Embrace the suck, as

they say, and remember that we did a lot of hard things as a team. We can do it again."

"Right," she said with a nod of her head and the clearing of her throat. "As I said, I don't know if central shipping got any of this."

"I thought Mina said they could see it all from a different computer or something."

"That depends on if the email sent or was stopped by the missile attack. You know how the tech was over there. Also, I don't know if the relics were found on the base afterward."

"Wait, you mean these twelve were actually on the base? They weren't spread out across other bases?"

"That's what I'm saying. I was finishing the catalog for a collection brought to us by a museum curator turned soldier. He wanted to protect the oldest relics of his collection."

"And then we go and lose them to history," Lucas said, whistling a low tune. "Doesn't look good on our end."

"Or his," she said, showing him the country of origin. "It was his government that attacked us. The thing is, I don't know if they're lost to history or not. Those twelve are an unknown to me."

"Ha," Lucas said with a shake of his head. "Okay, I feel less bad about it now. Do you think they want this information because they found the relics? Maybe they want to get them back to the right people or need the paper trail to get them back home?"

"First, they don't know I have this drive with the information on it, so why wouldn't they simply send me official army orders to return to a base and give them whatever information I could remember? Why all the games and the attempts to take me against my will?" she asked, motioning at her chin. "It doesn't make sense."

She was right, it didn't make sense. None of it made

sense. He stared at the computer screen and a folder caught his eye. He pointed at it. "What's that file?"

"That's a bit of a side project I was working on. It doesn't apply to these files." She motioned at the list before her.

"The Lost Key of Honor. It sounds important." He lifted a brow, and she sighed, bringing the cursor up but stopping before she clicked it open.

"I think it's important. Important enough that I'm not going to open this file and show you any part of it. What you don't know, you can't tell."

"I don't understand. Is it top secret or something?"

"I don't know what it is, Luca. Okay, I mean, I know what it is, but I don't know why there was so much subter-fuge based around it."

"You mean they didn't assign you this file?" When she shook her head, he got a bad feeling in his gut. A feeling that said the file was TNT. "Show me."

"No," she said with another shake of her head. "The less you know about all of this, the better. It still gives you plau-sible deniability."

"It also makes it impossible for me to protect you, Lilah. Plausible deniability is useless if you're dead or captured." His voice vibrated with all the fear bottled up in his gut. Haven walked over and sat next to him, leaning into his leg. Lucas found his head and stroked him, his gaze locked on the woman in the chair. Her face was drawn and drained of color, making the scars on her chin appear more prominent than ever before. Lucas traced the scar on her chin with his thumb, drawing a jagged breath from her lips. "You told me I had to trust you, so now I'm telling you the same thing. Trust me, Lilah, and we'll get through this."

Chapter Twelve

"You're sure?" she asked with a hard swallow punctuating the sentence. "Once you're involved, you're involved to the end."

"I'm already involved, Lilah," he reminded her, motioning at the room. "I've been involved since you walked out on me six years ago."

"That's not what I did, Luca! I was protecting you!" She shot up from her chair, but he grasped her upper arms to hold her in place. "I was protecting you," she whispered again, as though he hadn't heard her the first time.

"Which was honorable and, I'm sure, terribly difficult. I'm here now, and you've already involved me, so let me help you. If what you say about these guys is true, I can't go back to Secure One and carry on with my life as though the last few days didn't happen, right?" She shook her head, her lips in a thin line. "Then let me help you, really help you, end this situation so you can have your life back."

"You keep saying that, but if this ends and I'm still standing, I'm a woman with nothing. Now that's just as terrifying as facing down these guys."

"Now?" he asked, his thumb still tracing her chin.

Her heavy sigh said more as an answer than any words could have. She had relied on herself for so long that now, after finding him again, she found it difficult to walk away. He understood that sigh on a soul-deep level.

"You're sure you want to know all of this information?" she asked again, motioning at the computer. "We can't go back, so make sure you're prepared for what's to come."

"I'll be wading through what's to come with you whether I know or not, Lilah. I'm all in until you're safe. It's better to know what we're up against than fight an enemy without the knowledge needed to beat them."

Her curt nod and how she turned to the computer told him she accepted his decision. "This file refers to a trunk that a curator had brought in. It was a trunk they couldn't get open."

"He didn't bring the key along?"

"There is no key," she said, biting her lower lip. "The trunk is from ancient Iraq. It hasn't been opened for hundreds of years."

"The Lost Key of Honor," he said when the name struck him.

"Loosely translated," she agreed with a nod. "It was written in an old, dead language, but that was the best the curator could guess."

"He knew there was no key but wanted the trunk saved anyway?"

"There's a reason," she said, worrying her teeth across her lip as she clicked open the file. "It's been long believed that the trunk could hold—"

"The Holy Grail," he said with a breath as he pulled up a chair from the small table so he could sit. He took a moment to read the top paragraph of the file and let out a low whistle. "The trunk cannot be opened in any way other than with the key."

"There was little time to worry about it when it was

brought in at the beginning of the war, so it was shipped to the States to be held at a museum."

"This file says they were actively looking for intel on the key. How did they expect to find a hundreds-year-old key in that kind of rubble when the country's own people couldn't find it?"

"Because it's not a key," she said, facing him. "It's a piece of a stone tablet. The museum has long had half of the tablet that fits into the top of the trunk. The word *grail* is written several times on that half of the tablet. Without the other half, they can't translate the entire tablet or open the trunk."

"Okay, but grail can just mean something sought after, too. That doesn't mean it's the Holy Grail, and why would it be in Iraq?"

"The four rivers of Eden are said to converge in southern Mesopotamia, which we know is modern-day Iraq. How it got there or why, I can't say, but as you can see, they have put together a strong argument for it being the Holy Grail. If you believe in all of that, of course."

"You don't?" Lucas asked, holding her gaze for a heart-beat before dragging it away to read the file. The information on the drive was extensive and would take more than a cursory glance to understand it all. He didn't have that kind of time, so he would have to depend on her to give him the highlights.

"I believe that others believe it to be true, Luca. Regardless of what is inside the trunk, the trunk itself is a relic and should be preserved. It could be empty, but it existed at that time for a reason. I never saw it in person. It was sent off the base before I arrived. I've only seen the images in the file."

"How do you have the file if you weren't in charge of the trunk?"

"It wasn't meant for my eyes, but I didn't know that then.

I found it on a flash drive still in a computer on the base. I didn't know who the flash drive belonged to, but it was the only file on it. I may have transferred the file to my drive before I turned in the original."

"Why?"

"It intrigued me—The Lost Key of Honor. It drew me in and made me want to find it. I was intrigued by the question, where is it, and how could it even exist hundreds of years later?"

"It can't exist," he said with assuredness. "Not anymore. That country has been bombed and destroyed to the point no stone tablet from that time would ever be anything but dust."

"Unless it was protected somewhere," she said with a lift of one brow.

"Protected?"

After scrolling with the mouse several times, she pointed at the screen. "This picture shows the trunk with the half tablet in place. What do you notice?"

Once she enlarged the image so he could see it better, he stared for quite some time before pointing at a ridge. "There. Why would a ridge be in the center if it was one tablet? It's more like there are two separate tablets."

"Exactly," she said, a grin on her face. "Do you see the complicated notches on the side without the tablet?"

"All the indents?" he asked, and she nodded. "That's the key to opening it?"

"Best I can figure," she agreed. "The file indicates that several molds were made in an attempt to make a new key for it, but they all failed to open it."

"Strange. I'm surprised someone hasn't just busted the trunk apart by now. Why continue to search for something likely long gone?"

"Human nature? Spiritual beliefs? Fear?"

"Fear?" Lucas asked, holding her gaze, wholly engaged in the conversation even as he kept his ears open to the noises outside the motel. Cars speeding past on the highway. Tires at an even speed, not slowing or turning. No footsteps crunching across the snow. All was quiet.

"Fear of what might happen if they break the trunk to get it open. What does the other half of the tablet say? Is it a curse to open it without certain people present? That kind of thing. If people think this trunk holds the Holy Grail, they would never destroy it to get it open."

"Okay, I get that, but we both know that the other half of the tablet is long gone. Even if it's not, if the people of Iraq can't find it, how could we as foreigners?"

"I don't have the answer to that, only that they were trying."

"As a good faith mission for Iraq or…?"

"Again, I don't have the answer to that. I don't know who started this file or sanctioned the search. It's been six years. For all I know, the trunk has been returned and none of it matters now. I've been running for six years from some unknown enemy who wants me dead, and I don't know why! I just want to know what's going on!"

On instinct, he pulled her into him and held her tightly. "It's okay," he promised, soothing her by rocking her gently. "I know you're stressed, scared and exhausted. You're not alone anymore, and we might not be able to solve this in one night, but you have help now."

Lucas fell silent, rubbing her back as he held her, letting her rest her chin over his shoulder, heavy with fatigue. It was time for her to get some sleep, but he would be selfish a bit longer and continue to languish in the feel of her wrapped around him. He'd missed her warmth and how she made him feel safe in an unsafe world. Now it was his turn to do that for her, and he would. First, she needed someone to take care of her. He was grateful to be the one to get that chance again.

"Come on," he said, hoisting her from the chair and helping her to the bed. "It's time to let your mind rest and your body recover. You're exhausted. You need to sleep in a bed where you can stretch out and recoup."

Lilah didn't argue. Instead, she lowered herself to the bed and let him remove her boots before she slid her legs under the covers. "You're safe here tonight," he promised, pulling her spectacles off her face and setting them on the nightstand. That was a blanket statement he shouldn't be promising, but he willed it to be true. "I'm going to contact the team and stand watch."

"Just a few hours," she murmured, her eyes drooping as he stroked her forehead. It was an old trick he used to use when she refused to sleep that summer, worried he'd do something terrible to himself while she did.

"I'll wake you in two hours," he promised, but he wouldn't. He'd let her sleep in the safety of another human being for as long as he could. While Lilah slept, he hoped Mina would find something they could use to move this investigation forward and get the target off her back. They'd already been shot at twice. As he lowered himself to the computer and minimized the file that might hold the answer to everything, the only thought running through his head was, the third time was the charm.

Chapter Thirteen

"Lilah, wake up." She opened her eyes to see Lucas looming over her. "Time to go."

Without question, she sat up and tied on her boots. "Did they find us already?" she asked, slipping her glasses onto her face again.

"Hard to know, but Cal reported that someone is sniffing around the vicinity of the medal. He wants us to move again to be on the safe side."

The room was dark as she stood from the bed and took in her surroundings. He'd packed up all the equipment, and the bags sat ready by the door. He handed her his Secure One parka, the sleeves already rolled up.

"Here, put this on. I know it's a bit too big, but it's snowing now, and if we go off the road, you need something warmer than the coat Mina gave you."

"What about you?" she asked, slipping her arms into the coat that was, in fact, a bit too big, but with the sleeves rolled up, it would be wearable and keep her legs warm, too.

He slid into his field coat and buttoned it up. "We might as well use it to our advantage, right?" His tone told her he needed her to agree.

"Right," she said, grabbing the front of it and planting a kiss on his cheek. "I'm proud of you, Luca."

His smile told her she'd given him the answer he needed. "Wait here. I'll take the bags to the van and see what I see."

After her nod, he turned to Haven, already dressed for the weather. "Rest, Haven. Stay with Lilah." As though the dog understood the assignment, he walked over and sat, his ears at attention. "Good boy."

Lilah wanted to reach down and scratch his ears, but she knew better than to touch any service dog while they were working. Instead, she motioned for Luca to go and stepped back so she wasn't visible when he opened the door. Watching through the window, he threw the bags where they could reach them quickly and then checked for anyone on the road before he pulled off the magnet on the side of the van and switched it out.

"Get ready, boy," she said to Haven. "It's going to be cold."

She pulled the hood up on the parka and was ready when he opened the door. "Haven, fall in." The dog headed straight for the open van door while Luca helped her out of the motel and into the passenger seat. "Buckle up," he said, shutting the door for her before he secured Haven and slammed the side door.

Once they were on the move, she glanced over at him. "Where are we headed?"

"Somewhere southwest. Mina says we're supposed to drive out of the snow quickly. I hope she's right. The conditions aren't great."

Lilah tried to see through the falling snow, but it was nearly impossible in the dark, even with the windshield wipers on high. "Try the conditions are terrible, and no plows will be out way up here."

"The only upside is we have the road to ourselves. If nothing else, it will be a white Christmas."

"I can't argue with you there." After a glance in the side mirror, she started to chuckle. "Larry's Computer Repair. If we can't fix it, it ain't broke," she read from the sign on the side of the van. "Really?"

Luca wore a grin when she glanced back at him. "What can I say? Cal has a sense of humor. It's not much in the way of camouflage, but it does say something different than the last one, which was pizza delivery. With a little snow packed on the license plate, no one will know it's us immediately."

"You said Cal has eyes on someone stalking the medal?" She hadn't wanted to ask the question, but at the same time, she wanted to know the answer.

"That's what his eyes in the sky say, but he's waiting it out to see if they're just in the area or specifically searching for something."

"Or someone. I can't believe you might be right about this," she said, chewing on her lip. "It never occurred to me, mostly because I can't believe they could be tracking me with something so small for so long."

"Technology has evolved, Lilah. They make trackers now that only use power when they're pinged. The rest of the time, they're off. These small military trackers only use solar power to charge them, so it wouldn't take much time out of your pocket each month to keep it charged. For instance, having it out on a dresser for a day would give it charge for months."

"But why?" she asked, her hand grasping the door handle as the wheels slid toward the shoulder of the road. He got it under control again just before hitting the rumble strips, wherever they may be under the snow.

"I think we both know why," he said, tightly gripping the wheel. "They want to know where you are at all times. They may not know about the flash drive, but you exist, and you know things about what went down there."

Lilah fell silent as she watched the wipers clear the glass and the snow cover it again in a comforting pattern. She did know things. Things she wished she didn't and things she wished she knew about now that she was faced with people hunting her. She rubbed her chin absently as though that would make the jagged scar disappear. A thought struck her, and she gasped, the sound loud in the quiet van.

"What if I didn't even earn the medal and they just gave it to me to keep track of me?" To her ears, the sentence was incredulous but also wholly possible.

"No," Luca said, shaking his head as he steered the van around a sharp corner. They were doing barely twenty in a fifty-five, but until this snow quit, they were at its mercy. "Don't think like that. We don't even know if it is the medal. It's just a hypothesis right now."

"But you said Cal has seen activity around it."

"I also said he's waiting to see if it's approached, so just give him time to get back to me."

"What else did Mina say?"

"She's looking into the news archives about antiquities or tablets discovered or displayed over the last six years. She's also trying to get more information about the accusations against Major Burris."

"Something is fishy there," Lilah agreed. "The major was always professional and was scarily knowledgeable about the laws and customs that applied in armed conflicts."

"Even knowledgeable men have a price, Lilah."

She fell silent for several more minutes as she thought about Burris. Was he the kind of man who willingly stole precious artifacts for money? Not the man she'd worked under, but then again, everyone has a face they show the world and a face that hides below. She had to wonder if the face Burris hid was one of corruption and theft. "I hope she finds something helpful. Tell me how you started working at Secure One," she said to change the subject.

Luca's chuckle was self-deprecating if she'd ever heard it. "When I left the training program with Haven, my first job was working security for Senator Dorian in Minneapolis. Secure One worked an on-site event for the senator's daughter during the Red River Slayer's reign. Do you remember that?"

"Of course," she said with a nod. "That was a terrifying time for women around the country. It was hard to believe when the whole story came out."

"Truth. While Secure One was at the estate, I helped them protect the property's perimeter when the senator's daughter was at risk. Once the case was wrapped up and Secure One went home, Cal reached out and thanked me for helping them with everything. I replied that if there were ever any openings on his team, I would love to interview, with his understanding that it was two for the price of one," he explained, his gaze flicking to the rearview mirror to check on his dog. "He had me drive up within days, and I was hired on the spot. They had so much work coming in after being in the public eye so often over the previous years with high-profile cases that they were turning down jobs."

"That's fabulous to hear, Luca," she said, touching his arm as he drove. "I'm glad you took the chance and asked."

"I almost didn't," he admitted with a tip of his head. "High-stress situations were always difficult for me after we returned, but I'd worked for the senator for three years without problems. Not that it was high stress, other than Senator Dorian loved nothing more than to yell about everything that went on across the property, right or wrong.

My therapy from the VA and training with Haven was put to the test during those few days that the property was locked down, and I was able to handle it without difficulty. That was the only reason I inquired about working at Secure One. Well, that and the fact that his core team was all ex-military and understood the ups and downs of PTSD."

"Mina indicated that was the case to me, too," she agreed. "Understanding helps, but so does having a brotherhood again, right?"

"At first, I thought that might work against me," he admitted, letting the van pick up speed a bit more now that the snow had turned to just flurries. "I was afraid the environment would remind me too much of my military years, but I quickly saw that wasn't how Cal ran the business. He was a participant in the company and not the boss. It all works, despite our different experiences and reactions to them."

"No, it works *because* of your different experiences and reactions to them," she clarified. "You all bring different perspectives and knowledge to the table about different aspects of the security world. That's what makes it work. You're an expert at weapons but need a sharpshooter like Efren to use your knowledge practically."

"You know Efren was a sharpshooter?" She noticed the quizzical look he wore when he asked the question.

"Mina gave me a bit of a rundown on everyone as I was changing clothes," she explained. "She didn't want me walking into a meeting completely uninformed."

"That sounds like Mina," Luca said with a chuckle. "She's always about keeping the playing field level, which is funny coming from her."

"Why?"

"Mina is the smartest person in the company, male or female, and we all know it. None of us can do what she can with a computer and a few hours on her side. Before Mina joined the team, from what they tell me, they were nothing more than glorified security camera installers. Cal was doing work on the side to fund the company."

"What kind of work on the side?"

Luca cleared his throat and kept his eyes straight ahead. "Let's just say he did many things he didn't want to do to help good people who were suffering."

Her military experience translated that statement quickly into one word. Mercenary. "Understood."

"Now that Mina is part of the team, the business has grown, so Cal is starting a cybersecurity division. Mina will be heading it up. I foresee it quickly overtaking the personal security aspect of the business."

"There will be no doubt," she said, noticing a sign pointing them back toward Whiplash, Minnesota. Secure One was located on the town's southern border, but they wouldn't go there again until her situation was cleared up. Then again, she'd probably never return to Secure One, no matter how much she wanted to. "I worked remotely for a company for three of the six years I was on the run. My job was to keep their server safe, build their website utilizing hidden pages and code everything into a box. If anyone tried to brick their system, mine would do it first, allowing me to unbrick it again once the hackers were caught."

He glanced at her quickly before putting his eyes back on the road. "You can do that?"

"I could, back then," she agreed. "It was difficult work but worth it. These days, those techniques may not work anymore."

"It couldn't have been that long ago, Lilah. You were only gone six years."

"I quit three years ago, and things change at lightning speed in the tech world."

"Why did you quit?"

"I didn't see any other choice when they found me for the fourth time in three years. My only hope was to go completely underground and stay off their radar. Little did I know I may have been carrying that radar with me. Anyway, I banked a lot of money during the years I worked, and since it was remote work, it didn't matter if I had to move to a different town. I saved every penny I could over the years by living in some disgusting places, but it paid off. I survived on what I had for years and only needed to do odd jobs here and there to keep myself fed and clothed. I've spent so long on the run, I'm not sure I know how to stay in one place anymore."

"It's easy," he said with his lips quirked. "You find someplace that feels like home and you stay there."

"Easy coming from your side of the van, yes," she agreed, leaning her head on the cool glass of the window. "Not so easy when where you feel at home is off-limits."

"Where do you feel at home?"

"I've only ever felt at home with you, Luca."

Chapter Fourteen

I've only ever felt at home with you, Luca.

Try as he might, he couldn't get those words out of his head. Her sweet voice telling him how she felt even when she couldn't tell him how she felt made him want to stop the van and drag her across the console to finish that kiss from the motel room. He knew better. Whatever had stopped her last time was still between them, and while he wished he knew what it was, all he could do was let her reveal it in her own time.

Those words had kept him alert and awake on a long drive through bad weather. He wanted to keep her safe, so he'd driven as long as he could before fatigue set in. They'd found another small motel and pulled over for the night, knowing if he didn't, they wouldn't see morning.

"Secure one, Whiskey," the voice said, and Lucas hit the microphone button to connect.

"Secure two, Lima."

Mina's face filled the screen, and she immediately assessed the room around them. "You're safe?"

"For now," he said with a nod. "We're in a new motel south of the Minnesota border. We didn't pick up any tails, and all's quiet on the western front."

"Do you have enough supplies?" Cal's voice asked from

off in the distance. Mina zoomed the screen out and included the rest of the room in the shot. Cal and Roman were there with her.

"We stopped and picked up food at a small grocery on the way down the hill."

"Wearing Secure One gear?" Mina asked with her lips in a thin line.

"No, I, uh, actually wore my field coat. Found it in my duffel and thought it would be good cover." All three sets of brows went up, but they said nothing, so he cleared his throat. "Would you thank Sadie for dumping that giant bag of food in the back for Haven? It's less stressful when I don't worry about him."

"You know she's got her little dude," Mina said with a wink.

Lilah laughed, and he sat silently until the sound died away, soaking it up in case he never heard it again. "Have you learned anything since we last talked?"

"Yes," Cal and Mina said in unison, but Mina motioned for him to go first.

Cal spun his computer screen around to face the camera in the conference room. "We've been monitoring the house where I put the medal. It's an old abandoned place north of town and within a thirty-minute walk of the storage units."

"To make it look like I escaped and took shelter there?" Lilah asked.

"Exactly. I did it because you wouldn't stay there long if you were with us. They would need to move quickly to get another team there."

"Or there was already another team waiting."

Cal pointed at her and nodded. "I believe that's the case. As you'll see." He hit a button on the computer, and they watched as four men approached the house with their rifles raised.

"Are those AR-15s?" Lucas asked immediately.

"No, M4 Carbine EPRs," Cal answered.

"I thought M4 Carbines were for military only," Delilah said.

"These are law enforcement guns. The ERP stands for an enhanced patrol rifle. Better sights. Better stock. There's more room for mounting optics and accessories. The guys at the storage unit debacle had the same ones," Cal said, his face wearing a grim expression.

"That's odd because an AR-15 is much cheaper these days. If you're a gun for hire, you're carrying an AR-15, not an M4," Lucas said, confused by the whole thing.

"Unless someone is buying them for you," Lilah whispered. They all went silent as the four men left the house like ninjas in the night. "Do you think they found the medal?" she asked, gazing at the screen. Lucas could hear how much courage it took her to ask.

"No. It's inaccessible to them, but it will have to remain there for now," Cal said.

"Either way, they know we're on to them," Lucas said, reaching over and squeezing Lilah's hand. She held on for dear life, so he didn't let go. Instead, he ran his thumb over her hand to keep her calm.

"How did you even get that footage?" Lilah asked, her head cocked as though the thought just struck her.

"Drone in a tree," Cal explained. "Easier and faster than putting up a camera when your timeline is short."

"Okay, we know they're still looking for Lilah," Lucas said, getting them back on track. "We also know some of them are ex-military or law enforcement. Mina, did you find out anything?"

"So many things," Mina said with laughter on her lips. It brought a smile to his, and he glanced at Lilah to see her wearing one, too. Leave it to Mina to keep the moment light.

"I did some digging into Major Burris. He was never tried for the war crimes he was accused of because, according to JAG, the case was weak, with little evidence. However, he was within a year of retirement, so he served it at a desk and was ushered out on his last day."

"I bet he was," Lilah murmured. "I would love to know who brought those charges against him. Burris was always professional and the person we could go to when we had an issue. It seems off for his level of command and his personality."

"War does funny things to people," Mina gently said. "Kindness to his people doesn't mean he was kind to the enemy."

"That's true, I know," Lilah agreed. "I would just like to find out who was at the heart of those charges."

"Burris is now living near Rochester, Minnesota. I'll see if I can dig deeper and find more information about his accusers," Mina said, making a note. "Colonel Swenson is still working but is now a general in Minneapolis."

"Not surprised," Lucas said. "I worked a few ops with him, and he was voted most likely to be in the army for his career. He lived for the accolades and back patting he got moving up the ranks. He went into a funk if someone didn't tell him how wonderful he was every day. We used to call him Major Payne and Captain Fantastic."

Cal snorted while biting back a smile, but Lucas saw it. There wasn't a guy who had served who didn't know someone like Swenson.

"You'll find a lot of that kind of guy in the military," Roman said, still chuckling. "I guess that's one of the reasons we have career army men. They thrive in that environment. Anything else, Mina?"

"Yes," she said, leaning in on the table to address Lucas personally. "I called about that trunk you asked me to check on. The museum doesn't have and never has had a trunk like you described."

"What?" Lilah asked in surprise. "I have documented paperwork that it went to them."

"Not according to the museum curator who I spoke with there. He said they are sometimes sent to a different museum during shipping because one may have more room. I haven't had time to call other museums, nor would I know where to start."

Lilah cut her gaze to Lucas for a moment, and he recognized the look. She wasn't convinced that Mina was right. "I'll take care of it," Lilah said before Mina could say more. "As long as I can use the Secure One computer for a little questionable hacking?"

"As long as you're only looking," Cal said with a brow raised.

"Look, but don't touch. Got it," Lilah said with a wink.

"We can split the list if you send me the information," Mina said, elbows on the table. "I'm at your disposal."

When Lilah shot a look Lucas's way, he read in it that she wanted no one else involved more than they had to be. "It's no problem. I can do the museums while you keep looking into Burris's accusers?"

"Sure," Mina said. "I'm just worried you're both running on little to no sleep."

"I got to sleep last night while Lucas drove. He can sleep while I work."

"No," Lucas said immediately and without hesitation. "Someone has to be on watch. We can assume the medal was their dowsing rod, but we can't be sure. We can't let our guard down."

"You also can't go without sleep," Cal said, his words pointed. "Everyone in this room knows what happens when we push ourselves past the brink of exhaustion."

"I can keep watch and do the work," Lilah said, emphasizing her sentence by squeezing his hand no one else knew she was holding. "We're a team, and I can carry my weight on it."

Cal pointed at the computer screen. "What she said. We'll let you get to it. It's 6:00 a.m. now. The next check-in will be at noon unless something imperative arises. If you need backup, you know how to reach us. I still have the van monitored, so I know your exact location. You should be good for the day as the snow is about to hit your area and no one will move anywhere until it passes."

"Tell me about it," Lucas muttered. "Driving down from the North Shore last night was one of the most dangerous things I've done, and I worked munitions."

"You don't mess with Mother Nature," Roman said. "Take advantage of the break. Hopefully, by the time the snow passes, Min and Delilah will have what you need to take the next step."

"Charlie, out," Cal said, and the screen went blank.

Lucas turned to Lilah and took her other hand. "Why wouldn't the museum have the trunk?"

"That's what I want to know, too," she agreed.

"Can it just happen that a shipment is diverted?"

"Not unless the museum it's going to has burned down and closed. Then it would just get returned to sender, essentially, and routed back to central shipping. All of these antiquities have well-documented shipping papers for a reason. We never want to be accused of stealing other countries' precious art or artifacts."

"Maybe it did get returned to sender and sent somewhere else? There would be no way for you to know once we left the base."

"Except that the trunk was shipped before I got to the base, remember? I have images of that trunk in a museum in The Lost Key of Honor file."

"Are you sure it's a museum?" he asked, his brow raised.

She paused and tipped her head, probably thinking about the pictures she'd seen. "No, I can't be sure. I'll go through the images and inspect them closer."

"If it was at a museum, how would you track it down? Mina is right. There are a lot of museums."

"I'm going to do it the easy way."

"The easy way? Only contacting the museums you know took in antiquities during that time of the war?"

"No," she said, turning to the computer and inserting the flash drive. "I'll start by looking for the first six I sent out when I arrived. I know those left the base."

"To what end?"

"It's a first step. I'll know if some of the artifacts made it to their destination or if none of them did. It's a place to start while you sleep."

"No. I'm not leaving you without protection."

"If you don't sleep, you'll be useless to me if we need to run, Luca. Cal is right. Exhaustion makes everything worse, and I need you to be able to think on your feet. Look, the snow has already started." She moved the curtain aside so he could see the flakes falling. "No one is going anywhere, including us."

His shoulders slumped in defeat. "Only a few hours. Wake me the moment you think you hear something. I mean it, Lilah. It's easier to be proactive in these situations than reactive."

"On my honor, I will wake you at the wisp of a worry that there's trouble."

She stood and held his hand as she walked him to the bed. The motel only had rooms with one queen, and they'd taken it, but he had seen how her eyes grew when they walked in. She was hiding something he was determined to figure out. Once he had laid down on the bed, boots on, she covered him with a blanket and turned off the light. It was early and the sun wasn't up yet, but the way the storm was howling, he doubted they'd see much daylight over the next twelve hours.

Lilah kissed his cheek and lingered as though she were fighting a war with herself before she walked back to the desk to sit. Lucas fell asleep to the backdrop of her keys clacking as she set about her work. He couldn't help but wonder if the secrets were really hidden within that file or if they had been hidden in her all along.

Chapter Fifteen

Confusion and frustration filled Lilah as she stared at the screen. She had been working her way down the list of the dozens of shipping logs for the antiquities she had on the flash drive. She was nine deep, and so far, none of them had found their way to where they were supposed to be. In fact, it was as though they had just disappeared into thin air.

Lilah started typing again, trying to cross match the item across museums in case the schedule got screwed up when the base fell. Maybe one didn't reach the intended place but went to the museum where a different artifact was scheduled. Her fingers paused on the keyboard. If that were the case, they would have been returned to central shipping. It didn't make sense. She had no other ideas, so she tried it anyway, just in case museums were told to keep the item rather than return it.

After another hour of digging, it was easy to see that the theory was also incorrect. How was it that all these items had gone poof into thin air? The antiquities she was searching for weren't even on the base when it fell, so there would be no reason to think they didn't get shipped correctly.

Her neck and back aching, she stood and stretched, her shirt pulling up to reveal what she was trying to hide from the man sleeping on the bed behind her. She quickly pulled her shirt down and tucked it back into her pants. She had been working for nearly five hours, meaning Lucas had been sleeping for as long. Everything was quiet, and she was confident they'd have until the snow stopped before they had to worry about being on guard. Then again, if the medal had been to blame for leading these guys to her door, it would be much more difficult for them to find her now.

The idea that they took something she had pride in and turned it against her made her sick to her stomach. Had she earned the medal or was it just how they decided to keep track of her? That was risky, considering she could have done what Lucas did and stored the medal. Her mind drifted back to some of her conversations with other soldiers. She had said more than once that if given a medal, she would carry it with her always as a reminder that she could do hard things. Someone could have easily overheard her and used that statement to their advantage.

Now, here she was, six years of her life gone. Six years she didn't get to spend with the man sleeping behind her because someone played her strength as her weakness. Ironic. None of it made sense, though. Why would the government want or need to track her?

"Hey," Lucas said, sitting up and stretching. "How long have I been out?"

"Almost five hours," she said, the room nearly dark even in the middle of the day. The snow was falling so hard it felt like night rather than morning. "Feel better?"

"Much," he admitted. "That drive wore me out last night. Everything quiet?"

"As a church mouse. No one is out in this. You can't see your hand in front of your face. Why don't you take a shower?"

"No," he said, shaking his head at the suggestion. "Vulnerability could get you killed."

Her sigh was heavy when she stood to face him. "I'm capable of taking care of myself, Lucas Porter. I took Haven outside to do his business while you were sleeping and look, we're both fine."

"You did what? Why didn't you wake me up? You shouldn't have gone out there!"

"I was trained by the United States Army and kept myself alive through attack after attack for the last six years. I have a gun and know how to use it. Stop acting like my bodyguard and start acting like my partner." She tapped his chest with each syllable to drive her point home.

She didn't miss his small step back as he raised his brows. "Your partner?"

"We always made great partners, Lucas. No matter what we were doing, we played to each other's strengths and weaknesses without the need to communicate them. It was that way from when you picked me up off the tarmac and we pushed that old golf cart out of our way. I know it's been years, but you can trust me to have your back."

The look in his eye told her he remembered when they were partners in crime *and* between the bedsheets. "I'll be out in a few. The rifle is by the door if you need it."

Her salute was jaunty, bringing a smile to his lips for the first time since he woke up. "When you get out, I'll share what I learned while you slept."

After grabbing his bag and giving her a nod, he jogged into the small bathroom and closed the door. Lilah lowered herself to the chair and wondered if the Luca she used to know was still under those black fatigues or if he had become someone completely different since their summer on the island. Spending time with him the last few days told her that he was someone completely different from everyone but her. He had a hard edge to him now that he had never carried before, but maybe that was how he managed his emotions in the workplace and kept himself grounded during high-stress events. He was never sharp with her, and when their eyes met, it was as though the last six years had been stripped away. That was when she saw the same vulnerable, scared, resilient man before her.

Lifting her shirt, she ran her hand over her belly, the scarred ridges of puckered flesh under her fingers a reminder of how she had changed. When she stripped her clothes off, she was no longer the same woman he remembered. She was alive but dead inside, her heart only beating at the thought of, or the sight of, the man in the shower. Even though she knew she couldn't be with him again, a tiny piece of her heart wanted that chance. A second chance at a fleeting love of youthful innocence. It wasn't youthful innocence, though. It was a shared understanding of a shared experience that shaped who they would become. The love wasn't fleeting, either. It was still there. She could feel it every time they touched, but it was a different kind of love now. Instead of a roaring flame of desire, it was a barely-there ember that could remember what they had together but could never flare strong enough to start that fire again.

Lilah shook her head and sighed, rubbing her face while she tried to refocus on the things she learned during her search. She had sent Mina a message asking if she had more information about the charges against Burris, but she hadn't replied yet. It had only been a few hours, but she was anxious to make some part of this complicated, frustrated puzzle fit together. She had purposely not mentioned what she found to Mina, hoping that Lucas could help her understand it before relaying the information to the team.

When she heard Lucas rustling about in the bathroom to dress, she made him a cup of coffee from the single cup maker on the counter and handed it to him when he came out.

"Thanks," he said, lifting it in the air. "Did you track down the trunk?"

He lowered himself to the end of the bed to sit opposite her while they talked. She liked how he was always dialed in on her and was never distracted by outside factors. She could tell he had a firm handle on everything outside the motel, which was very quiet right now.

"I didn't track it down. It's nowhere to be found, but that's not all," Delilah said, spinning in her chair and showing him how she had made a spreadsheet as she cross-referenced all the items she couldn't find.

"Wait, all of them are missing?"

"Missing in the respect that I can't find any of them in the places I sent them or even as being checked into a museum. My original thought was maybe they got the wrong shipping labels put on, so I looked for each one at each of the six museums, but there was nothing."

"How is that possible?"

"That's what I've been asking myself for hours. I'll keep checking the remaining items, but I feel squishy inside."

"Squishy?" he asked, his head tipped to the side in confusion.

"That two plus two doesn't equal four in this case. Squishy in my gut, wondering if I blindly participated in something I shouldn't have."

"You were following orders, Lilah. Don't take whatever this is on your shoulders. Can you tell me first why these items needed to be protected and second why they would disappear?"

"No," she said with a shake of her head. "Well, I know they were being protected from theft or destruction from war. Why they'd disappear is anyone's guess. They may not have disappeared. They could be in a warehouse somewhere. All I can do is follow the paper trail that leads me nowhere."

"It's been six years. Maybe they were returned to their respective countries already?"

"I would say that's possible if there was any evidence that they had been checked into a museum and back out again. We don't have that evidence, and like anything in the military, it should be there with bells on."

"True," he agreed, his hands massaging her shoulders as he stood over her chair to read the screen. He worked at the knotted muscles that were the consequences of too much time hunched over the laptop, stress and too many years away. But with his hands on her again, she melted under the familiarity of his touch. "Did Mina find anything while I was asleep?"

"I messaged her but haven't heard back." An idea came to her, and she glanced up at him. "I just thought of something!"

Her fingers flew across the keyboard until a website popped up.

"The Smithsonian?" he asked, his hands pausing on her shoulders.

"They were going to host one of the full exhibits we sent over."

"Six years ago, darling," he said in that familiar drawl that sent her right back to the first time they met. He'd driven her to the cafeteria where they'd had lunch together. When it was time to part, he'd said, "If I never see you again, I want you to know I think you're darling. A bright spot in a place where there are few to go around and little is charming. I do hope to see you again, my darling Delilah." I guess that was the moment she'd become smitten with Warrant Officer Porter.

"Right, and I don't expect them to still have the exhibit open, but their archives are open to the public to search. Since I have the names of those exhibits on the flash drive, it's easy to see if they were ever on display at the museum."

She typed the name of one of the exhibits into the search box, changing spellings and the order of the words every way she could to get a hit, but nothing came up, no matter what she typed in. He continued to massage her shoulders, which relaxed her and keyed her up simultaneously. Being with this man again was hard enough, but having his hands on her and knowing she couldn't have him was torture.

"There's nothing here."

"I'm starting to share your squishy feeling," he said, gazing at the screen. "Something should have come up, right?"

"Many somethings," she agreed, facing him to break the connection between his hands and her body.

Delilah stood and started pacing, trying to think of other ways to search for these exhibits. There were so many museums they could have gone to if they'd been routed wrong, but after all these years, it was anyone's guess where.

"There you go, buddy," Lucas said, lowering himself to the bed again after he put food in Haven's bowl. "We slept through breakfast." The dog tucked into the bowl, crunching kibble as she continued to pace. "The question is, why were none of these things put on exhibit if that was why they were sent here?"

She tapped her chin and stared at the window, the ugly, brown floral curtains blocking the snow and the daylight from the room. She was wrapped in a cocoon of safety that she knew would dissipate when she stepped out those doors. Someone was still after her, and she needed to figure out why.

"No!" she exclaimed as her heart started to pound. "The question isn't why weren't they on exhibit."

Luca was leaning back on the bed, braced on both hands, when he glanced up at her. "Okay, what is the question then?"

"The question is and always has been, why do they keep trying to kill me?"

In one fluid motion, Lucas stood in front of her. "Kill you? I thought they were trying to take you against your will."

"In the beginning," she agreed, intimidated by his stance before her. As she gazed into his eyes, she accepted it wasn't intimidation. It was protection. He would take a bullet for her before he let her get hurt. She leaned into his chest with her fist and forearm, the memories of the last few days hitting her square in the chest. "You might remember that the last few attempts have been all bullets and no brawn."

Instinctively, he grasped the fist she had against his chest and held it there. "We haven't stopped moving long enough for me to consider that, but you're right. They weren't trying to take you hostage. They were trying to kill you."

"The last time they found me, right before I sent you the message, they came in guns blazing, too. I think they shot my neighbor." Her eyes closed, and her voice broke on the last word. "That's on me."

"No," he said, tenderly kissing her forehead. "That's on the guy with the gun and no one else. He didn't need to shoot your neighbor. He chose to shoot your neighbor. You can't blame yourself for anything that's happened over the years since we were discharged."

"I do, though. I made choices that had ripples of consequences both for me and the people around me without them even knowing."

"What dictated those choices?"

She leaned her head against his chest to avoid his gaze. "The people after me. The alerts that I'd been found. The fear that filled me all day, every day."

"The people after you. That's who is responsible for any fallout around us, Lilah. I think it's time to go back to the beginning if we want to sort this out."

"Back to the beginning?" she asked, lifting her head.

"To the first time you were attacked. I want to know everything day by day, year by year, until we met up again on that island."

"Luca, that would take all day."

His hands went out to his sides to motion around the room. "We have no place to be. In fact, we have nowhere to go until we come up with some reason why ex-military hitmen keep knocking on your door, so let's do our due diligence now in the hopes that a week from now, you'll have your life back."

She held his gaze, read his thoughts and understood his frustrations. There was more in those chocolate eyes than determination and frustration, though. There was desire. A heat she knew all too well. A need left unfulfilled for too long. Her reckoning was coming, but she had an ace in the hole that would squelch that desire and extinguish the ember once and for all. She just had to be strong enough to play it.

Chapter Sixteen

Lucas listened to Lilah walk him step-by-step through the horrifying events she'd lived through over the last six years. Delilah was stronger than anyone he'd ever known, and he let her slip through his fingers. The moment she didn't show up to visit at the hospital as promised, he should have checked himself out and gone after her before her trail went cold. Instead, he let his past abandonment issues with his mother color the situation. He let his pain and his pride prevent him from tearing apart the entire country to find her.

"Why did I allow this to happen to you?" he muttered when she turned from the makeshift whiteboard they'd made with paper on the motel wall.

"Luca, you didn't allow anything. You had no control over it."

"I had control over what I did the moment you didn't come back to visit me. I had control over the way I let my hurt and embarrassment at being discarded by another woman I loved consume me. I should have stopped to remember the Delilah Hartman I knew. That woman always kept her promises. If I had looked at it in the proper light, I would have realized that you didn't abandon me. No, that's what I did to you!" he exclaimed, his finger jabbing himself in the chest.

Lilah laid the marker down on the desk and walked to him, slipping her arms around his waist to rest her head on his chest. The memories hit him from the early days, but when he gazed down at her, the reality of the situation was evident in the jagged scars across her chin.

"You have to stop, Luca. I would have thought the same if I had been in your shoes. This isn't about who did the right or the wrong thing. This situation is about circumstances neither of us controlled, okay?"

Rather than agree or disagree, he held her, his chin resting on her head as he swallowed every bit of her warmth and comfort. His gaze was pinned on the wall of information that she'd been writing down, searching for any pattern or clue as to who was terrorizing her and why.

"What does 'The Mask' mean?" he asked, looking at the four events she'd written the words next to, including one just a few weeks ago.

She stepped out of his arms, and while he mourned the loss of her heat, he had finally found a pattern. He walked to the board and pointed to the four dates. The first was the night she'd dropped him at the hospital. The second was several years later, the third was about ten months ago and the final one was the night her neighbor had been shot.

"Those are the times I was approached by the guy I call 'The Mask.' He wore one of those extremely cold weather military masks."

"The ones that cover the nose and mouth and only leave the eyes uncovered?"

"Creepy as all get-out up close on a dark street," she said, a shudder going through her. "He covered his eyes with reflective sunglasses or goggles, which made it more terrifying. You could see your reflection in the lenses. You were a witness to your own agony splashed across your face with the jab of his knife. All you could wonder was what sick pleasure he took in being anonymous while he hurt you."

Lucas walked to her and ran his finger down the scar on her chin. "He's responsible for this?" Her nod was short. "Tell me exactly what he said to you that night, Lilah."

"The other guy always did the talking, but The Mask, he came in hot with the knife, sliced me up and left me for the other two guys to acquire—"

"Who always failed to?"

"Oddly enough, yes," she said with a shrug. "I could always escape their grip and run, but I knew they'd be back."

"Could that have been on purpose?"

"Like, they let me go?" she asked, and he nodded, adding a half a head tilt to make it questionable. Another shudder went through her before she answered. "You think they were just playing with me?"

"I don't know what to think other than he had a chance to slit your throat that night and didn't," he said, pointing at her chin and neck. "Instead, he stopped just short of slicing your carotid. He could have ended you being a problem six years ago instead of 'hunting' you for all of them," he said, adding air quotes. "It doesn't make sense." The more he studied the map and the list of attacks, the less sense it made. "What happened in year three when he showed up?"

If she thought he missed the subtle way she crossed her arms over her belly, she was wrong. "Same type of situation. He came in, tortured me a little and left me for the other two." She held up her hand. "Except he whispered that time."

"What did he say?"

Her tender throat bobbed once as her eyes went closed. "That the next time would be our last visit together. As the pawn, I can only move forward, not backward or sideways, the way he could as the king. He said I was surrounded and he'd made sure I had nowhere to go but where he sent me. He also said no one could help me now and that he'd be back to collect his pawn when he needed her to win the game."

An expletive fell from Lucas's lips before he walked to her and wrapped her in his arms. "I'm so sorry, darling. He's playing a game that only he understands. He didn't attack you with a knife the last two times?"

"Oh, yes," she whispered, a shiver spiking through her until he rubbed it away with his warm hand against her back. "He definitely attacked with a knife. He took extreme pleasure in hurting me."

Lucas stepped back and eyed her. "Where?"

"It doesn't matter, Luca," she said, but he caught the spike of fear in her eyes. "What matters is now I can't stop thinking that those guys let me go each time at The Mask's orders."

"Where, Lilah?" he asked again as though he hadn't heard her last sentence. "Tell me where."

He waited and watched the war reflected in her eyes until she shook her head. "I'm not showing you." Her swallow was so harsh it was audible, and he stepped toward her again. "I will say that when he found me ten months ago, it was so bad I shouldn't have been able to fight them off or escape, but I did. Why didn't I think of that? They never wanted to capture me. They wanted to toy with me."

"Why do you think that is?"

She walked to the wall and stood in front of it. "They wanted to keep me off balance? They wanted me to move?"

"They wanted you too scared to go to the authorities?" Lucas asked, coming up behind her.

"Or to think the police wouldn't help me if I did go to them," she agreed. "Not that I ever did or could. With my clearance level, walking into a police station was a sure way to put Delilah Hartman back on the map."

"I hadn't thought of that, but you're right," he agreed. "Then they'd ask why you were using a different name. When he attacked you ten months ago, the words he whispered were chilling. He would come and collect his pawn, 'when he needed her to win the game.' Is that what made you believe this had something to do with the flash drive of information?"

"I didn't know what else it could be about, Lucas. I was afraid they knew I had read The Lost Key of Honor file and had information I shouldn't have."

"If that were the case, killing you would have been the right answer. The fact that they didn't makes me think you know something—"

"Or they think I know something," she interrupted. "Something I don't know."

"That you think you don't know, but you don't know what it is, so there's no way to know if you know it or not."

Lilah burst out laughing, nearly doubling over as her shoulders shook. When she got herself under control, even he was grinning despite the grim circumstances. "That was the most convoluted but understandable sentence I've ever heard. Whether I know something or not is beside the point because they think I do. What are we going to do with this mess?" she asked, letting her hand flick at the wall until it fell to her side.

"We're going to contact Mina and see if she can find out where Major Burris was on the dates The Mask attacked you."

Rather than respond, she just stood in one place and stared at him open-mouthed. "Are you—have you lost it? Major Burris?"

Lucas took her shoulders and forced eye contact with her. "We know your medal was most likely what they used to track you. That indicates military involvement. We also know the guys who are tracking you are ex-military. We know that all those artifacts that are missing shouldn't be. It's not a stretch to think Burris is somehow involved in this."

"It wasn't him," she said, shaking her head. "I know it wasn't him behind that mask. I didn't recognize his voice."

"Maybe not, but it doesn't hurt to have Mina find out where he was, right?"

"It's not him, Lucas."

"Humor me?"

Lilah motioned at the phone on the table and sat on the bed to watch him type. He kept his facial expression neutral despite the fire raging through his veins. He wanted to find the man tormenting her and give him a taste of his own medicine. Right or wrong. He would do anything to protect Lilah now that she was back in his life, but he couldn't protect her from the pain and fear she suffered in the past, and that filled him with rage. He snapped the phone down on the desk and stalked toward her. "Show me."

"Show you what?" she asked, her head cocked to the side in confusion.

"Where The Mask cut you."

"Absolutely not," she said between clenched teeth.

"What are you afraid of, Lilah?"

"I'm not afraid of anything, Luca. What happened in the past should stay in the past."

"If I had a million dollars, I would bet all of it that where he cut you is why you turned me down on the once-and-done request yesterday."

"Wow," she said, drawing out the last *w*. "You do think highly of yourself."

"Not at all," he said, taking another step closer. "But I know you—"

"No, you knew me. There's a difference, Luca. I'm not the same woman who left that hospital. That woman is gone."

"Maybe some of her is gone, but the woman I held on my lap with my lips on hers in an old motel was the same woman I held on my lap with my lips on hers on a beach in the middle of Lake Superior. At least until that woman remembered she had something to hide."

The phone beeped, and she let out a relieved breath. "You better get that. It's Mina."

"She's on it," he said, dropping the phone to the desk. "Said she'd get back to us, as she had just gotten into the files on Burris's trial."

"Good. Maybe we'll finally get the information to move forward and clear my name." She turned and walked to Haven, patting him on the top of his head where he slept. When she turned back around, Lucas grasped her arm.

"You can pretend the past doesn't matter if that makes you feel better, but one day, I will find out what that animal did to you and I will kiss every last scar."

He dropped his voice to the timbre he knew always made her melt inside. The timbre that said he meant every word and what he said could be trusted.

"Just in case the destruction of my face isn't enough for you," she said, righteous indignation filling her words, "let me make it incredibly clear that I'm your past, Lucas, and you should be glad I am!"

With her fingers shaking and tears in her eyes, she lifted

her shirt to reveal what she'd been hiding all this time. Unable to process the scene before him, he stumbled backward onto the bed without a word.

Chapter Seventeen

Pain flooded Delilah as the look on his face transformed from caring to stunned to horrified. She hated that she had to destroy the memory of what she used to be to him, but it didn't matter. When this was over, they'd part ways and this moment of humiliation could be stored in the box where she kept all of her Lucas Porter memories.

She turned away and walked to the window, pulling back the curtain to see the snow still falling and the sky getting darker. The sun set early as Christmas approached, and she couldn't help but wonder if she'd live to see her thirty-fourth Christmas. It used to be her favorite season—not for the decorations, goodies or gifts, but for the sense of hope and renewal it ushered in. When she was a child, her father was the one who made Christmas merry. He loved everything about the season, from the carols to the candy to the tree and treats. After he died, her mom worked hard to keep joy in the holiday, but there was always something missing.

Then she joined the service and spent her first Christmas away from home. She had struggled to find joy that first year, so she was surprised it came so easily to her in the midst of war. Delilah had found joy in singing Christmas carols around a tiny tree and sharing treats sent by caring family members simply by reminding herself that Christmas, no matter the place, was a time for family. The soldiers on the base were her family, and she took comfort in having them. During war, Christmas was a time of hope for peace, even if that hope was always short-lived. That hadn't changed since she left the service. The last six Christmases she had spent alone but always took a moment to find joy in the day, and hope that it would be her last Christmas under wraps. It was then she realized, one way or the other, this was the end.

Her heart pulsed hard, and she rubbed her chest, but it didn't relieve the pain. Luca was everything she had wanted in her past life, but now he could be nothing to her, even if she wished their lives could be different. This would be their first and last Christmas together, leaving her with nothing but memories for every Christmas season to come—if she made it out of this alive, that is.

"My God," he whispered, his breath whooshing out again. "How did you survive something like that, Lilah?"

"He made sure to slice me just deep enough that I was maimed but not deep enough to kill me. It took forty-four stitches the first time and seventy-seven the second time to put me back together. The hospitals forced me to file a police report, but it didn't matter. The woman who walked into that hospital ceased to exist the moment she left."

"This sick animal needs to be stopped," Lucas said between clenched teeth. "We've got you now," he said, walking to where she stood at the window. "I know you don't need protecting, but I'm going to be here to fight with you until we find him and end this game he's playing."

"I want to believe that, but we've been together for two days and are no further ahead than when you found me."

"You're wrong. We have pieces of the puzzle, but we're missing the one pivotal piece that will bring the picture into focus and reveal the artist behind the design. You've fought too long and worked too hard to give up now."

Delilah knew that to be the truth. "But I only did it for you, Luca. I wanted to protect you."

"Then let me protect you now, my darling Delilah."

His words were desperate, and she turned just as he pulled her into him and took her lips, reminding her of all the reasons she had to keep those memories of Lucas locked up in a box. Allowing herself to feel them was too painful. Her heart and body couldn't take more pain. Still, she kissed him back, unable to deny herself the feel of his lips and the way his hot tongue cuddled hers.

"Lucas, we can't," she said, her lips still pressed to his. "We can't do this. It's not fair to either of us."

"Do you know what's not fair?" he asked, walking her backward to the bed. "Thinking I desire you less than I did before because of superficial scars on your skin. It's unfair to yourself and me. It's as though you think I'm superficial and never really cared about you."

"I don't think that, Luca," she whispered as he set her down on the edge of the bed and hoisted her up to the pillows. "When I say it's unfair, I mean it's unfair to ourselves knowing we can never be together again."

"Never is a dangerous word, Delilah Hartman. I never thought I'd see you again, but here you are, under my lips, reminding me why you never left my mind all these years. Why you were the last thought I had every day and the first every morning."

He lifted her shirt while he whispered sweet nothings, letting the cool air brush across her tender skin. She had a decision to make. Stop this now and continue to fight against the current trying to pull them under, or let herself have a moment of pleasure in a world full of pain.

His lips feathered a kiss across where her naval used to be before the ropy scar took over in a morbid smiley face. With a sharp intake of breath, her belly quivered as he moved his lips to the left and kissed her again, following the trail of the scar to her rib cage. His hands, so familiar against her skin, wrapped around her torso and pushed the shirt to her bra, making room for his lips as he traced another jagged scar to the right and down to her hip.

How was she supposed to fight against this when it felt so good? So right? His words came back to her. Once and done. It would never be done for her, but as he trailed his tongue across another scar, she decided once was better than none.

"Luca," she whispered, her breath heavy in her chest. When he lifted his head, his pupils were dilated and filled with heady need. "We don't have any protection."

A wicked smile lifted his lips as he rose and rifled through a bag beside the bed. He came up with a silver package in his hand. "Secure One has us covered," he promised, tossing it on the nightstand before he went back to kissing her belly, drawing a moan from her lips.

The sound was fuel to his flame, and he tossed her glasses on the nightstand, stripped her of her shirt and, just as quickly, her bra. He leaned back on his knees, his gaze raking her breasts. "You're even more beautiful than the last time I made love to you. I didn't think that was possible. Softer. Sweeter," he whispered, his head dipping to tease a nipple with his tongue.

"The last six years haven't been kind to my body," she whispered, her hands sliding into his soft locks.

He lifted his head and took her lips for a hot ride through the past. "Darling, your body is my resting place. Always has been. That hasn't changed."

Rather than answer, she slid her hands under his shirt

until he grasped the hem and pulled it over his head, letting it sail across the room. Her hands roamed over his muscles while he quickly did away with their boots and cargo pants. He loomed over her, his gaze filled with flames, and then, slowly and with the utmost tenderness, he lowered himself to rest gently across her body, their lips perfectly aligned.

He closed his eyes as his lips neared hers. "I have dreamed about this day for so long, Lilah. To cover you again and let your aura raise my soul from its resting place. To forget about everything for the moments that we're joined as one."

His honesty brought tears to her eyes, and she reached up to stroke his cheek before she grasped the package from the nightstand and tore it open. "Let's be one then and forget about anything but how we make each other feel."

Lucas dove in for a kiss while she deftly rolled the sheath over him, drawing a moan from deep in his throat. The room quieted for a single breath as he filled her before he swallowed her soft moan with his lips. Fire built in her belly, spiraling until her legs shook and her nails raked his back while she begged him to let her go. To let her fly into the sky and for him to be there with her, holding her hand as they soared.

"Patience, beautiful," he whispered, thrusting forward again as he nipped her earlobe. "We only get one second chance, and I'm going to cherish every last second of it."

With her head pressed into the pillow, she raised her hips, allowing him to slip a bit deeper to nestle in the place he loved the most. He told her that spot, that little piece of heaven, was his dwelling place.

"Lilah!" he exclaimed, his hips pressed tightly to hers. "I'm home." He whispered those two words into her ear as he thrust one more time and carried her over the threshold and into a second chance at life together.

"SECURE ONE, WHISKEY."

Lucas quickly moved to the desk and connected the computer. "Secure two, Lima." His gaze darted to Lilah, who was asleep on the bed. After they'd made love twice, she had showered and fallen into an exhausted slumber. He didn't want to wake her, so he addressed Mina quickly with a finger to his lips.

"She's exhausted," he said, without adding the part about how he was responsible for it.

"I can understand why. This is a nightmare of a dumpster fire, and none of us have an extinguisher."

Lucas couldn't help but chuckle. Leave it to Mina to sum it up so perfectly. "I couldn't agree more."

"I can't even imagine dealing with this alone the way she has been for so many years. It's one twisted mess. I'm not sure we'll ever get to the bottom of it, but I'm not giving up. That said, dealing with the government is like entering the second level of hell whenever you need information."

"You're not wrong," he agreed, his gaze sliding to the bed again to check on Lilah. "Did you find anything?"

"I found some interesting tidbits, but still no trunk. It's like it never existed in the world, even though we know it did."

"Lilah searched a bunch of archives, too, but never found proof that it was in the possession of a history museum in the United States. There was also no history of it being returned to its rightful country."

"What's going on?" Lilah asked behind him, rubbing her face several times before climbing out from under the blanket he'd covered her with when she fell asleep. Thankfully, she had been fully dressed.

Lucas's cheeks heated, and his body stirred at the thought of holding her again, but he had to accept that their second chance had come and gone. Once she was free, the last place she'd want to be was confined within the walls of Secure One. Unfortunately for him, he needed those confines to feel safe. For a brief moment, while buried deep inside her, he wondered if he could be safe wherever she was, but he knew the truth. He was far more likely to hurt her when his world wasn't stable, and that was the last thing he wanted. She was happy with one and done, so he had no choice but to accept the same—even if it had been two and never done for him.

"I was just telling Lucas what a dumpster fire this mess is."

Lilah's laughter filled the room as she walked toward him until he could feel her heat wrap him up tightly again. "I wish I could say you're wrong, but I can't. It makes less and less sense the deeper we dig."

"Well, what I have to tell you also aligns with that."

"Oh, boy," Lucas said as he stood and offered Lilah the chair. "What did you find?"

"I'm glad you're sitting down," Mina said, her lips twisted into a grimaced smile. "When I got down to the paperwork regarding Burris's war crimes—" she put the words in quotations "—you're listed as a key witness to the events."

"I'm what now?" she asked, leaning in as though she hadn't heard her right. "I'm not sure I understand. The paperwork says I turned him in?"

"No, I can't see who turned him in. Just that you are listed as a key witness to the crimes."

"The crimes he didn't commit or go to jail for?"

Mina pointed at her with a nod. "Did you witness Major Burris commit any war crimes?"

"Seriously?" Lilah asked, her voice full of frustration and anger. "I worked with him only while I was in Germany.

I was a computer geek. I had nothing to do with what was happening on the field."

"That's not true," Lucas said, leaning on the back of her chair with both hands to avoid touching her how he wanted to. Mina couldn't suspect there was more than friendship between them, or she'd insist that Cal replace him with someone who could be impartial about the situation. That wouldn't be necessary. As a soldier, he'd learned to separate his personal life from his professional, and he could do the same now, even if his personal life was at the heart of this professional situation. "You were tracking the ops and fielding any issues with the technology."

"Which," Mina said with a tip of her head, "if Burris was committing war crimes using the operations you were tracking, would make you a key witness."

"Even if I wasn't aware?"

"That is the question," Mina agreed. "You can be a witness to a crime without knowing, but that doesn't mean you can testify to those crimes in any way."

"The next question is, why wasn't I notified that I was considered a witness?" Lilah asked, her voice loud and clear now that the sleep and shock had disappeared. "And why wasn't I called to make a statement before they released him from the charges?"

"Those are also questions I can't answer other than…" She paused and shifted in her chair, obviously uncomfortable and not because of the pregnancy. She wasn't comfortable with what she had to say next.

"Other than?" Lilah asked. "Be straight with me, Mina. If this all comes down to something that happened in the service that I'm not aware of, I'd like to get it straightened out and get my life back before more years are stolen." Delilah tipped her head up to make eye contact with Lucas. He tried to keep his smile easy, when all he wanted to do was pull her into his arms and protect her from all of this.

"I wonder if the information I can see has been doctored."

"Whatever for?" Lilah asked. "Why would they need to doctor paperwork to make it look like I was a witness to something I wasn't a witness to?"

"As a reason to track you," Lucas said without hesitation.

Mina tipped her head in agreement. "That was my first thought, too."

"Tracking me is one thing. Attempted murder is something else entirely."

"I did warn you that this would make no sense," Mina said with a shrug. "As for Burris, he's living near Rochester now with his wife. He isn't working anywhere, but is heavily involved in several veteran organizations."

"Nothing else nefarious?" Lilah asked.

"On Burris? Not yet, but I will search property records, vehicles and bank situations. I came across something else that I thought was definitely concerning."

That got Lucas's attention, and he spun around a chair to straddle it. "How concerning?"

"Deadly," she said, her lips thinning for a moment. "It may be nothing, but I was hoping Delilah could shed some light on it."

"I'll do my best, but I've been out of touch with the world for years."

"While I was researching Burris," she said, shuffling papers around until she grabbed one from the pile, "I found the names of four other logistics officers listed as key witnesses to his war crimes."

"That's not surprising," Lilah said. "The supply chain in the military is massive. There were a lot of logistics officers."

"Agreed," Mina said, flicking her eyes to Lucas. The

look she gave him said what came next was the surprising part. He put his arm around Lilah to ground her. "When I searched those women, I discovered all four of them are dead."

The room was silent for two beats before Lilah spoke. "They're what now?"

"Dead," Mina repeated. "All victims of violent crimes."

"Did they involve knives?" Lilah asked, and Lucas heard her voice quiver on the last word.

"Three of the four," Mina answered. "This is the part that confuses me. All four of them were living under an alias like you. The first two women were found in an alley, as though it was a mugging gone wrong. Ultimately, their fingerprints were used to identify them since their identifications were poor fakes. Another woman was found naked in bed. It was staged to look like a BDSM scene gone wrong, but she had been strangled and moved to the bed. The final woman was pulled from a river. Whoever killed her made it look like she jumped, but the police have questions since she was obviously stabbed before she went into the river. That victim was also using a false name."

"I have questions," Lucas said, rubbing Lilah's back to keep her grounded. A shudder went through her, and he gently squeezed her neck to comfort her. As her anxiety built, Haven raised his head, assessed the situation and walked to Lilah, resting his head on her leg. Lucas noticed her stroke his head, and her shoulders relaxed as she did.

"The deaths of four women who did the same job I did is not a coincidence, Mina."

"You won't get an argument out of me. It is a dead end since the crimes were never solved. They remain open, but the last death was a year ago, so they're all cold cases now."

"Wait," Lucas said, leaning forward. "When did they find the first woman?"

Mina searched the paper and counted backward. "Almost five years ago. The next woman was found three years ago, the third was two years ago, and the river victim was last year."

"I was next," Lilah said, her voice surprisingly steady. "That's why The Mask showed up at the apartment building this time. It was my turn to die."

"The Mask?" Mina asked, glancing between them.

"That's what she called him," Lucas said before Lilah could. He didn't want her to have to explain it. "He did that to her chin and cut her several other places."

"I noticed the scars when you were dressing," Mina admitted, addressing Lilah now. "I'm so sorry that happened to you."

"Lucas pointed out that any of the three times he attacked me, he could have killed me." Mina nodded her agreement. "It was about ten months ago when he showed up and whispered in my ear. He said I was his pawn and he'd come for me when it was time for him to win the game."

"That's what finally spurred her to contact me," Lucas explained. "When he showed up a few weeks ago, she knew she was out of time."

"I was hoping to use the flash drive as a bargaining chip for my life," Lilah said, sarcastic laughter filling the room. "That was never going to happen."

"I'm curious as to why these other women were killed, though," Mina said, flipping the camera to show the entire room since Cal and Eric had walked in.

"Is it possible you weren't the only one shipping artifacts back to the States?" Cal asked, sitting down at the table.

"I never considered it, but there had to be people on other

bases also taking in antiquities to protect, right? There were other bases in other parts of those countries. You would think word would spread like wildfire throughout the curator community that we would keep their treasures safe. Do you have the real names of the women who were killed, Mina?"

Mina nodded and read off the women's names and ranks, but Delilah shook her head before she finished.

"I don't know any of them. Not that unusual, as I was working more cybersecurity than supply chain by that point in the war, but what is unusual is that they all died questionable deaths."

"And the timeline is scarily precise," Mina finished. "As though someone was checking off a box once something was completed."

"We just need to know what that something was and who was killing them," Lilah said with a groan. "Were there any other witnesses listed on the paperwork?"

"No, it was the five of you, and you're the only one left standing."

Lucas tipped his head to the side. "Mina, did any of those women get medals for their service?"

"Boy, I didn't dig that far. Do you think it's important?"

"I do," Cal said. "That's why we're here. Eric retrieved the medal from the abandoned house today."

"It was still there?" Lilah asked. "I figured if they were tracking me with it, they'd take it."

"They might have if they had time to search for it," Eric said, pulling out a chair. "But the medal was in the tree with the camera. I put it there to protect it. It would lead them to the house, but my gut said the tracker wasn't pinpoint accurate."

"Meaning it just gave them a general area she was in?" Lucas asked.

"Exactly," Eric agreed as he pulled it from his pocket. The medal was in two parts now as he laid them on the table. "I apologize that it's ruined," he said to Lilah, who shrugged as though she no longer cared. "When I broke it open, inside was the smallest GPS I've ever seen. Lucas, you were right. It was solar powered."

"You didn't bring it back to base with you, right?" Lucas asked, and Eric shook his head.

"No, that's why I did it in the field. I left the tracker in the tree. If they tag it again, it will get plenty of power to keep it active. I wasn't sure if we'd need it for evidence, so I didn't want to destroy it."

"All of that said, what's our next move?" Lucas asked.

The room fell silent until Lilah spoke. "I think it's time we pay my old major a little visit."

"No. Not happening," Lucas said, leaning over the chair and grasping her shoulders. "You're not going anywhere near him."

"Do you have a better idea?" Delilah asked, her gaze locked with his as though the rest of the team no longer existed in the conversation. "You know what they say. If you want the truth, get it straight from the horse's mouth."

"She's not wrong," Mina said from the computer.

"You're not helping, Mina," Lucas snapped.

"She is, though," Lilah reminded him. "That's why this has to end. I've gotten so many people involved in this nightmare, including you. It's my responsibility to get you back out of it alive and in one piece. I can't do that holed up in this motel room!"

"I don't like it," Lucas said, his hand fisted in his hair.

"We don't have enough information to walk into a mission we don't understand and expect to come out unscathed."

"I don't like it, either," Mina and Cal said in unison, giving the moment a bit of levity. "But she's right," Mina finished. "There is no way to solve this from that motel room. Let us talk together as a team about options. We'll call you back?"

Lucas shook his head in defeat. "Fine, but I already know this is not smart."

"Maybe, but I'm not sure we have any other move on the board. Whiskey, out."

The screen went black, and the room went silent.

"Luca," Lilah finally said, her voice soft in the quiet of the room. "You know I'm right about this."

The answer he had to give was one she wouldn't like, so he said nothing while he shrugged on his field coat and grabbed Haven's lead. "We're going to check the perimeter. Lock the door behind me."

"Luca," she called as he opened the door and walked out into the blackness, but he let the night swallow anything else she had to say.

Chapter Eighteen

If Lucas was going to agree to this plan, Delilah needed to find a tidbit of information to prove that going to Burris was the only answer, even if she already knew it was the only answer. She didn't know how she knew, but something told her the only way to find the end was to start at the beginning.

That was her plan as she opened The Lost Key of Honor file again and started scrolling. She had read it so many times that nothing stuck out to her as applicable. There had to be something, though. Claiming five women were witnesses to something they couldn't back up with facts just to kill them didn't make sense otherwise. Then again, if Lucas was right, and the war crimes occurred during the ops, she'd be in charge of troubleshooting, so it was possible she had information and didn't know it. That honestly felt like the only answer as she scrolled down the rows, because the file revealed nothing it hadn't already. All this correspondence was nothing more than a back-and-forth sharing of buildings checked, people contacted and the next steps.

While she read, her mind wandered back to the time spent in bed with Lucas. They'd gone as slow as they could the first time they'd made love, but it was still too fast. The second time had been more about learning how they had changed and discovering how they had stayed the same.

Their touch had been gentler, longer and more precise, leading to an intimacy they hadn't shared that first summer. She knew why, too. That summer, they thought they'd be together forever. This Christmas, they knew their time together was fleeting.

Someone in the room next door dropped something, and Delilah jumped, accidentally clicking the mouse on the file. That click brought up a box asking her if she wanted to go to the link provided. Did she? Yes. Could she? Her gaze tracked to the VPN that had her as a user based in Switzerland. There were ways to see a VPN, but she hoped the file no longer mattered or they would take it at face value if they noticed anyone on the link. Her laughter filled the room. No, they'd know immediately that Delilah Hartman had clicked the link, but Cal's stealth VPN was impossible to get around. It offered her a cloak of invisibility she never had before when online. If ever there was a time to take advantage of it, now was that time.

A click on the yes button took her to a chat website and into a private room. There was a chat transcript going back eight years, with the latest entries from someone named *Iamthatguy* being one month ago when he'd replied to someone called *Bigmanoncampus*.

Any luck this time?

None. I don't believe this tablet exists anymore. If it did, it surely would have been found by now.

I don't care what you believe. The tablet is out there.

Do you have any new leads? I sure as hell don't. It may be time to let it go, boss.

Don't tell me to let it go! We're a month from the big event and we still don't have the main attraction! I've got a new lead, but I'll need you to go back to where this started. The information will come in the usual manner. I'll be waiting to hear.

When *Iamthatguy* responded, he certainly didn't sound happy.

Back to the beginning? This is exhausting and I'm not getting any younger. I'll go one last time, but after that, I'm out.

You're out when I say you're out! *Bigmanoncampus* replied. Delilah could almost hear the venom dripping from his words. Get the job done, we're running out of time! If you don't, you'll be spending your Christmas in a very small box.

Delilah had no doubt they were talking about the tablet to open the trunk. Undeterred, she scrolled up to a feature where items could be pinned, curious about the files and why they would pin them there. She clicked open the first file and was surprised to see a map of a small village in Iraq. It had been methodically marked off with a red *x* through each building on the image. The following three files she opened were the same. The fourth was a list of names with red lines drawn through each one.

"The snow has stopped, but with that fresh layer on the ground, it's cold," Lucas said, coming back inside with a snow-covered Haven. His return surprised her, and she glanced up to see him strip off his coat and pull off Haven's boots.

"How long have you been out there?"

"Too long," he answered, motioning for Haven to follow him to his food bowl. "But I cleared the van of snow so we can go."

"You agree that we need to find Burris?" she asked, her tone giving away her surprise.

"No, but we also can't stay here much longer." She could tell he was trying not to be short with her when all he wanted to do was shake her silly until she understood what a bad idea it was to show up on Burris's doorstep. She completely understood what a bad idea it was, but that didn't mean she had a choice. Lucas would end up on the run with her if they didn't do something soon. While she wouldn't mind that, something told her Cal and the other guys at Secure One would. No, it was time, once and for all, to find out what they wanted from her and give it to them. If they wanted her, she'd turn herself over to the US government and hope for the best. She couldn't continue to put other people at risk because she was afraid.

Her spine stiffened with the thought, and she turned back to the computer. There was one more file, and she clicked it open, but this time, page after page after page opened. "What is going on?" she muttered as Lucas came up behind her.

"What are you looking at?"

Without turning, she quickly flipped through the pages, stopping long enough to glance through each one. "I accidentally clicked inside the file for The Lost Key of Honor. It took me to this chat room–type website where *Iamthatguy* and *Bigmanoncampus* discuss their search for the missing tablet. This," she said, motioning at the screen, "has maps of villages in Iraq that were searched, and these," she tapped the open file on her screen, "are detailed dossiers on what I think are other artifacts they found during the search." She took a moment to read more of each file, a whistle escaping as she recognized several artifacts on the list she had been told to catalog. "What in the world?" The question was barely whispered as her hand froze on the mouse.

"What did you find?" he asked, kneeling beside her chair.

Her finger shaking, she pointed at the screen. "The trunk hasn't disappeared. Whoever these two guys are have it in their possession."

"They want access to it so when they find the tablet, they can open the trunk."

"Feels a little Indiana Jones in here, right?" Delilah asked, leaning back in the chair. "We all know that never ended well for the greedy treasure hunters."

Lucas stood and started to massage her shoulders again, almost like he knew she needed a calming hand at the helm. "It's not going to work out for these guys, either, once we find out who they are, that is. Is there a way to send these to Mina?"

"I can't download them," she said, checking the files' properties. "I could just send her the whole file." She bit her lip and stared at the screen. If she shared The Lost Key of Honor file with Mina, that made her a witness to anything illegal they found in the files and an accomplice to data theft. She didn't want to put that on Mina's or Secure One's back. Then again, considering what Mina did there, it wouldn't be her first rodeo with backdoor access to files.

"What are you thinking? Walk me through it," he encouraged, still massaging her shoulders.

"I could send Mina a digital copy of the entire flash drive. Then she'd have The Lost Key of Honor file and access to all of this and the full dossier on each artifact. The problem is that makes her a witness to any crimes we discover and an accomplice to any data we use to bring this to an end."

"Darling, if Mina was worried about being an accomplice to data theft, she wouldn't be doing what she's doing. Send her the file."

"Somehow, I knew you were going to say that." Laughter spilled from her lips, and it felt good amid all the angst that filled her.

Delilah enlarged the first open file and opened the snipping tool app.

"What are you doing? I thought you said you can't save the files."

"I can't, not in the traditional way, but I can take screenshots. There's a fifty-fifty chance that the chat room ceases to exist as soon as I close this tab."

"What now?" he asked, leaning on the desk, ankles crossed. "Why would it cease to exist?"

"There could be a failsafe on it, so if anyone but them login, it shuts itself down."

"Wouldn't that happen right away? It's letting you read it."

Delilah kept at her task as she talked, afraid he was right and the screen could go black any second. "I followed the link from the file, making the page think I was one of them, but I'm not taking any chances that Mina can't get back in to read this stuff." After a few more clicks of the mouse, she saved everything in a new file. While at it, she saved the chat in a sequence of screenshots and then highlighted the dates for Mina to see. "Okay, I think I have it all." She clicked out of the chat room and let out a sigh.

"Package that up and send it to Mina. Then, we're leaving."

"To go where?" she asked, adding the files to the flash drive and zipping the contents.

He held up his phone. "We're about to find out. Is that

ready to go to her?" Delilah nodded, and Lucas hit the call button, holding the screen out for her to see. "Secure one, Lima," Luca said, waiting for a beat until they heard Mina's reply. When her face filled the screen, it was lined with fatigue. Delilah immediately felt guilty for putting this on their shoulders. What made her feel a little better was knowing this was almost over. They could all go back to their lives, even if she was lost to time forever.

THE VAN WAS unnaturally quiet. It was as though they were holding their breath, knowing something big was coming but unsure if they'd survive whatever it was. When the team called back, they sent them south, sticking to back roads and two-lane highways to avoid the freeway. Mina programmed the van's GPS with the location of Burris's house in Rochester. They'd head in that direction while she went through the files on the flash drive Lilah had sent.

He glanced at the woman in the seat next to him and fought back the wave of protectiveness that filled him. Hard as it was, he couldn't protect her from this. The only way out of it was through it. He feared the through part would leave them both shredded and bleeding. Four women were already dead. There was no way he would let her be the next one. What he was struggling to understand was, while a pet project wasn't unusual for the military, hiding other countries' treasures was immoral at best and illegal at worst. The US government would never sanction that. The only thing worse would be auctioning them off to the highest bidder. Lucas gasped.

Lilah glanced at him immediately. "What?" she asked. "Are you okay?"

"Fine, but I was just thinking. Do you think the two

guys from the chat room plan to sell the artifacts on the black market?"

"Well, yeah. Going by the dates in the chat room, my bet is, they have an auction scheduled on Christmas Day. They want the tablet to complete the trunk, thereby making it the main attraction. It will surely bring a bidding war unlike any ever seen."

"Christmas Day?"

"He said the big event was in a month, counting forward that makes it Christmas Day. I see the allure of the ultrarich wanting a new trinket on that day."

"Okay, but how do you find buyers for stolen artifacts? It's not like you can use Sotheby's."

He couldn't help but smile when she laughed. He loved being the one to make her laugh now that they were together again. At least for however long they were together. This second chance of theirs could end quickly and without warning. That thought stole the smile from his lips.

"The black market is deep and dark, Luca. There are plenty of buyers for these artifacts who are all too happy to keep them locked away from the world forever. We can't let that happen."

"This *Bigmanoncampus* and *Iamthatguy*, do you think they're military?"

"I did get to the page via the file, so that would make the most sense."

"True." Lucas drove in silence for a few moments. "But what if the military is monitoring the page for intel?"

"Could be that, too," she agreed. "There's no way to know unless we can see who's behind the fake names, which I doubt even Mina can do. Not on the dark web like that."

"Wait, that was the dark web?"

"Uh, yeah," she said, biting her lip. "I thought you knew."

"I'm not a computer nerd, Lilah. I thought it was just a web page."

"Who you calling a computer nerd?" she asked haughtily before they both giggled.

It was several miles down the road before they got themselves together again. "Okay, this is serious business," Lucas said, but his smile defied that statement. He loved being with her again and refused to think about how boring life would be when she was gone.

"We already know these artifacts aren't in the museums," Lilah said, leaning back into the seat. "Which means they have to be somewhere else. They may not even be in the country at this point."

"I wish we knew if that chat room was being monitored by the military, created by them or owned by someone else entirely."

Lilah nodded, ready to speak, when the phone rang, making them both jump. Lucas hit the answer button on the dashboard. "Secure one, Lima."

"Secure two, Whiskey," Mina said.

"Did you find something?" Lilah asked, sitting forward in her seat to turn up the volume. Lucas scanned the road for somewhere to pull over and noticed an old rest stop ahead.

"Hang on, Mina, I'm going to pull over." He slowed, turned and pulled the van under overgrown trees before he doused the headlights. There was no sense in being a sitting target if someone was looking for them. "Go ahead."

"I haven't had time to go through all of the flash drive files yet, but I did get results for the property search on Burris."

Lilah glanced at Lucas quizzically. "I thought we knew that already. Isn't that why we're driving to Rochester?"

"Yes, he has a home in Rochester, but he also has hunting land southwest of the Rochester airport."

"There's hunting land all over that part of Minnesota. I'm not sure how that helps us," Lucas said, frustrated by the lack of answers at every turn.

"It may be nothing, but he applied for a building permit to put up a garage on that land. Said he was going to store his hunting equipment in it."

"That makes sense," Lucas said, a huff leaving his lips as he let out a long, frustrated breath. "We're in hunting country. You know that, Mina."

"I do," she agreed, "which is why I checked DNR records next. George Burris has never had a hunting license in his life."

Chapter Nineteen

Lilah's heart pounded hard at Mina's revelation. "You think he built the garage for other purposes?"

"I see no other reason than to store something," Mina agreed. "It could be innocent, but I'm starting to think it's not."

"Me, too," Luca agreed.

"Especially since we can't find evidence that any of those artifacts in your files ever made it to a museum."

"What is the working theory then, Mina?" Lucas asked, rubbing his hands on his thighs before he tapped out a rhythm in threes. He felt exposed sitting in such an isolated location and wanted to get out of there. Haven stuck his snout around the side of the seat to bop his arm. It was a reminder to breathe, so he inhaled to three and held it, counting to three while he waited for Mina to answer.

"I think we all know the answer to that question," Mina said.

"That Burris has somehow managed to funnel all these artifacts to a garage in Minnesota?" Lilah asked.

"With or without help from someone else," Mina agreed. "The how—I can't answer that. The why, well, the simple answer is money."

"Did you get into the chat room?" Lilah asked out of curiosity.

"No, you were right about it locking me out. I clicked around on the file, but it went nowhere."

"Let me give you the highlights," Lilah said. "I think they're planning an auction for Christmas Day and wanted the trunk complete to encourage a bidding war."

"We can't let that happen," Mina vehemently said. "If that's the case, we have three days to stop it."

"Are they onto us?" Luca asked, his gaze tracking the area around the van with caution.

"No, they're onto the fact that someone else was in the chat room. I assume they were notified. The dark web is tricky, as Lilah knows."

"That's why I took the screenshots," she said. "I was relatively sure that's what was going to happen."

"You told me it was a fifty-fifty chance," Luca said, turning to face her.

"I didn't want to freak you out," Lilah admitted to Mina's laughter.

"We still have no proof that Burris is behind this, though," Lilah said. "It's just a gut feeling on our part."

"I always go with the gut," Mina said. "It's rarely wrong."

"I'm feeling exposed out here without backup," Lucas said. "I don't want to approach this place alone."

"That's why the main team is getting ready to leave. They'll meet you at the Rochester airport at 0800 hours."

"We'll be in Rochester in an hour," Luca said, eyeing the clock that read 5:00 a.m.

"Head to the airport and wait for the rest of the team. Since the chat room won't let me in, I can't dig into who the two people are conversing on it. I'd bet my firstborn that one of them is Burris."

Luca's laughter filled the van. "Roman wouldn't be happy with you betting his little girl, but I agree."

"Me, too," Lilah said, a lead weight settling into her gut. "That would explain the tracker in the medal. If he'd been led to believe I was a witness, he'd be nervous since we worked so closely together on what I thought was preserving these artifacts. Instead, he was looting them to sell illegally and killing anyone who knew about it. I guess, in a way, that does make me culpable."

"No," Luca and Mina said together. "You were following orders," Mina said. "You had no way to know that the artifacts weren't going where you sent them. Someone was cutting them off at the pass. I aim to find that person, but so many years have passed that it may be impossible."

"I need to get back on the road," Lucas said, his nerves frayed. "We'll meet the team at 0800 hours unless we hear otherwise. If you need anything, you know how to reach us."

"Ten-four. Whiskey out."

Luca glanced at her. "With any luck, we'll find something useful at the property."

"And then what?" Lilah asked. "If we find proof of something, and I report it, they're going to accuse me of the crime since I have no proof that I didn't know the artifacts weren't being shipped properly."

"You've been on the run for six years!" Luca ground out. "Why else would you run?"

"On the run can mean a lot of things. They could say I was running from the law, not for my life."

"I think the scars covering your body would say otherwise, Lilah."

She sat nodding, trying to figure out what was bothering her. "Burris isn't The Mask, though. I know for sure he's not the guy coming after me."

"That doesn't mean he isn't involved," Luca responded, flipping on the headlights and putting the van back into Drive. "The Mask could be another hired thug."

"True, but it felt far too personal for any old thug. It's like the man behind the mask has a personal vendetta against me."

"Like he couldn't kill you yet, but he needed to keep you off-kilter and afraid."

"That," she said without thought. "It makes me wonder if that's why he came at me at regular intervals. He never wanted me to get comfortable with the idea that he was gone for good or that I wasn't being watched. Regardless, I could still get trapped in this, Luca. I could go to prison for all of this."

"That's where you're wrong. The information on that flash drive proves that you didn't know what was happening. It shows a straight chain of command. The items went to central shipping when they left your hands. Your major signed off on that. There was no way for you to know they didn't get to their next destination. Your responsibility ended when Burris signed off."

"When Burris signed off," she said slowly. "Burris had to sign off, which means he could have easily changed or deleted all of my shipping labels. He could have shipped them elsewhere or moved them out of the countries in other ways. That might be our proof that Burris is behind this. Regardless, I'm scared this will blow up in my face and I'll be left holding the bag. Worse yet, it blows back on you and Secure One."

"Let's take this one step at a time, okay?" he asked, reaching out to take her hand and squeeze it.

"What happens if we don't find anything at Burris's property?"

"I guess we wait for Mina to find us another lead."

"No," she said, her head shaking as she thought about the future. "I'm done running. If we don't find anything at the property, I'll confront Burris—alone."

"You are absolutely not doing that," Lucas said between clenched teeth. "Selina tried that and nearly died at the hands of the person after her. On the off chance Burris is The Mask, I refuse to let you take that risk. Backed into a corner, he might stop cutting and start killing."

Lilah bit her tongue to keep from arguing with him. He was wrong, but he was also right. She was stuck between a rock and a hard place that might only be solved by her sticking her neck out. Luca may not understand that, but as the final puzzle piece snapped into place, she did. Burris wasn't The Mask. With a sinking heart, she realized who it was.

"CAL IS NOT going to be happy about this," Lucas whispered for the third time, but Lilah wasn't listening. "We were supposed to wait for them."

"We are waiting," she answered. "He didn't say we couldn't approach Burris's other property."

"I'm rather sure he meant in general, Lilah," he said between clenched teeth. He'd been trying to get her to listen to him for the last hour, but she wasn't budging. She was keeping something from him, and he didn't know what it was, but ever since they left that rest stop, she'd been withdrawn and somber.

"Hold up a minute," he said, pulling her and Haven into a grove of trees near Burris's property line. The houses were spaced far apart, with at least an acre of land surrounded by woods that made for natural fencing. They would have to do it methodically if they approached the Burris home. The last thing he wanted was for someone to call the cops. "What is going on with you? Since Mina called about Burris's other property, you've been uncommunicative, combative and bossy."

She stood before him with stubbornness written across her features in a way that said she wanted to tell him the truth but was determined not to in order to protect him. Lucas wasn't having it. He wrapped his arms around her and pulled him into her, kissing her forehead before he leaned down near her ear. "I'm already involved in this, Lilah. I'm already involved with you. We can't deny that, but I can protect you. Just tell me what you're thinking. Have you even thought this through?" He paused and put his lips on hers, but sensing her hesitation and fear, he pulled back. "You haven't, but you know it needs to end, so you're willing to sacrifice yourself to protect me."

"You're right, I am!" she exclaimed, tapping him in the chest. "I need to stop dragging other people into this nightmare and stand ready to defend myself and my country. That's the oath I took in the army and the one I hold myself to today. You don't have to like that choice, but you do have to respect it." A tear tracked down her cheek, and he pulled off her glasses, wiping the tears with his thumb. "No more innocents can lose their lives because of me, Luca. Enough people have already died due to greed and corruption. It's on me to stop this now. I understand if you want no part of it. Take Haven, get in the van and go home. You can't save me now. I'll pay the piper, whatever the cost, so no one else has to. That's the only right and fair thing to do."

A tendril of anger worked its way from his gut into his throat. Anger for the men who started this mess and at her for thinking she had to go this alone. "For the longest time, I was mad at you, Delilah Hartman, but never as mad as I am now. I'm standing alongside you, ready to defend you or go down trying, but you want to play the hero and do it all yourself!"

"That's not what I'm doing! I'm giving you a damn out before things get real, Luca. This isn't your war to fight. It's mine. I won't ask you to walk back into battle for me again."

He grasped her face in his hands and brought her lips to his, drinking from her like a man who hadn't had water in days. When the kiss ended, he held her gaze, the sky lightening enough for him to see the look in her eyes that said he had to go all in if he wanted her to listen. "You're not asking me. I'm volunteering. I would walk into any battle with you, Delilah Hartman. I'd rather die by your side than live without you again. Do you understand what I'm saying?" Her nod was enough for him. "You haven't been able to trust anyone for a long time, and I understand that, but you could always trust me, right?"

"Always," she said, her words breathy on the cold morning air.

"Then trust me this time, the most important time of your life, Lilah. Let us help you end this war. No one fights alone. You have special ops cops and a sharpshooter headed here to fight with you. They wouldn't do that if they didn't think the fight was worth it. You can trust them for the simple reason that I trust them."

The silent morning stretched between them as smoky tendrils rose from the trees, warmed by the rising sun. Haven leaned into him, checking his handler for shakiness that wasn't there. Lucas was firm in his declaration to this woman, and he would wait however long it took for her to accept it and make the right decision.

"I'm terrified, Luca. Terrified that I'll die and terrified that you will. I don't know what the right answer is anymore."

He rubbed his thumb across her forehead and smiled. "I

know you don't. That's understandable. You want this to be over, but you see no other way than to walk in guns blazing. Trust me when I say Secure One has your back."

When her shoulders deflated a hair, Lucas knew she'd made her decision. His heart nearly broke in two when she nodded, biting her lip to keep it from trembling. "Let's go meet the rest of the team and make a better plan. I'm not in the mood to die today."

The truth spoken, he leaned in and kissed her, gently this time, pouring all of his soothing care into her. No one needed it more than her after all these years alone. When the kiss ended, she smiled at him, her gloved hand patting his face. "Thank you for being my voice of reason in a world where nothing makes sense."

"I'll continue to be until this is over," he promised as they returned to the van. He secured Haven while she climbed in, then joined her and started the van. He cranked the heat up to warm them after being out in the cold.

"Secure one, Charlie." Cal's voice filled the van, and Lucas hit the answer button on the dashboard.

"Secure two, Lima."

"Why in the hell is my van outside George Burris's home? I will not have another team member go rogue on me!"

"It's my fault, sir," Lilah said without hesitation. "I thought I had to fight this battle alone, but Luca convinced me otherwise. Don't be upset with him."

"I was never going to let her go in there, boss."

"I didn't think you would, son."

"You don't sound like you're in the air yet," Lilah said, her head tipped as she listened to the background noise.

"We're not. Plans changed. I decided filing a flight plan might tip someone off to your presence there. Besides, bringing mobile command is easier when we don't know what we're up against. Roman, what's our ETA?"

"We'll hit Rochester proper in an hour and thirty-seven minutes. I need you to scout a location for us to circle the wagons and then send us the coordinates."

"We're headed in the direction of the airport now. You'll have the coordinates in forty-five minutes or less."

"Counting on you, brother," Cal said. "Charlie, out."

The line went dead as Lucas sucked in a breath of surprise.

"Are you okay?" Lilah asked. At the same time, Haven rose from sleep and put his head on his handler's shoulder.

"Wow," Lucas said with a shake of his head as he pressed a fist to his chest. "That was the first time he called me brother instead of kid. I wasn't expecting it."

"I'm confused?"

Lucas reached back to stroke Haven's head while he processed the moment. Once he had, he turned to her with a smile. "The guys always called me son or kid, but it didn't bother me. I'm the youngest and the newest on the crew, so I accepted it as being under their wing and learning the ropes."

"Now you're equals."

He tipped his head in agreement as he put the van into Drive and let off the brake. "And I'm not going to let them, or you, down now."

"You won't let me down, Luca," she promised, squeezing his shoulder. "We're a team, but you're the leader. How do I help?"

"Watch our six," he answered, pulling onto the road again just as dawn finished breaking. "Let me know if we pick up company. I need to concentrate on finding a place to meet the team. One way or the other, this war ends today."

There was no greater feeling in the world than knowing he had found a brotherhood again, and that was what Cal had given him with one simple word. It was time to prove to the team that he'd earned it. Glancing at the woman beside him, with all her attention focused on the side mirror, made him wonder if they could be a team when this mission ended. The part of him who remembered their summer together said yes, but the other part of him, the part that needed Haven to live his life, reminded him that she deserved better than the life he could give her. He'd do well to remember that.

Chapter Twenty

The truth of the situation settled low in Delilah's belly when she lowered the binoculars. "There's not much for cover anywhere."

Cal grunted his agreement. "The forest on the western edge will help, but you still have to cross three acres to reach the garage from the woods, while the other three sides would remain unprotected."

When Luca found an abandoned gas station to use as a meeting place, they parked the van behind it and got busy gearing up while they waited for the rest of the team. Their first step was to check out the property, which they'd been doing for three hours, and there'd been no movement in or around it other than four-legged visitors. Unfortunately, their options were limited with their approach to the garage, something she suspected Burris had planned for.

"Anyone else wonder why he built a garage smack-dab in the middle of a field without easy accessibility?" Luca asked, lowering his binoculars, too.

"It crossed my mind," Cal agreed. "I'm starting to think we're barking up the wrong tree. If they're hiding priceless artifacts in that garage, there's no way to move them in and out without being seen. There's no power out here, so there can't be cameras or a security system unless it's solar powered."

"You could move them under the cover of darkness," Luca said, glancing up at the darkening sky as another snow shower approached. "Still not ideal for vehicle access or moving about unnoticed, though."

"Or it's the perfect situation," Lilah said slowly, bringing the binoculars back to her face. "All you need is a shotgun, boots and a camo jacket with an ATV parked outside the door. Not a soul pays attention to a hunter on their own land. Not in this part of the country."

"She's got a point," Roman agreed, setting his notebook down. "For right or wrong, we have to make a decision."

"We're going in," Delilah said without hesitation. "There's no choice. If we're correct, the auction will be in three days. We can't allow it to happen. If we can rule this place out, we know our next target is confronting Burris at home."

"Agreed," Luca said. She smiled, happy to have him on her side. "Chances are, it won't take long to clear the place, but if we're lucky, we find something that tells us where to go next. Cal, Roman, Lilah and I will go through the woods on the west side. Cal and Roman will hold coverage there while Lilah and I approach the building."

"What about the other three sides of the building?" Cal asked, a brow raised.

"Mack keeps mobile command secure and the communications running while Eric runs the drone overhead," Luca said. "Selina," he said, turning to the woman who had kept them all alive for years. "You and Efren take our van behind the property and find a place for him to set up his gun. You may have to trespass, but again, we have few options."

"We'll go through the forest on the west side and find a tree stand. Burris may not hunt, but I assure you, others do, so there's bound to be a few stands out there. That will give me a view from above that will cover the entire perimeter of the garage," Efren said, having thought it out already.

"Excellent," Lucas said with a thankful nod. "We'll give you a head start. If you see anything, alert Cal and Roman. It's not ideal, but again, we have few options in this situation."

"Agreed," Cal said with finality.

Selina and Efren were already getting their gear on. "We're heading out now. Give us twenty minutes of scout time, but we'll be on coms," Selina said, fitting one in her ear. "We'll let you know if we encounter anything that will change the current plan."

"Ten-four," Cal said as they exited the mobile command station and disappeared. He addressed Lucas again. "All of that said, you'll have to hold your own out there if someone approaches. We're easily—" he put the binoculars to his face and swung them back and forth between the woods and the garage "—five minutes out, and that's if we're not dodging bullets."

"Understood," Luca said. "I say we move soon. The snow will give us cover."

With everyone's jobs defined, they prepared their gear for the trip, including lights for Delilah's pistol and Luca's long gun. She didn't want to carry a rifle, fearing it would slow her down. Lucas was taller, stronger and better suited for carrying a gun that size through knee-deep snow. Besides, the garage was small, which made her think this was all a lesson in futility, but when it came to her life, she could leave no stone unturned.

"Ready?" she asked, checking that her pistol was easily accessible.

"I'm in the lead," Luca said, taking her hand and pulling

her to the door where Haven waited. "I'll plow through the snow, and you follow in my footprints with Haven."

"We're on your rudder," Cal said as he and Roman lined up behind them.

With a nod, they exited mobile command and found their way into the woods. The walk would be long, but it was the only way to keep their vehicles away from Burris's land on the off chance it was being monitored, or he showed up.

Lucas moved quicker than expected, and she found it challenging to keep up with him, especially trying to keep clear of Haven. She bent over to catch her breath when they reached the forest's edge.

"I'm short, Luca," she said, puffing air from her lips. "Give me a second to catch up."

Luca hung back and waited for Cal and Roman to approach them. Once they were together, she stood, and Cal motioned to his right. "There's a thicker grouping of trees that will give us good cover about a hundred yards down. Give us a few to get set up before you head toward the garage. Tango and Sierra, are you in place?" He was addressing Efren and Selina now, as they'd been quiet throughout the walk.

"Ten-four," Efren whispered. "Just made it into a tree stand. Sierra is on the spotting scope. So far, it's still clear. Proceed with usual caution."

Cal nodded at them before he and Roman broke off and headed away. Luca clicked off their microphones before resting his forehead on hers. As the snow melted on her glasses, he shimmered before her like an angel come to save her. "No heroics, got it?"

"I don't see any reason why they'll be needed, but I'll say the same to you," she whispered. "I also want to say thank you. Thank you for stepping up and helping me when you didn't have to."

"Thank you for reminding me that I can do hard things."

She smiled then, her heart cracking open as he used her words in a way that held so much honesty and truth. "Let's do one more hard thing and find justice for our fallen soldiers. Right?"

"Right, but first…" He removed his glove and pulled a cloth from his pocket before gently removing her glasses. Carefully, he wiped them down with the cloth and slid them back on her face. "There's the pair of eyes I see in my dreams," he said with a wink before he stowed the cloth.

Her heart nearly melted into a pool of mush on the forest floor, knowing he had brought the cloth to keep her vision clear. Even with Cal's special coating applied to them, he knew the snow would be a problem for her. He still cared about her, which gave her hope that they could remain friends when this was over.

Once Luca was ready again, he grabbed her hand and pulled her to the edge of the trees. "On my lead." She nodded, and he took off, Haven tight by his side this time.

The closer she got to the building, the more fear and dread built in her belly. A garage in the middle of a field felt like hiding in plain sight, and she worried whatever they were hiding was going to get her killed.

Once they were through the open space, they stood tight to the side of the building and took a moment to catch their breath. Their earlier assessment had been correct. There were no cameras under the eave of the garage. There may not be power out here, but you could buy solar-powered camera units, so that was another red flag as far as she was concerned.

"I'm telling you, Lucas. Burris isn't dumb. There's no

way he'd put anything here without cameras or more security. This is a futile endeavor."

"Maybe, but there may be something else in there that will help us sort this out. Old paperwork or equipment that we can jack the black box on," he answered. "Mina is still running down Burris's finances and doing another property search."

"I wish she could have gotten into that chat room," Lilah whispered. "If we knew who *Iamthatguy* and *Bigmanoncampus* are, then we'd know if we're on the right track." A little voice said she did know who they were. She just didn't want to admit it to herself.

"Unfortunately, that's lost to us for good, so all we can do is the legwork. Eventually, something will break. Keep your light off until we're inside and I've secured the door."

"Got it," she said, flipping her microphone back on as she crouched low and worked their way down the side of the garage.

Delilah stood behind Lucas while he inspected the side door, pulling his lock-picking kit from his vest. He glanced at her and checked the knob, a look of shock crossing his face when the door swung open. Haven was at his side as he swung his gun around the opening before stepping inside. Delilah followed from the rear and pushed the door closed.

"Door secure," she whispered, knowing the team could hear them, too. "Why wasn't it locked?" Before Lucas could answer, Haven growled low in his throat in a way she had never heard before. "What's wrong with him?"

"I don't know," Luca answered. "Haven, rest."

The dog didn't follow his handler's orders. Instead, he bolted to the right behind a pile of boxes.

"Haven. Return," Lucas hissed as he flicked on the gun's

flashlight. She did the same with hers, illuminating a simple one-car garage filled with boxes.

"Do you smell the copper, too?" she asked, moving closer to where Haven had disappeared.

"Haven, return!" Luca said again as they walked around the boxes, but he stopped short. Lilah bumped into him before she could stop herself. "That explains the smell."

"What?" Cal asked through their earpiece. "Give me an update."

"Dead body," Lilah said, strangely detached. "Haven found him behind a pile of boxes."

"Him?"

"Definitely male," Luca said. "I haven't rolled him yet."

"There's no need," Lilah said, knowing who it was. "It's George Burris," she whispered, motioning at his left knee for Luca to see. "He had that knee brace made after he was hurt on a mission. He had to wear it all the time."

"Repeat. You've found Major George Burris dead?" Cal asked through their earpiece.

"Affirmative," Lilah said with her lips in a thin line.

"Looks like a round to the chest from the exit wound I can see on his back, as well as a round to his temple," Lucas reported.

"Where is his weapon?" Efren asked.

"Sidearm on his belt," Lilah answered.

"Rifle resting on a box five feet away," Lucas added. "Not staged as a suicide."

"He knew his attacker then and didn't feel threatened," Efren responded.

"You need to get out of there," Cal said. "I'm not ready to deal with the murder of an army major."

"We haven't had a chance to look around. Give us five?" Lilah asked.

"Negative. Get out while the snow is falling to cover your tracks. I do not want to deal with the police and the army."

"Not the army," Lilah said, motioning to Lucas to spread out and search. "He's been discharged, so he's a civilian now."

"All the same," Cal said, and she could picture him rolling his eyes. "We need to move out."

"No one wants to know why someone shot a former army major in his garage?" Efren asked, making Lilah snort internally. "Can you tell how long he's been down?"

"Not long. Maybe twelve hours," Lucas said. "Doubtful anyone would be worried yet."

Lilah was walking around the garage, which was big enough for a car or a boat but not much else. "These boxes are empty," she said, pushing on one until it fell to the ground. "There's nothing in this garage."

"Except for a dead army major and you two. Get out. Now," Cal repeated, and they looked at each other, their brows raised.

"Ten-four," Luca said, shaking his head at Lilah and clicking his mic off. She did the same while he walked over to her. "We have two minutes. Go."

Lilah walked behind the boxes she dumped, shining her flashlight around the floor and the walls, looking for anything that shouldn't be there or didn't belong there, but the garage was filled with empty boxes and nothing else. Haven had his nose on the ground as he sniffed through the garage. His ears pointed to the ceiling as he went, and his concentration was undeterred by Luca's commands.

"Why didn't they pour a concrete pad for this building?" Lucas asked, bouncing on the floor a bit. "Plywood is going to rot in these conditions."

"It feels temporary to me," Lilah said, motioning at the

walls that were nothing more than studs and particle board. "Like they had no intention of using it very long."

Haven growled again, the sound raising the hair on the back of her neck. "Luca, we need to get out of here. Haven is a mess."

Luca walked to his dog and crouched low. "Haven is a retired war dog, but he's acting like an active one now. He's reacting to the major's death."

Lilah walked up behind him, her boots thudding across the cheap plywood. It was her final step that made her pause. "Did you hear that?" She stepped back on her right foot just as there was a metallic snap. The floor bounced, and they jumped back, their eyes locking when the floor no longer sat flush.

"Trapdoor?" she mouthed to Luca, who nodded. He motioned her to flip her mic back on as Cal demanded to know where they were.

"Secure one, Lima," he said, letting them know they were now in a situation that required rapt attention. "On our way out, Lilah tripped a trapdoor. Give us three to investigate it."

"Negative," Cal instructed. "Get out of there now. There's already one dead body in there. I don't want three."

"There's no one here, boss. I suspect whatever is below us is empty, but this is why we're here. It could be the answer we're looking for right below our feet."

They both heard Cal's heavy sigh on the other end of the mic. "Fine. Charlie and Romeo will approach."

"Affirmative," Luca said, flipping the mic off while motioning for Lilah to stand back. She stepped out of the way and grabbed the handle on Haven's vest to hold him back. She nodded, and he lifted the door, sweeping his gun across the opening. "Empty," he said, motioning for her to look down the hole. "Notice the stairs?"

"Well made." There were even handrails on each side of the staircase going down. "I was expecting a rung ladder."

"Me, too, but this tells a different story."

"A story of someone with a bad knee using them frequently?"

Luca nodded with his foot on the first step. "Haven, return." As soon as Lilah released the dog, he followed Lucas. They went down the stairs back-to-back so he could sweep the space on the way down as she kept her sidearm pointed at the top. It was possible Burris's killer might show up before Cal and Roman.

"These steps are better made than the floor above them." He swung his flashlight around, assessing the situation. "Old shipping container," he said. "They must have buried it and built the garage above it."

Their feet hit the container floor and Lilah swung her flashlight along the wall, illuminating shelves that ran the entire length on both sides, all filled with relics of a different time and place.

"I believe it's time to call in the cavalry," she whispered, her heart sinking at the thought. Once again, her problem would become his and Secure One's by default, but it was too late to back out. All she could do was go forward and pray that of the two left who knew about these artifacts, she was the last one standing.

NONE OF THIS made sense. Lucas walked along the side of the wall in shock and horror to see so many treasures from other countries. "Someone has done all the provenance on these," Lilah said, pointing to documentation next to each treasure. "They're ready for an auction."

"That probably explains why Burris is upstairs dead," Lucas said, his gaze trained on two bronze chalices on a shelf. "Whoever he's working with double-crossed him." He stared at the cups on the shelf, willing his memory to recall where he'd seen them.

"Mack, we need to contact the local police, military police, homeland security and JAG. We must establish a chain of command and custody for these relics, not to mention, deal with the murder victim," he heard Lilah say. Still, his mind was off in a different time and place.

"Porter, let no one through these doors until we return."

"Yes, Colonel Swenson." He held the door for the colonel and two other men that Swenson had simply introduced as "men of faith." Lucas could only assume they were local church leaders or priests who had information for the government, but that was above his pay grade. His job was to make sure the colonel didn't die on this social visit.

He climbed inside the Humvee and sat at the gun turret. He wasn't happy when he'd been assigned to take the colonel out alone, but Swenson had insisted they weren't in combat territory and the locals were their allies. Lucas didn't believe for a hot second that anyone in this hellhole of a country was their ally. He'd seen far too many of them blow up his friends. He trusted no one except his K-9, Hercules, who stood at attention by the door, his head swinging right and left as he scanned for enemies and listened for vehicles approaching.

As a munitions officer, it wasn't Lucas's job to be out using the ammunition. It was his job to make sure they had enough. He wasn't given a choice today when Colonel Swenson needed backup immediately and no one else was available.

"In and out, right, Hercules?" he asked the dog while they waited in the hot desert sun. Sweat dripped down his spine, running a shiver through him. Something was off. He

swung the gun around, expecting an ambush, but finding nothing in any direction. "Come on," he hummed, glancing at the building door and praying it would open. His sixth sense was telling him to get out of there now. He pressed the button on his walkie-talkie. "Porter to Colonel Swenson. ETA?"

"Coming now," was the answer.

Lucas hopped down from the gun and opened the passenger side door of the Humvee. He commanded Hercules to stand next to him. Swenson was the first to emerge, and then the two men, one carrying a large white bag.

Lucas didn't get a word out to the colonel before a barrage of bullets struck the stucco wall behind them. Lucas swung his gun around and sprayed the area, unsure where the enemy was. "Get in!" he yelled to the colonel, standing over the two men sprawled on the ground. "Get in, now!"

Swenson grabbed the white bag and jumped in the open passenger door. Hercules followed him in while Lucas sent another burst of gunfire and then slid into the driver's side. He threw it into gear and took off, sand and gravel flying from under the tires.

"I thought the locals were our allies!" Lucas yelled, angry that, once again, they'd been lied to. "Who were those guys?"

"Men of faith," Swenson said again. "They're the only two dead, which should tell you something."

"Why would anyone want men of faith dead?"

"I can't answer that, Porter. Just get us back to base in one piece."

"Yes, sir," Lucas answered between clenched teeth. He pretended not to notice the bag by the colonel's feet that had fallen open and revealed a bronze chalice...

"Luca?" He turned his head as reality filtered back in.

Haven had his nose pressed hard into his thigh, so he took a minute to breathe in threes, noting his heart rate slowing as he stroked Haven's head. "Thanks, buddy. I'm fine."

"You look like you saw a ghost," Lilah said, still swinging her flashlight around the space. There were dark corners he didn't like. He was praying Cal arrived soon with backup.

"I may have," he said, motioning at the chalices. "I've seen these before."

"What? Where?"

"I'd been on the base about two weeks when Colonel Swenson wanted transport with two other men to a building in a small village. Everyone else was busy, so he demanded I take him."

"Alone?"

He nodded. "I told him it wasn't a good idea, but he wasn't budging."

"Which meant you couldn't ignore a direct order."

"Not without spending time in the brig. Four of us went out, but two came back, along with these chalices. Do you remember putting these through for shipping?"

Lilah shook her head, her lips in a thin line. "I recognize only about half of these items, Luca. I'm starting to think those dead women were doing the same thing for him as I was, but on different bases."

"Only they weren't going to museums. My logical mind had Burris building a personal collection, but with him upstairs dead, I'm starting to think he was the grunt man for someone much higher up."

"That memory you had is the answer."

"Colonel Swenson?"

Before she could nod, clapping started from the darkness. Lucas swung around, bringing his gun to his shoulder as a man stepped into the beam of his flashlight. Lucas felt his world tip when the man before him was indeed Colonel Swenson. "Aren't you smart?" he asked as Lilah's flashlight illuminated the item they'd been searching for all this time. Behind Swenson was the trunk—half a tablet present in the top.

"Colonel Swenson?"

"That's Major General to you, Porter," he spat. "And you," he said, addressing Lilah. "You have been a trial. I have to say, I'm glad this is over." He kept his gun at his shoulder but stretched his back. "Thank goodness you finally arrived. Do you know how uncomfortable the floor is in a storage container?"

"You knew we were coming?"

"The alert that someone accessed the chat room told me it was time to take care of some final business. I always knew you had the file, but as long as you didn't click on it, I could keep you alive. Now, I'm afraid that's no longer possible. Especially since you know of my involvement in this. Since I couldn't track you—you finally caught on to the medal. Good job," he said with a sarcastic smirk. "I hedged my bets that you'd end up looking for Burris once you decided he had the answers. Sad, but you know what they say, dead men don't speak."

"Just tell me why," Lilah said, stepping closer to Lucas as Swenson advanced on them. "Tell me why I was tracked and harassed for so long."

"You were a real pain in my back quarter, Hartman. You were tracked because you had all the information in your head about these little baubles," he said, swinging his arm out at the wall. "Not to mention, you saw The Lost Key of Honor file. I had to keep you quiet until the auction."

Lilah whistled, and a shiver ran down Lucas's spine.

"It's a shame that I saved all the information about

these—what did you call them?—baubles to a flash drive before the base fell," Lilah said, doing exactly that. "It's already in the hands of the authorities. It would have been smarter to kill me, but you didn't. You took great pleasure in slicing me up, but why play the game with me when you killed the other four women?"

Lucas tried not to react to the information that Swenson was The Mask. He wondered if Delilah knew who was behind it before they even set foot in this basement and never told him. Haven leaned in hard against his leg, a steady low growl coming from his throat as he glared at the man before him.

Swenson raked Lilah lasciviously. "I have to say, I always wondered what my creations looked like once they healed. Your chin," he said, motioning at her face. "Not bad work there. I do hope your gut healed well."

"You son of a—"

Lilah cut Lucas off. "You didn't answer my question. Why didn't you just kill me like you did the other women?"

"We were still looking for one more artifact. On the off chance I needed to have a little chat with you about something you may have seen or heard, you had to be breathing."

"The Lost Key of Honor," Lilah said as Swenson smiled like an animated horror puppet.

"Such a powerful name, right?" he asked, almost giddy as he advanced on them. "I'm sure you can understand why it was important to keep you out of the picture until I could ascertain the piece and finish the auction."

"And did you?" Lucas asked. "Ascertain the piece, that is."

Swenson's smile dissipated, and he shook his head. "Unfortunately, no, but the auction will still happen. I have too many people looking for these trinkets, and I can't disappoint them on Christmas morning. I still have a few days to decide what to do with the trunk. Our time together is over, though. I do wish I had my knife and an unlimited amount of time to turn you into beautiful artwork, but I don't, so a bullet to the head for each of you will have to do."

There was commotion overhead, and then Cal yelled, "Secure One, drop your weapon!"

Cal and Roman came barreling down the stairs, and Haven pounced at Swenson. A gunshot rang out, and Lucas stumbled backward into Cal, who lowered him to the ground. Lilah fired three times in quick succession.

"Haven!" Lucas screamed, afraid the dog was in the line of fire. "Haven! Return!"

The small space quickly became chaotic as it filled with team members yelling different things simultaneously. Lucas sat there, detached from the room and his body as he breathed in to three, held it for three and let it out to three.

"Luca!" Lilah said, dropping the gun and running to him. "Call an ambulance!" she yelled as Lucas watched Cal handcuff a raving Swenson. Lilah's bullets had found a home in his shoulder, arm and knee. None of them were life-threatening, but satisfying nonetheless to inflict a little pain on someone who had tortured her for years.

"You're going to be okay," she said, but the expression on her face said something else entirely. She stripped off her jacket and held it to his chest, pushing so hard it made him grunt with pain. "I know. I'm sorry to hurt you, but I need to keep pressure on this wound."

"Wound?" he asked, his voice holding disbelief.

"Swenson shot you," she explained. "If Haven hadn't pounced on his arm at the last second, the bullet would be in your head. You'd be dead."

"That rhymes," he said, laughing once before he started to cough, the taste of blood in his mouth.

"Don't talk, just conserve your energy," she ordered, so close he could kiss her.

"Don't leave me, Delilah Porter," he whispered, his words stuttering as he spoke. "I will follow you anywhere."

She brushed the hair back off his forehead and kissed him. "All the days since I left you, I've wished my name was Delilah Porter," she whispered. "I'm not going anywhere. Everything I've done for the last six years has been for you. To protect you. To keep you safe, but in the end, I couldn't do that. You can't die on me now, do you understand? You have to hang on. Hang on, Luca."

It wasn't lost on him that he had this woman back in his life because death came calling and he'd answered the phone. He'd been given the gift of a little more time, something others often weren't fortunate enough to get, and he hadn't wasted a moment of it. Lucas had brought closure to a situation he never thought he would, and for that, he was grateful. If death took him this time, he would accept that his work here was done. Then she pressed her lips to his, and he knew he'd die a very happy man.

Chapter Twenty-One

The old adage that no good deed goes unpunished had settled deep in Delilah's bones as soon as the military and homeland security arrived at the shipping container. The man she loved was hauled away by ambulance while she was forced into custody as a party to real war crimes. While she'd been treated well and was comfortable, she'd spent the last two days under lock and key while they tried to sort out who knew what in this bizarre case of unabashed greed.

Thankfully, she could use the flash drive and screenshots of the chat room to her advantage. It turned out that *Iamthatguy* was Burris and *Bigmanoncampus* was Swenson. She should have thought of that sooner, but honestly, she didn't have officers of the US Army stealing antiquities to sell on the black market on her bingo card. That was what they had planned to do, though.

The way Swenson told it, they started with good intentions, wanting to help the locals, but they quickly realized what the relics were worth on the black market and how easy it was to make them disappear. Sadly, the one thing she wasn't expecting was to learn that the base was attacked because of Swenson's and Burris's actions. They had systematically gone out and killed every person who had turned in relics to the base. It was easy to make it look like they died in the war, but if there was no one left who knew where the relics went, there was no one to thwart their plan. No one but her, that is. The locals didn't believe that revenge was best served cold. They believed in immediate revenge in the most brutal of ways. A shudder went through her at the memory.

"Are you cold? I can turn the heat up," Mina said.

"No, I'm fine," she answered, staring out the window at the white fields stretching as far as the eye could see. "I was just thinking about what Swenson told the police. Evil on a level I never want to see again, Mina. How could I be so wrong about them? How did I not see the evil?"

"The true psychopaths in our midst never reveal themselves, Delilah. We've seen it so many times. Look at my situation with the FBI. No one would have seen that coming."

"True," she whispered, staring at her hands as they drove silently for a few miles. "The army offered me veteran benefits."

Mina lifted a brow as she steered the van around a curve. "Disability benefits?"

"Yep, as well as the Secretary of the Army Award for Valor along with the Purple Heart, neither of which I want."

"The Purple Heart is for those wounded in battle during active duty."

"True, but PTSD and a traumatic brain injury may not be visible but still qualify. Also, these are quite visible," she said, motioning at her chin. "The stabbings weren't while I was on active duty, but from what I understand, it came down from rather high up on the chain of command. The other four women will also be receiving them posthumously. I want to refuse them both."

"Unfortunately, that's not how it works, Delilah," Mina said with a chuckle. "When you're the pivotal person to help return priceless artwork and antiques to their respective home countries and paid heavily because of it, you get medals."

"And a whole lot of memories I'd rather not have."

"Now, that's a true story." She nodded. "Cal told us they offered you a job."

"Ha! Yeah, like I'm going to go back to work for the government. Hard pass."

Mina's lips tipped up. "Can't say that I blame you there. You've been through enough."

"How bad was it for Cal, Mina?"

"Secure One came out just fine, so don't worry. Don't forget that Cal is an army veteran. He was looking out for another, and we had plenty of paperwork to prove it. We were out of there within a day. I wish the same had been true for you."

"Me, too. I want to see Luca. How is he? I talked to him yesterday and he said he was feeling fine, but he hasn't responded to my text from this morning."

"He's only alive because Haven pounced on Swenson. He was using armor-piercing rounds in that gun. Lucas would be dead."

"I'm not sure a bullet to the chest is much better, but I'm glad that he's healing." She sighed, and it was heavily weighted with sadness. "When we talk now, it's awkward because I don't know what to say to the man who saved my life. I can't face him knowing he took two bullets for me in the span of a week."

Mina's laughter filled the van as she turned right and guided them down a narrow road. "Sweetheart, that man would take all the bullets for you. You'll know the right things to say when you see him again. Just trust your heart."

Sure, trust your heart, she says. That's hard to do when

you aren't sure if it'll get stomped on. Would Luca stomp on her heart intentionally? No, but she was afraid of the unintentional consequences of this event, especially since she had no one else in her life but him and the team at Secure One.

When Delilah glanced out the car window, she was surprised. "Why are we at a cemetery? You said I had to talk to the Rochester Police about the incident."

"You do, but someone else will be taking you there. I'm officially off duty."

She barely heard a word Mina said as she stared through the windshield, the sun making it hard to see anything, but she did notice a man standing in front of a grave with a dog at his side. "Luca?"

"Go to him. You need each other right now."

"But, Mina, what do I say?" Her question was desperate as she turned to the woman she had come to count on as a friend and confidant.

"The truth." Mina reached into the back of the van and grabbed Delilah's winter coat, which she shrugged on, along with a hat, scarf and gloves.

Was she prolonging the inevitable? Maybe, but knowing it was time to face the man she had loved for six long years made her pause and search her heart for the words she'd need when she faced him again. She slung her purse around her shoulder and let out a sigh.

"Thanks for the ride and the advice, Mina. Merry Christmas," she said, throwing her arms around her friend. "Be careful on the drive home."

"Roman is waiting at the police station. I'll pick him up and head home while you ride with Lucas and Haven."

With a nod, Delilah pushed the van door open and

climbed out, her eyes glued to the man just a few feet in front of her, his back turned as he stared at a gravestone.

"Hey, there, Lilah," he said, his back still to her.

"Luca," she said, but blinked twice when she realized he was wearing his dress uniform, his polished black shoes reflecting the sunlight as she glanced down at the grave marker. It read Tamara Porter. "Your mom's grave?"

"I thought since I was down here, I'd let her see me in my dress uniform on Christmas morning. Better late than never, right?"

Her heart wanted to burst at the implications of this moment. "Luca, I'm stunned."

"You shouldn't be. You were right, Lilah. I gave that bag way too much power, and it was time I stopped. It's time to change the way I think about what I did in the service, and that's already helped with my anxiety. You reminded me to stop feeling guilty about who I lost by remembering who I saved. It's still a work in progress, but now I wake up with less burden from the past and more hope for the future."

"I'm happy for you, Luca," she said, leaning into him. "Are you okay? I need to know that you aren't in pain."

He took her hand and brought it to his chest, pushing it against his skin. He didn't flinch. "No pain. It was a through and through, so a few stitches and a few weeks means it will be nothing more than a scar. We all have them, right?"

"Some of us more than others." That was when she saw it. "Luca," she whispered, glancing up at him. "Your medals." She ran her hand across the row of medals now attached to his uniform.

He shrugged but avoided her gaze. "If there was one thing my mother was proud of me for, it was my service. I wore them for her this morning."

"She was a proud army mom," she agreed with a smile.

"Nice touch. I know wherever she is over the rainbow, she's never been prouder."

"One down then," he said, finally turning to her and taking her hands.

"One down then?" she asked, confusion filling her voice. "I don't understand."

"Being here in this uniform is a reminder that one woman I love is proud of me. Now I need to know if the other woman I love is proud of me, too."

"Me?" Delilah asked, and he nodded, smiling as she nearly melted into the snow with relief.

"I've loved you since the moment I picked you up off that tarmac, Delilah Hartman. I told myself that day I was going to marry you. I intend to keep that promise or die trying."

"You've nearly died trying enough times, Lucas Porter!" she exclaimed, watching a smile grow on his face. "You don't need to keep trying. I love you, Luca, and I'm overwhelmingly proud of what you've overcome to be standing in this uniform today. I sent you to that clinic alone six years ago because I loved you. I walked away from you that day and stayed away for the same reason. I would do anything to protect and keep you safe, even if it meant we could never be together."

"That's over now, my darling Delilah," he promised, lowering his head for a kiss that warmed her head to toe even on this cold Christmas morning. When he lifted his head, his eyes glowed with happiness in a way she had never seen. "I want to explore us," he said, holding her tightly. "I don't know how that will work since we live such different lives, but I know one thing. I'll follow you anywhere. I know you got a job offer from the army. If you want to take it, say the word. I'll be right behind you—"

Delilah put her finger to his lips. "Secure one, Delta."

Her smile grew when his brows went up. "What now?"

"Turns out, another job offer awaited me in the civilian sector. Cal offered me a position as a cybersecurity tech to work with Mina, building Secure Watch, the new division for Secure One. I accepted this morning. I want to be with you, Luca, through the good times and the bad. I know that sometimes our memories paint outside the lines of the present, but we'll face those together, too. How do you feel about that?" Her question held a tinge of nervousness as she waited for his answer.

"I think there's only one thing left to say, Delilah Hartman."

"Then say it, Lucas Porter."

"Secure two, Lima."

Then his lips were back on hers as they stood in the bright sunshine of a day that, for the first time in years, offered her true joy, hope and peace. They shared the first kiss of the rest of their lives, ready to focus on a future they could build together from a place of love, understanding and acceptance of their past that led them to this place in time. His tender kiss was a layer of comfort over the jagged scars in her soul, assuring her that he'd heal them completely with enough time.

"Happy?" he asked, lifting his lips from hers.

"Better than happy," she whispered.

"What's better than happy?"

"Being healed."

A smile lifted his lips as they neared hers again. "I couldn't agree more. Merry Christmas, my darling Delilah," he said, pulling her steamed-up glasses from her face.

"Merry Christmas, Luca," she whispered before they shared another kiss to the sound of Haven's joyful barking.

* * * * *

BODYGUARD
RANCHER

KACY CROSS

To my firstborn—It means the world to me that you're still the most enthusiastic supporter of my books. This one is for you.

Chapter One

Charli could feel the ranch hand watching her. Not in the I'm-being-paid-to-keep-you-safe way, like she'd expect given the fact that he'd been employed to do exactly that. But in the way a man watched a woman when he wanted her to know he was interested.

Well, *she* wasn't interested.

She refused to so much as glance in his direction as she strolled from the back door of the house to the barn. Heath McKay was the opposite of easy on the eyes. The man was so hot he could burn a woman's retinas if she stared directly at him.

He knew it too. He was in that category of male who could charm a nun out of her habit. Who always had the next woman waiting in the wings—or maybe even right on stage at the same time as his current woman. How did Charli know? Because Heath McKay was Exactly Her Type in huge ten-foot-tall letters and she had crappy taste in men.

Her sister, Sophia, whom Charli secretly called Super Sophia, had hired him to make sure no one kidnapped any other Lang women from the ranch. After Sophia's harrowing experience of being taken from their home at gunpoint, she'd laid down some serious cash to ensure there were no repeats. Charli could have saved her the trouble. No one paid enough attention to The Other Lang Sister to bother kidnapping her.

She was about to change things, though. She had a plan. A good one. She was going to rise from the ashes of her old life and be the superhero of her new life. Maybe not Super Sophia, because her sister already had that locked. But someone else just as good, like Black Widow.

That was it. Charli could be Black Widow, eater of men, completely and utterly fearsome to the opposite sex. Black Widow was also awesome at her job and beautiful.

She could dye her hair red and buy some black outfits. It could work. She'd been telling herself to have a goal, hadn't she?

Now she just needed the right man to complete this picture.

"Paxton," she trilled as Heath's partner, the lean computer whiz, exited the new barn directly in her path. Lucky break. "Exactly who I was looking for."

Or rather, he was good enough.

"Me?" Paxton Pierce pointed at himself, a thin sheen of panic glazing his eyes that could be considered offensive if she let herself stop and think about it. "I was just…uh, Jonas is expecting me to move the horses from the south pasture with some of the other guys."

"You still have to do cowboy stuff even though you're technically doing security now?" she asked innocently, despite knowing that Paxton, Heath and Sophia's boyfriend, Ace Madden, were still working undercover as ranch hands. The fewer people who were aware of their real jobs, the better. "What if I have a security emergency? I might need you to subdue an intruder."

Heath was still watching her. She could feel his gaze between her shoulder blades, and it set off something inside that she could only describe as *delicious*. But she'd take that to her grave.

Charli let her fingertips graze Paxton's arm the way Black Widow might when she was being coy and flirty. It wasn't a chore. He was so cute with his clean looks and even cleaner Stetson, which looked like it had never hit the dirt. When she'd decided to move to the ranch and find a nice cowboy, Paxton Pierce was exactly what she'd pictured in her head.

Paxton could be the one to break her streak of cheating SOBs. He was clearly a great guy, one who called his mother every Sunday and had likely never seen the inside of a jail cell. Probably. This was her fantasy, and he could totally star in it.

Paxton's Adam's apple bobbed as he stepped just out of her reach. "If you have a security emergency, that's what McKay is for."

Yeah. Heath McKay was the problem, with his square jaw sporting a perpetual five o'clock shadow, and hooded gaze with even more shadows, and biceps that could make a woman drool. There was not one lick of *nice* anywhere in that man's body.

"Can't I switch babysitters midstream if I want to? Ask Ace to assign you to me instead?"

Man, there was an idea. Why hadn't she thought of that before now?

"Because—well, actually…" Poor guy swallowed so fast that he almost choked. "I'm what you call the brains. McKay is the brawn. Not that he's not smart, but his talents are definitely in the physical realm."

Oh, there was absolutely no question about the validity of that statement. But seriously. They'd caught the guy who had been terrorizing Sophia. The university people had squirreled away the gold coin she and Ace had found. What was there, really, to protect Charli from?

"I like a man with brains," she said with a little laugh.

Paxton did not seem bowled over by her charm. That was deflating. Maybe she should reel it back a little. Come at this from another angle. What would Black Widow do? She wouldn't sit around and wait for a man to figure out how awesome she was.

"Maybe you could find some time to ride with me out to the west pasture?" Charli fluttered her lashes. "I need to do a practice trail ride run before the guests start arriving next week."

That's when she'd start being taken seriously around the ranch. When people would see her as the other Ms. Lang instead of Charli, the screwup sister of the boss. As soon as she and Sophia welcomed the first guests, this place would stop being an inheritance and start being a dude ranch.

The Cowboy Experience. It had been her idea, one that she was secretly so proud of that she sometimes danced around in a circle of glee that Sophia had taken the suggestion.

Soon, she'd be able to forget she'd gotten fired from her last job at a pet store. A *pet store* for crying out loud. Where she'd been in charge of cleaning birdcages.

"Uh." Paxton glanced around feverishly. "I'd love to go on a trail ride but I, uh, I have to go do a thing with Jonas?"

"Are you sure? You don't sound sure."

Paxton edged away, pulling at his shirt collar as he practically tripped over his own two cowboy boots. "I'm sure. Ask McKay to ride with you on your trail ride, uh…thing."

She watched him go, the sun beating down on her back, vaguely disappointed Black Widow channeling had not gone well. But what did she expect? That she'd magically figure out in the course of two minutes how to not be a train wreck when it came to her love life? More practice needed, stat.

But when she turned around, Heath was standing a scant two feet away.

Not the sun on her back, then. *Him.* It was always him, right there, leaning against the fence, arms crossed in that insolent slouch that screamed Lock Up Your Daughters. His battered hat had seen more than its share of action, as had the very lived-in body underneath it. A scar ran along the base of his neck as if someone had tried to slice his throat but then abruptly stopped.

The man reeked of promise and next-level decadence.

Heath tipped his chin, his heated blue eyes tracking her with a lazy, practiced sweep. "Maybe you should try on someone your own size."

"Like who? You?"

She crossed her arms and stared him down in kind, but she had a feeling her own sweep of his cut torso and legs that went on forever had a lot more intensity in it than she'd like. It wasn't fair. No human should be that perfectly put together.

"Yeah. You could do worse."

"I have," she informed him sweetly. "That's how I know exactly what I'd find inside your box of chocolates. No interest in a repeat, thanks. You can toddle off and go do whatever undercover security agents do when they're pretending to be cowboys. I'm sure you're bored out of your mind watching me anyway."

"Bored is not the word I'd use."

Nonchalance rolled from him in waves, as if nothing bothered him, which pushed every single one of her buttons. A man this hot must have a volcano under his skin and she'd pay money to see it erupt. It would serve him right for harassing her.

"Well, when you think of the right word, don't come find me," she shot back and pivoted to walk away, speaking to him over her shoulder. "I'm going back to the house. Where I'll be doing very boring things that don't need your attention."

"Pierce is all wrong for you," he called, and she could almost hear his mouth tipping up in that amused smile that fooled no one. "You need someone you can't run rough-shod over."

"I'll keep that in mind."

She escaped into the house, shutting the door of the blue Victorian behind her, then leaned on it, her lungs curiously unable to drag in air all at once. That man drove her bananas. But that didn't stop the frappé mode activating on her insides whenever he was around.

There had to be a cure for that. She'd tried going out with him once, just to see if she could burn off the attraction by feeding it. No dice. She'd spent the whole time with a heightened awareness that it wouldn't take Heath McKay more than about five minutes to break her heart. And she'd yet to patch it back together after the last loser had finished with it.

Careful to stay away from the windows in case *he* was peering through one, Charli skirted the kitchen island and dashed for the front door. Her babysitter was likely still stationed near the back door, his gaze trained on it in the event she made a reappearance.

Joke was on him. She lived to give him the slip.

No one put Charli in the corner. Well, except for the times she did it to herself. Which was most times. But that was the beauty of her brand-new plan. She was reinventing herself. No more screwing up. The time for that had long passed.

Skipping out the front door was a piece of cake. She had a lot of practice exiting a building without making a sound. She'd done it as a teenager plenty of times—it was easier to sneak out than it was to upset her single mother who was doing the best she could to raise three daughters after Charli's deadbeat dad had taken off.

Then there was the time she'd had to back up quickly after coming home to her apartment early to find Toby in bed with a very enthusiastic woman who was not Charli. Definitely not the time to hit a squeaky floor joist.

Better to stay off that subject before she forgot she was over Toby's cheating hide.

Back outside, Charli rounded the house near the long drive and headed for the woods. She really did have to scout the area for her trail ride, but she'd skip the horse this time. Too visible. Heath would insist on coming along and she wasn't about to fall for that trap. The more time they spent together, the harder it would be to convince herself she wasn't attracted to him.

This circular path to the woods meant she had to veer close to the encampment where all the university people lived. They had said it would be temporary, but it was starting to feel like they'd never leave. Over two dozen tents lined the south pasture, most of them housing archaeologists or anthropologists or some other kinds of *ologists* with names that were largely unpronounceable by regular humans. There were some museum people thrown into the mix too, or at least that was her understanding, after they'd found the jade beads from some dead guy's tomb in Mexico. Pakal the Great.

Apparently, her deadbeat father had actually found some kind of treasure during his frequent jaunts to the Yucatan. The whole time he'd been busy ignoring his family, he'd scored some priceless artifacts and then buried them in various places around his father's ranch.

Grandpa Lang had died, then left the ranch to Sophia, Charli and their baby sister, Veronica, who had yet to check out her inheritance. Ergo, they now owned the treasure too, for whatever good that did when Sophia had unilaterally decided all the stuff should go back to Mexico.

As long as the *ologists* left before the guests got here, they could have the dead guy's tomb decorations.

And then Heath would be free to leave the ranch. No more laser beams between her shoulder blades. No more lying awake at night fantasizing about threading her fingers through his almost shoulder-length thick, curly hair, mussed from a day of hat-wearing, cowboy things.

"Hello, luv," a silky voice said from behind her.

Charli glanced over her shoulder to see one of the university guys with his eyes glued to her butt. He wore a Harvard T-shirt and a smirk that he'd likely developed around the silver spoon in his mouth.

"Hey. My eyes are up here." She pointed with two fingers to her face. "And it's Ms. Lang."

"Ah. You're one of the sisters." His gaze traveled up her front to land on her face as instructed, but his attention still felt a tad...off. "I'm Trevor Longley. Which Ms. Lang are you, Sophia or Charlotte?"

"Neither one." Not that she owed him any sort of explanation, but she couldn't stand it when someone called her Charlotte. "I'm Charli. Charlotte is a spider or a princess, take your pick, but don't address me that way if you expect an answer."

"Charli, then," he adapted smoothly, catching her hand in his and bringing it to his mouth in some kind of weird eighteenth-century mannerism that she'd seen a dozen times on *Bridgerton*.

In real life, it wasn't so charming. It was kind of creepy. Plus, this guy wasn't British. He did have that moneyed New England look about him, though, so maybe he thought that counted for some reason?

"Well, see you around, Trevor," she said in hopes he would take the hint.

He didn't. He fell into step beside her, hooking their elbows together as if they were old pals and she'd invited him along on her trail ride scouting trip. This was getting a little tiresome and a lot out of hand.

She disentangled their arms and scowled at him, which obviously didn't mean the same thing to Harvard guys as it did to everyone else, since he just laughed.

"That's no way to be," he said with what felt like forced cheerfulness. "We're going to be good friends, I can tell."

"Because I'm giving you all sorts of come-on-to-me vibes?" she asked witheringly. "Maybe you need your vision checked."

Trevor's smile got a little less friendly and developed an edge she didn't like. "That's no way to speak to a guest."

No, it wasn't. Should she reel it back? Practice being a little more friendly? She kind of sucked at that. But there was something off about Trevor that tripped her radar.

"You're not a guest, Trevor," she emphasized. "You're a grad student who is quickly wearing out his welcome."

Where was everyone else? There were supposed to be approximately nine trillion dig nerds around here. Every time she left the house, she tripped over more than her share, yet there was no movement from the temporary campground. The woods behind her felt eerily quiet.

Why hadn't she thought to scout for a trail in the front

part of ranch land where the grad students usually didn't go? Because she'd been thinking about Heath, not anything that mattered.

"You're going to want to watch your mouth, Charlotte," he said sharply and that's when he grabbed her.

His fingers bit into her arm as she yelped. What was this guy's problem?

She couldn't get free. No amount of yanking pulled her arm loose and the last tug wrenched her shoulder. "You're hurting me."

And if she didn't figure this out, he could do a lot more than that. Genuine fear coated her throat.

"Good," he snarled, all traces of his previous cheer gone. "I'm trying to be nice to you but you're obviously a bi—"

"Take your hand off Ms. Lang."

Heath. His voice saturated the tense atmosphere, flooding her with relief.

His expression as hard as his body, Heath materialized at her side, towering over her. And Trevor. Who didn't seem to be aware of the fact that Heath McKay stood a head taller and outweighed him by fifty pounds of muscle.

"Find your own amusement, friend," Trevor tossed out, his fingernails cutting into her skin. Also known as not following orders.

Heath cracked his neck, his gaze lethally honed into Trevor's face. "Looks like I have."

Chapter Two

Heath didn't like most people. He liked them even less when they came with a big sign on their forehead that read *I'm Entitled*.

This Harvard guy was going for some kind of prize, though, with a how-fast-can-I-die vibe, putting his hands on Charli like he had every right to, even as she was telling him no. Freaking dig nerds. They'd scurried into every nook and cranny on the ranch, causing problems and creating security nightmares.

Now this.

"Looks like you have? What's that supposed to mean?" Harvard snarled. "You think I'm going to share?"

Heath leveled his gaze, boring straight into the dude, giving him a giant opportunity to do the right thing so everyone could walk away. "I think you're going to provide me with about fourteen seconds of very satisfying entertainment. And then I'm going to deposit you in the back of a squad car to face assault charges. Or you can reassess the situation and make your own course adjustment."

Harvard glanced at Charli and then back at Heath and laughed. *Laughed*, like Heath habitually walked around issuing empty threats.

Just because he'd made a vow to stop solving things with

his fists didn't mean he couldn't take a brief hiatus from his new, calmer persona. In fact, it would be his pleasure.

No. No punching the idiot. That wasn't how this should go down. Heath wasn't that guy anymore.

Okay, deep breath. He could do this without resorting to violence. There were other ways to handle handsy jerkoffs. Even when Heath had a signed contract that said he was responsible for keeping Charli safe and had unwritten latitude to do that however he saw fit.

"You're going to want to take a step back, *friend,*" Heath informed Harvard with as much venom in his voice as he could muster.

"Or what?"

That was the million-dollar question, wasn't it? Old Heath would have put this guy in traction and enjoyed every second of it. But Margo's exact words when she'd dumped him zinged through his head 24/7, leaving no room for his temper to make an appearance. If he wanted to prove to her that he wasn't the hothead brawler she'd labeled him as, he had to stop acting like one.

He *wanted* to stop. He wasn't a SEAL any longer. Reacting with a cooler head worked much better for civilian life.

Another deep breath didn't soothe the seething mass of anger simmering under Heath's skin. Dark edges crowded his vision.

And Harvard's hand was still clamped around Charli's arm. She didn't look quite as terrified as she had, but she was still in distress and Heath needed to fix that.

"Or I'll help you take a step back," Heath said silkily without specifying how he'd accomplish that. "How do you think your bosses would feel about you manhandling the owner of the ranch where you've been invited to dig?"

Harvard tossed his head. "My father's lawyers will handle any trouble you stir up."

Of course they would. His father probably paid a retainer fee specifically for this jerk-wad, much of which would have likely been spent erasing previous assault charges. It wouldn't shock him to discover Harvard had the rap sheet of a choir boy working on his Eagle Scout.

Now Heath was good and righteously pissed. Some trash deserved to be taken out, ex-girlfriends' opinions aside. "Then this is for both Charli and all the other women who have been standing in her shoes."

He popped the guy right in the nose. A good, hard, wholly satisfying jab that broke a lot of stuff that held his face together. The dark edges around Heath's vision dissolved. The dig nerd screamed and finally released Charli in favor of cupping his nose, which was currently pouring blood into his palm.

Nice. Heath took the opportunity to shuffle Charli behind him, where he could feel the heat of her warming his back. She clutched his arm, peering around it at her former assailant, clearly quite happy to have the wall of Heath between them.

It made him happy, too.

"I'll have you arrested for this!" Harvard announced, his bravado still in full force even after being treated to what amounted to the opening volley. "Do you know who my parents are?"

"Equally entitled brats?" he hazarded a guess, rolling up on the balls of his feet in case Harvard got some kind of idea that whatever dozen or so boxing classes he'd taken last semester would in fact help him here. This guy was the type who seemed incapable of taking a hint. Or a hit.

"My father—"

"Is not here," he finished for him. "And I would ask myself how hard it will be to dial him up after I break every single one of your fingers."

Finally, Harvard developed a slight glint of panic somewhere in the vast unreached places of his brain. "You can't do that."

"Well, let's deconstruct that, shall we?" Heath offered, crossing his arms lazily as if he had all the time in the world for a chat. Which he did, since Charli was his only job, but he'd already broken his vow once, and he'd rather not do it a second time. With his fists tucked away, it might be easier to remember to use his words instead. "If by 'can't' you mean I'm incapable, try me. Happy to give you a demonstration. If by 'can't', you mean you're going to stop me, thanks. I needed that laugh today. Or maybe you meant 'can't' as in it's a reprehensible thing to do and my moral fiber will prevent me from taking such a heinous step? Which is it?"

Harvard looked confused. Not a surprise. Most people didn't expect a guy they called the Enforcer in the Teams to have a vocabulary too. His ability to spit out twenty-dollar words was what had first won over Margo. She'd often told him how sexy the combo of muscles and a mouth was. Until he used the muscles. That, she wasn't so fond of.

"Heath, it's okay," Charli murmured from behind him, her palm still wrapped around his arm. "I'm fine. We can go."

"It's not okay," he growled, his gaze still boring into the dig nerd. "Because Harvard here isn't quite convinced that he should be taking a new path in life, one that leads him away from the wages of sin and toward the kingdom of righteousness where he respects women and fully understands the meaning of the word no."

He could practically hear Charli's eye roll. "I don't think you're going to convert him in the space of five minutes."

"I definitely won't if you don't let me continue."

Harvard tipped his head back, presumably to help with the blood flow issues his broken nose was causing him. "I need to go to the hospital."

Reluctantly, Heath nodded. "That you do. I'll let you live on one condition. That you swear never to touch another woman unless she asks you to. Square?"

"Whatever, dude. I'm walking away. Leave me alone."

"That is also up to you. I would be thrilled to never look at your face again," Heath informed him pleasantly. "You come near Charli, you get to find out what broken fingers feel like. You stay away from her, we never speak again. Your choice."

In what amounted to the smartest decision he'd made thus far, Harvard marched away, blood dripping from his fingers. Which left Heath with an even bigger problem— Charli. The thorn in his side. The Lang sister Madden had dubbed a loose cannon.

Heath just called her trouble. She even smelled like it, a infuriatingly indecipherable combo scent that was both feminine and dangerous at the same time. Probably because every time he caught wind of it, his body tensed for what followed: a punch of arousal to his gut and an unsettled certainty that she was about to piss him off.

"You're something else, McKay," Charli said, her voice a lot stronger now that Harvard wasn't around. "I thought you were going to talk him to death. Breaking his fingers would have been a lot more satisfying."

For him too. But he'd reeled it back, letting the dragon inside sleep. Maybe he could do this after all. Wouldn't it be something when he could show Margo that she'd called it wrong? That he was capable of being husband material.

But what would be more awesome—Charli not putting him in a position to have to break anyone's bones. He spun. "On that note, Ms. Lang, let's talk about why you went out the front door, like that was going to stop me from knowing you'd left the house?"

Charli had the grace to look embarrassed. "You have freakish stealth senses. It's infuriating."

"That's not an answer." He didn't uncross his arms, mostly because he hadn't lost the urge to break something and the only things around were a large rock or a tree, and he'd grown attached to the skin on his knuckles. "You can't give me the slip, so it's baffling to me that you keep trying. Maybe stop?"

"Maybe quit following me around?" she suggested sweetly, lifting her brown hair off her neck in an unpracticed way that would make a lesser man salivate.

Yeah, it was hot outside. Which was why he'd much rather be sitting in the shade doing surveillance with Charli safe in the house. "Talk to Sophia and Madden if you don't like it."

"Maybe I will. Paxton would be a much better choice to play bodyguard."

No. He wouldn't. Charli terrified him, which was amusing. But it was also not a good mix when trying to handle the difficult task of keeping her safe. Especially since she seemed determined to increase the complexity by refusing to cooperate.

"Good luck with that," he told her. "In the meantime, I need you to help me do my job. Go back to the house and stay there."

That way, he could circle back with their mutual friend Harvard and make sure the dude understood he'd made an ironclad promise that Heath would be helping him keep for the foreseeable future. It would be best if the dig nerd went back to New England and saved everyone some grief, but odds of that happening were slim, unless Heath encouraged him to further consider the idea.

"I have things to do." Charli's crossed arms mirrored his.

He fought the urge to uncross them for her. Touching her would open up a whole can of worms he'd rather leave sealed tight, and he'd already pushed the limits of his restraint by not breaking more of Harvard's face than he had.

"I'm a fan of things," he told her with feigned nonchalance that he wished would magically calm down all the stuff writhing to get out. "I can do things, too."

"I bet you can," she muttered. "I should have qualified that with *solo* things."

"There is no solo at Hidden Creek Ranch. Not for you." He left off the implied bit, namely that she caused her own problems by not trusting him to do his job.

"I'll just sneak out again," she told him pertly. "So there's really no point in insisting that I go back to the house."

"Then I'll just come inside with you," he insisted through gritted teeth, willing his tone back into the realm of tranquil and collected. "You can't win this, Charli."

She stared at him, the air crackling between them with tension and a lot of other stuff that he'd refused to examine too hard. The whole point of New Heath was to show Margo what he was capable of in a relationship. Margo was it for him. He just needed to figure out how to get her back. He had zero interest in Charli Lang. The weird sparks between them didn't count.

"Fine. I'll go back to the house but only because I have a headache," she conceded. To her credit, she didn't protest nearly as much as he'd expected her to when he proceeded to escort her back the way she'd come, restricting herself to only a bit of jostling and thrown elbows.

Once he clicked the door shut—with her on the right side of it this time—he texted Madden to double up on rounds to ensure someone had eyes on all sides of the house while Heath made a short side trip to help the dig nerd pack up and leave.

Okay, and maybe to give himself some time to cool off. Because he was not cool. At all.

Replaying the scene in his head where the jerk-wad put his hands on Charli wasn't helping. Neither was reliving the feel of her standing behind him as he faced down the threat. He liked protecting those who couldn't do it for themselves. It was in his blood.

What he did not like was the sheer difficulty of stuffing his feelings into a tight container. It should be easier to handle a simple thing like reining in his temper. Granted, he'd made the vow to give up Old Heath before being assigned to watch over a champion button-pusher like Charli Lang.

But still. He'd done a lot of hard things in his life, not the least of which was earning his Trident after BUD/S training. Lots of guys rang out. But Heath had persevered, then spent a decade serving Uncle Sam overseas, ridding the world of filth one deployment at a time.

The loose-cannon Lang sister was not going to beat him.

Determined to ride off his anger, Heath saddled a horse and rode out to the university encampment. His mood didn't improve. Instead of tempting himself twice in one day, he found Harvard's project manager and had a civil word about reassigning the jerk-wad to another dig. The less people put him in a situation that required him to reel it back, the better.

Then he did a perimeter sweep along the east fence line at a full gallop that put enough endorphins in his bloodstream to take the edge off. Who knew that horseback riding would be the magic ticket to getting his sanity back?

Slowing to a walk to allow his mount—both of them, really—a chance to breathe, Heath focused on his surroundings, gradually aware of a prickle along the back of his neck. It was a warning sign he'd learned never to ignore, which was the reason he'd come home from Afghanistan alive.

Something wasn't right. What?

There. A circular patch of grass lay in the wrong direction from the surrounding area.

Heath cantered over to it, peering down at the green someone had stomped flat. No question it was a human, because in the center lay a couple of cigarette butts.

No ranch hand would have left behind something like that, not if they wanted to keep their job and their hide, because Jonas would have both if he caught one of his guys littering where the horses grazed. Not to mention how harmful a cigarette butt would be to a horse if one accidentally ingested it.

One of the university or museum people, then?

Or two of them… Heath homed in on the second circle, not as obvious as the first. It had been a meeting. One orchestrated outside of security camera range. For Heath's money, he'd say because one or both weren't supposed to be on site, or they would have just chatted anywhere on the property.

It was hard to tell from the evidence how long ago this meeting had taken place, but Heath recalled it had rained about a week ago, so probably since then. But the horses had been in this pasture two days ago, and several of them liked to eat the grass on the other side of the fence. Odds were, they would have trod all over these circles, destroying them.

So within the last two days. At least one, maybe even

both these people weren't supposed to be here, which made them a threat to Charli and Sophia.

Oh, no. Not on his watch.

Adrenaline poured into his system, priming him for battle. A haze clouded his vision. He kicked the horse into gear, a warrior on the warpath.

Just as the horse hit a full gallop, he remembered. Forced a breath, like he'd been training himself to do. He wasn't the Enforcer anymore. He couldn't be. But then what did that make him? Who was this post-SEAL Heath McKay if he wasn't that guy?

Heath pulled the horse back into a trot and then stopped, rubbing the back of his neck as the sun baked his shirt into his sweat-soaked skin. What could New Heath do to handle this situation calmly and without violence?

Inform. Madden and Pierce needed to be updated on the situation.

Track. Heath could follow the trail and see where it led. Nothing more. And then he'd see what was what.

Chapter Three

"Earth to Charli."

Charli blinked and focused on Sophia's face across the desk that they were sharing for the moment. "Sorry. Did you say something?"

Sophia set her pen down on the pad that held her written to-do list, the one that she regularly vetted to see if the task would make it to the real to-do list on her phone. It was exhausting even thinking about having a tryout to-do list, as if one list wasn't good enough—the tasks actually had to *audition* for a spot.

"I said, is everything on track for the decorator to finish tomorrow?" her sister told her. "For the third time. I guess I don't have to ask what's taking all your attention after that big production Heath made to escort you into the house."

The wry twist of Sophia's lips set off a lick of guilt in Charli's gut and she glanced away, toward the wall of the office. "It's not what you think."

Nor did Charli think telling Sophia exactly what had happened with Trevor the Handsy Harvard grad student would be a great plan either. She'd just side with Heath and that would make it twice as hard for Charli to leave the house without her bodyguard in tow.

"I get it. I have a hard time concentrating sometimes too,

when I know there's just a couple of walls between me and Ace." Sophia's voice took on this dreamy quality that she didn't have to explain at all.

Or rather, Charli would prefer that she didn't. Everyone knew Sophia and Ace were gaga over each other and they'd happily rub it in everyone's faces if given half a chance. It was both nauseating and jealousy-inducing.

"Yeah, you don't actually get it," she grumbled. "McKay is a pain in my butt, that's all."

"I thought you guys were dating."

There was a glint in Sophia's eye that Charli didn't like. It was part *I'm about to interfere* and part *what in the world is wrong with Ace's partner?*

"It didn't work out."

"Oh."

She could see Sophia trying to reason out in her head what the issue could have possibly been, and odds were high that telling her Heath was *exactly* Charli's type wouldn't actually explain anything. Neither did Charli feel like spelling out why Heath being her type wasn't a good thing. Sophia never made bad choices or screwed up anything.

This ranch—the Cowboy Experience—was Charli's chance to change her fate. Falling back into the same old same old traps wasn't happening. Except that meant she had to focus and stop making Sophia repeat herself.

More to the point, she had to stop daydreaming about Heath's biceps. And his unexpected chivalrous streak. Really, what woman could resist a man who *defended* her, and then threatened the loser who'd cornered her?

She'd never felt so feminine and important and protected in her life. Because of *Heath*.

It was messing with her.

Charli squared her shoulders. "The decorator will be done tomorrow. Guaranteed. I paid a little extra for a rush job."

"You did what?" Sophia set down the pen she'd just picked up. "Char, you can't do that without talking to me. We have a budget."

"Yeah, but I'm an equal partner," she argued, thrilled to have that leg to stand on. "I have to make decisions sometimes without consulting you due to time constraints. I'm trying to get a job done on schedule and did what I deemed best in that moment. Doing this together means you have to trust me."

Spoken like a true Black Widow in the making. Black Widow wouldn't flinch when faced with questions about her choices.

Sophia blew out a breath and nodded. "Okay. You're right."

She was? Charli stared at Sophia, convinced she'd misheard. "Okay? As in...okay? You're fine that I spent the extra money?"

This was a test. A trap. Something. Sophia never thought Charli was right about much of anything.

Shrugging, Sophia gave her a look. "I'm trying to do as suggested. Trust you. I don't like it, but I can't be in control of everything or there's no point in doing this together. So, yes. You're right."

Well. Charli crossed her arms and sank down a little bit in her chair as something light and fluttery beat at her heart. "That was a lovely apology."

Sophia rolled her eyes. "Don't get used to it. Switching gears after a lifetime of being a control freak isn't something I'm going to accomplish with a lot of grace."

A grin tugged at Charli's mouth. "I can give you a lot more chances to practice."

"Please—" Sophia cut off whatever she was about to say when someone knocked at the door.

Ace poked his head in without waiting for Sophia to call out to him, his trademark cowboy hat the color of beach sand set low on his forehead. "We have a situation."

Her sister's boyfriend had two modes: mushy in love with Sophia and all business. This was definitely the latter. He bristled with authority, looking like he could handle anything thrown at him with efficiency and expertise. And he had. He'd gone searching for Sophia with righteous fury when she'd been kidnapped, yet still managed to give off the impression he'd invented cold calculation. He was attractive, if you liked the clean-cut all-American type.

In short, he was the opposite of his partners. An iceberg to Heath's volcano and Paxton's computer brain. Charli often wondered how in the world they'd become friends.

Sophia sat up straighter, her expression alert. "What's going on?"

Ace stepped inside the office, his hat automatically in his hand because he was that kind of guy. "McKay found evidence in the south pasture that we might have some unwelcome company on the property."

"There are a lot of people on the ranch who are unwelcome," Charli said with an arched brow. "You're going to have to be more specific."

Ace glanced at her. "It was a meeting between at least two people, conducted out of range of the security cameras. That means at least one of them isn't on the official roster of those authorized to be on site as part of the excavation team. In the digital age, we assume that a face-to-face conversation means someone didn't want their association tracked and also has a good handle on the ranch routine since they picked a time with low risk of being seen together by a staff member. All of that adds up to a problem."

Sophia's expression flattened. "An associate of Cortez?"

That was the name of the guy who had kidnapped her sister, but he was in jail with no chance of bail. Charli recalled that he'd given the authorities a very limited amount of information about his associates, but the one name he'd offered up had landed like a bomb: Karl Davenport. Her father's treasure hunting partner.

"It's possible," Ace admitted.

"Cortez only had one associate who matters." Sophia and Ace both looked at Charli. "It's true. I'm just saying it. It's Karl, right? That's who you think it is. Isn't that why Ace is here having this chat with us?"

The implications of that—she couldn't even wrap her brain around it. But she did know one thing. It meant there was a lot of Heath in her future unless she figured out something else superfast.

"My liaison at the sheriff's office confirmed that Karl Davenport is still at large, yes," Ace said. "And most certainly dangerous, given that he hired Cortez to rough up Sophia and scare her away from the ranch."

"Oh, man, this is not good." Sophia tapped her pen against her paper to-do list, her mind obviously on the hundreds of things that they still had to do to get the ranch ready to open its doors to guests in less than a week. What she did not look like was scared. Nothing scared Sophia. It was a skill Charli would like to learn.

"Maybe it's someone else," Charli suggested with a confidence she wasn't sure she felt.

This was the last thing they needed. The guests would be here soon, and it was already going to be hard enough to navigate around all the dig nerds. Throwing another threat into the mix didn't help.

Sophia stared at her. "Like who? Dad?"

"Well, maybe." That had honestly never occurred to her, but she latched onto the alternative with gusto. "Why isn't that possible? Just because we haven't seen him in years doesn't mean he won't make an appearance now that the university people are digging up his cache. Maybe he wants it back."

"That's also a possibility," Ace said with zero inflection, giving away nothing of what he was thinking. "Which doesn't mean David Lang isn't a threat to either of you. You'll forgive me if I wait to pass judgment on his paternal instincts until I have a reason to trust him."

"That's fair," Sophia said, and Charli nodded. "You'll certainly not get an argument from either of us on that front."

"Yeah, I'm happy to pass full judgment of his father skills right here and now," Charli said with a scowl. "David Lang is a name on my birth certificate. That's it."

Honestly, the idea of their father roaming around the ranch that he'd never bothered to claim as his birthright might sit worse with Charli than knowing it was Karl Davenport out there plotting harm to people she loved. David Lang was a parasite on humanity. The kind of man who dumped his responsibilities at the drop of a hat, who thought nothing of donating sperm and skipping town in favor of gold over his family.

"We're assuming nothing at this point," Ace told them. "Other than the fact that whoever it is doesn't intend to march up to us with identification and his hands raised. So we have a security issue that my team is handling. Needs to be allowed to handle."

And that was the real reason he was here. Charli could

see it plastered all over his face. "You came to make sure I'm properly chastised about ditching my shadow earlier."

Sophia glared at her. "Charli. We talked about this. You can't roam around without Heath. That's the whole reason he's here. To keep you safe."

"I know," she grumbled as the reality crashed over her. If she wanted to cross the finish line with the Cowboy Experience, she had to give a little—and that meant agreeing to be babysat. "I hear everyone loud and clear. I solemnly swear I will drag McKay around with me everywhere I go, including the shower and to bed."

And that was precisely where she assumed he'd end up if given half an inch of latitude. She could see it now, the way he'd disarm her with the perfectly logical excuse that he could protect her much better if he never left her side and wouldn't it be handy to have someone to wash her hair while he was there and already naked?

Yeah. She could see it. Her brain seemed pretty set on looping that scene through her mind's eye over and over again. She nearly groaned as she pictured exactly how much of her bed Heath would take up.

Ace's expression, to his credit, didn't budge an inch. "The logistics of how he protects you are between you and him. I'm only asking that you don't leave the house unless you're in the company of the man tasked with ensuring you don't end up on the wrong end of a nine millimeter."

"Do you think we need to consider delaying the opening of the ranch?" Sophia asked Ace in all seriousness, like that was an option she was considering.

"Hold on," Charli protested as it felt an awful lot like the office floor had turned into quicksand. "I said I wouldn't go anywhere without Heath. You have Ace watching out for you. The guests will be fine. No one cares about them."

"Well, we don't know what these new intruders might want," Ace said, hesitating. "We can't be sure they aren't unknown threats with unknown motives. They could be after the treasure themselves, hoping to beat Davenport and the university people to the punch. Pierce ran a lot of analyses, but we don't have enough evidence to be certain about anything."

"We should consider delaying the opening, then," Sophia said with a nod, her mouth tight.

"No, we can't consider that." Charli pinched the bridge of her nose, as her plan started circling the drain. "Just give it a few days. Ace and his team will be stepping up surveillance and stuff, right?"

Ace confirmed that with a nod, tapping his hat against his wrist. "I'm hiring a couple of guys to start doing perimeter sweeps in rotation. We're not leaving anything to chance. The more information we can get, the better prepared we'll be to handle whoever these guys are."

"We don't have a couple of days," Sophia countered. "We have one day. If we're going to delay the opening, we have to give people enough notice to cancel flights and rebook."

Charli's temples started throbbing. "We're not telling people to cancel flights. The opening is happening."

Otherwise, her stake in this would slip away. This was the only thing she'd ever had in her life that she could point to and say, *This is mine. The Cowboy Experience is happening because of me.*

"Give it a day, Soph," Ace told her, and something passed between them that made Charli's throat hurt. They had something special that most people would never get to experience, herself included. Why couldn't she get interested in a straight arrow like Ace? Surely there were more guys like him out there.

Heath McKay wasn't one of them, though. That fact presented itself to her loud and clear when she texted him that she had to go to the store later, like a good girl who did what she was told.

She stepped out of the house and into the maelstrom of testosterone and biceps on her porch. "Punctual. I like that in a man."

Heath reset his hat on his head, the new angle highlighting his amazing cheekbones. "Agreeable. I like that in a woman."

She made a face at him. "Don't get used to it. As soon as you figure out who had the clandestine meeting in the south pasture, I'm back to inventing creative ways to frustrate you."

"Pretty sure that's still going on," he muttered as he opened the passenger door to his truck, an ancient flatbed that she'd always assumed he'd procured from somewhere as part of his cover. It didn't fit him in the slightest. A sleek Jaguar was more his speed, with a deep, throaty engine, ready to pounce or sprint away pending his mood.

"I'm here. In the truck with you," she pointed out when he slid into the driver's seat, then nearly swallowed her tongue as the cab filled with Heath.

It was more than a physical presence. She could feel him along her skin even though both of his hands were on the wheel. Delicious. And then some. But she had no intention of feeding his ego by letting him see her reaction.

"You in here is what's frustrating," he commented mildly as he backed out of the circular drive in front of the main house. "What store are we going to?"

"Whatever one in town carries tampons," she said and grinned as he shot her a look. "What? You wanted to spend twenty-four seven following around a woman, congrats. This is part of life."

"Do you hate all men or am I just special?"

"Men are generally the spawn of Satan, but I will admit a particular pleasure at riling you specifically," she informed him with genuine cheer, a minor miracle given the way her day had gone thus far.

Heath rolled to a stop at a red light and turned his head to treat her to a once-over that wiped the smile right off her face. It was the first time she'd registered him really *looking* at her, and she suddenly had the worst feeling she'd turned to glass. As if he could see everything, even the things she didn't want him to.

"What?" she croaked out defensively. "Is my shirt backward?"

"Not all men are evil," he countered. "Though before too long, I'm going to be asking for the name of the one who left you with that impression."

Oh, man, he'd definitely walked right in and helped himself to a whole heap of Charli's vulnerabilities without her consent. That was not okay.

What would Black Widow do?

She'd kick the man on her way to the curb. "Beg to differ. You can ask for a name, but you're not going to get it. And for your information, more than one man has given me my set-in-stone viewpoint about the origins of the male species, so the odds of you changing my mind are zero."

"Wanna bet?"

Chapter Four

Wanna bet?

A throwaway phrase. One Heath hadn't necessarily meant for her to take literally. But Charli's brows lifted as she contemplated Heath, and dang if he didn't like being the subject of her perusal. Even if she was looking at him as though he'd started spouting sonnets. And yes, he did know what a sonnet was, but he wasn't planning on reciting any to her.

What had just instantly scrolled through his mind was way better.

"Do I want to bet what?" she asked.

"Whether I can change your mind. About men," he clarified because she was totally the type to misread this very specific offer, which definitely needed about a hundred guardrails to keep it from going south. "You've obviously got an ex in your rearview mirror who treated you like a disposable wipe. I'm saying I can prove to you that not all men are like that. I'm not like that."

Charli threw back her head and laughed, a silvery sound that shouldn't be coaxing ripples along his skin, especially not when he was reasonably sure he was the source of her amusement.

"It's not funny," he growled.

"It is on so many levels that I can't fully address each

one fast enough." She held up a finger. "But really, I only need the one point. You have nothing I want, so there's nothing to bet."

Now she was talking his language. There was nothing on this earth Heath liked more than a challenge, and she'd just dropped one right in his lap. Never mind that he'd come up with this idea strictly because they had to spend every minute in each other's company. Why not be productive at the same time? Practice being New Heath a little.

Except she'd turned it on its head because that's what Charli did—disrupt things.

"Darling, you are such a liar. I have plenty you want," he drawled and grinned when a telltale flush rose up high on her cheekbones. "But I wasn't talking about that kind of bet. As much as I am thinking about some very interesting images you've kindly put into my head, I'm suggesting totally different stakes that I am positive even you will appreciate."

Heath kept his gaze trained on the road ahead, giving Charli plenty of space to work up a healthy curiosity. He could practically hear her teeth grinding from here, which put a nice little kick in his chest to know he'd managed to get her worked up. Finally, she crossed her arms.

"Spill it, McKay. You clearly have something up your sleeve. The sooner you lay it out, the sooner I can shoot it down."

"Shame signs."

The hard cross of her arms over her midsection went slack. "Go on."

"The bet is simple. If I don't change your mind about men, I'll wear a shame sign and post it to social media. You get to decide what it says. Heck, I'll even let you make the sign."

The exact moment when she got interested in this idea

played out in a very subtle head tilt. A lesser man might have missed it, particularly one who paid a lot of attention to driving. But Heath had stayed alive in Afghanistan by honing his ability to read everything about his surroundings.

And she was frothing at the mouth to watch him lose. Game on.

"You're serious."

"As an undertaker at a hanging."

Her mouth twitched. "You're something else, my guy. I'm assuming that the reverse is true. If you somehow pull a rabbit out of that Stetson and hit whatever criteria I come up with that proves you've changed my mind about men, I have to wear your shame sign."

"Of course." He reset his hat on his head, already contemplating the sheer number of bunnies that he'd be forced to conjure before too long. Because she was going to say yes. He could feel it. "I already have the wording picked out. 'I was wrong, and Heath was right.'"

"You know my problem with men is that they're all horn dogs who can't keep their pants on around other women, right?"

Yeah, he wasn't confused. Trying not to be too stung by her tone, he glanced at her as he parked in the lot at the Walmart in Gun Barrel City. "What exactly happened with the former Mr. Charli that gave you the idea that's difficult?"

Her expression iced over. "There's no former Mr. Charli. And that's not part of the deal. No history lesson included. Take it or leave it. And note that my idea of faithful is extremely stringent. You'll get zero freebies like a random woman's number in your phone who's 'just a friend.'"

She accompanied this with exaggerated air quotes and a sneer that hooked him in a place he was pretty sure she hadn't been trying to reach. He stared at her, trying to figure out why the rock she'd stuck in her chest to replace her heart bothered him so much.

Charli meant nothing to him. What did he care if she'd been burned so badly by her crappy ex?

"For the record, I'm not a player," he murmured. That had never been Margo's problem. "But I'm game for leaving our history out of the mix."

He was more than happy to keep his motivation for all this to himself, though he would have explained it if pressed. Probably. Maybe not all of it. Actually, he wasn't even sure he could fully express why this bet had become such a big deal so quickly, but it was.

Because if he could prove to Charli that he was different than her cheating ex-boyfriend, that he had what it took to treat a woman like a queen, then he could prove to Margo that he was husband material. Right? Charli would get to see a man who knew how to toe the line. One who could be more righteous than a choirboy on Easter Sunday with zero passionate outbursts to his name.

And Heath got a free pass to practice for the real thing. No one would get hurt. Everyone wins.

It was the most brilliant plan in the universe.

"How is this even going to work, McKay?" Charli asked, the thread of incredulity lifting the ends of her words past the point where it sounded like she was still on board. "To prove you're not a serial cheater, we'd have to get married and be together until the day we die. And you and I would probably kill each other before we hit our one-week anniversary."

He had to laugh because yeah. "That's what makes this such a great deal for you. You get the Heath McKay special and don't even have to worry about whether you can do your part long-term."

"Wait. What?" He had her attention now.

People streamed by his flatbed on their way into the store, but neither of them got out of the truck. With one hand draped over the steering wheel, he lifted a shoulder as if it was obvious. "This is a bet. You have to do something for me in exchange. This is not just a one-way street."

Though if this worked, he would get the most benefit. Old Heath would be laid to rest forever. New Heath would emerge as a man worthy of an elegant, classy woman like Margo.

"You're saying you don't think I can do my part?" she ground out and then seemed to think better of doing her own digging in. "What are you even talking about? Is there more to this than you bringing me flowers or whatever passes in your head as a lame attempt to change my opinion about men?"

"Yeah. You have to give me a fair shot. Unlike the last time."

Clearly stymied by the direction of the conversation, Charli stared out the front windshield as if she hoped to glimpse whatever had captured his interest on the other side of the glass. Ha. Little did she know that every iota of his focus was on her. The shift of her leg against the seat. The way her index finger tapped against her elbow. A restless energy that his own recognized. It was part of what fascinated him about her, that she could be so magnetically alluring without a power suit or a pair of ice pick stilettos in sight.

And he didn't have any better handle on her this time than he had last time.

Nor had he realized that her previous rejection still prickled a little. Maybe that had snuck a few tendrils into the roots of this deal. She didn't have to know that.

"For your information, I gave you a fair shot last time," she informed him loftily.

Also known as the one and only time he'd tried to breach her defenses with the atrocious crime of taking her to dinner at the steak place one street over. He still wasn't sure what had spooked her, but since his heart belonged to Margo, the way it had ended—with her fleeing from his truck the moment he'd pulled up at the ranch—was for the best.

He'd only been trying to move on with the one woman who had sparked his interest in the months since Margo had kicked him to the curb. See if he did that again. This bet wasn't about that.

"We have different definitions of what constitutes a fair shot," he countered mildly. "So different that I'm making it part of the terms of the bet. For this to work, you have to commit. Three weeks. No arguments. No weaseling out of it because you have a headache."

Suspicion narrowed her eyes as she swung her gaze to meet his. "What do you get out of this?"

The million-dollar question. Suddenly he wasn't so keen to lay all of his cards on the table, after all. "An opportunity to do my job without having to hunt you down for one. We have to spend time together, whether you like it or not. This at least gives us both a chance to relax a bit."

Truth. Or as much of it as he planned to give her.

Her chuckle caught him off guard. "You're the least relaxing person I've ever met and you're the liar if you don't say the same about me."

"I meant relax in the knowledge that we're stuck together," he shot back with a smirk. "You can't ditch me for three weeks. During that time, you treat it like we're in a relationship. I'm betting you can't do it."

Man, she was good. Not a muscle in her body twitched.

He would know. He was so dialed into her that he might be able to detect if she so much as moved a hair. That's the only reason the slow smile that spread across her face punched him so hard in the gut.

"You're one more stipulation away from a straitjacket," she said and that's when he knew he had her. "Counter term. You have to take me on official dates. One a week for every single week of the three. You're paying. And no cop-outs. McDonald's doesn't count."

Shocked that she'd fallen right into his trap like that, he contemplated her, his own suspicions raising one of his brows. "You'd agree to that?"

She lifted her hands. "What, to letting a man turn himself inside out to impress me with his imaginative ability to conjure new and noteworthy date locales week after week? Yeah. I'd sign up for that in a heartbeat."

"Then we have a deal." He stuck out his hand, wondering if she even realized he'd already won.

Because whatever number her ex had done on her, the creep had done him a huge favor. Heath McKay knew how to treat a woman. Where she'd gotten the idea that he couldn't keep it in his pants, he had no clue, but commitment was his middle name.

Where he struggled was tamping back his tendency to be over the top with it. Margo wanted refinement—that's what he'd give her. After he spent the next three weeks getting his technique honed. New Heath had free rein from here on out. No letting his emotions off the leash. Should be easy. This was Charli after all.

Charli stuck her hand in his and the jolt sang up his arm. She'd felt it too, judging by the way she snatched her hand back and turned to look out the passenger window. "You're going to a lot of trouble just to get me to stop ditching you."

"I'm a workaholic. Sue me," he commented with a grin. "Besides, I like to win."

"Same goes."

Oh, he had no doubt. There was only a certain kind of woman who would take a deal like this one, and it wasn't the sort who looked forward to having a man pick up the check. Odds were, she'd go hard in the direction of trying to trip him up, stringing women across his path in hopes of goading him into violating the terms.

On that note—since he hadn't been born yesterday—they needed to put a few things in blood before he'd ever agree that he'd lost this bet at the end of the three weeks. Which he already knew she'd try to claim regardless. "When we get back to the ranch, we're each going to write down our criteria for how we judge who wins. It goes in a sealed envelope. Mine to Sophia, yours to Ace."

"What good is that going to do?" she complained, instantly dismissing it with a curt slice of her hand. "I'm just going to write down something that will stack the deck toward me, and you'll write down the same for you and we'll argue about it till the cows come home."

"I mean we'll write it down for each other. And then if it's sealed, no one can argue that the criteria wasn't met."

For who knew what reason, that was the thing that got a reaction from her. And it was the strangest mix of slightly dazzled and a whole lot unhappy about it. "You're a lot slicker than I give you credit for."

"I'll take that as a compliment."

And the bet as a challenge. In more ways than one. He certainly hadn't climbed into this truck with the intention of using Charli's shenanigans as a way to practice being New Heath. But if this was what it took to get Margo back, great. He could do his job keeping Charli safe at the same time. Brilliant.

That's when she slid out of the truck and sashayed into Walmart without so much as a by-your-leave, forcing him to scramble after her. As she walked, she tossed a smirk over her shoulder.

His chest iced over. She was planning something.

What, he had no idea. He'd missed that crucial point during the negotiations, too set on his own agenda to realize she had one of her own. Of course she did. No woman with the personality of a bottle rocket about to explode agreed to a bet that a mere man could change her opinion about much of anything, let alone whether he could change her mind about men as a whole.

Too late. She hadn't fallen into his trap. He'd fallen into hers.

Chapter Five

For better or worse, Charli had a new boyfriend. The best kind—one that would vanish in three weeks. Or sooner.

Not that she thought for a millisecond that any of this nonsense meant anything to Heath, which was most of the reason she'd agreed to the bet. Okay, maybe more like fifty percent, the other fifty percent being the absolute need to win. Not just because of the shame sign potential, though that had sweet bonus written all over it.

But because Heath McKay needed to be taken down a peg or twelve. He thought he could change her mind about *men*? Heath—who defined everything that was wrong with men and then tacked on a few more of his own unique surprises. That guy thought his moves would be smooth enough to make Charli forget that the whole time, he was trying to win a bet. And would do anything to get there.

That alone put her blood on boil.

Besides, Heath didn't know that Black Widow's superpowers lay in driving men away.

Nor did she have any plans to inform him. He had three weeks to do his best to resist her natural man repellent, but in the end, Charli would prevail. She always did.

Even her own father hadn't bothered sticking around.

Sometimes late at night, she relived that early childhood

trauma of lying awake, straining for the sound of her dad coming back home. She'd wanted to be the first one to hear him, to realize that all her prayers had been answered. Eventually, she'd grown into an adult who'd gotten used to disappointments and a silent God.

This bet would be no different. She'd put Heath in his place and move on.

Except when she came out of her room, she practically tripped over her new boyfriend, who was waiting for her outside her door in a casual lean that made it seem like he was holding up the wall with his sheer physical presence, instead of the other way around.

Gah, how did he look so good in the morning? Any woman with naturally curly hair like his would have to spend hours taming it. Not Heath McKay. No, he stuck his chocolate brown hat over it and instantly turned into a cowboy supermodel, complete with the rugged five o'clock shadow that would make any breathing female wonder what it felt like against her skin.

"Do you ever shave?" she grumbled by way of greeting because pre-coffee, that was the best he was going to get. Better to get used to it now.

Heath rubbed his chin absently. "Only if I remember. Why, are you worried about beard burn when I kiss you?"

Gravity ceased to exist and nearly threw Charli to the ground, but of course, he was right there, grasping her arm the moment she faltered. Annoyed at his quick reflexes and even quicker grin, she scowled at him. "You never said anything about kissing."

"I never said anything about not kissing. Besides, if I have to be monogamous for the next three weeks, who else am I going to kiss?"

"A pig that flies by?" she suggested sweetly. "Because you'd have a better shot, frankly."

He just squeezed her arm with a slight thumb caress, which set off a flurry of tingles that she didn't hate. But she wasn't about to let Heath know that.

Only the look on his face shut down her throat, freezing it.

"Trust me, Charlotte," he murmured. "There will be kissing. We're supposed to be acting like we're in a relationship. It's a natural progression considering how much time we're going to be spending together. You're eventually going to realize you actually like me."

That was enough to get a laugh out of her icy throat. And make her forget to spit out a reminder at how much she hated being called Charlotte. "You keep right on dreaming, McKay. With an imagination like that, you should go work for Disney."

"Fine. No kissing. Unless you start it," he said, crossing his arms to show off his biceps, which she suspected he did to remind people that he could deadlift a half-grown horse if he had a mind to. "In the meantime, I have a job. Two jobs. Charli's babysitter and eventual Bet Winner. How smart of me to combine the two."

Yeah, she'd gotten the message yesterday. This whole bet was a scheme he'd cooked up to amuse himself while he did his job. That was another reason to lean into smearing him all over the pavement. Driving him into the arms of another woman would be oh-so-satisfying for a multitude of reasons.

Even though part of her wished it wouldn't be so easy. A small part. Tiny—way in the back.

Most of her just couldn't wait to shove his face in the fact that he'd done nothing but solidify her place in the world as a woman who had his number. It was zero. He had as much of a shot at changing her mind about men as she did of stumbling over one who could.

Which reminded her of the ground rules she'd come up with last night. She turned toward him to lay them out and misjudged the distance, smacking straight into his solid torso. His hands snaked around her waist instantly, holding her steady. Holding her against the magnificence that lay under his shirt, which she'd thought she'd already cataloged pretty well visually. Oh, she so had not.

"Are we starting the kissing already?" he murmured, his smoky gaze locked on hers with enough intensity to steal her breath. "Or are you just demonstrating your willingness to stick by my side? I'll admit, I didn't think you'd be so into that aspect of this deal."

"I'm not." She lifted her hands and slapped them onto his chest, fully intending to shove him back a healthy step, but kind of got lost along the way when the feel of him fully permeated her fingers.

The good Lord had definitely been in a mood when He'd built this one. Then Heath had added additional texture, like the scar along the base of this throat, highlighted by the sun-bronzed skin around it. There was so much to see and do and explore that he should sell tickets to the wonderland of his torso. There might be drool in her future.

"Charli." She slid her gaze to his face, which was this delightful combo of leashed and struggling with it. "Unless you're planning to spend the next three weeks with me in your room with the door shut, you're going to want to stop looking at me like that."

That was enough to put a fire under her feet, propelling her backward.

And enough to allow her brain to jump-start itself.

Plus give Heath the opportunity to let a dangerous smile spread across his chiseled jaw. "Miz Lang, I do believe you've already moved on to third date territory."

"Oh, don't be ridiculous," she snapped, completely aware that she'd just handed him a lot of ammunition that she'd likely be sorry for later. "I never said I wasn't attracted to you. I'd have to be blind and maybe from another planet not to realize you look like a movie poster for a *Magic Mike/Yellowstone* crossover."

Instead of laughing like she'd expected—like any other man would have—Heath cocked his head and gave her another one of those deep perusals, as if her skin had vanished, leaving her thoughts and dreams exposed for him to read. "Why does it bother you so much? That you're attracted to me?"

"Because it makes it harder for me to win the bet. Duh." She tossed her hair, terrified he'd see right through her lie.

If he found out he was exactly her type, no telling what he'd do with that knowledge. Plus, she didn't *like* that she naturally drove men into the arms of other women. It hurt. And allowing herself to admit an attraction to him gave him the power to do that.

"Maybe instead of pushing me away, you should try sliding into this," he suggested. "It's a freebie. No harm, no foul. Practice being in a healthy, long-term relationship with no strings."

The concept was so mind-boggling she could only stare at him for a hot second. "What is this nonsense you're babbling about?"

He shrugged. "It only makes logical sense. If we're in this bet and I have to shadow you in the first place, why not drop all this animosity and just enjoy spending time with me? I'm not a monster. A lot of women find me a pretty good guy to have around."

"I just bet," she mumbled before realizing that she already had, which slammed a scowl onto her face. "You've proven how handy you are in a crunch. I get it. You're the bestest bodyguard in East Texas. What you are not is boyfriend material."

The temperature in the hall dropped twenty degrees, along with his expression. Ice cubes might start forming at any minute. "One of the stipulations of the bet is that you have to give me a chance. Which you've so far failed to do. You have no idea what I'm made of. That's the point of the bet, isn't it? Besides, you act like I'm planning on losing. Nothing could be further from the truth. This is your chance too, to be wined and dined within an inch of your life, doted on by a man who knows a thing or two about it."

With that impassioned speech hanging in the air between them, he spun and stalked toward the stairs.

Well. Mr. Temper Tantrum had a long three weeks ahead of him if he couldn't take a hit.

"I'll be downstairs," Heath called over his shoulder. "Not getting in your space. But you can't leave the house without me, so don't bother."

Charli had been on her way downstairs, but changed her mind, since broody cowboys with hooded expressions might be even more her type than the flirty, troublemaking kind. Her room sounded like a lot more fun.

But the moment she shut the door, the four walls mocked her. No, she hadn't given Heath a fair shot. Nor did she intend to. That would be a very quick way to lose the bet, especially if she forgot for a minute that none of this was for real. It would be easy to get caught up in it. Begin to believe some of his rhetoric.

How did she know? He'd gotten a pretty good head start during their one and only date.

The only way to handle the next three weeks and arrive on the other side unscathed was to stay in the zone. Show him that Charli on the offensive was a force to be reckoned with, the kind of hurricane that spit men out on her way to wreak more destruction.

Basically, standard operating procedure. Instead of Black Widow, she'd embrace Hurricane Charlotte. Best part—she already knew how to destroy everything.

Because that had gotten her exactly what she wanted in the past? Charli flopped onto the bed.

Her eyes squeezed shut automatically as the sight of Toby with that waitress from Applebee's spilled into her brain uninvited. It happened less and less now, but there was a time when the image sat front and center any time she was awake. She'd recognized the waitress immediately because the tramp had flirted with Toby shamelessly, right in front of Charli. As if she hadn't been sitting there, or worse, provided absolutely zero threat to the woman's agenda.

It had messed with her head. She'd unleashed on him the moment they'd hit the threshold of their apartment, accusing him of exactly what she'd later walked in on. Only with distance had she started to question if he'd been unfaithful from the start—or if she'd driven him to it.

What if *she* was the problem? What if she turned men into cheaters, solely because they were looking for a scrap of affection and warmth, only to seek it elsewhere?

Ugh, no. She couldn't think like that. She was not the problem. *They* were.

And Heath McKay was exactly the man to prove it. All she had to do was exactly what he'd laid out—give him a fair shot.

Resolute, she stormed downstairs to find him, determined to get this bet rolling so she could win. As expected, he wasn't far away, standing in the kitchen chatting up Sophia, an easy smile on his face. Not the kind he ever gave Charli.

And the second he saw her at the entrance to the kitchen, underneath the arch that led to the dining room, his smile slipped into the self-satisfied smirk she'd long grown used to.

"Come to apologize?" he asked, crossing his arms, which she immediately realized was his way of putting a barrier between them.

He did that a lot.

Because he was always expecting Hurricane Charlotte to hit him full force in the chest?

Yeah, she needed to take a step back and reassess. Bigtime.

Like Heath had said, this was her one and only golden ticket to see what might happen if she didn't act like a banshee on the loose in a relationship. What would better solidify to her that she wasn't the problem than to take him up on what he was offering? She could ease into this bet. See what it was like to be in a relationship where she already knew the score, with a clear end in sight. It could be like…training.

Besides, the moment she caught Heath's eye wandering, which it would, she'd win. She could smugly start doodling some signs and call him a dog, content in the knowledge that she'd been right all along. It wouldn't be her fault and she wouldn't be the one to blame for whatever happened.

And in the event she ever found a man somewhere who could actually be faithful, she'd have some intel to use. No one had to know she was using this fake relationship as a proving ground for what happened if she just relaxed and had fun while waiting for Heath's true colors to eventually show.

"Yeah, I did," she said with a nod, more convinced than ever that this was the right track—especially since it would knock him off his. "Come to apologize."

Heath's eyes goggled so hard that she almost laughed. Men were so easy. Sophia glanced between the two of them and shook her head.

"Not getting in the middle of this," she said and held up her hands, backing away slowly.

Neither Charli nor Heath watched her go. His gaze was locked firmly on her, slightly squinty, as if he couldn't quite figure out what had happened.

"Are you feeling all right?" he asked.

"You can cut the sarcasm," she said with less venom than normal and didn't even choke on it. "Especially since you know you hit the nail on the head. I had no intention of giving you a fair shot. And it occurs to me that you probably put that down as your criteria for what I need to do to win, so I'm essentially beating you at your own game by apologizing."

"Which you have yet to do," he reminded her, his smirk softening into enough of a smile that it didn't hurt nearly as much to return it as she'd have assumed.

"I'm getting there. I'm sorry I was so prickly earlier. I'm done. Where are you taking me on our first date?"

That's when someone banged on the back door hard enough to rattle the frame.

Heath's entire demeanor shifted from casual to red alert, his shoulders thrown back as he expertly slid in front of her, angling his body as a shield. Just like he'd done when putting himself between her and the dig nerd. He rippled with authority and promise, as if advertising to the world that nothing would get through him.

It was his Protect Charli mode, and it was so affecting that her mouth went dry.

"Stay behind me," he murmured, and she didn't mistake it for a request.

Besides, where would she go? She was exactly where she wanted to be. Well, almost. There was still a lot of space between them, and the heat pumping from his body would feel delicious against her skin, she had no doubt.

She followed him as he took two steps toward the door and opened it only a crack so she couldn't see who it was through the solid male torso blocking her view.

"I need Miss Lang," a male voice rang out, high-pitched with excitement and urgency. "We found something."

"Who are you?" Heath demanded as Charli tried to peer under his arm. "What do you need her for? I'll give her the message."

"Oh, I'm one of the grad students. Ben Fuentes. But that's not important. Dr. Low sent me to get Miss Lang. She needs to come to the Harvard trailer so we can show her."

He meant Sophia. But guess what? Charli's last name was Lang too and she was standing right here.

"Show me what?" Charli called out, muscling her way around Heath's growling form, pretty sure any grad student named Ben wasn't carrying a gun under his T-shirt.

Ben turned out to be a scrawny, earnest kid who might outweigh her by five pounds. "The statue we found. It's solid gold. Dr. Low is conservatively estimating its worth at five million dollars."

Chapter Six

Chaos erupted at Hidden Creek Ranch after the Harvard find, and Heath wanted to punch whoever had unearthed the statue.

He shouldn't. But it was hard to remember why. None of the university people stood still long enough for him to wind up a fist anyway, another logistics nightmare that had become his reality in the four hours since Dr. Low's assistant had broken the news. Apparently, everyone on the ranch proper had heard about the artifact, and all of them wanted to see it.

Strangers milled around the Harvard trailer constantly, which wouldn't have normally hit his radar since Madden had made sure Heath knew Charli's safety was his number one priority, but the ranch operation had spiraled out of control more quickly than any of them could get a handle on.

No more undercover security. It was *all* out in the open now. Nice because Heath didn't have to help round up horses any longer, but that didn't make any of this easy.

With Charli safely in the house—for now—Heath tried to concentrate on his temporarily assigned task. There were too many people to account for. Anyone could slip into a crowd this size, and no one would know a threat had joined their ranks because they were all basically kids with academic degrees in stuff he could barely spell.

There should be lines. Check-ins. ID requirements.

That's why Heath was here. To instill order. Except the really smart ones were giving him a wide berth, clearly recognizing that the former SEAL with the glower might be the biggest threat around. The dumber ones stood in easy-to-pick-off circles, laughing and pushing up their glasses as they waited their turn to view the hunk of metal that had turned his life into a three-ring circus.

Madden stalked into his field of vision, likely from the house, but Heath wouldn't know because he'd completely lost his focus. And his cool.

"What?" Heath snapped. "Do you have a third job to hand me?"

Ace Madden, his oldest friend, didn't even blink at his tone, which was one of many reasons they jelled. "If I did, you'd handle it."

Yeah, like he was handling the first two so well? For all he knew, Charli had bolted out the front door like a prison escapee thirty seconds before the floodlights spilled into the yard. This would be the one and only time he'd be unable to follow her, which might account for at least half of the reason his skin felt so itchy.

The inability to punch something was the other fifty percent.

All he needed was an excuse, like another one of the dig nerds putting his hands on Charli. Of course, given Heath's current circumstances, someone could be dragging her off into the woods right now and he'd never know.

It was killing him.

And the longer he went without unleashing his frustration, the tighter his fists clenched.

"We need more guys, Madden," he muttered at about half the volume he'd like, but there were too many of the people they were here to keep safe milling around. And that was still his job, even if he didn't like the fact that he'd been temporarily reassigned.

"We do," Madden agreed. "Especially when Sophia is currently having a meltdown and I can't be there to provide the shoulder she needs."

Heath rolled his eyes. "Sure, and Sophia's version of a meltdown probably looks like a lesser woman having a bad hair day. I'm sure she's fine."

But Madden just gave him a look. "Let's have this conversation again when someone you love is kidnapped and held at gunpoint, which took about ten years off my life, by the way, then add in a complete monkey wrench like a priceless ancient artifact showing up at the ranch you're tasked with ensuring is secure while she's crying in the kitchen."

Aw, man. If it was anyone else, Heath wouldn't care how broken up about it the guy sounded, but it was Madden. He blew off some of his mad and breathed. Or tried to, anyway.

"Is Charli with her?" he asked. "Is she okay?"

"She's the one talking Sophia down right now." Clearly at his limit, Madden took off his hat and ran stiff fingers through his hair with the other hand. "I need these people in a line, McKay. I need to know everyone on this ranch at all times, where they are, what they're doing. How do I do that with a six-hundred acre ranch?"

Heath lifted his hands, mostly to cover the wash of relief that coursed through him to hear that Charli was still where he'd left her. "I'm the brawn. Shouldn't Pierce be running some numbers or something?"

"He is. He's holed up in Sophia's study throwing together a heat map that's supposed to cross-reference unique signatures with satellite imagery, but there are a lot of trees on the property, so it's taking a while for everything to do the whatever thing he calls it. Execute the code."

Heath nodded, focusing on breathing in hopes it would calm him down. Everyone was doing their part, but it didn't help his state of mind to hear that Sophia was upset. Was Charli upset too? What if she was crying and Madden hadn't even realized because he was too worried about Sophia? No one was there to pay attention to the other Lang sister.

Since he was the only one who seemed to be concerned about that, the only way for him to get back to his real assignment would be to fix the mess in front of him. At least the part he could control. And *should*, because his friend needed him to.

"All right, everyone," Heath bellowed over the chatter to the entire field full of grad students. They all froze and looked at him. Excellent. "We're going to play a game called help me do my job. Line up if you want to see the jaguar head or whatever it is. If you don't want to stand in line, go back to your designated area. No exceptions."

"What if we've already seen it?" one of the dig nerds asked, with a nervous glance at Madden, as if trying to assess whether the two of them would enforce the rule. "Can't we hang out and discuss? I mean, this is *our* job."

"Oh, I'm sorry, you must have mistaken me for someone who cares," Heath shot back with saccharine sweetness. "That statue thing has been exactly the same for a thousand years, give or take. I'm pretty sure you can talk about it tomorrow without losing anything important in your analysis."

The dig nerd licked his lips, apparently contemplating whether arguing would get him anywhere, but finally nodded and slunk off, his cell phone already in hand to switch his commentary to text messaging, most likely.

A dozen or more people followed him, shooting Heath the kind of dirty looks normally reserved for authority figures who broke up keg parties. Fine. He'd take that. Though when he'd turned into the guy on the other side of that equation, he had no clue.

An eternity later, some semblance of a line had formed, and Heath presided over it with his fists mostly by his side. There were a couple of dicey moments when a newcomer didn't realize how strictly enforceable "single file" was meant to be.

And he still didn't see any sort of opening that would allow him to peel off and check on Charli.

Madden had stalked off to oversee some other area of security that Heath didn't want to know about. Presumably to ride the back forty looking for intruders or possibly to check on Pierce's progress with his computer program. Not that Madden had any better of a shot at understanding that man's brain than anyone else did.

At seven o'clock, Heath's stomach had already started eating itself in protest for being so empty and the line had dwindled, so he cut it off, ordering everyone to go back to their campsites. He personally watched Dr. Low as she locked the jaguar head into the safe bolted to the trailer floor. Someone could drive off with the whole trailer, but it wasn't currently attached to a vehicle, and the ancillary security contractors they'd hired had showed up an hour ago to run perimeter sweeps overnight. Madden would probably put at least two of them on stationary sentry duty outside the trailer.

Word may have already gotten out to the world at large that the trailer held something worth five million dollars. It was Madden's job to make sure the quality of security matched the value. Heath had done his part. And now he needed to turn his focus to his slightly less relaxing second job—Charli. Assuming she'd stuck around this long.

An eternity later, he found her in the kitchen, leaning against the sink, phone in one hand and a beer in the other that she sipped absently. A couple of drops of condensation slid down the longneck, which meant it was cold, and he'd never seen anything he wanted more in his life.

Only he couldn't pick out whether it was the woman or the beer that had struck something inside him.

Until Charli glanced up, her gaze snapping onto his with…something. Not animosity. Not her usual trouble. Something else, which he had no vocabulary to explain, but wanted to.

"Hey, stranger," she called. "You look like you need this way more than I do."

She crossed and pressed the bottle into his hand, which was indeed chilled enough to cool him down a few blessed degrees. Without hesitation, he guzzled the sweet nectar of a wheat beer he'd have never touched otherwise, but thoroughly enjoyed after a hard day of herding nerds.

Maybe because the glass against his lips had been against hers not moments before. He tried not to think about that too hard.

"Thanks," he rasped, wholly unsettled at this dynamic between them that didn't seem to be veering toward a knock-down-drag-out, which he'd been braced for.

"Have you eaten?" she asked, peering up at him critically as if she might glean the answer for herself.

"Not since a million years ago," he admitted, hard pressed to even recall the last time he'd put food in his mouth, especially since his gut was currently registering the intensity of Charli's gaze instead of its lack of food.

She shook her head, lips pursed, and snagged his wrist,

leading him to the table. "Sit. I'll warm up some of the left-overs from dinner. It's hamburger helper, but with ground turkey, and it's not too bad if you don't think about it too much. Green beans or no?"

"Uh, yes, I guess?" Was there a right and wrong answer?

Charli's smile made him think there probably was, and he'd managed to find it. "You're a better man than Ace. He wouldn't touch a single green bean and Sophia threw one at him."

Before he could fully wrap his head around what was happening, she'd heated a plate of leftovers and slid it onto the table in front of him, adding a fork and a napkin. Then she plopped down on the bench seat next to him with a fresh bottle of beer, stuck her elbow on the table and leaned her face into her hand, her brown eyes huge and beautiful.

"What is going on here?" he blurted before realizing how accusatory it sounded.

But Charli's grin just widened. "If you have to ask, I must not be doing it right. Eat your dinner, McKay. You look like you're about to pass out."

From shock, yeah. "You're being nice to me. It's weird."

That made her laugh. "You've had a hard day handling university people. You deserve a break from Hurricane Charlotte. Don't get used to it."

No danger of that. No one had ever taken care of him, not like this. Well, maybe his mom back when he'd been a kid. But this was different. Completely. He took another sip of his beer that had previously been Charli's, unable to stop being dazzled by the entire scene.

Only he was too hungry to think about it too much. The hamburger helper wasn't terrible, even with the healthier option of ground turkey. As his arteries weren't getting any younger, it was a nice touch. The green beans crunched instead of turning to mush in his mouth, a surprise.

"Sophia is a good cook," he announced as he wolfed down the rest of it.

"I'd pass on your compliments, but I'm the one who made it," she countered wryly. "I can understand your confusion, though. Sophia reeks of the kind of woman who knows her way around a pot and a stove."

"It's definitely the best thing I've eaten in a while," he said and elbowed her. "Don't think I didn't notice that you kept your role as the chef a secret until you heard my opinion."

She made a face. "Not an accident. Tell me what's happening outside."

"You didn't poke your head out?" he asked. The hits, they kept on coming. "Frankly, I'm not even sure why you're still in the house. I expected you to be long gone."

The pause grew some teeth as she stared at him, and it took a lot to keep from fidgeting. Heath didn't fidget. But she'd always managed to get under his skin without much effort. Coupled with all the strange vibes running between them, he scarcely knew which end was up.

"This is me behaving," she finally said. "I told you I would. It's not your fault there's so much going on with the stupid statue."

This was such a revelation that Heath didn't bother to hide his reaction—which was caution and confusion and not a little disbelief. He put his fork down on the table and fully turned on the bench to peruse her without a barrier between them.

"I didn't believe you," he told her honestly. "Earlier, when I asked you to stay in the house and you said okay. I thought it was a throwaway line, one you'd immediately invalidate by climbing out the second-story window or something."

Her brief flash of a smile caught him in the gut. "It's too high. I broke my arm doing that when I was ten, by the way."

"Not a shock," he advised her and lifted his chin. "Madden said Sophia was crying earlier. It would be like him not to notice whether you were too. Are you okay?"

"Why, Heath McKay." She clutched a hand to her heart and gasped theatrically but not before he saw the emotional glint in her eyes that he suspected she was trying to cover. "Points for sincerity and since you went to the trouble to ask, I'll be honest. This jaguar head is a big problem. For more reasons than one. Let's just say I'm not a crier, but that doesn't make me okay."

Nodding, he didn't think. Just reached out and snagged her hand, squeezing it tight. Silently telling her that he got it. "If it makes you feel better, I'm not a crier either, but I almost made an exception when this one UT kid called me sir. Who did he think he was talking to? I'm barely old enough to be his...somewhat older brother."

That made her laugh and upped the emotion quotient in her eyes. Which he strangely liked a lot.

"You're being nice to me, too," she sniffed. "It's not as weird as I want it to be."

"I told you, most women think I'm a pretty good guy. It's not my fault you didn't believe me."

"Oh, I see." She did this thing where she rearranged their fingers in a fluid motion so they were interlaced. Like they were holding hands. On purpose. "This is you pretending we're in a relationship. I get it now."

Actually, he'd forgotten all about pretending. But he nodded anyway, as if she'd hit the nail on the head, and tried to conjure up an image of Margo. "Since you brought it up, I never did get around to setting a time for our first date."

She shot him a saucy grin that immediately drained Margo from his mind. "I hate to break it to you, but I think this is it."

Sharing a beer over the kitchen table while exhausted after a day of standing around in the sun? No. Not even a little bit. "This is *not* a date. Trust me, you'll know when it happens and it's going to be way better than this."

Tomorrow night. Maybe. If Madden could get all his security issues sorted by then. Actually, Heath would make sure he did. Because he suddenly didn't feel like waiting to flip this script and be the one to dazzle *her.*

Strictly for the bet. This time he'd remember it was practice.

Chapter Seven

Charli poured coffee into an extra-large Yeti cup she'd found in the back of the cupboard. It was probably meant for someone who had planned a long morning of riding clear out to the south end of the property, or maybe someone like Super Sophia, who needed the extra caffeine hit to mow through her gargantuan to-do list.

Well, Charli wasn't either of those, but she was a woman who couldn't get Heath McKay's blue eyes out of her head long enough to sleep. That counted. Especially when Sophia called a meeting at 8:00. In the morning! Like, who had meetings that early? Corporate weirdos and politicians probably. Not ranch owners.

Except this one, she thought. Her sister had no respect for how difficult it was to be an independent woman who didn't need a man but kind of wanted the one that had been dropped in her lap. Charli couldn't figure out how to admit that to herself, let alone out loud where it would become a quick path to losing the bet.

That was probably the most painful part—having to temper the stuff inside that Heath had stirred up last night with all his gentle consideration over how she was doing. This was what she got for agreeing to give him a fair shot. It was a quandary. Because, yes, she got it. He was actually not a bad guy. No news flash there. They *all* started out that way. They ended up the same, too—heartbreakers.

Charli eyed her coffee mug that suddenly didn't feel large enough to hold the amount of caffeine technically needed this morning. So, she gulped down a quarter of it, sticking her tongue out to cool it as she topped off the cup to the brim, then stirred in hazelnut creamer, the only way to fly.

Smug that she'd beaten Sophia to the office, she settled into the chair on the guest side of the desk, content to let her sister have the business side. Sure, they were equal partners, or at least Charli liked to think they both considered that the case, but that didn't change which Lang sister was good at organization and numbers and other stuff that crossed her eyes.

Sophia bustled in at eight o'clock on the dot, making it feel like a virtue to be precisely on time. And now Charli felt like an overeager golden retriever who couldn't wait for someone to play fetch with her.

"Good morning," Sophia said, her tone that of a well-rested woman who knew exactly her place in life. "I appreciate you being here bright and early. I know you're not a morning person."

"No one is a morning person," she grumbled. "Some people are just better at hiding it than others."

Sophia slid into her chair and set her own coffee mug, a regular-sized earthenware one with a blue rim, onto the desk, then steepled her fingers around it as if warming them. "I like mornings. Especially when it's quiet. I can actually think. Which is why I got up at five a.m. and sat on the porch."

The thought made Charli's head hurt. "What did you think about?"

"Whether we should start canceling bookings."

"What? No."

With that gauntlet thrown down, the meeting got serious. Charli's spine stiffened, driving her to the edge of the chair. This was definitely not enough coffee.

"Char." Sophia rubbed at one eye and that's when Charli noticed that her sister didn't look all that well-rested and it was probably the ranch that had kept her up, not Ace. "We talked about this. The jaguar statue is the last straw. You saw what it took to keep everyone in some semblance of order yesterday."

So she'd peeked out the window a time or twelve to watch Heath corral all the dig nerds. So what? It wasn't a crime, and the scenery had a lot to recommend it.

"Heath handled it," she countered. "With style. And they hired all those other guys too."

Who had come heavily armed, she'd noted. Every single one of the new security guards carried a semiautomatic rifle along with an expression that suggested he would not appreciate being tangled with. The ranch was in good hands.

Sophia stared at her as if she'd just suggested that they coat the new security guys in honey and stake them on an anthill. "You think the guests will consider armed guards a good addition to the staff? Think again. We have to depend on word of mouth for the first six months to generate new business. I don't think 'they have people with really impressive guns' is the kind of review we're going for."

Slouching down in her seat, Charli stalled with a big show of drinking her coffee. Yeah, of course she'd thought of that. Kind of. It felt like a plus to have extra security on staff because that meant Heath would have the capacity to take her on a date sooner rather than later. Which she was looking forward to—strictly because he'd piqued her curiosity, no other reason.

What she should be focused on was the ranch. And the guests. Which she was, right now, and it totally counted. "I get the point. But they're moving the jaguar thingy at the end of the week. Dr. Low promised."

That news had been the one thing to get Sophia to stop crying yesterday. It had put a lump in Charli's throat to see her sister so upset, but it was just a minor setback. Everything would work out.

"You think that's the extent of what there is to find here?" Rubbing her eye again, Sophia blew out a breath and picked up her coffee mug but didn't drink it. "I'm afraid it's the tip of the iceberg. This place is going to be crawling with additional search teams and new experts. I don't think we have a choice but to cancel bookings and delay the opening of the ranch."

The fatigue in her sister's face poked at Charli. "This is because you think you have to do this by yourself."

"What, run the ranch?"

"Yeah." She rolled a hand in the general direction of the window. "And make decisions. You don't trust me with the really heavy lifting. Just the decorating and such."

"I'm not... Char, this is a conversation. A meeting. If I was going to make all the decisions, I would have done that at five thirty, when my brain got to the end of a very long list of pros and cons for delaying."

Sure. Her sister had every intention of listening to Charli's point of view. That's why she'd framed the whole thing as "we don't have a choice."

"Fine. Let's talk. Tell me when you think we can open if we delay."

"I don't know."

"Exactly. Because there's always going to be one more thing they might possibly find if we let the university people keep looking." This was where Charli could shine—laying down the law. "So we tell them they're done. Take your jaguar head and go. Don't come back. Your welcome is officially worn out."

"We can't—"

"This is *our* ranch, Soph. We can." Warming to her subject, Charli jumped to her feet, scarcely registering the slosh of coffee in her cup. "We don't have to cater to the university people. Maybe we introduce a treasure hunt element for guests. Like the diamond field in Arkansas where you can sift through sand yourself in search of one. I read that a woman found one worth millions of dollars not too long ago. We'll advertise that you too can find valuable stuff on our land if you just come pay us a lot of money."

This idea had huge profits written all over it. The publication of the jaguar head find would fuel that fire. It was free publicity. All they had to do was get everyone with university or museum affiliations gone—and boot the security detail—then work out the new plan.

No more Cowboy Experience. This was all about gold, baby.

But Sophia's dubious look sent her suddenly jubilant mood back down to earth.

"What?" Charli spread her hands. "You don't love this idea? It's perfect."

"We already have a ton of work into the first idea," Sophia said wryly. "Expensive graphics on our website. Signage. No plan for security when a guest finds the other five-million-dollar jaguar head, the female one."

Wait, what? Charli's mouth dropped open. "There's a female one? Why didn't you mention this earlier?"

"I've been trying to get there but you keep shooting off in

another direction," Sophia supplied unhelpfully. "Dr. Low mentioned it when she came by last night. You were busy."

With Heath. And she wasn't even a little sorry. That scene in the kitchen last night had stirred up something inside her that she wasn't sure how to handle. But wanted to figure out.

It had felt like something real. How other people might interact in an adult relationship. She was starting to think she hadn't had one of those yet.

Sophia continued. "One of the people on her team authenticated the head they found as part of a cache of treasure cataloged in some cave drawings in Central Mexico. There are supposed to be two. Whoever hid the male head on the ranch property may not have possessed the second one. Or they might have and it's still here."

The weight of this information pulled at Charli's shoulders. Why did there have to be two? One priceless giant jaguar head couldn't be enough for the Pakal guy or whoever had commissioned the statues?

"That just means more publicity for us, right?" she suggested feebly, guessing that Sophia's implacable expression meant the treasure hunting idea wasn't happening. "Okay, fine. I get that we don't have the right kind of plan to manage a crap ton of people searching for something worth that much money. We stick with Cowboy Experience. But delaying the opening, dealing with cancellations, that's bad business, too."

Sophia was already shaking her head. "I'm trying to do the right thing here, Char. I don't want to screw up the Cowboy Experience before it starts. But we've got a lot of dominoes stacked up here that I don't know how to stop from falling and wiping us out permanently."

Yeah, that was the problem. Sophia didn't know. And that meant Charli couldn't know either. It didn't matter if she had four hundred and eighty-seven good ideas for how to manage these obstacles, no one in this room wanted to hear them.

She resisted crossing her arms and sinking down in her chair for a good long pout. Barely.

This was par for the course, though. Her sister didn't think she had a single thing to contribute, so that was that. They weren't opening the Cowboy Experience next week. Instead, they'd spend their time cleaning up after a bunch of grad students and wincing every time one of them scared the horses with their ridiculously loud videos they played on their phones, but never watched with earphones.

"I'm calling it," Sophia said. "Permanent delay of the opening."

"Compromise," Charli said and stood, willing it to come across as a position of power. "Delay the opening but set a deadline for the university people. Two weeks. If they don't find the female in that length of time, odds are it's not here. That'll have to be good enough."

Sophia blew out a breath. "Two weeks? That's so soon. Why not two months?"

Because that was too long. "Three weeks, final offer. And they have to publish the fact that the female head is lost forever on their way off our land."

Three weeks fit the terms of her bet with Heath, too. Then he could wear his shame sign and be gone from her life, taking all his confusing vibes with him.

Her sister nodded, but it didn't feel like a victory. "Okay."

Great. Three more weeks until Charli could point to the Cowboy Experience and say she'd done that. Until she could claim that she'd truly found her niche in the world. It was better than nothing, and meanwhile, she'd have Heath to entertain her.

Somehow, looking on the bright side hadn't fixed her frustration. Sophia had still driven a hard bargain and a compromise wasn't the same thing as trusting Charli. She had this. But her sister didn't have a single drop of faith.

Fuming and itching for a place to unleash her mood, she stalked out of Sophia's office. She found exactly who she was looking for outside, climbing from the driver's seat of one of the off-road UTVs that he and the other guys had started using in place of horses to ride the fence line.

"McKay," she called, and he swung around to face her, a grimace her reward for getting his attention.

Good. He was in a mood too. She could tell by the faint lines of annoyance around his mouth and eyes. Neither made him look happy to see her.

"You're not supposed to be outside," he said by way of greeting, his attention clearly split between her and whatever he'd been about to do when he'd arrived in the yard. "Go back to the house, Charli."

She crossed her arms. "You owe me a date. You can't keep using work as an excuse."

And here he thought she'd be the one trying to ditch their prescribed time together. But with the delay of the opening, everything was upside down and she did not do idle well at all.

No reason not to get this bet on the road. Especially since in her current state of mind, she'd be driving him away sooner rather than later. Men wisely steered clear of Hurricane Charlotte when she got a full head of steam.

Except Heath didn't cross his arms and glare at her in kind. He shut his eyes and sucked in a breath through his nose, then took off his hat to run a hand through his damp hair, which should look ridiculous after being squashed by a Stetson for hours. But nothing looked ridiculous on him.

This might as well be a commercial for something masculine and expensive that no one could remember the name of but sold out instantly.

"I'm sorry," he murmured, his eyes locking onto hers, the glacial color in complete opposition to the warmth there.

She couldn't look away all at once. "You're not allowed to apologize. I'm mad."

His gaze bored through her, and the rest of the yard fell away. It could have been full of circus monkeys instead of grad students and she'd never hear a single chirp.

What did he see when he looked at her like that?

"Not at me, you're not," he countered mildly and then unexpectedly lifted two fingers to her face, sweeping hair from her eyes in what was obviously a clear ploy to touch her, but she didn't mind so much. His fingertips lingered, sliding down her cheek in a wholly delicious way. "It's okay, though. You can yell at me as long as you want. I can take it."

The man scrambled her brain. "You can't do that. You have to fight back."

His smile was nothing short of diabolical. "You can count on that. Later. Seven o'clock. Dinner. No excuses."

Mollified in more ways than she cared to admit, she cocked out a hip. "What if I'm busy tonight?"

"You're not." His gaze swept down to her toes, curling them without anything more than the heat he always generated. "Wear something pretty."

Oh, man. She'd have to raid Sophia's closet. The black Dolce & Gabbana Charli had been eyeing would do nicely. Sophia's shoes lacked even an ounce of personality, but that was fine. She'd pull out her red stilettos and maybe have a shot at being able to whisper in Heath's ear if the mood struck.

She blinked. Speaking of moods, Heath had completely changed hers. It was a neat trick that had certainly never been in the arsenal of any man she'd ever dated before. Er, any man she'd *wagered* with before. The more she reminded herself this wasn't real, the better.

That didn't stop her from thinking about their date the rest of the day.

Chapter Eight

The stairs in the Victorian house that had belonged to Charli's grandpa did not mix well with five-inch heels. Side note: halfway down the flight was not a good time to discover this.

Fingers digging into the handrail, she clomped down two more steps cautiously. If she ended up in a heap at the bottom, she'd be spending date night in the hospital instead of giving Heath grief over his choice of locales.

Because there was no way he'd come up with anything that would impress her. She'd lived in Dallas her whole life basically, and there was very little she didn't have access to from Cirque du Soleil to Taylor Swift to high-end restaurants to world-class shopping.

What she did not have was a lot of practice wearing these shoes on a ranch. Lesson learned for next time. There was no way on God's green earth she'd change now—this dress fit her like a glove and the in-your-face red of the shoes gave her confidence.

She'd need it to spend more than five minutes with a man like Heath who oozed masculinity and authority.

By the time she hit the ground floor, one ankle twinged, but she ignored it and strode across the hardwood like a supermodel, grateful all at once for the flat surface to practice. She was doing that a lot lately.

Practice. It shouldn't sound like such a bad thing. Was there a point in life when you got to stop practicing and start *doing*, though? That was the crux of why Sophia forcing the Cowboy Experience delay still stuck in her craw.

She wanted action. Hurricane Charlotte was in the house and that persona suited her to the ground, way better than Black Widow had. It was past time for her to move forward with the plan that would fix her life.

She made it to the kitchen without stumbling once. Small wins. Now she could get on with her practice date. The thought almost didn't curl her lip.

What did she want, though? A real date and a real chance with Heath? She'd had that. No, thank you. Practice was far better. She'd go into this with her eyes wide open, category five gale force winds ready to blow his cheating hide from here to eternity.

Except when she answered the back door at precisely seven o'clock, most of her brain function shut down.

Heath McKay knew how to clean up.

Hatless, he'd obviously washed his hair with angel's wings. Nothing earthly could make his curls look so soft and so perfectly tousled around his face. He wore a pair of khaki pants with an impressive crease likely courtesy of a dry cleaner, but the fact that he'd ranked her as worth both the cost and effort struck an odd nerve.

When had that become a bar that men couldn't hit? And how dare Heath be the one to leap over it with ease and grace?

"You're wearing date clothes," she said and yes, it sounded every bit as accusatory out loud as it did in her head. He'd worn jeans the one and only time they'd done this before.

"You're not," he growled, his gaze heating as he swept her from head to toe, lingering on the shoes. "You don't listen very well. That dress is the exact opposite of pretty."

She scowled to cover the wave of goose bumps rising on her skin along the path of his scorching sweeps. "What's wrong with this dress? It looks fantastic on me."

"That it does," he agreed, but he didn't sound pleased about it at all. Then he twirled a finger. "Go on and let's get the torture out of the way. Give me all of it. I'm pretty sure I can handle it."

"I'm not playing fashion model for your enjoyment," she said primly and almost crossed her arms over her chest but that would only highlight the V of the dress.

"Too late." His grin bordered on wolfish as he hustled her backward and shut the door, leaning against it. "You can't pretend you didn't wear that outfit for me. I already know you did. And Charli? I am enjoying the daylights out of it."

Well, that was something. The heated appreciation glimmering from his gaze worked its way beneath her skin and she almost shivered. Okay, he wasn't wrong. She had pictured his reaction a time or two as she'd gotten dressed. Was she really going to balk because he'd come out of the gate with an attitude?

It was Heath. Torture sounded like a good punishment for his dictatorial arrogance.

Good thing she'd practiced. Without the slightest wobble, she did a slow spin and relished the almost inaudible sound of him sucking in a breath. Ha. Take that.

Her spin screeched to a halt, courtesy of Heath's arms. Which he'd just hauled her into.

Breathless all at once, she lifted her gaze to his, registering all at once that the stilettos did indeed put her at a much different height that worked extremely well with his.

"I wasn't done with my pirouette," she grumbled even as her entire body sang with some otherworldly chorus that hopefully only she could hear.

"Yeah, you were."

His voice had gone hoarse and the catch in it prickled her skin. She'd done that to him. She'd affected him. It was heady stuff. His hot hands at her waist didn't feel all that fake. Probably because the rest of her had made itself at home up against the hard planes of his body. Heath definitely didn't have an ounce of fat on him anywhere. Except maybe between his ears.

"You can unhand me," she informed him loftily, proud that their proximity hadn't affected *her* voice. "You'll wrinkle this dress and then I'll look like I just rolled out of bed for the rest of the evening."

Bad choice of words. Or good, pending how she was supposed to take the fact that his fingers spread across her back, nipping in deliciously. What he did not do was let her go.

"That happens to be my favorite look on a woman."

Of course it was. She nearly rolled her eyes. "If you're trying to lose the bet, you're well on your way."

"Funny, I don't see any other women around here," he countered. "Just you."

His gaze burned through her, and she had a bad moment when she realized she might have miscalculated with this dress. If her goal had been to keep all his attention on her, it would have been a brilliant move judging by his reaction thus far.

But that wasn't her goal, exactly. It didn't seem too likely that his eye would be wandering any time soon. In fact, he might not have peeled his gaze from her once from the moment she'd opened the door. It was…not a terrible feeling.

That's when it occurred to her that if she lost the bet, she might end up with a whole lot more than she'd bargained for. Because losing meant that he'd changed her mind. That she had to concede Heath wasn't like other men. It meant he was one of a kind. Special.

And she already knew that was true.

Her heart pounding, she stared up at him, terrified all at once that he'd read the things racing around in her heart. Dang it, even in the heels she hadn't gained enough of a height advantage to feel close to being on a level playing field. Which might have more to do with the vulnerabilities she'd only just started to uncover.

Being off-kilter pushed her into a dangerous mood.

"Seems like we're doing an awful lot of standing around on this date you promised me," she said snippily.

"I also promised you I'd fight back," he reminded her with a lethal grin. "How'm I doing?"

Oh.

She had to laugh, and it released a lot of the tension that had bunched her shoulders. This whole scene was a setup. He was practicing *and* making good on his promise from earlier.

"Better than I thought. You're a lot more diabolical than I'd bargained for."

"That's what happens when you make a deal with the devil."

That she had and she wasn't even a little sorry. Heath wasn't a simpering idiot like Toby. This whole thing wasn't real. How great was it that she could be completely herself, no holds barred, and Heath would just brush it off? He wasn't going anywhere, no matter what category strength Hurricane Charlotte reached.

Plus, he smelled divine.

Feeling a lot more solid, she made the mistake of relaxing, only to discover it nestled her deeper into his embrace, which he did not miss. The atmosphere around them fairly crackled and if there was ever a time in the history of the world for a first kiss, this was it.

Strictly in the name of practicing.

When her gaze dropped to his mouth, the corners lifted as if he knew exactly what she was thinking about. What she was considering.

Only odds were high he had no clue. Because what she was actually turning over in her head was how quickly they'd both dropped into this place where they were so easy with each other. It was slightly fascinating and wholly terrifying. But she didn't have the urge to flee. Not even a little bit.

"You're looking at me that way again," he murmured and lifted a lock of her hair away from her face. "I like your hair down."

"Yeah? I was going for a little less tomboy and a lot more 'I look like I belong on the arm of Heath McKay.' Did it work?"

"And then some."

He shoved his fingers through her loose hair, somehow making it feel like a caress. Suddenly dinner was the furthest thing from her mind. He'd given her all the latitude. He wouldn't kiss her—*she* had to make the move.

Would she? *Could* she?

That's when someone banged on the door behind Heath, startling them both.

He whirled instantly, reminiscent of the time when Ben

the grad student had brought news of the jaguar statue. Charli's pulse tripled as everything warm and lovely and languid inside froze.

Heath bristled as he yanked open the door. "What?"

This time, she had five inches on her past self and could partially see around Heath's shoulder. It was Dr. Low and a couple of the higher up university people. No grad students in sight.

Foreboding settled into Charli's stomach. She knew before Dr. Low opened her mouth that her date was ruined.

"Someone broke into our research trailer," Dr. Low explained, her faint Southern accent more pronounced as she pushed her salt-and-pepper hair back from her ears.

"What?" Charli shoved at the steel shoulder blocking her way and it was only because Heath let her that she succeeded in ducking under his arm. "We have armed security agents guarding all the trailers. Is the jaguar head missing? How is that possible?"

The guys Ace had hired had all looked so formidable that Charli herself had tiptoed around them, and she was paying their salaries. If someone had gotten around *them*, none of this was going to work.

Dr. Low shook her head. "No, not the trailer with the safe. That's our admin trailer. I'm talking about the research trailer we moved to the east pasture where we found the head."

Pieces of Charli's vision started going gray, which didn't help her focus on the trailer under discussion. They had more than one trailer, she knew that, but she couldn't have told anyone the difference for a million dollars. And she vaguely recalled that the trailers used to be sitting at a right angle in the grassy area near the barn, but so many people had started milling around the yard in hopes of peeking at the gold statue, they'd moved one somewhere else. The south pasture apparently.

And she really needed a better handle on the things happening on her own property. This was her job now.

She squared her shoulders. "What happened? Was anything taken?"

One of the other PhDs spoke up, a man wearing a sport coat with elbow patches so ancient that they'd half worn away. "It doesn't seem like it. A lot of the equipment is destroyed, though. It was a very expensive break-in for nothing being taken."

"We'll call the police," Heath said, his jaw clenched so tight it was a wonder he hadn't cracked a few teeth. "Start cataloging what you can with pictures."

"We're already doing that for insurance purposes," Dr. Low said. "But this is unacceptable. This kind of thing can't happen again. It's set us back weeks."

The gray in Charli's vision went black as this uncontrollable urge to break something swelled through her fingers. "You make it sound like it's our fault. What exactly are you accusing *us* of?"

"Can you excuse us a moment?" Heath said and it wasn't a question. He tugged Charli backward with a hand around her waist and shut the door in the faces of the university people.

And then he turned her in his arms and hauled her close. That's when she realized she was shaking. The solid lines of Heath soothed her instantly, though the gentle hand stroking the back of her head did wonders as well.

Her state of mind was in such a disarray that she decided to let him.

"This is a disaster," she said into his shirt, which was a

lovely, crisp white button-down that smelled like a heavenly combo of laundry detergent and man.

"For them, yes," he murmured. "Not for you."

"How can you say that?" she wailed. "I literally just talked Sophia into opening the doors in three weeks, only to find out our security is useless, and people are breaking into the wrong trailer. They didn't take anything because the jaguar head wasn't in that trailer. Why are criminals so stupid? Can you hire more guys with guns? We need like ten more—"

"Charli." Heath's voice was so firm and sharp that she glanced up. "Breathe. I'm handling this. This is my job, not yours."

His eyes snapped with an emotion she couldn't name. Maybe because she'd never seen it before on any man in existence. Coupled with the strong arms that were literally holding her together at the moment, it felt an awful lot like he cared about her.

That wasn't right.

It was part of the act.

For some reason that calmed her down. Sucking in a deep breath, she tamped down on her swirling thoughts. This was practice for a real relationship. Sure, it was fun to be Hurricane Charlotte with no worries about scaring off the guy. But taking a step back and handling a crisis like a mature adult counted, too, and she frankly needed a lot more practice at that than anything else.

"Okay." She nodded and heaved another breath. "I'm okay. I trust you."

Instead of clutching his chest in a mock heart attack like she'd expected him to, he did the oddest thing. He leaned into their embrace—somehow, she'd ended up with her arms around him too—and brushed his lips across her temple.

"Good," he murmured. "Remember that."

And then he released her. His heat vanished from her skin, leaving her cold and feeling as if he'd taken a huge chunk of her with him.

"Stay in the house," he ordered as he swung open the door, disappearing through it without a backward glance.

The second the door shut, she locked it. Wrapping her arms around herself, she slammed her eyes closed and let her head thunk back against the wood. How was he so good at reading her? At calming her? At being so thoroughly exactly what she needed when she needed it?

I'm okay, she repeated as instructed. Best way to remember that was to keep it front and center.

But that wasn't the only thing that reverberated through her head.

I trust you.

That's what he'd meant for her to remember.

Chapter Nine

The bad feeling in Heath's gut got worse by morning.

The officers from Gun Barrel City personified small-town cops who rarely dealt with anything more serious than burglary, jaywalking and the occasional 911 call from a resident who had seen a shadow outside their window. Despite the connotations, the city's name had come from an early observation that the main road through town lay as straight as a gun barrel.

Heath knew that because Pierce had done a thorough dossier on the town, as well as law enforcement all the way up to the state level. Madden had looped in the Texas Rangers recently—the law enforcement agency, not the baseball team—as a courtesy due to the value of the jaguar head, but thus far, there'd been no need to lean on those resources.

Unfortunately, even this recent break-in hadn't changed that. No one else was impressed with Heath's bad feeling. Or his insistence that something bigger was going on than everyone was crediting.

After all, if Karl Davenport could hire someone to rough up Sophia, he could hire someone to distract everyone on the ranch with a petty crime that amounted to nothing more than misdirection.

These two cops who looked like they'd come from directing traffic near the church weren't going to crack the case of who had broken into the trailer. The patrol car that had rolled up in the yard had the city's motto—We Shoot Straight with You!—for crying out loud, painted on the side. That pretty much said it all.

No problem. Heath didn't need anyone's help to do his job.

Madden took point on giving the locals the rundown while Heath and Pierce stood off to the side of the clearing, running perimeter control. Which mostly looked like keeping the dig nerds out of the way. Easier said than done thanks to the fanfare.

Heath eyed the newest pair of sightseers, both grad students. He'd learned to tell based on how they dressed, which usually consisted of a dirty pair of worn jeans and an even dirtier T-shirt emblazoned with either the name of an indie rock band or a saying that they thought was funny but really, really wasn't.

The scrawny one didn't disappoint. His T-shirt read Pardon My Trench. The other one, Heath didn't like the look of at all. Not only did his shirt have nothing on it—which was its own kind of tell if, say, he didn't want to stand out—but he wasn't skinny. All archeology grad students were skin and bones, apparently, because they had no money and forgot to eat, or at least that's what one of the chattier ones had told him.

Eyes narrowed, Heath watched as the no-logo-shirt guy edged forward, obviously misunderstanding the role of the two former SEALs standing between him and the crime scene.

"Trailer's off-limits," Heath announced and crossed his arms. Usually that gave the dig nerds enough of a warning that they backed off.

Not this guy. He edged forward again, completely breaking free of the small crowd that had gathered to watch the police proceedings.

"Yeah, no, I get it, dude," No-Logo said with nod and took a couple of test steps in the direction of the no-fly zone. "It's just that I left the artifact I'm researching in there and I need to check on it."

"It's off-limits to everyone," Heath repeated as nicely as he could with clenched teeth. "Including you."

No-Logo nodded again. "I'm not going to stay or anything. I just need to check on it and make sure it's still in one piece. It's a bone fragment and—"

"Everything in the trailer is evidence. No exceptions."

"Oh. I see." The guy looked him up and down with an expression on his face that would have earned him some expensive dental work a year ago. "You don't have a degree in anything academic, obviously, or you'd understand the importance of my research."

The frisson at the base of Heath's spine shook loose something black and sharp as he set his heels. "Correct on all counts. My degrees are in black belts. Care to test out which are the most relevant in this situation?"

No-Logo had the gall to laugh and actually take a few more steps toward the trailer. "Is that supposed to scare me? What are you, like a glorified mall cop?"

Must not punch the idiot. Must not punch the idiot. The refrain did not stop Heath from wanting to do exactly that. But unlike earlier, when he'd clocked the dig nerd who had gotten handsy with Charli, he didn't have an excuse this time.

Pierce strolled over at that opportune moment looking an awful lot like Heath's savior. "Problem?"

"Yeah, this guy is not taking the hint," he growled as he

shoved a thumb in the direction of the interloper, who had actually edged closer to the trailer, clearly working out in his head how to duck under the yellow police tape.

"You want me to talk to him?"

"No, I want you to rearrange his face," Heath spat.

If there was a way for Pierce to push up his metaphorical glasses, he would have. "I'm the brains. I don't hit people."

This from the guy Heath had watched dispatch three unlucky insurgents who had stumbled over him in what should have been a hard-to-find location in the top of a bell tower, where Pierce had hidden to operate a drone over hostile territory. If Heath hadn't been so far away, he'd have been there in a heartbeat to help, but it turned out Pierce hadn't needed it.

"But you could. You act like you sit in front of a computer for eighteen hours a day and have the complexion of bread dough."

"You're acting like you couldn't put him in traction with one hand tied behind your back." Pierce eyed him. "You feeling okay?"

"Fine," he snapped as No-Logo edged closer to the trailer. "I'm just…working on a new approach to how I handle situations like this. I'm not in the Teams any longer. Maybe it's time to hang up the Enforcer."

Pierce laughed and then broke it off abruptly when he caught sight of Heath's glower. "Oh, you were serious? What are you even talking about? That's who you are, man. You take care of things. I've never once thought that was a problem you should fix."

"Well, it is."

And he left it at that, even as Pierce shook his head.

"Happy to have you in my corner no matter what. Meanwhile, your rabbit is itching to cross the finish line."

Heath glanced at the trailer and swore as No-Logo dropped to his knees and crawled right under the yellow police tape, then stood, heading straight for the door of the trailer. With no time to waste and a trailer full of CSI who would not be thrilled with an interruption they'd specifically asked Madden's team to help prevent, he stalked across the clearing in two seconds flat.

His temper boiled over faster than that.

He ducked under the police tape easily thanks to a rigorous morning routine that included squats, and halted No-Logo's forward progress like a record scratch when he snatched the back of his jeans. "Not so fast."

The grad student glared at Heath over his shoulder. "Let me go. You can't stop me."

"I can. I am," Heath countered, forcibly keeping his fist by his side as he dragged No-Logo in the opposite direction, which to the guy's credit wasn't as easy as it sounded.

He fought the entire way, digging in his heels and babbling threats, all of which Heath ignored. Instead he focused on breathing in hopes it would do something to reel back the black edges riding shotgun through his bloodstream.

With a loud rip, No-Logo's jeans came apart in his hand. Great.

Instead of squawking about it, the guy actually reversed course again, heading back toward the trailer without the force of Heath pulling him away. Why? Why did it always come down to this?

Rolling his eyes, Heath took off after the idiot and didn't bother to check his strength when he gave him a hard shove to the ground, then dug his knee into the back of the dig nerd's neck. The black edges softened and immediately stopped trying to hack through his veins.

But they didn't vanish completely. Heath tried to make his peace with that.

"I said the trailer was off-limits. Which supervisor am I speaking with about banning you from the premises?"

No-Logo sputtered and spat out a mouthful of dirt. "I'll have you fired for this."

Yeah, good luck with that, kid. "Since you're not being forthcoming with the details, I'll drop you with Dr. Low and she can sort out your transfer paperwork."

This threat did the trick. No-Logo stopped struggling and blanched. Bingo. Dr. Low probably wasn't his academic advisor since she was at the top of the food chain, but she wouldn't take kindly to a grad student who couldn't follow the rules.

A few minutes later, No-Logo sat with his head in his hands outside of Dr. Low's personal trailer, which she used as an office. His duty done, Heath slapped the dirt from his jeans and stalked back to the clearing to ensure no one else thought they were above the law.

Apparently, his little show of force had convinced everyone else to scatter. Only Pierce remained, his expression unreadable. "Guess you figured it out."

"Save it," Heath suggested, his mood veering back toward black.

It wasn't that he was mad at Pierce for pointing out the obvious flaw in Heath's plan to hang up the Enforcer while on a job that required him to be exactly that. What else would he contribute to the team if it wasn't the muscle? But why did his resolve constantly have to be tested? Couldn't the universe find a way to allow him to just stand around and *look* threatening?

WHEN HE GOT back to the house, Charli was in the kitchen looking for all intents and purposes as if she might be waiting for him. Good night, the woman shouldn't be such a sight for sore eyes, but he couldn't stop himself from drinking her in, letting his eyes feast on the way her leggings clung to her thighs and the enormous T-shirt she wore sat kicked off to one side, exposing a healthy slice of shoulder that he imagined would smell divine.

She was just as sexy in casual clothes as she had been last night wearing couture and stilettos.

That put him a worse mood. Because he shouldn't be thinking about her as much as he was.

"What do you want?" he snapped, crowding into her space in hopes of picking a fight, which did not improve things as the light scent of woman curled through his senses.

She stopped him with a well-placed palm on his chest but the way her fingers curved to nip in told him that she enjoyed touching him as much as he enjoyed letting her.

"Food," she advised him, her brown eyes missing nothing. "I thought you might be interested in taking me out to make up for our cancelled date from last night. So I haven't eaten yet."

Oh, yeah, he was interested all right. But that didn't magically transform his life into something more manageable. Why everything seemed to be conspiring against him lately, he had no clue.

"I can't." He slapped a hand over hers, searing her palm into his chest before she got the idea that she should step back. Because he really liked her where she was. "The place is crawling with cops who may need extra security help at any moment. The best I can offer you is leftovers while watching a movie upstairs."

One of the bad things about being so far from Gun Barrel City—you couldn't order food for delivery way out here. Which made date night far less spontaneous. But he'd work with what he could.

"Guess I put on the right outfit for that," she said sunnily.

That she had. Almost as if she'd read the room ahead of time and realized he couldn't actually leave the premises. Which begged the question of why she'd opened with the invitation to go into town for to dinner.

Warily, he swept her with a once-over that revealed exactly nothing of her motives. She had one, though. "What gives? You're being far too conciliatory."

"Now, that is a word I don't hear often in conversation with a hot cowboy." Her gaze burned with a thousand other things that she'd elected not to voice. "Would you like me to argue with you a little bit? Sock you on the arm to make a point?"

"It would make me a lot less suspicious, yeah."

She laughed and smoothed her thumb along the ridge of one rib as if she didn't mind that he'd captured her hand there the slightest bit. "I heard from Sophia that you've had a tough day. I figured you didn't need my crap heaped on top of it."

Really. "So you're fine with having a date night here at the house?"

"Oh, no, sport. Do not get ahead of yourself." She gave him the slip and waltzed out of reach to check out the contents of the refrigerator, presumably for the aforementioned leftovers. "This is not a date. You promised me something spectacular for our first date, so this doesn't count."

She was giving him a pass. That's what this was. Slightly dumbfounded, he scrubbed at his beard. "Then why would you take me up on the offer of warmed-up leftovers and a movie? You should go back to your room and do something you want to do."

"I am doing something I want to do."

The grin she shot him was full of mischief that he couldn't quite wrap his head around Charli's angle here. "Sure. You're volunteering to hang out with me but not insisting on counting it as one of the three dates you agreed to. And you're not giving me grief. What's your game, Charlotte?"

"You've cracked the code. I was totally trying to get you to full-name me," she said with a smirk that was so animated it almost came with its own soundtrack. "Don't bust a gut trying to figure it out. You're not the only one who can practice being in a relationship at a time when it's not strictly required."

That pronouncement whacked him upside the head so hard that it rendered him speechless. Heath didn't have a lot of relationship experience himself, but Margo had never once given him the impression she'd be fine with it if he suggested a movie at home. And as far as he knew, she didn't own a single T-shirt, nor would she be caught dead in leggings. Stilettos she had dozens of, but they were more arsenal than accessory. Most of what Margo owned could be considered as such.

Honestly, he'd describe Margo as high maintenance on a good day. Usually he hadn't minded that, but today it sounded…exhausting.

Practice sounded a whole lot less demanding. It loosened his spine a notch. None of this counted. Not even toward their bet. He didn't have to do anything except eat and pretend to like whatever lame chick flick Charli threw on the TV.

There was zero pressure—from any direction—for the

first time in ages. Heath rolled his neck and realized all the tension in his shoulders had eased off. He might even be able to describe himself as relaxed if this kept up.

Instead of standing there like a bump on a log, he helped Charli heat up the leftover tacos she'd found in the refrigerator, but she didn't put them on a plate. In a stroke of genius, she broke up the shells and dumped all the filling in a bowl with some shredded lettuce for an instant taco salad.

"I'm a fan of the way you practice being in a relationship," he mumbled around the first bite as they settled into the ancient couch on the second floor of the house.

This room had been deemed off-limits to future guests and would be for family use only once the ranch began operating as a hotel. That meant it had stayed comfortable instead of getting a makeover like the rest of the place.

"You haven't seen nothing yet," she advised him with an eyebrow wiggle. "Tell me about your terrible day. There was a guy giving you problems?"

Heath scowled at the mention of No-Logo. "Yeah, let's just leave it at that."

"I hope you broke his nose," she said so matter-of-factly that he blinked.

"I, uh…didn't. Not every problem should be solved with fists," he quoted without meaning to drag Margo into this conversation, but since her aversion to violence was to blame for his current sabbatical, it wasn't inappropriate.

Besides, he *should* be thinking about Margo. And how nice it was going to be when she smiled as he told her— showed her—that he'd changed.

"And sometimes it just feels good to watch cartilage crunch," she countered darkly. "Like when you hit that guy who was bothering me. That was hot."

Since none of those words belonged in a sentence together, his immediate response was to stare at her. "Come again?"

She sighed dramatically. "You're going to make me say it, aren't you? It was one of the sexiest things a guy has ever done in my presence. And I mean that exactly the way it sounds. I'm not proud of it. But there you go. You're my hero and you can't make me stop thinking that way."

What way? As if it was perfectly fine in Charli's world if he flexed the muscles in his arms instead of just the ones in his head? As if she found him *more* attractive when he took care of things according to his natural inclination?

If that wasn't enough of a revelation, he spent the rest of the night wondering if this was Charli practicing a relationship, what did the real thing look like?

Chapter Ten

If Heath on the ground got Charli's motor humming, Heath on a horse should come with a surgeon general's warning—Caution: may cause heart palpitations, sudden swooning and temporary loss of feeling in your legs.

He also should have mentioned that he wasn't a slouch in the saddle, or she'd have totally brushed up on her equestrian skills. As it stood, they'd barely cantered out of the yard, and she'd already had to resituate herself twice. Though that might have more to do with the fact that she'd been watching him handle the reins and letting her mind connect a few dots about how well he'd grip other things in a wholly different scenario.

Which she should not be thinking about.

She and Heath were barely friends, let alone in a place where any *scenarios* would happen. There had been that almost-kiss, though…

"Thanks for coming with me on this practice trail ride," she said when they slowed their mounts to a walk once they cleared the split-rail fence enclosing the pasture the dig nerds had claimed for their campground. She was riding Ricky, a sorrel male and her favorite horse, while Heath rode the unimaginatively named Hershey, a brown gelding the color of chocolate.

"You say that like I had a choice in the matter," Heath said with a quirked-up mouth that made it seem like he wasn't too unhappy about it. "You're my primary job."

"And this is my job," she reminded him. "Or at least what will be my job in nine million years when we finally open the Cowboy Experience."

Assuming Sophia agreed to open it ever. The three-week delay seemed like a pipe dream at this point after the trailer break-in, but she'd been too heartsick to bother asking her sister for confirmation that the delay might be a lot more permanent now. The police had no leads, but that wasn't a surprise given Heath's professional opinion that Gun Barrel City's finest couldn't find their butt with a map and two hands.

"Honestly, you gave me an excuse to get out of Dodge," he admitted, and she nearly fell off her horse. Again.

"What is this?" she demanded. "You can't be okay with it when I make you follow me some place unpleasant to do your bodyguard duties."

"The sky is blue, the sun is warm. The horses are sprightly, and you needed to practice trail riding. What's not to like?" he asked nonchalantly. "If this is your definition of unpleasant, we need to have a serious conversation."

This was going to be a long ride if he was already this agreeable. Was this how he lulled her into a false sense of security and then pounced? It had been a while since he'd done that, but he still had the capacity to knock her totally off-balance if he wanted to. "Are you trying to get me back for the other night? The non-date?"

He grinned and it was the kind that lit up his whole face, making her sorry he was wearing sunglasses. She liked watching it when his eyes warmed up, turning a pretty color that reminded her of Nordic fjords.

"If by *get you back*, you mean practicing being in a relationship, it's only fair," he informed her. "I can't have you getting better at it than me."

That crossed her eyes a bit. "I didn't know we'd turned it into a contest. Don't we already have a bet going?"

He shrugged without jerking on the reins, and that was hot too. The man knew his way around a horse because of course he did. There was nothing that Heath McKay didn't excel at, including the ability to handle a horse. And Hurricane Charlotte. What was the point of pushing him if he just rose to the occasion and proved he could match her, time and time again? That's why she'd banked the Mach 5 storm surge and just relaxed.

Only it was totally not okay for him to do the same. What would they talk about if they weren't giving each other grief?

"Nothing like raising the stakes, I always say," he commented mildly. "I guess this doesn't count as a date either."

"It absolutely does not."

Though if someone had asked her to list out the qualities of a perfect date, this one had a lot of them: a gorgeous man in a battered Stetson and jeans that fit him so well that they might as well be painted on; an enormous blue sky stretching endlessly to the horizon; nowhere to be and all the time in the world to enjoy being outside with someone who made being with him easy.

Of all things. When had being with Heath become *easy*?

He was right—it was glorious to have an excuse to leave the ranch behind and forget all the mess, the continual cycle of a new crisis every five minutes. There was no one on earth she'd rather do that with than Heath. Practicing had started feeling like the only time she could be herself.

And she'd just keep that information to herself, thank you.

"Just checking," Heath drawled lazily. "At this rate, we'll never get to our first date."

"Nice try," she returned, even as she considered if maybe that might not be a bad thing—wouldn't a real date be sort of anticlimactic by now? "We're not canceling the bet. You'll get your shot at impressing me soon enough."

"I never said anything about canceling the bet."

It was implied, though, as if he'd perhaps caught the slightest hint that she'd started entertaining the idea way in the back of her mind that she might actually lose. Which she'd never admit to, even under threat of death.

So she spent a lot of time not thinking about how different Heath was from any man she'd ever met. And by not thinking about it, she meant obsessively turning it over in her head and then forcing the notion to vanish, only to have it reappear later when her guard was down.

They fell into a companionable silence as they rode abreast toward the back pasture, which stretched almost a mile away from the house, following the trail that skirted the woods. It was a pretty easy ride, which was the intent. This route would be the one she set for guests, assuming that most had never been on a horse before. It wasn't a short ride, though, and guests would feel it by the second hour.

Charli's mount, Ricky, skittered sideways out of nowhere.

"Easy, boy," she murmured and stroked his neck.

Then Hershey did a similar half prance to the side, yanking a few choice words out of Heath as he fought to get control.

Charli exchanged a glance with Heath as their horses continued to shy and spook, snorting loudly with eyes rolled back. He was enough at home in the saddle that he knew something was wrong too. She scanned the trail ahead, braced for literally anything to appear that might explain what had caused their mounts to freak out.

Only the ghastly sight that came into view around a bend eclipsed everything her brain had conjured—several skinned animal carcasses strewn haphazardly across the path. The bloody, flayed bodies of small animals lay in gruesome piles, buzzing with flies and other stuff she didn't want to think about.

She cut her eyes away, but the scene had burned itself into her mind's eyes. So, no sleeping tonight, then.

Ricky spun in frantic circles, fighting the bit. She struggled to calm the agitated animal while Heath dealt with his own panicked Hershey nearby. The stench of death and the visceral carnage was doing a number on her; she could only imagine what the horses were going through.

"I've got to get Ricky calmed down," Charli called over to Heath. "He might throw a shoe if he keeps this up."

"Probably a good idea to check out the scene anyway." His tone had a steel thread running through it that told her he wasn't unaffected. But Heath handled his disquiet a lot better than she did.

They both dismounted with extra care. The animals shifted nervously as Charli and Heath patted their noses. Heath slowly approached the horrific scene. Crouching down, he examined the torn flesh and trailing entrails of the skinned animals.

"What are they?" Charli whispered, not wanted to say out loud that without skins, it was really hard to identify the animal. Refusing to look at them played a factor in that too.

"Foxes and raccoons, mostly. A coyote." Heath's voice got steelier.

Anyone who could kneel down in that kind of horror for

the time it must have taken to do this job had more than a couple of screws loose.

A shrill whinny snapped Charli's focus back. She turned just in time to see both horses rearing up in terror before pivoting and galloping full-tilt back down the trail.

"Ricky! Stop!" Charli cried out in vain.

Stupid horses. Except they were actually a lot smarter than the humans. Of the four, who was still standing around near the crime scene of a disturbed individual? Not the horses.

Now Charli and Heath were stranded deep in a remote part of the ranch. With zero weapons except the ones attached to Heath's shoulders.

"Do you think whoever did that is still around?" she whispered, hand to her mouth and nose to filter the stench.

"Nah." Heath wasn't speaking at a normal volume either, contradicting his denial. "The carcasses are not fresh. Probably closing in on six or eight hours old. Someone staged that scene, probably because they knew ranch personnel use this trail."

His meaning sank in. "Wait, you think someone did this on purpose?"

"No one skins a bunch of animals and accidentally leaves them spread over a trail." To his credit, he didn't add the *duh*, but it was implied.

"This is my first skinned animal crime scene," she shot back defensively. "It's a crime, right? You can't go around doing stuff like this on people's private property."

"Trespassing. At best," he practically spat. "You might could make animal cruelty stick and possibly harassment or some other minor intimidation charges. But this is unfortunately not going to be very high on local law enforcement's radar. Not with the break-in occupying most of their brain cells."

But coupled with the break-in, this was too much to be a coincidence in her mind. "This is sabotage."

Heath lifted his hands. "What? No one even knew you were going to be out here today. Why would someone sabotage your practice trail ride?"

"I don't know, but they did. Pretty effectively too. You said yourself that someone staged the scene here because they knew people used the trail. I'm people. I own the ranch too. Why not sabotage?"

Oh, goodness. What if she'd been leading an actual group of guests? This sort of horror would stick with a person, and they would definitely put it in their Yelp review. Her stomach squelched for a wholly different reason as she instantly became a fan of the delay in opening that Sophia had forced.

"I can't stand here a second longer," she announced as breakfast threatened to make a reappearance. "I guess we're walking."

Heath nodded. "I'll send some of the rookies out here to clean this up later."

A procedure she wanted to know nothing about. But as the ranch owner, probably she should? Maybe she'd ask him later. At the moment, she was full up on the subject.

As they started back toward the house, Charli pulled out her cell phone. No bars. Not that she was surprised. Reception was spotty at best, especially this far from the house. Sophia had installed a satellite dish for internet service, but the signal didn't extend out here.

They were in for a very long walk. In boots.

"You okay?" Heath asked, his arm bumping hers companionably.

Was she? A quick inventory gave her an answer she wasn't too happy with. "I'm pretty shaky."

"Given the circumstances, that's not too bad." Without a

drop of fanfare, he slid his fingers through hers, lacing them tight as they walked. "I won't let anything happen to you."

"I'm aware," she said with a short laugh. "And I wasn't worried, for the record. It's just…a lot to process with the break-in and now this. It's like the whole universe is conspiring against me."

Not that her lack of success was anything new. If she thought about it too hard, she'd land on the conclusion that *she* was the problem. The Cowboy Experience would be fraught with issues for the whole of its existence solely because she'd touched it. After all, those animals had been carefully placed on the horse trail. The horses were *hers*.

"Don't talk about that, then," he said. "Tell me about what you did before you came to the ranch."

She shot him a sideways glance. "Small talk, McKay? Really?"

"Shh. It's a distraction."

His grin went a long way toward clearing out the squishiness inside, which left a lot of room for her to register complete awareness of the fact that they were holding hands as if they did it all the time, as if this stroll had all been planned from the get-go.

Practice. That's all this was. If she'd been his real girlfriend, he'd do something similar.

And honestly, a distraction sounded heavenly. Especially in the form of an endless conversation with the one person who made her feel like she was standing on solid ground.

"I worked at a pet store. Bird section mostly."

His eyebrows lifted. "A pet store? I expected you to say you came from corporate America. Man-eater division."

"Ha, that was Sophia." One hundred percent, designer clothes and everything. Maybe if Charli had stuck with college, she could have followed in her sister's footsteps, but Charli and school had not gotten along. "Birds paid the bills."

"Did you like it?"

"No," she responded instantly despite not ever having considered the question either way. "The birds were mean to me. They pecked my fingers any chance they got. I think they knew I wasn't really a pet person, deep in my heart. Can we find another distraction? Tell me about being in the service."

"That's not a subject for mixed company." He said it so shortly that she glanced at him. His jaw was clenched the way that usually indicated she'd vexed him in some way.

But this time, she hadn't been trying to. "I'm sorry. I didn't know it was off-limits."

His jaw relaxed a fraction. "It's not. It's just...a lot of stuff along the lines of the scene we left behind. Whatever romantic notions you might have about Special Forces, wipe them from your mind. It's bloody, thankless and soul-draining."

"Well, I'm thanking you," she announced pertly. "For your service. You did something difficult and special, and it means something."

Heath swallowed. And swallowed again. And she realized he was dealing with some emotions she had no idea how to help him through. Or that she'd desperately want to. So she just held his hand the way he'd held hers and they walked in silence.

If he could practice, so could she. And keep her mouth shut about how much she longed to feel like this for real, as if a man like Heath would always be there for her, exactly like this.

After a few minutes, he cleared his throat. "Sorry. That's a bit of a sore subject. I didn't mean to make you feel like you picked up a rock, only to find a rattlesnake under it."

"I didn't feel like that at all," she told him truthfully. "This is a safe space, Heath. No judgment. We won't speak of it again."

"The thing is," he said so carefully that she couldn't help but glance over at him. "Maybe I want to."

Chapter Eleven

This is a safe space.

The strange thing was that it felt like one. Not just because Charli had articulated it into being. He'd felt like that with her for a while now. As if he could be fully himself, no holds barred.

She certainly wasn't like any woman he'd ever met. He couldn't have come up with the name of one who would have stood in that grisly animal carcass dumping ground and kept their cool the way she had.

Margo would have screamed and thrown a hysterical fit, probably strictly for the attention and to ensure Heath spent a lot of time soothing her emotional distress. Not once would she have clued in on whether he had his own brand of emotional distress.

Charli had, though.

"I know we said no history lesson," he said, and she glanced at him, then back at the trail, which he appreciated. It was a lot harder to talk about some things than others, but she seemed to get that. Almost as if she knew that if she stared at him, he'd never get the words out.

"That was before," she said nonchalantly. "I don't know if you know this about me, but I like to break rules."

For whatever reason, that actually got a laugh out of him.

Which he also appreciated. "I feel like you deserve to understand a few things. And since this isn't a date, I don't have to worry about impressing you."

"Oh, you manage to find ways regardless," she said in a singsong voice. "I don't know any men who excel at identifying skinless animals."

If that impressed her, he really wanted to know more about the ex who had done a number on her. But he wouldn't push—that was hers to share if and when she chose to. At the moment, his most important objective was getting the fifty-ton boulder off his chest. The one that had dropped into place when she'd asked him about being in the service.

"Job hazard, I guess. I learned a lot of things they don't teach you in school while in the navy. I loved being a SEAL," he murmured. "But there's a lot of other stuff wrapped up inside that package that I haven't processed well. It's taken me a while to unpack it, especially because there are complexities."

"That has a woman written all over it," she interjected so matter-of-factly that he did a double take.

"How did you guess that?"

She shrugged, a small smile gracing her face that had a glow from their walk in the sunshine. "No one can introduce complexities like an ex."

Now his need to know about hers had risen to an epic level. He shoved that back in favor of the bigger elephant in the room. "Her name is Margo."

Oddly, voicing the name of the ghost living in his chest lifted some of the weight. As if speaking her name had loosened something inside, something he'd only just become aware of—Margo Malloy had a hold over him that wasn't entirely healthy.

And little by little, he was picking his way through the

obstacles Margo had strewn around him in all directions as far as the eye could see. Only here with Charli in this moment had he paused long enough to see the impediments for what they were—a field of land mines.

"I hate her already," Charli commented and stuck her tongue out. "She sounds exquisitely beautiful and probably speaks three languages. Does she compete in marathons too?"

Heath chuckled. "I think she speaks more like fourteen languages, but if she's ever run a day in her life, I'll keel over in shock. I don't even think she owns a pair of shoes that don't have four-inch heels."

"Oh, one of those." Nodding wisely, Charli squeezed his hand. "Is she like an interpreter or something?"

"What? Oh, you mean because she speaks so many languages. No, she's JSOC." And then Heath had to roll his eyes at himself because even now, he fell into acronyms to describe things that had been a part of his life for so long but weren't anymore. "Joint Special Operations Command. Margo is an SO intelligence analyst."

The face Charli made had him biting back another grin. Who would have thought she could get him to laugh in the midst of unloading all the crap Margo had piled up inside of him?

"Smart and beautiful. I definitely hate her."

"Jealousy might be my favorite look on you," he mused, earning a sock on the arm courtesy of Charli's non-handholding fist. "Y'all are completely different women, and trust me, that's a good thing."

She got quiet for a long minute. "Can I ask what happened with Margo?"

"Why wouldn't you be allowed to ask? I wouldn't have brought it up if I was just going to shut it all down."

They'd been walking long enough that the sun had shifted, throwing the shadows of tree branches across her face. "Because that gives you the right to ask me similar questions."

She didn't want him to. That much was clear. So he wouldn't, no matter what. "Safe space, Charli."

That's when she let her gaze slide toward his, locking in place. A wealth of things passed between them, and he found himself stroking her thumb in some kind of half-comfort, half-caress combo that felt so completely right that he couldn't fathom how he and Charli hadn't always been like this with each other. How he hadn't known instantly what *wrong* felt like—the same wrong he'd felt for so much of his life.

"Duh," she returned loftily. "Do you think I walk through scary woods possibly hiding serial animal killers with just anyone?"

Holding hands, to boot. But he didn't point that out in case she had a mind to change that part of the equation and he was not done touching her. Not by a long shot.

"Margo coordinated missions," he said, figuring it was better to get this part over with before he forgot the whole reason he'd brought up Margo. "Mine, a lot of times. We worked together. Pierce was her go-to guy since he did intelligence for our team, but we were often in the same meetings. One thing led to another and before long, I was dreaming up perfect proposal scenarios in my head. Spoiler alert. She wasn't rehearsing how to say yes."

"Ouch," was her only contribution to the conversation, a rarity. Usually, she had plenty of commentary or a smart-aleck comment. Or both.

Apparently, she was taking the safe space rules to heart. Despite the fact that they were wholly unspoken, they both seemed to know what they were. No grief. No giving each other a hard time. Not out here.

This wasn't *practice*. It was something else entirely.

"Margo hated my job," he said bluntly. "She's not a fan of violence."

Charli blinked. "Maybe she should have picked a different career. And a different boyfriend."

Yeah, the irony wasn't lost on him, but if his Trident had been her only problem, they'd still be together. "You have to understand that Spec Ops is nuanced. Sure, I did my share of cleaning out terrorist hidey-holes in godforsaken places, but a lot of warfare is strategy. That's what JSOC does. They're analyzing intercepted data. Making decisions about strike zones and drone range. Margo and her team fight our enemies from a war room. They're somewhat removed from the actual logistics."

"So?" Charli's scowl plucked at a string inside him that he didn't know was pulled so taut. "What's that got to do with the price of rice in China?"

"She didn't like that my fondness for getting physical is pretty much my default," he admitted, scrubbing at the back of his neck, which had grown hot enough to get itchy. From the sun. Probably. "Even when it's not strictly warranted."

Throwing up a hand, she waved it in a broad circle as if shooing away flies. "What in the Sam Hill is that supposed to mean? Last time I checked, you have a body that won't quit and a very good command of it. That's sexy, no two ways about it. Which part of getting physical did she have a problem with and are you sure she's smart? She doesn't sound smart."

Oh, yeah, the back of his neck was hot all right. Along with the rest of him. Charli hadn't meant all of that as a compliment—at least he didn't think so—but he *felt* complimented. And a little objectified. Which worked for him in *so* many ways.

"Not that kind of physical," he growled. Though now that the subject had been broached, he had to stop himself from the instant denial that had sprung to his lips. Because honestly, Margo hadn't appreciated his tendency to be touchy-feely. And he'd never thought about the correlation. "Okay, yeah, maybe that kind too. She mostly didn't like that I get into fights occasionally."

She'd called him a brawler at heart often enough and he knew *she* hadn't meant it as a compliment.

"Sounds like Margo needs to date one of her robot drones," Charli informed him with an animated fierceness that dug into his skin. "She picked a guy with one of the most physically demanding jobs on the planet. One who likes being in the moment, who gets a sense of satisfaction from protecting those who can't do it themselves and then tells you she doesn't like the thing that makes you who you are at your core. If I ever meet her, I'm going to punch her for you."

Heath stopped in the dead center of the trail, accidentally swinging Charli around to face him since their hands were still connected. But that was fine. He wanted to see her the way she saw him. Unlikely. Her skill at peeling back his layers was unparalleled.

"I do like being in the moment," he said, a sense of wonder coating the realization. "Do you really think about me like that? As someone who uses his fists to defend people?"

"Duh," she murmured. "Instead of stopping you, Margo the Idiot should have sat back and watched occasionally. You're like a poem in motion sometimes and it's so beautiful it hurts my chest."

She was looking at him again, the way she did sometimes,

the way that made him think she had things on her mind that were best taken behind closed doors. He liked that look on her. Liked the way she made him feel.

Except the whole point of *practicing* with Charli had been to win Margo back. That's what he should've been focusing on, not the fact that Charli had called him beautiful with that catch in her throat.

"I'm sorry Margo did that to you," she murmured. "She made you think you needed to do something different."

"Yeah," he admitted readily, grasping at the threads of the conversation. At all his reasons for why Margo's opinion counted. "I need to become someone she could see herself marrying. Because she couldn't. Said I handled myself like a hormone-hopped-up teenager who wasn't husband material, whatever that means."

"I wondered why you'd make that bet with me," she said, her expression lightening with dawning certainty. "It didn't seem like there was anything in it for you. But I get it now. That's what you wanted to practice. Being husband material for Margo."

The reminder was a bucket of cold water.

With that, Charli stepped back and pulled her hand loose. His felt strange and empty without hers in it, which shouldn't be a thing. The moment was over, if there had ever even been a moment in the first place.

She dusted off her hands and smiled, clearly of the same mind. But her smile had an edge he didn't like.

"You should have said so from the beginning," she told him brightly, almost too much so. It felt a little forced. "I had no idea we were whipping you into shape so you could strut your husband-material stuff in Margo's face. That is a challenge I can get behind in a hurry. When we're done, she'll be asking you to marry *her*."

And then Charli set off toward the house again, the intimacy between them completely broken. What was he supposed to do, tell her she was wrong? She wasn't.

This whole bet had been strictly to get Margo back. That's all he'd wanted for ages. Charli was on board with helping him get there—and she'd provided the much-needed reminder that Margo was the goal, not cozying up to Charli. What wasn't to like about this plan?

Everything. And he had no idea when that had changed.

Chapter Twelve

Charli's relationship with Heath was *practice*. It always had been. No matter how real it had started to feel.

Thankfully, he'd reminded her before she'd done something totally stupid, like kiss him.

Heath was still in love with Margo. That much had been obvious from the way he talked about her. Good. *Great.* This was perfect. One more step toward winning the bet—after all, if he spent a lot of time pining after another woman while on a date with Charli, that totally violated the whole point of the bet. It was basically over before it started if he couldn't focus on Charli for more than five minutes.

Granted, they'd have to go on a date for that to be a factor. During which, she'd be totally aware the entire time that he was thinking about Margo as he practiced being the perfect mate on Charli.

She'd give him points for the excellent distraction. Not once on the walk home had she thought about the skinned animals.

When they got back to the ranch, she had to think about them, though. Heath called a meeting that he conducted at the kitchen table and for once, she wished she could bow out. Not only was the subject terrible, Ace sat next to Sophia and Paxton took the very far end of the table, leaving Charli to sit next to Heath.

Her knee brushed his thigh as she slid onto the long bench seat that she'd never minded before, but not having her own chair meant that it was completely obvious that she'd opted to sit as far away from him as possible. He spared her a glance laden with meaning, but what was she supposed to do, sidle up to him and coo all over his manly muscles while he treated her to that megawatt smile that she'd started thinking he only gave to her?

Firming her mouth in a straight line, she stared at the table as Heath outlined what had happened, leaving out the grisly details, which she appreciated for both her sake and Sophia's. Her sister didn't need the image of all those animals in her head, the way they were in Charli's, and neither did she want to relive them.

"They were planted?" Ace asked, his tone razor-sharp.

Heath nodded once. "Very clearly. The carcasses were stacked in pyramids."

She hadn't noticed that detail. Not surprising since she'd studiously avoided looking at the scene with much care. But she had opinions none the less. "Whoever did this knew it was a trail for horseback riding. And was probably aware I was planning to do a practice trail ride today. So that means it's someone on the ranch."

Sophia looked like she'd been punched in the face. "Great. That means we only have a hundred and forty-seven suspects."

"It's okay," Ace said softly and gathered her closer with the arm he slung around her sister's waist. "This is what I'm here for. We'll handle it, Soph."

Soph. The cutesy nicknames and being there for each other with casual intimacy made Charli's eyes sting with jealousy and longing. Sure, she was happy for them, but she wanted a man to look at her the way Ace looked at Sophia. As if he *saw* her. As if he'd cut a swath through hell itself if it stood between him and her.

The way Heath talked about Margo. He was going to enormous lengths to get her back, obviously because he thought Margo was worth it.

And what did Charli have to look forward to? *Practice.*

She glanced over at Heath almost involuntarily. It was her default lately, to seek out his steady gaze, to let him settle her. Except he was already watching her, his expression hooded and stormy. Searching for something. An answer.

What did it mean that she knew exactly what he'd been trying to figure out?

Yeah, she'd been the one to put the distance between them. For a *reason*, one she didn't feel like explaining. Everything was standard operating procedure to him, and why wouldn't it be? Nothing had changed on his side.

He'd talked her into the bet for a very specific reason—to figure out how to be the man Margo wanted him to be—and Charli's job was to help him get there. *While* he treated her with the reverence and respect a man should treat a woman he planned to be in a long-term relationship with. Only Charli wasn't the actual woman he dreamed about at night.

Squaring her shoulders, she tapped on the table to get everyone's attention. "What's the next move, guys? How are you going to handle this?"

Preferably as quickly as possible. But she didn't say that. Honestly, she didn't have a lot of faith that it mattered. They still didn't know who had broken into the lab trailer and even if they caught both guys, it didn't mean nothing else bad would happen.

This ranch might as well be cursed.

And if the Cowboy Experience never got off the ground, she'd have nothing.

"We're going to report it to the police first," Ace said and nodded to Paxton. "Pierce will take point on analyzing all the video footage from the property. Our guy must have left a trail of some sort. We'll find it."

They talked logistics for another thirty minutes, complete with a warning that neither Lang sister should leave the house without an escort. Well, that's what was *said* but they really meant Charli shouldn't. Sophia wasn't the flight risk, apparently.

When the totally useless meeting ended, Charli stalked out of the kitchen, intent on a hot bath and a mindless book. But Heath caught up with her well before she hit the staircase.

"A word with you, Ms. Lang," he drawled, and she rolled her eyes at the firm hand on her elbow that told her it wasn't a request.

Back to that, were they? "I have a date, McKay, and it's not with you."

The volcano in his irises bubbled and frothed. "No dates with anyone other than me. Nonnegotiable."

Well, well, she'd struck a nerve. Looked like her plans for the evening might have changed slightly. He wanted to go a round? She cracked her neck.

This was where they'd find out what he was made of, per his own request. A husband test, so to speak, because she couldn't think of anything more on point than a knockdown drag-out fight that would prove he couldn't hang in there when a woman had righteous indignation on her side.

"Jealousy is *not* my favorite look on you," she lied with a totally straight smile while secretly reveling in the nip of his fingers against her skin. "Careful or I might get the impression you care who I go out with."

"In case it's slipped your mind, my job is to keep you from resembling one of the skinned animals we found in the woods," he shot back with an impressively saccharine tone. "That's my only priority and there is nowhere in my contract that states I have to do it while third-wheeling it with you and another man. Besides, that violates the terms of our bet."

"What in the world are you blathering on about?" she said, shoving her face in the direction of his but he hadn't gotten any shorter, so she only ended up with a nose full of Heath's woodsy-piney-clean-male scent that wafted from the V of his button-down shirt. "I never agreed I wouldn't date other men."

He showed his teeth. "You did. When you agreed to give me a fair shot. Allowing another man to romance you cannot be described in any way, shape or form as a fair shot. Look it up in the dictionary."

A fair shot? Yeah, she'd given him that. Enough of one that she forgot that it wasn't real. Enough of one that she'd fallen for his sorcery and had actually started to think they were being authentic with each other.

"Oh, I see," she sneered, one hand on her hip. "It's totally fine if you're sitting around mooning over Margo while holding hands with me, but the moment I start making eyes at someone else, that's off-limits. What was I thinking? Oh, that's right. That you're a two-timing misogynist who can't spell monogamy with three sets of Scrabble tiles."

Instead, Heath crowded into her space, his frame fairly vibrating with tension that she could feel through her thin shirt. Oh, he was in a mood. She liked it when he was in a mood, especially when it matched her own.

Let's go, McKay.

She slapped two hands on his chest to force distance between them. He was so finely crafted that she forgot for a minute that she wasn't supposed to touch the artwork and let the pads of her fingers slide into the grooves of his ribs.

That's when she made the mistake of meeting his gaze dead-on. The volcano erupted, blue flames engulfing her with heat that rippled across her skin. Oh, my, that was delicious.

"I'm not thinking about anyone but you, Charlotte," he growled, and it rumbled through her fingers. "It's not what I was expecting when I proposed this bet."

That lovely confession melted all over her, softening her ire as she stared up at him. "What were you expecting?"

"A way to make spending every waking second in each other's company tolerable." The brief flash in his gaze spoke volumes. "I may have gotten more than I bargained for."

Two for two. A man who could admit when he was wrong was dead sexy. It was enough to get her to take a step back, even as she recognized that he didn't mean he thought about her the way she thought about him.

"My date is with my bathtub and a book," she murmured but he was still close enough that she could feel the exact moment when his body released its coiled tension. "It wouldn't be entirely inaccurate to say I wasn't expecting to prefer that to going out with another man. As your punishment for assuming that's what I meant, I'll let you think about me in my bath outfit."

It was something she'd say to a boyfriend. Wasn't this practice? Two could play this game.

He made a strangled sound deep in his throat, his expression darkening. "You might have just become the proud owner of a bathing partner. What kind of bodyguard would

I be if I didn't ensure your complete and utter safety in all situations?"

Okay, practicing had just gotten a quadrillion times more interesting. And dangerous. But first—interesting. She swept him with a cool, assessing glance. "I don't believe you'd actually fit in my bathtub."

"Wanna bet?"

The laugh that got out of her felt a lot like a palate cleanser. "I'm still in the middle of the last bet you bamboozled me into."

His smile warmed her immensely. "And doing a stellar job at it too, I might add, despite the big mistake I made dragging Margo into this equation. For that, I'm sorry."

The apology was so unexpected and so sincere, it nearly buckled her knees. What was this twist? How dare he change the rules midstream. *This* was the man his ex-girlfriend thought needed a major overhaul before she'd contemplate the idea of marriage?

Nothing inside her skin felt right. When she'd started this fight, she'd expected him to career off the rails, maybe land a few of his own verbal hits. Get back to that place where they barely tolerated each other, and everything made sense. They'd always sparred pretty well with nothing more than their vocal cords and a healthy amount of chemistry. Why would this be any different?

Except it was. Because something *had* changed. What, she couldn't put her finger on, but this was not Heath conducting business as usual. This was Heath being… Heath. Solid. Unyielding, even when she pushed him. Matching her, toe to toe, giving as good as he got, and never, ever dropping the ball.

It was more than sexy. It was…something else she had no vocabulary for.

"I don't know how to have this conversation if you're going to fight dirty with the only thing guaranteed to render me speechless," she grumbled.

"And yet, you're still talking," he pointed out without a drop of irony. "But you still haven't told me what set you off in the woods. That was what I thought we'd be fighting about."

The volcano in his gaze had receded. Slightly. Actually, his eyes still burned pretty bright, but the energy didn't feel like it might lash out and burn her alive at any moment. It just felt…focused. On her. She didn't hate it.

But she did hate the question marks in his comment, and she was woman enough to admit she had played a part in the vibe going south between them.

"It's stupid. I just didn't like the idea of being your testing ground, only to have to give up my spoils to Miss Special Operations. I mean, she already won the interview question and probably the evening gown competition. Thanks to me, she's getting the husband of her dreams and all I get is the satisfaction of watching your shame sign video."

His lips quirked. "If you wanted to poke the bull, you picked the right way. That sounds a lot like you think you're winning our bet. Nothing could be further from the truth."

"Except the bet is that you'll change my mind about men," she reminded him, though why she had to was beyond her. "And here we are with another woman in the wings. The exact scenario I was expecting. Which means you lose."

Instead of immediately flaying her with his argument to the contrary, his gaze softened, drawing her in, settling around her like a soft blanket. Swallowing her whole before she could blink, wrapping her in something that felt a lot like gentleness.

That, she had no defense against.

"The difference here is that I'm being up-front with you," he murmured. "Isn't that the whole point? You're mad at men who keep secrets. Jerkoffs who tell you one thing and do another. Make you believe something that isn't true. I'm not hiding anything from you. Margo is the reason I made the bet and I've never given you one reason to think this is anything other than practice."

Oh geez. He wasn't wrong. That mean *Charli* was the other woman in this scenario.

And she had it totally backward. The more he practiced with Charli, the closer he'd come to winning. Because it wasn't real. Because the more he didn't put the moves on Charli, the more apparent it would become that he could, in fact, spend a great deal of time with another woman and not cheat on Margo.

Completely off-balance, she scowled. "You have a long way to go before you convince me you're different."

"How long? Tell me what I'm up against," he suggested with the gentleness that might be her undoing, but the point still stuck in her gut like a word spear that shouldn't hurt as much as a real one.

He'd been nothing but honest with her and she'd thus far refused to return the favor. How could she say she'd won the bet if she didn't tell him what was on the mind that he'd volunteered to change?

"His name is Toby."

"I hate him already," Heath ground out with gritted teeth in a parody of her comment about Margo, which oddly re-laxed her spine. Unexpectedly.

"Not so much fun being on the other side, is it?" she commented with a tiny smile. "I'll make it worse by telling you *her* name is Mandy. Which I know because she came on to him right in front of me. Then I had the pleasure of realizing he'd taken her up on the blatant invitation later when I walked in on them."

Heath's hands had curled into fists by his side, the white knuckles giving her an unparalleled amount of joy. This was what someone having your back looked like.

"I hope you punched her."

"I didn't, no." Though now she was thinking she should have. It might have been a form of closure that she'd thus far been denied. "I turned around and walked out. It was easier. At least until I tried to get my stuff back and he refused to open the door. He was in there too. I could hear his phone buzzing when I called it."

"Please tell me he then gathered everything up and placed it carefully in a box for you to retrieve later."

She shook her head. "I've made my peace with the fact that I'll never get my stuff. He's probably dumped it in the trash by now."

Heath's glower could have singed the paint off an iron fence and she should probably be ashamed at how giddy his rage made her, but come on. No one in her life had ever been even slightly ticked off on her behalf. Heath didn't even know Toby and she had a feeling if they happened to be in the same place at the same time, Cheater McCheaterpants would not come out the better for it.

"Get your purse," he growled. "We're going to pay Toby a visit."

Chapter Thirteen

"You know you can't actually break any of Toby's bones, right?" Charli commented from the passenger seat of Heath's truck where she was sitting way too far away from him.

"Says who?" he snarled, aware that he'd done very little actual talking since she'd confessed the details of the raw deal her ex had treated her to.

Pieces of work like Toby needed a few broken bones. It wasn't quite the same as crushing his spirit the way he'd done to Charli, but it was a close second, and it was the only pain Heath had the capacity to inflict.

"Margo, apparently," she informed him with a smirk that did not improve his mood. "And since you've appointed me as the judge, jury and executioner of your Win Back campaign, I guess me too."

The face she made distracted him from his grim determination as his flatbed ate up the miles between Gun Barrel City and Dallas, where they were headed for the reckoning she'd been denied. He would fix that for her. Possibly with a few less fists than he'd set out to use.

But not because his temper had abated even one tiny iota. Because she wasn't wrong and that pissed him off even more. "Your job is to keep an open mind about relationships and my role in one. Not tell me what to do."

Now he was snapping at her. Mostly because she was still too far away, and his fingertips ached to feel her skin against them. Just one little hit of Charli would soothe him, he was sure, but he refused to reach out. If he could power through without that fix, it meant he wasn't addicted, right?

Everything was fine. Just because he'd started craving Charli's brand of humor and her tendency to be 100 percent on his side no matter what didn't mean anything. They were spending a lot of time together. It stood to reason they'd start to appreciate things about each other.

"Beg to differ," she said mildly, not even the slightest bit cowed by his mood. "When you're on a mission to right a wrong on my behalf, the least I can do is make sure you're staying on the straight and narrow. It's what you asked for, McKay. If this was up to me, I'd pay extra to see Toby in traction."

"You're not paying me in the first place." But the sudden image of her jackhole ex in a full-body cast did cheer him up a bit. Instead of sitting here stewing in his own righteous fury, maybe he could lean into this unexpected fantasy she'd introduced. "What else would you like me to do to him? If it was up to you."

The look she shot him said she knew exactly why he'd asked. When she smiled, it was purely diabolical, and he had a very hard time tearing his gaze away from her in favor of focusing on the road to Dallas.

"Oh, I like this game," she announced with undisguised glee and clapped her hands. "You could break all his fingers. You threatened to do that to Trevor, and I have to admit it was a nice touch."

Heath lifted a brow, amused all at once. His knuckles gained some color as he eased off his grip on the steering wheel. "Trevor? That was the dig nerd's name? Precious."

"He introduced himself to me," she explained, distaste coating her tone. "Like we were at a club, and he was gracing me with his presence."

Now he wished he *had* broken all of Trevor's fingers, even though the university had kicked him off the project. Couldn't dig up many treasures if you couldn't hold a shovel, and surely he'd dialed up Daddy as quickly as he could to get a new assignment.

"What else?" Heath demanded. "And let's stick with Toby since he's the one who hasn't suffered yet."

"Well, let me think. It's not often I'm asked to get creative about how to torture someone who hurt me."

Charli shifted in her seat, angling toward him and lifting one knee onto the bench seat so that it grazed his thigh. She didn't pull away. It was a subtle move, but it was clearly not accidental, and it tore through him with unexpected fire.

Margo, Margo, Margo. It shouldn't be this hard to remember why he'd cared so much about her.

"Let your imagination run free," he insisted magnanimously, since this was all hypothetical anyway, and his mood had just mysteriously improved.

Toby might not even be home, which would be a shame. Heath wouldn't hesitate to break down the door to ensure Charli had a chance to search the entire apartment for any item she wished to retrieve—whether it originally belonged to her or not—but scaring the bejesus out of her ex would be the likely extent of his satisfaction given the warning he'd just received.

No, he couldn't punch Toby in the solar plexus like the jerk deserved. And wasn't that a kick to know that Charli had appointed herself his keeper?

"You know what would really set him off?" she mused thoughtfully. "If you kissed me in front of him."

The sudden image of doing exactly that flooded him and he had a hard time shutting off the accompanying heat for more reasons than one. But he did have enough brain cells left over to be impressed with her brutal brand of retribution, which so neatly fit the crime.

That didn't make it a good idea. "I'm not kissing you for the first time in front of Toby."

"Eliminate that as a factor, then. Pull over and kiss me now."

Heath nearly swerved off the road and it was only the steady drum of the rumble strips that jolted him into correcting course. Her smile held way too much satisfaction for his taste. Oh, she didn't even have the first clue how much he wanted to do exactly as instructed.

And how conflicted the whole thing made him.

"Let's keep thinking," he suggested darkly as she laughed.

"I'm only kidding, of course. I know your heart belongs to Margo." She waved a hand at him abracadabra style. "But it's not my fault that you have all of that going on along with a healthy side of Neanderthal. It's apparently working for me."

And it worked for him that she appreciated the full package. What was he supposed to do with all of this?

A road sign for Dallas flashed by, indicating they had another twenty minutes until the city limit, which wasn't nearly enough time to sort out the mixed messages his body was giving him. Guilt at the mention of Margo wasn't pairing well with the sizzle in his blood. Hyperawareness of Charli's knee against his thigh wasn't slowing down the sizzle any. And knowing that she'd be totally fine with it if he did rearrange Toby's face might be the best adrenaline high he'd ever had.

Scratch that. *Worst.*

It was the *worst* high. Adrenaline wasn't his friend. If he ever hoped to reel back the part of his personality that would always be the Enforcer, he had to stop enjoying it when Charli encouraged him to be himself. She wasn't the one he needed to be thinking about impressing.

But he couldn't stop himself from imagining how Charli would react if he did pull over and kiss her. That occupied him until she told him to take the next exit and soon, they'd pulled up to a nondescript beige apartment building in Richardson that refused to distinguish itself from the ninety others they'd passed on the way here.

"Far cry from a six-hundred-acre ranch and a three-story Victorian house," Charli commented, her voice flat enough for Heath to figure out that she had some emotions about this trip that she hadn't shared.

He didn't hesitate to lace their fingers together—strictly for her comfort, not because the contact skimmed through his blood quicker than lightning. "You're better off. Let's get your stuff back."

Logistically, it made sense for Charli to lead since he had no idea where they were going, but it chafed not to be the one in front. It hardly mattered. There wasn't a single thing in a hundred-mile radius that could get the drop on him, even if it had been months since he'd depended on his reflexes to keep himself and his team alive.

Some things would never change, though. As they mounted the stairs to the second-floor apartment near the parking lot, his senses cleared and the slight uptick in his pulse flooded him with crackling energy.

The fact that Charli had opted to keep their fingers laced had something to do with it too. And he didn't even mind that it had probably been for show. This arrangement benefited him as well for reasons he didn't want to spend a lot of time analyzing.

He did steal the task of announcing their presence from her, though. When Heath beat on the door, the sound reverberated through the wood with some oomph that gave Loverboy plenty of warning that answering it wasn't optional.

Unfortunately, Jackhole Toby was slightly smarter than he sounded and swung open the door, ruining Heath's plan to kick it in. He shuffled Charli behind him, just in case, but honestly, she could probably take Toby in a fair fight.

"You Toby?" he growled at the scrawny weakling who either used a ridiculous amount of sunscreen or never went outside. Plus, he had *gel* in his hair that sculpted it into a fan over his forehead. It was literally the most nauseating hairstyle Heath had ever seen.

"Yeah. Who are you?" Toby gaze shifted to Heath's hat and then swept him with an assessing glance all the way down to his boots. Which took a minute since the guy was a head shorter than him.

Then he caught sight of Charli peeking out from behind Heath's arm.

"What are you doing here?" he said with a scowl.

"No. You don't talk to her." Heath snapped his fingers in Toby's face and reversed his index finger to point at himself. "You talk to me if you decide you have something to say. Meanwhile, you're going to stand aside while Charli spends as long as she likes gathering whatever from this residence she wishes to take. Got it?"

"What is with this guy?" Toby asked Charli, completely ignoring Heath and his very patient explanation of what was about to go down. "If you want to talk, I have a few min—"

Heath pushed open the door, effectively shoving Toby out

of the way. "You listen about as well as you do relationships. Move aside and keep your filthy mouth away from Charli."

Then he crossed his arms and crowded Toby until he backed up defensively, trapping him against the wall of the entryway, which allowed Charli plenty of room to navigate behind him into the apartment. In another subtle move, she pressed her hand to Heath's back as she passed.

"It's okay. This won't take me very long," she said.

Her tone was off. The Charli he knew spit fire when she got riled and if there was ever a right time to be riled, this was it. But he hadn't imagined the warble in the last couple of syllables. Whatever it was about this situation that had made her feel vulnerable wasn't okay, and he had his guess about where to place the blame.

Heath eyed Toby, who was frowning at him as if he had a right to be annoyed or put out by this surprise visit.

"Problem?" Heath growled.

"Yeah. But it's between me and Charli. I don't know who you are—"

"The person who is going to break your face if you so much as look at her again," he informed Toby succinctly. "She doesn't owe you one second of her time. And you don't deserve a millisecond."

"Look, man, I don't know what she told you, but—"

"She didn't tell me anything. I just don't like the look of your face." Heath's fist ached to plow right into the jaw-line of Loverboy, to inflict more pain than this loser would have the ability to deal with. But he kept his arms crossed.

Because as his newly appointed Win Back campaign manager, Charli expected him to. And he didn't want to disappoint her.

He'd finally gotten his chance to stand around and look

threatening instead of being forced into using his strength to make a point. Was he really going to waste it?

Toby scratched his neck, finally looking a little uneasy. "I didn't think she'd move on so fast."

Heath didn't bother to respond to that statement when the reason for that should be perfectly obvious—that's what a woman did when she found a real man. Except she hadn't moved on, not the way Jackhole thought she had. This was all for show. And wasn't that a shame?

Charli deserved to have a man treat her well, especially after the way this one had treated her. Yet, she'd have a pretty difficult time meeting one when Heath was the only man she was spending time with.

The thought should have him stepping aside. He shouldn't care who she went out with. But when she'd told him she had a date, a red haze had filled his vision. Kind of like what was happening now.

Imagine if he actually had to watch her go on a real date. And he would have to watch. His job would still be his job, even if Charli elected to give him a taste of his own medicine and find some other guy to take her to dinner since Heath couldn't seem to find the time to do it.

More to the point, a date with Charli still wouldn't be anything other than practice. It shouldn't bother him so much.

"Where did you meet Charli?" Toby asked, as if they were having a chat in his foyer and he had every right to ask questions. "She's never been into country music. I can't believe she went to a honky-tonk."

The sneer was implied. Amusing.

"She's my boss," Heath told him just for fun.

Technically it was true, though he doubted Charli had ever thought about it that way. Neither had he, honestly, and now he had a lovely fantasy about her sitting on a desk with her legs crossed primly as she bossed him around with that smart mouth of hers.

Charli reappeared from the back of the apartment, lugging a box filled haphazardly with stuff, including a hoodie slung across the top that hid the majority of the other contents.

"Hey, that's mine," Toby protested and actually took a step toward Charli like he planned to wrestle the hoodie from her fingertips.

"You gave it to me," she insisted.

She paused near the door, releasing the box, but grabbing the hoodie protectively in a way that made Heath's stomach clench. Maybe he'd misread some of her cryptic emotions from earlier. Did she miss this guy? Seriously? Was that why she hadn't found a replacement yet?

"To wear, not to keep," Toby informed her and reached out, as if he intended to grab the hoodie in a forcible takeback.

Heath stepped between them. "She gets the hoodie. You get the waitress. Everyone wins."

Toby glared at him. "I didn't think she told you about that. You don't understand, it was a one-time thing. A mistake." Then, he actually tried to step around Heath to speak to Charli. "She meant nothing to me, I swear. I tried to call you, but—"

Heath stepped between them again, and this time, it was easier to keep his fists from clenching. This guy wasn't worth it. "Charli, go to the truck. I'll carry the box down. We're done here."

Thankfully, she did as ordered. Heath hefted the box into his arms and walked out of Loverboy's apartment, leaving him sputtering about the hoodie. The fact that he was more concerned about the sweatshirt than Charli pretty much summed up the entire altercation.

After stowing the box in the bed of the truck, Heath slid into the driver's seat. Charli was already in the passenger seat, buckled in, and uncharacteristically quiet as she sat there clutching the hoodie.

"I'm sorry," he offered since it was clear she still had big emotions seething around inside. He got it.

She glanced up at him, her gaze snapping. "For what? You're the only person in this equation who did the right thing. I should have been the one to smash a fist into his nose after he had the audacity to try to explain away his cheating."

Heath grinned. "I would have paid extra to see that."

The joke seemed to break the dam and Charli rewarded him with a watery laugh as she tossed the hoodie to the floorboard and stomped on it. "I cannot wait to get home and burn that thing."

"Oh, is that what you wanted it for?" he commented with far less glee than what was happening on the inside. What was wrong with him that he felt such a blinding sense of satisfaction that she wasn't pining over Loverboy?

"It certainly wasn't to wear," she shot back and then her eyes widened. "That's not what you thought, right?"

She smacked him in the arm, and he caught her hand, pulling her close with it until he could see the slight smattering of freckles over her nose. "Your decisions are your own. Wear it if you want to. But I would have a very hard time not ripping it off you."

Charli shuddered but he didn't mistake it for a temperature-related reaction when heat climbed through her expression simultaneously. "Well, that just sounds like a challenge."

They stared at each other as the atmosphere sizzled between them. "You're not supposed to be challenging me to get physical. It's the other way around."

"That's the thing, though, Heath," she murmured. "Everything you do makes me feel safe and protected. No one has ever stood up for me like that before. You're amazing and you did it without grinding Toby into the carpet. If you'd needed to, you would have. I trust your judgment because you know the difference between when to stand down and when you can't."

The clearest sense of awe flooded Heath's chest as Charli's lips tipped up in a small smile.

"Now I need you to trust yourself," she said.

Chapter Fourteen

Heath was waiting for Charli outside the door of her bedroom by the time she rolled out of the shower the next morning. Despite the door being closed, she knew he was there. She could feel his energy seeping through the walls. That was the problem with a man who had as much going on inside him as Heath McKay—he couldn't contain himself even if he tried.

Most of the time, she didn't mind just soaking him up. It was a guilty pleasure that she'd deny if asked. Thankfully, there was no enforcement agency questioning her motives when she allowed herself to bask in the way he made her feel. *Feminine. Heard. Understood.*

They might even be friends at this point.

Except she'd never had a friend who treated her like Heath did. Nor had she ever had a friend who set her blood on snap, crackle, pop mode with nothing more than a look.

That's why she couldn't face him today. Not after the way he'd handled Toby. Yeah, she'd heard every word of their exchange yesterday. The whole scene had settled into her bones—along with Heath. She didn't think she could dislodge him if she tried.

So that was a problem. This thing she'd developed for him, it had to go.

They called it a crush for a reason. It perfectly described what was going to happen to her sooner rather than later. Like the moment Heath realized he was already husband material times infinity.

And then he'd go back to Margo.

Miss Special Forces would take him back because of course she would. The woman had probably already cried herself dry over her idiocy at letting him go in the first place.

The broken heart in Charli's future was exactly what she'd been trying to avoid by not going out with him the first time around. The bet should have provided enough of a cushion to fall back on. But no. He had to be wonderful and strong and perfect at pretty much everything. Handling her ex had been the straw that squished the camel's heart.

How was she supposed to avoid Heath when she'd agreed to be joined at his hip? How was she supposed to stay away when all she wanted to do was throw open the door, drag him inside and start something he would never finish?

Or would he?

That was the other thing that was burning her up. If this was all practice, why did it seem like he wanted to kiss her for real sometimes? Why hadn't he taken the bait in the truck yesterday? Sure, she'd used her flirty I'm-not-really-serious voice when she'd dared him to pull over. No, she hadn't missed the way he'd said he didn't want to kiss her the *first* time in front of Toby. Like there'd be a second and third and fourth time.

There weren't going to be *any* times. She had zero desire to find out how principled he was. Because if he did kiss her, then he was even more of a dog than she'd pegged him to be. But if he didn't, she'd lose the bet. And know forever that he'd found a better woman, one he couldn't get over ever. Charli wasn't even a blip of temptation on his journey back to happily-ever-after with Margo.

It was killing her. That's why she'd slept a measly two hours last night. Why she was pacing in front of the door, glancing at the knob every forty seconds as she contemplated opening it and acting like everything was fine. Or not opening it and leaving Heath to cool his heels for a few hours while he guarded the pathway to her door, a grumbly bear who would gladly bite the head off anyone who tried to get to her.

That part might be the worst of all. It was becoming way too easy to believe he'd started to care about her the longer he defended her against all manner of evil in the world.

Before she drove herself to the brink, she grabbed her phone and pulled up a calendar. They still had two more weeks before the arbitrary deadline she and Sophia had agreed to. Two weeks to find the other jaguar head before word got out that it existed.

The university people had agreed to keep it a secret as much as they could, given that everyone involved had cell phones and social media accounts. Charli knew they'd focused almost all their dig nerds' efforts toward locating the hiding place of the other head—assuming it was also hidden somewhere on the ranch.

It was highly likely that the jaguar head was here somewhere. Charli's luck didn't work any other way.

And if she had a prayer of getting her life going, the stupid thing needed to be in that safe on its way to Fort Knox, or wherever university people kept ancient statues worth millions of dollars.

"I can hear you pacing, you know," Heath called through the door with barely concealed amusement.

"So?" she shot back. "This is my room. I'm allowed to pace if I feel like it."

"Fair. It just feels like restless pacing. Something on your mind?"

Trust Heath to correctly interpret the way she paced. She rolled her eyes. The man paid far too much attention to her, and she liked it far too much. "I have so many things on my mind I couldn't possibly describe them all to you."

"Do any of them have something to do with breakfast? I'm starving."

"I'm not hungry," she lied. "You can go on without me. I'm working on ranch plans."

That much was true. But if she didn't send him away, the temptation would still be out there in the hall, wearing jeans so worn they were practically a butter-soft second skin.

And the fact that she knew the texture of his jeans might be at least half the reason she'd had trouble sleeping. The other half could be the fact that she also knew the density of the powerful thighs encased in those jeans. The things you could catalog by firmly wedging your knee against a man's leg in a truck could not be overstated.

Heath wasn't leaving. His presence hadn't budged from the hall. "The day you're not hungry hasn't arrived. What's going on?"

This was the one time she wished he wasn't so dialed into her. Other times, it felt…nice to know that he'd started to figure out some of her tells. That was part of the problem. She enjoyed the way he paid attention to her. It was going to her head.

"Nothing," she responded brightly. "I'm just rearranging some of the stuff I got back."

Honestly, she hadn't bothered. The box of her belongings

had been meager at best. The retrieval had been largely symbolic, and instrumental in bringing about her current mood.

Because it had solidified something for her. She'd never felt like her life had really started back in Dallas. Walking back into that apartment she'd shared with Toby had rung some of her bells the wrong way.

It had never felt like her place.

This ranch? *Home.* Just not *her* home. Not yet. Making her mark with the Cowboy Experience would go a long way toward fixing that. That's why she needed to focus on figuring out how to move forward. Sophia had all of her own tasks laid out in her millions of planners. Charli had never been one for making lists, but she had a running agenda in her head. That counted.

And the first item on her mental to-do was finding that jaguar head. It could lead to clearing out the entire place of dig nerds because why would they stay after that? Even the single jaguar head was the find of the century. Once they had the other one, it was all over. They couldn't possibly justify hanging out in hopes of hitting a third jackpot. Right?

So that meant Charli had a vested interest in being the one to locate the head.

"You're still pacing," Heath called.

"You're still not eating," she pointed out. "I'm fine. Go eat."

Just to throw him off, she scampered to the box and pulled out the handful of paperbacks she'd never gotten around to reading but liked the look of on her bookshelf. It made her feel like she could be the kind of person who read for fun. Eventually. If things settled down enough and she found some downtime, she could totally be a reader.

Carefully, she placed the books on the dresser since this bedroom she'd chosen didn't have actual bookshelves.

Which was fine since she didn't have an actual library. The four slim volumes of classics fell over immediately.

"What was that?"

"A noise," she informed Heath grumpily. "One you wouldn't have heard if you'd gone to the kitchen like I told you to. My books fell over."

"You have books?"

"I can have books," she returned defensively, hoping he didn't ask her the titles because obviously he was the type who did actually read, and he'd probably read all of these multiple times. She'd fail the quiz and then he'd ask her why she didn't have bookends.

And the answer was that she'd never had bookends because she'd leaned the books up against the end of the bookcase, but she didn't have a bookcase anymore so that was a logistical issue she hadn't solved yet. The whole thing was giving her a headache and all she wanted was for Heath to leave her alone so she didn't have to spend 24/7 trying to figure out how he'd gotten under her skin.

"Do you want some help putting your stuff away?"

Oh, he'd like that, wouldn't he? An invitation into Charli's room where his Heathness would spill over into all the empty spaces, including the ones inside her, and warm up everything, reminding her how bleak and horrible it felt to be in here alone.

She hugged her abdomen with both arms, wondering if it was actually possible for a person's guts to spill out strictly from longing.

"That's okay. Thanks," she called as an afterthought.

"Now I know something is wrong," he said with an edge to his voice. "You never say thank-you."

"That's not true, I say it all the time." Didn't she?

"Not to me," he commented. "I'm starting to get a complex about it."

She rolled her eyes again. "Thank you, Heath. You're the best, Heath. I don't know what I would do without you, Heath."

"Never mind," he muttered. "I definitely didn't have a lack of your sarcasm in my life."

Now he sounded vaguely…something. She frowned. That was one thing she couldn't do with the door closed—read what was going on in his eyes. So maybe she *was* a reader. Huh.

When she flung open the door, against her better judgment, mind you, he was leaning against the wall with that loose, lazy pose that screamed exactly how comfortable in his body he was, one booted foot crossed over the other. That hat pulled down low over his face that he hadn't bothered to shave. Again. Even the scar near his collarbone screamed *too hot to handle*.

He was so delicious that her skin actually reacted, a swath of goose bumps racing across it, chasing the flush of heat that accompanied her first visual smorgasbord of the day.

Then she met his gaze and what she saw there set her back a step.

"Did I hurt your feelings?" she whispered as something flickered in his depths.

She had. She'd stumbled somehow while wallowing in her own crap.

"Men don't have feelings." His voice was oddly flat. "We have urges. Mine is usually to break something."

She suspected he hadn't meant to answer the question, but he actually had. "I'm sorry. I'm not in my right head yet. Thank you for taking me to get my stuff yesterday. It was implied, but that's not good enough for the effort. It was really amazing."

Heath's arms were still crossed but they relaxed a fraction as he tipped his head in acknowledgement.

"I'm fine," she told him. "I also appreciate that you're concerned. No one else pays enough attention to me to figure out if I'm anything, let alone not okay. Thank you for that too."

He eyed her suspiciously. "That sounds like a lead-in if I've ever heard one."

What was wrong with her that the one person who spent the most time in her company accused her of never saying thank-you and of having an ulterior motive when she did?

No wonder he preferred Margo. Charli was a hot mess who destroyed stuff simply by breathing on it. She had to do better. That's what this bet was about, after all. Practice. On both sides. If she'd never had an adult relationship before, one where each of them treated the other with respect, how could she expect to get it right unless she started figuring it out right now?

Despite knowing it would set off a chain reaction of butterflies in her stomach, she reached out and placed a hand on his arm. "No agenda. Just…thank you."

Without a lot of fanfare, he covered her hand with his. "You're welcome."

Something passed between them, and it was so light and bright that it filled her chest so fully that she couldn't breathe.

She yanked her hand free. "I'm really not hungry. Go. I'm going to finish putting my stuff away."

Thankfully, he nodded, his gaze searching hers, but he didn't seem to find whatever he was looking for. "I'll be back later to catch up with you on your plans for the day."

Since she didn't have any, other than making doubly sure she avoided Heath the rest of the day, that wouldn't take long. "Have a good breakfast."

The moment his bootsteps faded from the stairs, she bolted back into her room and slathered on some sunscreen, then changed into old clothes, shoving a baseball cap over her hair. Giant sunglasses hid her face and with any luck, she'd pass for a dig nerd if none of them looked at her too hard.

Hiking boots in hand—no reason to alert anyone to the fact that she was creeping down the stairs—she made it to the front porch without anyone seeing her. Sophia would have ratted her out in a heartbeat and Ace probably would have too, but thankfully they were nowhere to be found.

She had to get out of this house. Out of the sphere of Heath's influence before she lost her mind. She needed fresh air, stat.

Taking a horse would be too obvious, so she laced up her boots and put her legs to good use, vanishing into the trees as quickly as possible, her back on fire as she braced to be stopped with a solid hand attached to Heath's body.

Nothing happened. Somehow, she'd legit managed to give her bodyguard the slip.

Now she could breathe again. And find that jaguar head.

Chapter Fifteen

Clear air. Yes, that definitely should have topped Charli's list a lot sooner. This was her ranch, and she should be spending a lot more time on it—all of it. She'd headed in the opposite direction of the university people's camp, not that it mattered. They'd spread like ants over the entire property.

No problem. She could avoid the dig nerds if she tried hard enough.

The ranch property opened up into a number of pastures just down the hill from the new barn. Sophia had filled her in on how the old barn had collapsed, which had happened before Charli had gotten her head wrapped around the concept of being named as one of the new owners.

Inheritance. It was one of those words that you heard applied to other people. Not to yourself. It hadn't meant much to Charli at the time, for sure. Some money maybe. But Sophia hadn't wanted to sell. Veronica, their younger sister, emphatically insisted they shouldn't keep the ranch.

Charli had been caught in the middle, totally unsure which side she should pick. Story of her life. The money from the sale would have been nice, but she knew herself. It would have slipped through her fingers with little to show for it other than a new car and some expensive shoes. The rest would have gone unaccounted for.

Veronica would have used the money to do something smart like start her own business or invest it. Sophia would have stuck it in a savings account and kept on being Super Sophia at whatever corporation she'd elected to tame next. The only one who would have kept drifting was Charli.

Because she was the most like their father.

It was an ugly truth she'd always known in the part of her heart way in the back. That's why it had been so important for her to put a stake in the ground at the ranch. To make it a home. Her home.

Being out here in the midst of it—*alone*—did wonders for her state of mind. This was hers. All of it. Sure, technically she owned one third of it, but there wasn't a way to divide it up like a pie chart. She liked to think of it as all three of them owning the entire ranch. As if their shares sat on top of each other instead of side by side.

This was what she'd expected to feel during the horseback ride. A sense of pride. Ownership. *That's my tree. This stretch of grass? Mine. That fence post belongs to me.*

Instead, she'd spent the entire day engrossed in her riding companion, even after they'd found the animals. That's what Heath did to her—took her brain hostage—and if she was being honest, he commanded the attention of most of the rest of her too.

That's why this break from him had been so sorely needed. She could think about important ranch things and forget about Heath. He certainly didn't think about her when he wasn't in her presence. All his mental energy went toward Margo.

This part of the ranch contained remarkably few people. Most of the nerds had focused their dig sites in the woods, which stretched along the east side of the property. That's where the creek ran, but you had to know where to look for it. She remembered that from the few times she'd visited her grandparents. It was a bit of an inside joke for Sophia to have named the place Hidden Creek Ranch, but Charli appreciated it.

Since she'd wanted to avoid the university people, she'd veered toward the pastureland. Plus, if the dig nerds spent all their time in the woods, odds were high they'd find the jaguar head...or they wouldn't because it wasn't hidden there. No reason for Charli to duplicate their efforts.

No one was in this far-south pasture. Jonas, the ranch manager, kept the horses closer to the house in deference to all the treasure hunt activity. It was more work to feed them, but it eliminated a lot of hassle and prevented the university people spooking them. Which just proved the urgency of finding the female head—the sooner they got these extra people out of here, the sooner the ranch could return to normal. And the sooner they could get the Cowboy Experience up and running.

And finally, Charli would have a place to belong.

No more Tobys. No more pet stores with the pecky birds. No more running from real life, her default. *That* was the inheritance she'd gotten from David Lang. That was what she was up against—the DNA her father had infused into her blood. She could consciously put that behind her and *belong*.

Charli's boots crunched through the tall grass as she trudged across the neglected pastureland. A slight breeze blew against the long grasses, rifling through the split ends for acres upon acres. It would take forever to search every square inch, especially without tools, which she'd forgotten about in her haste to give Heath the slip.

Well, this wasn't wasted effort. She could still enjoy the breeze and feeling her own earth beneath her feet.

The breeze picked up, flattening the grass and then releasing it to gently bob. There was one place where the grass seemed shorter, as if it had been trampled or mowed recently. Except that would be really weird, considering the horses hadn't been in this area for weeks.

Curiosity piqued, Charli set off for the cleared-out area because, why not investigate? As she got closer, she could see the outline of a circular something, overgrown with weeds and vines.

She pulled one of the vines away and saw that it clung to stone covered in moss. What was this, some kind of grave marker? She knelt down, wishing she'd worn gloves, and yanked another vine free, a long one that curled over the top of the circle. A lizard darted away from her hand, and she yelped, jumping a solid four inches.

Oh, thank god. One of the little green ones. Those she didn't mind but there were probably other ones—and maybe snakes too—that she did not want to come across.

She shuddered. Well, too late to worry about that now. If she cared about snakes, traipsing around in a big field full of things they liked to eat was not the way to avoid them.

Another yank and she had partially uncovered the circle. It was a hole in the ground ringed by stones, so deep that she couldn't see the bottom. A well. Right? What else would be out here in a pasture meant to hold animals who would need to drink a lot of water?

More to the point, it was a deep hole in the ground that would be a great hiding place for stuff. Like a gold jaguar head worth a lot of money. Best of all, probably no one else had found it yet since it was out here in the middle of a field the university teams cared nothing about.

Enthused by her find, Charli leaned closer to inspect the well. The ancient stones creaked beneath her weight. Wow, this thing might be older than she'd first assumed. She shone her phone's flashlight down into the darkness, cursing her lack of foresight in bringing a real flashlight.

There were still a few stupid vines stretching over the opening, casting too many shadows. She pulled at a couple with her left hand. The earth shifted and she lost her balance. And her grip on her phone, which tumbled into the hole.

That had *not* just happened. Charli cursed.

Her phone's flashlight was still shining, and she hadn't heard a splash. That was a good sign, right? But geez, it was so far down the hole. She could barely see it, even if she angled herself right over the opening.

The stones of the well's edge crumbled under her weight. With a *crack*, the whole edge collapsed. Flailing, she grasped at thin air as she fell into darkness.

The fall was quick and brutal. Her wrist absorbed most of the impact, sending a searing pain through her arm. Her hip glanced against something hard. Maybe her phone. Or the well floor.

Her lungs on fire, she struggled to catch her breath, heaving great gasps of air. The opening above her let in a bit of light but not nearly enough. Given her luck, she'd landed on her phone and killed it, which had also effectively eliminated her one light source.

It was dark. She was in a hole. No one knew where she was. She was *so* screwed.

Panic edged in faster than she could check it. A scream clawed its way out of her throat, which did zero good and got the rest of her body in on the panic. She started to shake as pain forked up her arm, sharp and agonizing.

Okay, this was probably the worst thing that had ever happened to her, but just like anything else, there was no one to rescue her. She had to figure this out on her own. What would Black Widow Hurricane do?

Climb.

Sucking back the panic, she crawled to her hands and knees, whimpering as she accidentally put some weight on her wrist.

So that was a problem. Broken probably.

Well, she'd just have to use it anyway. This well wasn't going to lift her out via a magic carpet. She felt around for some crevices in the well wall. It seemed to be made of the same stone as the part above ground. If her arm didn't hurt so badly, she might have a second to appreciate the construction quality of this well. How had they gotten the stones all the way down here?

And where was all the water? Had this well dried up at some point—or was it not a well at all?

Honestly, she didn't care enough to spend a second more of her precious brain power wondering about the creation and maintenance of whatever this hole in the ground was. Tentatively, she reached up to search for a niche or a ledge to hoist herself up, the fingers of her good hand scrabbling for purchase. Finally she got a solid enough grip to try to pull.

Okay, good. This was working. She levered herself up, slamming her feet into tiny cracks between stones, gasping as one boot slipped off the weatherworn stone. Barely managing to avoid sliding back to the floor, she froze, locking her fingers in place.

Somehow, she kept her position. But she had to *move*.

Now came the hard part. She stretched her left hand high, wincing as pain radiated from her wrist, but she didn't have the luxury of being a baby about this. Her fingertips found the next ledge about a foot higher than the stone she clung to with her right hand.

The second she put her weight on her injured wrist, a lightning bolt sailed down her arm and lit up her entire body with agony. It was so bad that she lost her grip and fell back to the floor in a heap, a torrent of angry tears cascading into the dirt beneath her cheek.

She felt sorry for herself for exactly thirty seconds, during which she cursed Heath for not realizing she'd given him the slip and then following her on this ill-advised adventure, Sophia for telling the university people they could look for more Maya crap, and David Lang for giving her not only a tendency to drift but a healthy amount of curiosity and zero fear.

Except for right this minute. She had a lot of fear. It was suffocating her.

But she couldn't give up. Something was poking her hip and that needed to stop. She felt around and her fingers slid over a smooth flat object. Her phone. She nipped her fingertips around the edges and when she tilted it, the screen lit up. Glory be. She'd been sure she'd smashed it in the fall. Somehow, she'd managed to switch off the flashlight with her hip. Bet she'd never be able to do that twice.

No bars. Not that she'd thought for a second cell service would pop up on the screen. She'd had to check, though. At least she had light for as long as the battery lasted. This was a positive. *Focus on that.*

Rolling—carefully—she sat up and fumbled with her phone, shining it around the bottom of the well. Or whatever it was. Because it didn't really seem like it had ever held water. Wouldn't it have mold or something along the edges? And it was kind of wider at the bottom, like a…cave. Sort of similar to the ones closer to Austin in the Hill Country, where the water table had carved out the limestone.

She ran the light along the edges until she couldn't swivel

any further, then scooched around until she could sweep behind her. Oh, man. There was a wide passageway from the main area, which would have been super handy if it had still been another exit point, but it looked like it had caved in on itself several feet back.

And there was something over there. A few piles of what looked like old fabric.

Charli blinked and held the phone up higher. Had someone used this area for storage at one point? That seemed so unlikely. Wouldn't it have flooded when it rained?

But if there used to be a different entrance, anything might be possible.

She climbed to her feet, wincing as her abused body let her know that she'd fallen twice in the last few minutes, and limped toward the piles. She nudged the one closest to her with her foot, expecting the fabric to disintegrate, but whatever was under it was pretty solid.

Kneeling gingerly, she used her good hand to pull on the fabric, but it was wrapped tight. One good push up allowed her to free the dusty covering, which reminded her of the stuff that covered patio chairs with the rough texture, and then the wrapping came loose.

She yanked it free and gasped. Never, never again could she claim she had anything but pure, blind dumb luck because holy ancient Maya gods, she held the other jaguar head.

The statue gleamed in the light from her phone, unmistakable even though she hadn't studied the other one at length. This one had the same burnish to it, as if it needed to be polished, the black markings of the jaguar's spots fading into the gold along the edges. The flat, black eyes stared at her.

This one, which surely was the female, had a similar

round, collar-type thing ringing the base of the head, like the other one. That's what the statue stood on and the collar was covered in what looked almost like cartoons, but she was pretty sure it was the Mayan language, which kind of resembled Egyptian hieroglyphs but not really.

Oh, man. She definitely couldn't climb out of here with *that* tucked under her arm, even if she felt stronger in an hour or so. Which wasn't likely with no food and water.

Okay, think. Could she dig out where the tunnel had collapsed? She stumbled over to the giant pile of dirt, rock and a few tree branches, but she couldn't budge even the very top layer.

Frustrated, she stepped back and kicked one of the other piles of fabric, the ones she had forgotten about instantly. Boy, she was some kind of adventurer. What if she'd hit the mother lode of Maya treasure and all she could think about was escape? Wasn't there some saying about one jaguar head in the hand meant there were two more in the bush?

She poked at the pile of fabric, but this one wasn't solid like the other one. Plus, it was a lot longer and thinner. Running her light up the length, she got a funny squiggle in her gut that the pile of fabric looked like…pants. That led to a shirt. And a face. Or what was left of it.

Not a Maya treasure. But a body. A dead one. And she was trapped with it.

Chapter Sixteen

Heath shoved his hat back further on his head and jammed his finger in the direction of the pastures.

"Spread out," he barked. They'd been messing around in the woods too long and had almost lost the light. "Do not miss a single inch of ground. You shoot a flare if you find so much as a piece of thread that might be from Charli's clothes. Got it?"

The group of dig nerds nodded solemnly, and the leader held up his flare gun, the one Heath had painstakingly showed him how to use. Meanwhile, he was counting down the seconds with his thundering pulse because it was yet another delay in getting to Charli.

The woman was going to kill him. Only fair. He was pretty sure he was going to return the favor. As soon as they found her. *Assuming* they found her, which given their lack of success over the last eight hours wasn't a given.

"Move," he instructed the dig nerd team, who'd volunteered to take the front section of pastureland. They meekly complied, trotting off like a herd of lazy buffalo.

Heath, Pierce and Madden were leading a second team including Sophia and a few of the ranch hands. Their objective: combing the back section of pasture along with the dogs, where they obviously should have started instead of wasting time in the woods. The dogs strained on their leashes, and Jonas spoke to them in the same soothing voice he would use with a spooked horse. They were itching to get going and so was Heath.

Pierce settled a hand on Heath's shoulder, his expression calm. "We're going to find her."

If only faith worked in these situations. Heath bit back a testy reply because they'd all been at this for eons already. He wasn't the only one who was hot, tired and terrified. Sophia hadn't stopped pacing on the porch, even though she'd personally walked the entire front half of the fence line with Madden earlier this morning. This was after she'd called every single person she could think of who knew Charli or had spoken to her recently.

Nada. Just like everything else they'd tried. Charli was missing. Like, full tilt, dropped off the face of the earth, no note, car in the half-circle driveway, purse and wallet still in her room, missing. Just…gone.

He'd do a repeat call to everyone in the county if he could do that and ride a horse at the same time, but so far, he'd been wildly unsuccessful dialing while at a full gallop.

Madden crossed the yard and shoved a sandwich into Heath's hand, obviously sensing it was the opportune moment since this was the first time in over eight hours that he'd been in the same spot for more than five minutes.

"Passing out from lack of protein isn't going to help anyone, McKay, least of all you," Madden murmured and jerked his head. "Sophia called her mom. She's on the way."

Oh, God. If Sophia had finally given in and called Mrs. Lang, that meant she didn't have a lot of hope for a positive outcome. Well, he wasn't giving up. Period. Guess he hadn't lost his blind faith after all.

After all, Heath had extracted a high-profile Taliban prisoner from a compound hidden in the extensive cave system of the Spin Ghar Mountains. In the dark. He could find Charli.

He'd been standing here immobile during their regroup session for too long, that was the problem. It made his mind spiral, worrying that she'd been kidnapped by one of the unsavory characters lurking in the shadows of this long-drawn-out assignment.

And that was the rub, right? He had no clue who he was up against, if so.

What if they'd taken her somewhere off the ranch? He'd never find her. And he was way past the point where he'd deny caring if asked. This went beyond an assignment, and it wouldn't surprise him if everyone had guessed that already. Madden and Pierce had wisely kept their cracks about it to themselves, which he appreciated, because he did not want to break his vow of nonviolence by knocking out the teeth of one of his friends.

But that didn't mean he planned to spend a lot of time examining the curl of panic in his gut or why it was making his throat hurt. Why everything inside screamed at him to move, to find her. What if she was hurt? What if she was lost? She needed him and he was failing her.

Plus, this whole situation had smacked him in the face with the fact that he needed her too.

Sophia paused midwhirl and buried her head in her hands, scrubbing at her eyes. "If she just took off for a spa day and didn't bother telling anyone, I'm going to disown her."

"She didn't just take off," Heath said for the millionth time. The worst part was that he almost wished she had. That would be better than the alternative. "If she had, she'd be back by now. Or she'd have called."

Anyone with a cell phone had been tasked with trying

to call her but she never picked up. So that eliminated any possibility that she was ducking Heath or Sophia's calls. They'd even tried getting Veronica to call her. She had nothing to do with the ranch, so even if Charli had descended into some sort of temper tantrum over Heath's method of personal security, she wouldn't have suspected her younger sister of wanting to locate her.

And honestly, Charli had stopped causing him problems a while back. They'd been on the same page lately. She wouldn't do this to him deliberately.

This was a bad situation. He could feel it in his gut. And it was getting worse. Statistically speaking, the odds of finding Charli went down exponentially with each hour that ticked by.

They'd crisscrossed the woods twice already, working in teams since he couldn't physically search an entire six-hundred-acre ranch himself, not in a few hours. If something didn't break soon, he had a feeling he would be personally going over every inch with a flashlight before too long.

Shoving the last of his sandwich into his mouth, he chewed and swallowed, wordlessly taking the bottled water Pierce had pressed into his hand. He checked his walkie-talkie—again—as the others did the same.

"Let's go," Madden said and led the charge, but only because Heath's knees had gone a little weak. From lack of food combined with physical exertion. Probably.

Was it worse to admit he was out of practice at executing an operation with stone-cold reflexes or that the mission itself had personal undertones that were messing him up?

Stalking ahead, he ignored everything but the terrain beneath his feet.

They were walking this time, at Heath's insistence. He'd been so sure they'd find Charli in the woods and in his arrogance, he'd also made the wrong call of being on horse-back. Better to cover a lot of ground, in his mind. Wrong. They'd do this section on foot and that's what was going to make a difference. It had to.

"Cut the dogs loose," he instructed Jonas, who had maneuvered the hounds to the search party's twelve o'clock position.

Another necessary shift in strategy that he'd felt in his gut. Jonas unsnapped the leashes, still stone-faced as always.

Madden glanced at Heath as Pierce caught up to them both, but it was a testament to their partnership that neither of them questioned his directive. These guys had his back no matter what. It was nice.

Shrugging, Heath kept his gaze on the ground, scanning for visual clues as he explained anyway. "We tried following the dogs in the woods, hoping they would lead us to her. That didn't work. We don't have time for that now."

The sun had started to set. Charli had been missing since nine twenty this morning, when he'd realized she wasn't refusing to answer the door for some mysterious reason, but because she wasn't actually in her room. After an hour of assuming she'd reappear, he'd known in his soul that she was in trouble.

The dogs seemed to sense that they were the stars of the show, eagerly pushing their noses along the ground despite not being trained bloodhounds. Putting his faith in them might be another problem, but Heath had few options.

If this had been Afghanistan, he'd have military-grade equipment at his disposal, complete with infrared scanners, drones and night vision goggles. In East Texas, he had his eyes, his brain and some dogs Charli petted occasionally.

The breeze from the north fluttered the split-seeded tips of the overgrowth in this pasture. Another problem. Under normal ranch operations, Jonas would be rotating the horses through these pastures, which would have naturally mowed down the grasses as they grazed.

Instead, the search party got to contend with acres and acres of tall foliage that would easily hide a small woman who might be passed out cold from who knew what.

Heath bit back an order to hurry. The dogs needed to be thorough, not rushed.

As he scanned the field to the left, the breeze ruffled the grass differently in one particular section. He shaded his eyes against the glow of the setting sun. It definitely looked like the grass was flattened in that area in comparison to the rest.

It might be Charli.

Without a word, he shifted his trajectory to head in that direction. Pierce automatically split off from the group and followed him. Madden stayed on the group's course with Sophia, but he'd redirect everyone in a heartbeat if Heath called him on his walkie-talkie.

The flat grass area was a hole in the ground. An old well by the looks of it, but the stones around the edges were crumbled in on the edges closest to the center. It looked fresh.

"Charli?" he called, and his heart stumbled as he heard scrabbling inside.

"I'm here."

The sound of her voice emanating from the hole unleashed a slew of sensations that swept through Heath's body and not one of them he could name. Except mad. That he knew he was plenty of.

"Why don't you climb out now," he instructed as calmly as he could, given the adrenaline levels currently flooding his veins. "I'll grab you when you get close to the top."

"As fine an idea as that is, McKay, don't you think I would have already done that if I could?" she shot back with far less sarcasm than he would have expected.

She sounded so weak. It was alarming. "Is the shaft blocked or something?"

After a long pause, he heard her response drift up to him. "I broke my wrist when I fell. I can't put any weight on it."

"Call the others," he instructed Pierce over his shoulder. "Have them bring a rope."

Then he wasted no more time, slinging a leg over the edge of the hole. He couldn't wait for proper gear, not if Charli was hurt. If he'd known he would be descending into the pits of hell with nothing more than his best ninja skills, he'd have worn something other than cowboy boots, but he'd done worse in far more desperate circumstances.

Never with someone he cared about deep in a hole in the ground, though.

Calf muscles screaming, he braced both legs against the outer walls, pushing out to keep from sliding. Gymnast he was not, but he could brute-force his way down in a controlled descent with the best of them. As he shimmied down the stones one agonizing inch at a time, the flashlight and walkie-talkie clipped to his belt loops slapped his hips with each jerky movement.

That was going to leave a mark.

"Are you practicing to be Spider-Man for Halloween?" Charli called up the shaft wryly. "Because you're nailing it."

His chest heaved from the exertion. Man, he was out of shape. Something like this wouldn't have even winded him a year ago. "If you want to be rescued, save the small talk."

Finally, he hit the dirt floor and shook out his aching biceps, then resituated his hat, which he hadn't lost in the descent, so he'd count that as a plus. It was pretty dark down in the depths, but he could sense Charli just off to the right. His fingers yearned to reach out, just to assure himself she was safe. The rest of him just wanted to fold her into his embrace and never let go.

He crossed his arms. "Not the locale I would have picked for a date."

"Good thing this isn't a date. How did you find me?"

Heath switched on the flashlight. The glow lit up her face, highlighting the smears of dirt across her cheeks. She had a twig in her hair, and she cradled her right wrist against her body. The sight of Charli injured put him in a dangerous mood.

"Well, it was simple really. I read the note you left and decided to let you suffer for your sins, then went to a bar to live it up since you so magnanimously gave me the day off." The edge in his voice echoed off the worn, dingy stone surrounding them. "How do you think I found you? I kept looking until I did. Eight hours we've been at this, Charli. Everyone. The entire ranch. Your mom says hi, by the way."

Charli's mouth tightened. "I didn't ask you to come after me. I didn't leave a note for specifically that reason."

His laugh sounded as forced as it felt. "You're so welcome, Charli. I'm glad you appreciate the effort. No, no, I refuse to leave you here despite your very compelling arguments to the contrary."

"Don't be a jerk," she returned and shifted her arm, wincing.

"Let me look at that."

The mulish look she shot him didn't do his mood any favors, but he wasn't here to make friends. Setting the flashlight down, he pulled her closer by the shoulders and took her hand, gently turning the wrist over. When she cried out, his stomach clenched.

"Yeah, it's broken," he said gruffly.

"Thanks, Sherlock, I am thrilled to hear expert medical opinion comes along with your manly muscles. Whatever would I have done without you?"

Her exhausted expression pulled at some other parts of his chest that he'd rather remain unaffected, but that ship had sailed a long time ago. He sighed.

"Let's not do this, okay?"

"Do what? Practice being a couple?" she practically sneered. "Guess what? The bet was your idea, and this is what people in a relationship do. Fight. Especially when one of them is being horrible to the other one."

Heath checked his eye roll because yeah. She wasn't wrong. "I'm tired. It's been a long day."

"Back atcha," she said with one hip jutted out like a supermodel on the catwalk with plenty of lip and attitude that convicted him for that crappy non-apology. "You didn't ask, so I have zero motivation to tell you, but we're not alone down here."

Instantly, his spine stiffened, and he hustled her behind him, his feet spread and arms poised to take apart any threat that tried to get to her. They'd have to come through him and hope he let whoever had threatened her keep their limbs attached.

"Relax, Rambo," she huffed on a half laugh, half snort. "It's of the not-currently-alive variety. And I don't mind telling you that being stuck down here with a corpse has scarred me for life."

"A…did you say a corpse?" Heath swept the well area beyond where he stood with Charli and saw the body in question that was decaying enough to have him cover his mouth with his shirt.

"You get used to it," Charli commented with a wrinkled nose. "But that pales in comparison to what else I found."

She pulled something shiny out from under a tarp and he blinked. "Is that the other jaguar head?"

Dumb question. It matched the first almost exactly and what else would anyone expect to find in the hiding place of a five-million-dollar statue but a dead body—which he'd lay odds had not ended up that way accidentally. But why kill whoever the unfortunate soul was, only to leave the ancient statue behind?

"The one and only." Her grin came out as a half grimace. "I quit feeling lucky about three hours ago when I started accepting the fact that there would be two corpses in here before too long. I…well, I had a lot of time to reflect on how dumb it was to ditch you. I shouldn't have. If you promise not to look at me while I do it, I'm going to admit I was wrong and say I'm sorry."

The catch in her voice undid him. Flat unwound everything that held his heart, his lungs—his soul—together, all of it uncoiling in the depths of his stomach. He muttered a curse and yanked her into his arms, tucking her deep into the place that she'd just emptied out.

Charli snuffled against his shirt, her bad arm hanging at her side, but the other one clung to his waist and she felt like heaven against his body.

"I'm sorry too," he murmured into her hair as she filled him up again to the brim, with heat and light and pure bliss. Whatever he'd been furious about blew away in an instant and he forgot everything but this woman, here, now. "You scared me."

"I'm sorry," she whispered again against his shirt and repeated it mournfully. "All I could think about was you. That I'd never see you again and how mad you must be. I thought I was going to die and the last memory you'd have of me is how crappy a practice girlfriend I am."

"This is not practice, Charlotte," he growled. "Safe space. Take a time-out for a minute."

Just as she drew back, her gaze searching his, a rope hit the ground behind him. He looked up to see a dark head leaning over the edge of the well.

"You guys ready to get out of there?" Pierce called.

Chapter Seventeen

Charli's brand-new cast sucked. All she wanted to do was sleep when they finally got home from the emergency clinic in Gun Barrel City, but the skin under the plaster itched and everything hurt. Especially her throat. From holding back the screams, most likely.

Predictably, Heath followed her up the stairs to her room, his hand at the small of her back like he was afraid she might pitch backward down the stairs if he wasn't there to catch her.

Well, that made two of them afraid of that, dang it. She had plenty of other things to worry about too, like blubbering gratitude for his heroic efforts to make sure she didn't die. And maybe some other stupid feelings churning around in the mix that felt an awful lot like fodder for losing the bet.

He *was* different. He'd proven that over and over again. What he was not? *Hers.* The time-out at the bottom of the well notwithstanding.

Whatever that had been about. A time-out from what? The bet? Practicing? That wasn't a thing, not in her world.

Heath paused at her door, dropping his hand. "Want me to help you get ready for bed?"

"You'd like that, wouldn't you?" she said with a smirk, desperate to get back to a place where she understood the dynamic between them. Understood why her chest hurt when she looked at him.

"Yeah, a woman with a broken arm is my kind of hot date," he muttered, his eyes on the ceiling in what looked like a not-so-veiled attempt to keep his temper in check. "But sure, try to take your clothes off with one arm. I'll wait."

"I can call Sophia."

"The same sister who walked all over half this ranch today and is currently about to slide into a bubble bath drawn by her equally exhausted boyfriend?" Heath crossed his arms and leaned on the doorjamb. "That sister?"

Yeah, she hadn't thought that through. She sighed.

The man would not stop showing up for her and she was sick and tired of pushing back the tendrils he'd snaked around her heart. Especially when he said confusing things like *this is not practice*.

Was he saying it didn't feel like practice because she'd messed it up or because he'd truly been worried about her? As a friend. Right? And why didn't she know? Because she didn't want to ask. Didn't want to have it clarified so she knew for sure it had been a friendly hug that had felt anything but.

As soon as his partners had lifted them out of the hole via the sturdy rope they'd thrown down, Heath had driven her into town to have her wrist checked out with Sophia and Ace in tow. Sophia because she'd refused to let Charli out of her sight and Ace because he'd refused to let Sophia out of his. Heath had stayed glued to her side because he was Heath.

Paxton had stayed behind to call in the body they'd found, then planned to assist the local police with securing the scene. No one knew about the jaguar head except the five of them, per Sophia's directive. Which Charli appreciated.

Tomorrow morning, they'd figure out how to manage what would surely become a forty-seven-ring circus combined with a petting zoo and a rave once word got out that they'd located the second head.

There better not be any jaguar babies or extended family statues out there somewhere or she'd punch something.

"I'm running on fumes, McKay," she said as it all hit her like a ton of bricks. "I can't do this now. Please just let me be for tonight and I promise, tomorrow you can go back to being your domineering, confounding, hotter than asphalt self and I'll be in a much better place to take you down a few pegs. Deal?"

Heath nodded once, though his expression could give a mule a run for its money. He didn't argue thankfully, and it felt like a small win as she shut the door in his face. Until she tried to wrench her shirt off with her good hand and wound up smacking herself in the face.

Cursing, she eased off her hiking boots and jeans, which went easier, then padded into the en suite bathroom. Dear God, was that her face? It was practically unrecognizable under a layer of dust and some black streaks of who knew what. Bat poop probably.

It took four million years to scrub her face clean with one hand, only to find some of the black was bruising—nice—and another four to get a brush through the bird's nest on top of her head. An actual twig fell out, so that was lovely.

Exhausted all over again, she opted to get into bed with her shirt still on. She could surely wash sheets with one hand after she'd slept for twelve hours. But her brain would not shut off long enough to sleep. For one, she was still filthy, and she had a hard time not thinking about what kind of ick she might be spreading around in her bed.

She eased off the mattress and trudged back into the

bathroom to wet a washcloth, then ran it all over her body, only to realize as she collapsed back into bed that she'd just splatted right in the middle of the dirt she'd transferred there earlier.

Another futile struggle with her shirt later, she sank to the floor and slumped against the wooded rail of her bed frame, cradling her cast. Angry tears pricked at her eyelids. For what? Because she was in pain, emotionally overwhelmed, and weak from not eating but not hungry enough to actually put something in her stomach.

And her throat still hurt.

Maybe a glass of water would help. She stumbled to the door and flung it open, nearly tripping over the cowboy spread out on the wooden floor of the hall with his back to the doorframe, which had to be uncomfortable.

"What are you doing out here?" she grumbled, annoyed that her McKay-dar seemed to be busted. How had she not realized he'd made himself at home outside her door?

He rolled and climbed to his feet with a grace that shouldn't seem so effortless on a body with so much bulk. Even bootless, Heath towered over her, his hair adorably rumpled and untamed without his hat. Good gravy. This version of him might be even more delicious than the put-together one.

"Dancing the cha-cha, obviously." His voice sounded like he'd gargled gravel and the lines of exhaustion around his eyes aged him instantly.

Nope, no feeling sorry for him. She clamped down on the wash of emotions, especially the tender ones. Coupled with the precarious vibe between them, she had no choice but to go on the defensive until she knew how to manage the things zinging around in her heart. Preferably without giving him an advantage that would crush her, at least until she understood what he meant by *this isn't practice*.

"I wasn't going to ditch you again," she told him. "At least not tonight."

Heath's gaze flickered. "That wasn't my concern."

It took her a second to figure out what he meant. Because they'd found a body. And a jaguar head. He'd been worried about someone trying to get to her in the middle of the night, and instead of scaring her, he'd elected to forgo his own comfortable bed.

Her heart stopped zinging and started tumbling.

"I didn't ask you to do this. I can take care of myself," she returned hotly.

"Yeah, I can see that," he said without a drop of irony as he eyed her dirt-streaked shirt. "Meanwhile, I'll sleep better knowing that you're inside your room, safe and sound."

Sleep better on the floor? Sure. The warmth of his stupid self-righteous hero complex would definitely lull him into a peaceful slumber. "This is not one of those times I'm going to say thank-you."

"I wasn't confused."

Her eyelids fluttered shut. Could he be any more unflappable at midnight? Or anytime? They were standing in a semi-dark hallway, the house hushed for the night, and all she could think about was this man spider-crawling his way down a well shaft to get to her. There was no reason for him to have done that. He could have told her to hang on while he went to fetch the rope or waited for the others to get it, then lowered himself down.

But he hadn't.

She ached to ask why. She wanted to hear him confess that hearing her voice after spending a very long stretch of time convinced he never would again had opened up a place inside him that he'd had no clue existed. That's what had happened to her. She'd basically given up hope and then her name had floated down from heaven on the lips of Heath McKay and everything had shifted.

And she'd thought her feelings for him had been jumbled *before* she'd fallen into the well. Add the ghost of Margo into the mix and she had no clue how to be in her own skin.

The angry tears resurfaced. One splashed down on her cheek and she swiped it away, but not before Heath noticed. His expression caved and he muttered an expletive, drawing her into his arms without explanation. Since that was exactly where she wanted to be, why would she argue?

"Don't cry, slugger," he murmured into her hair, which quite frankly might be her favorite way for him to speak to her. "Let's reel it all back for a while and just…"

"Stop practicing?" she suggested as he walked her into her bedroom, leaving it open.

"I was going to say sleep."

Apparently, only he could call a time-out. She clamped her mouth shut as Heath gently spun her around and peeled her shirt from her sore body. It wasn't the slightest bit sexual. It was worse. Tender and intimate, as if they'd done this so many times that the ritual had become as familiar as her own skin.

With only two false starts, Heath found the drawer in her dresser with the oversize T-shirts she slept in and expertly drew one over her head, settling it on her shoulders as he threaded her arms through the holes. Who knew a man *dressing* you could be so…actually she had no idea what this feeling was.

Wordlessly, Heath led her to the bed, settling her into the correct side of the mattress without asking because of course he would be observant like that, then nodded once.

"I'll be in the hall if you need anything."

She needed *him*. How pathetic was that, to yearn for a man she couldn't have? "You can't sleep on the floor. It's ridiculously uncomfortable."

Hands shoved in his back pockets, he shrugged. "I've done worse."

"Not after spending all day searching for me without stopping," she correctly him crossly. "Get in the bed and don't argue with me. It's big enough for two adults who have a tenuous friendship and one of them is in love with someone else besides."

He hesitated long enough that she almost called his name, worried that bringing Margo into the mix had been a mistake. But she'd wanted him to know that she got it. He'd never pick Charli. It was fine.

"I won't maul you in your sleep," she said, the scowl on face hurting the bruised places. "And think how much better you'll be able to take out an intruder if you're well rested."

That seemed to be the deciding factor since he shed his clothes without a word and slid beneath the covers.

Oh, my. When she'd offered, she'd sort of expected him to stay dressed. Every drop of moisture fled her mouth. She lay there, senses on such full alert, so painfully aware of Heath that her teeth hurt.

She'd promised not to maul him in his sleep, but she'd never said a word about what she might do while he was awake. All that Heath-ness was right there in touching distance, and she wanted to reach out more than she wanted to breathe. But she wanted to be shut down far less.

Plus, she wasn't that woman. His heart belonged to someone else. She could not in good conscience go after a man who was committed. Even as a part of her knew deep down that she didn't have a prayer of dislodging Margo in the first place.

"The sound of you not sleeping is so loud, I can hear it way over here, you know," he murmured, flipping to face her and that was so much worse.

She rolled away, facing the wall. "I'm overtired. It's not a big deal."

"Yeah, same," he admitted, sounding as weary as advertised.

Her fault. She'd led him on an exhausting search and rescue mission that shouldn't have happened. Finding the other head via her pure, dumb luck remained the only good thing that had come out of it.

She owed him. She rolled back. "Turn over."

"What? Why?"

"Just do it, McKay." She didn't even have the strength to snap at him but he did it anyway. Probably too tired to argue.

When she threaded her hand through his hair and started massaging his head, he let out a husky moan that nearly undid her.

If he kept that up, she'd forget all her principles in under point-zero seconds. Because now all she could think about was getting a repeat of that sound, but in wholly different circumstances.

"How did you know that's exactly what I needed?" he murmured.

Her eyelids slammed shut. His rich, decadent voice in the dark did sinful things to her body, things that she hurt too much to enjoy. And she really, really wanted to savor all the sensations Heath caused, even if he didn't mean to do it. Even if all of this wasn't real.

"Oh, you know me. Always practicing," she said lightly, reveling in the feel of his hair against her fingertips since this was the perfect excuse to touch it. "Since there's no time-outs tonight."

He fell silent for a beat. "Is that what we're doing? Practicing?"

"Sure. You're exhausted thanks to me. This is what I would do for you if we were together for real. Take care of you. Isn't that what an adult relationship is all about? Seeing that the person you love needs something and doing it."

"Your arm is in a cast," he pointed out needlessly since it currently lay wedged against her leg, probably adding to her bruise count.

But she wouldn't move for a million dollars. His masculine, clean scent had drifted over her, winnowing down into her blood. "So? My other arm is fine."

"I should be taking care of you," he grumbled and suddenly rolled to face her so unexpectedly that she didn't have time to fully prepare.

Who was the genius who had decided to switch off the lights? She was missing out on a whole experience here of seeing his beautiful cheekbones up close and personal, plus the chance to memorize what he looked like in her bed so she could conjure up the image later.

"My turn," he told her. "Roll over."

Oh, that was an unexpected twist. She couldn't comply fast enough.

But he didn't rub her head or even stroke her hair, which would have felt nice. Instead, he gathered her in his arms and spooned her against his delicious heat.

Instantly, she relaxed despite her previous conviction that having a hot cowboy in her bed would produce the exact opposite reaction. But this was something else. Something she'd craved without knowing it would be the glue that fixed broken places inside.

She'd never been this warm and this content in the whole of her life.

"Just to be clear," she murmured against his well-defined arm muscle that shouldn't be such an excellent pillow. "I do not sleep with men on a first date."

She could feel his lips turn up against her cheek. "This is not a date, Charlotte."

"Why don't I hate it when you call me that?" The claws came out when anyone else full-named her.

He was silent for a beat. "Because you know I only use it when we're being genuine with each other."

How could she be anything but genuine? She'd never succeed at being anything else with him. "I generally only think of myself that way when I'm at my worst. Hurricane Charlotte, at your service."

His thumb brushed against hers. "But that's when you are your truest self."

The certainty of that settled inside of her, not feeling as foreign as she would have expected. Neither was the hard press of his legs against the backs of hers. All of it over-whelmed her, beating against her rib cage to escape. "What are we doing, Heath?"

His thumb stilled. "Practicing?"

With a question mark and an implied *duh*. Because what else would it be? That's what he meant by being genuine— he genuinely didn't feel anything for her. Fine. That was perfect. It allowed her to stuff everything back in the box, where it should be.

"Yep," she agreed brightly. Too brightly for the middle of the night. "I've never slept like this with anyone, so we'll have to see how it goes. I might be terrible at it. It's a good thing—"

"Shh," he said into her hair and his breath floated over her. "You're still not sleeping. That was the point of this. So we can both rest."

And he needed to. He'd more than earned the right to rest, to have a respite from her. She could read between the lines. What she could not do was sleep, not with all the stuff churning through her head and her heart.

She was falling for him.

She could feel it happening, powerless to stop it. This man could break her. Shatter her into a billion unrecoverable shards.

It was exactly what she deserved for putting herself in this position, for pining after another woman's man. For letting him scoop her up into this wholly improper, wholly delicious embrace under the guise of *practicing*.

None of this felt like practicing. Worse, whatever she learned here would go to waste because she couldn't imagine being like this with any other man.

Apparently, Heath could also market himself as a sleeping pill because the next thing she knew, it was morning, and she woke draped over him. He slept flat on his back, and she'd wiggled her way into the crook of his arm, one leg thrown over his.

Shameful.

But when she tried to work herself free without waking him, his arm tightened, clamping her in place. And then Heath opened his eyes, still heavy with sleep, and the bottomless abyss of blue scored her on the inside where a man should never have been able to touch.

Which scared her more than anything else that had happened to her in the last twenty-four hours and that was saying something.

"Hi, good morning," she said with fake cheer. "I need food and ibuprofen stat."

Prying herself loose only worked because he let her and then she fled.

Chapter Eighteen

When Heath came back to the house after taking a shower in the ranch hand's quarters where he normally slept, Charli was right where he'd left her, sitting at the breakfast table sipping coffee like he'd asked her to.

He paused before announcing his presence to just…take a minute. Man, she was so much stronger than any woman he'd ever met. Not only had she survived a fall into a well, she'd found the jaguar head and a human body, and somehow resisted curling up in a ball in the corner after finding herself trapped with a corpse.

She was something else. Someone he'd never have said he'd be attracted to, but here they were. His skin still tingled from the feel of her against his fingertips.

Nothing in his head or his chest lined up quite right when he looked at Charli. She'd destroyed him and then knit him back together with nothing more than her fingers in his hair. Tending to him. Because that's what a woman did for someone she cared about in Charli's world.

Not in his. He'd never even dreamed that someone could pay that kind of attention to him. Or would. Especially after a day that included her being trapped in a well and breaking an arm.

What was he supposed to do with her?

Charli wasn't alone in the kitchen. An older woman who must be her mother sat with her, both of them glancing up when he made a noise to let them know he was here before his silent reckoning got creepy. Yep. They had the same eyes.

Mrs. Lang insisted that Heath call her Patricia, taking his hand and warmly thanking him for saving her daughter. Which was a totally legit thing to be grateful for, but geez. What was it about mothers that made him want to duck his head and get a haircut?

Maybe it was because he and Charli had crossed some kind of line last night. What line, he didn't know, but everything had changed and yet nothing had. It had always felt like they were entangled in ways that were difficult to explain.

Nor was anyone asking him to, least of all Charli. She couldn't leave the bed they'd slept in together last night fast enough. He got it. Everything had turned upside down and it was big and strange. He should probably check in with her.

But the security company that bore his name had multiple things going on today and he owed it to his partners to show up. Despite the fact that all of them needed some downtime after the long darkness of the day before, no one was going to get it.

Before the craziness started, he planned to dump copious amounts of caffeine down his throat. As he pulled a mug out of the cupboard above the coffee maker, Charli joined him, sliding right into his space as if they'd always stood here together in a scene straight out of the domestic bliss playbook. She even smelled perfect, like vanilla and woman.

"Let me," she murmured and took the mug from his hand. "I owe you this, plus about a million other things."

Speechless, he watched as she grabbed the carafe and

poured the coffee, then dumped two spoonfuls of sugar into it, stirred, then added the exact right amount of creamer. She'd even done it in the same order as he always did, which he'd honestly never even thought about as a routine, but she'd somehow learned his coffee preferences expertly as if she'd memorized the steps.

"What is all of this?" he asked suspiciously.

"Do I need a reason?" When she glanced over her shoulder, she must have realized the answer to that was *duh*. She rolled her eyes. "I like being able to take care of something for you. You run around being all capable and stuff. Makes it hard for me to reciprocate. Deal with it."

She handed him the mug and he sipped, biting back a moan as the first rich taste hit his system. "How did you know how to make this for me?"

She flashed him a guilty grin. "I can't tell you on the grounds that it might incriminate me."

"You have a spy camera set up in here?" he guessed and glanced around for show despite being 100 percent aware there was no such thing thanks to Pierce's careful sweeps for any foreign equipment.

"Which part of *I can't tell you* wasn't clear?" She hip-checked him and winced, instantly sobering the vibe between them. "I guess I fell on that one."

That hip and a lot of other places that he'd personally cataloged while helping her change into her T-shirt last night. She'd heal but the rage that had built in his chest as he'd noted the marks on her skin roared right back. There wasn't anything he could break that would fix it for her. That was the problem. She hurt and he couldn't do anything about that or his urge to plow a fist through something.

"I'm sorry," he murmured. "Want me to kiss it and make it better?"

She glanced at her mother, still seated at the table on the other side of the kitchen and turned her back to the table deliberately, leaning in to whisper. "Heath McKay, are you flirting with me?"

That teased a smile out of him, because of course Charli would have the power to amuse him even in the midst of his physical response to her pain. "Yes. Strictly for practice, of course."

Her expression instantly flattened as she nodded. "Of course. I knew that. The coffee is practice too."

That was the same voice she'd used last night, after she'd asked what they were doing and he'd answered the question with a question because he had no idea. He loved Margo or at least that's what he'd been trying to tell himself for quite some time. But at this point, he didn't have a lot of confidence he'd be able to pick love out of a lineup.

Margo had never done anything like rub his head or make his coffee. What did that mean? He was driving himself nuts with questions that shouldn't be so hard to answer.

Heath tipped up Charli's chin with his thumb so she could see his sincerity. "The coffee was a nice touch. I'd like to stand here and flirt some more, but I'm afraid today is going to be a nightmare. For both of us."

Which started almost immediately when Madden, Sophia and Pierce rolled into the kitchen, business faces on. Everyone took a spot at the table.

Beneath it, Charli slipped her hand into his, warming him in places he hadn't realized were cold. He suspected she'd needed the connection to settle something inside.

At least he could do that for her. And would, as much as she wanted. It worked out that it settled something inside him too. Who knew secret hand-holding would be so affecting?

"Logistics meeting," Madden announced.

Sophia touched her mother's shoulder. "Mom, this is going to be so boring. You're welcome to stay if you would like but Ace is going to be talking about some of the security changes that have to happen now that we've located another jaguar head."

And a dead body. But Heath kept that to himself. Everyone was enough on edge without the added fear that there might be a killer on the loose. Though it had to be on Madden's mind.

"*Another* head?" Charli stressed. "You mean *the other* head. Right? The only one. Say that's what you meant."

Sophia glanced over at Charli, her expression grim. "I talked to Dr. Low about that. She's pulling in some other experts from the museum in Mexico who might be able to verify if there are more."

Charli groaned and tried to rub her forehead with the arm encased in the cast and nearly hit herself in the eye. "No more heads. We need these people to leave, not bring more experts to the ranch. We might as well move the opening date of the Cowboy Experience to next year at this rate."

"Actually," Madden interjected. "That's not a bad idea."

If Heath hadn't been holding her hand, he might have missed how agitated that statement made Charli. He stroked a thumb down hers, but her spine didn't loosen, and he needed it to.

"Can we table that conversation for the moment?" Heath wasn't asking, though, and plowed ahead. "We need double the number of armed guards pronto."

That did the trick. She relaxed, letting her shoulder graze his arm in a way that set off sparks in places that needed to stop sparking ASAP. This game required his head in it with no distractions, and all he wanted to do was wrap himself and Charli back up in the cocoon of darkness where they could keep pretending the real world didn't exist, that they hadn't made the stupid bet, and he'd never let Margo get her hooks into him in the first place.

"Already on it," Madden confirmed with a nod. "They'll be here by noon."

"No one leaves the house without one of the three of us," Heath continued, wagging a finger between himself, Madden and Pierce. "I'm thinking it wouldn't be out of place for us all to renew our acquaintance with our friends Smith & Wesson."

Sophia glanced at Madden and the look they exchanged carried a lot of unspoken language meant to leave everyone else out of the conversation. Normally Heath would be the one Madden shared his concerns with, but things had subtly shifted with the introduction of his friend's relationship with Sophia. It should bother him more, but given the vibe between him and Charli, and the ways they'd been learning to read each other, he got it all at once.

This was what a relationship looked like. It was mind-blowing how wrong he'd gotten it with Margo. How right it felt with Charli. Did she feel it too?

"Everyone should make that decision for themselves," Madden said quietly.

"Can I have a gun then?" Charli wanted to know.

"No," Sophia and Heath answered at the same time. Charli looked so crestfallen he rushed to amend that with, "At least not until I teach you how to use one."

That got him a smile and a head bop on the arm, which seemed to raise her spirits. Until there was a knock at the front door and Sophia left to answer it, then returned in seconds with the sheriff in tow. His badge gleamed against his sedate brown uniform, both ominous this early in the morning.

"I'm glad you're all here," the sheriff announced gravely, his hat in his hand. "Thought I would come by personally to tell you some difficult news. We've positively identified the deceased as David Lang."

Forget a pin—you could have heard a feather drop in the room.

Heath immediately removed his hat in kind, wishing he hadn't seen that bombshell coming a mile away. Charli sucked in a breath, her grip on his hand tightening, but otherwise, she accepted the news stoically.

Sophia, not so much. She started crying and Madden folded her into his embrace, murmuring to her while he stroked her back. Which Heath totally would have done for Charli if she'd seemed like she needed it, but in her typical fashion, she met this challenge head-on.

"Are you sure?" she demanded of the sheriff. "No question?"

The sheriff nodded. "We used two corroboration methods to verify."

Because of the level of decomposition, no doubt. The sheriff was being discreet by leaving out the details, but most likely the police had access to Lang's dental records and possibly existing DNA samples since he'd grown up here at the ranch, likely utilizing still-existing medical services in town.

Mrs. Lang, who had returned to the room with the arrival of the sheriff, stepped forward, her face frozen. "Do you know how long he's been dead?"

The sheriff met her halfway and extended his hand to shake hers. "You must be Mrs. Lang. I am very sorry for your loss and to be meeting you under these circumstances. I'm afraid I can't give you specifics yet. We've ordered an autopsy, which will help us determine cause of death as well as the date. Rest assured we'll open an investigation immediately if foul play was involved."

Mrs. Lang murmured her thanks and put a comforting hand on each of her daughters' shoulders. Heath's skin got tight and started feeling like it was on backward, so he bowed out, catching Madden's eye and jerking his head toward the door.

Figuring it was better to let the Lang women grieve without an audience, he hightailed it to Charli's bedroom to wait it out. Man, that was a rough scene. He didn't do grief well in the first place. It was one of the few things that couldn't be pounded out of his system, and it hurt to watch other people hurting.

Especially Charli. And wasn't that a kicker to find out that he could bleed just as easily when someone else took the hit.

Some forty-five minutes later, Charli wandered through the door, not seeming overly shocked to find him lounging on her bed, boots kicked off and hat on the floor next to them. Which he'd done strictly to show her that he was here and present for as long as she wanted him there.

"Heath," she croaked, looking as if she might faint at any second. Before he could spring out of the bed to catch her, she held up a finger. "Time-out. No questions."

He nodded. As if he'd have denied her anything.

Without a word, she crawled onto the bed and right on top of him, collapsing against his chest. Automatically, his arms came around her, cradling her close. She was shaking.

"Hey," he murmured, inhaling her scent, which inexplicably calmed him. "I've got you. Breathe with me."

She did, falling into the rhythm that he set. He stroked her hair, pausing occasionally to circle her temples soothingly.

After an eternity of his heart feeling like she'd seared it with a hot knife, the trembling eased off, finally stopping entirely.

"Good girl," he whispered and lifted her face with his thumbs. Then wished he hadn't.

Charli's expression was ravaged. Coupled with everything else, it put his body on simmer, the edges of his vision going black. Not a good thing, especially when there wasn't a target for him to punch. But this was where he would temper his tendencies, pull it all back. For her. Because she needed him to.

"What can I do?" he almost bit out and course-corrected quickly, leveling his voice on the last syllables.

"You're already doing it."

Her accompanying sigh reverberated through his chest, the sentiment likewise spreading through him like warm honey, soothing him in the same vein as he'd tried to do for her. Who knew that they'd be so good like this? That they could pull each other off the roller coaster at a time when they both so desperately needed it?

She sat back on the bedspread, her legs under her, taking all her heat and light and vanilla-y scent with her. But she threaded her fingers through his and it was enough. They clung to each other as they each processed their own very different emotions.

"It doesn't feel like enough," he muttered. "I hate seeing you so upset."

Charli shook her head. "The terrible part is that I'm not upset that he's dead. It's fine, he's basically been the equivalent of dead for a long time anyway. But now it's like... final. We can't ever have a conversation where I tell him what a lousy piece of filth he is for leaving us."

"And what if you find out he's been dead for years?" he added because he got it. It was a lot to take in.

"Exactly. It changes things. It changes how I think about myself." She eyed him. "Why are you here? You left the kitchen and I thought I'd find out you'd galloped off on a horse or something."

He scowled. What kind of man did she take him for? "And leave you to deal with all of this by yourself?"

To be fair, he had actually left her in the kitchen, but he had good reasons for that. She'd needed to be with her family, not a bunch of onlookers.

She stared at him, and he had the distinct impression she wasn't at all sure what to make of what she saw. That made two of them. "I don't get any of this, Heath. Why the bet? Why frame all of this as practice? Because it doesn't feel like you need much."

Oh, he definitely did. Whatever had just happened between them, whatever you called it, he could do that a hundred more times and still not feel like he'd mastered it—but more to the point, no other woman had ever made him want to try. Or afforded him the opportunity to.

This bet with Charli was 100 percent practice, but not for the reasons he'd originally laid out. Not anymore.

He forced a chuckle. "If it makes you feel any better, this is not the kind of thing I've ever done before."

Disbelief climbed its way up Charli's expression. "What? Show up for me? That's what you do, Heath. It's like you can read my mind and know exactly what I need from you."

"Took me way too long to find you yesterday," he muttered as everything inside revolted against what she was telling him. That he was good at this relationship business when in reality, he was stumbling around blindfolded, depending on his senses to guide him. "I meant I've never done *this* before. Whatever *this* is."

He waved his hand in a circle to encompass the two of them, punctuating the point.

"It's practice. Isn't it?" She stared at him, her eyes huge and damp and full of something he couldn't look away from. "That's what we agreed to. The bet is almost an afterthought now. Because somewhere along the way, I realized how much I want to get it right."

He let himself fall into the possibilities that she meant she felt the way he did, that it had stopped feeling like rehearsal a long time ago. That this might be the realest real deal there was.

"I want to get it right too," he murmured.

"Of course you do," she said and squeezed her eyes shut. "For Margo. It's a lot easier for you because you have her in mind when we're practicing. I'm turning myself inside out for some nameless, faceless dude I haven't met yet. He's going to be different. What if getting it right with you is wrong with him?"

White-hot rage stole his vision as he processed the idea that for one, he and Charli were not in fact on the same page with what was happening between them and two, at some point she'd move on. Into someone else's arms. Who was not Heath.

He wanted to destroy that nameless, faceless dude.

Just as the black edges bled into the field of white, she squeezed his hand. It centered him. Brought him back from the edge in a blink.

"Thank you for introducing the concept of a time-out," she told him. "Our friendship means a lot to me. In a lot of ways, that's practice for a relationship too. Because this matters to me in a way a romantic relationship wouldn't. I can tell you things I would never say to someone I was dating for real."

So…that's what all of this was to her? Them becoming *friends*?

The tiny sound he heard inside could quite possibly be his heart breaking a little. But honestly, it was the best scenario. He did love Margo. Probably. And did want to impress her with his new personality, the one that could come back from the brink of hulk-smashing drywall with nothing more than a squeeze of someone's hand.

"That's what I'm here for," he said weakly but meant it.

This was how it should be. If he got back together with Margo, she'd become better too, simply by virtue of seeing what lengths Heath had gone to in order to win her back. That's how it worked with Charli. They both tried, they both gave, they both course-corrected when needed.

Like he needed to do now. Charli expected him to act like a friend—that's what he'd be.

Feeling as if he still wasn't quite on the track he'd expected to be, he ran his thumb over Charli's, gratified she'd never released his hand. "We're both learning how to have an adult relationship without the risk of screwing it up."

Her expression grew thoughtful. "I'm realizing I've never had one. An adult relationship. You see what my model for relationships is. My dad ending up at the bottom of a well, leaving all of us to believe he abandoned us. My ability to take things at face value is broken. It scares me. Maybe I'll do all this practicing and screw it up when it comes to the real thing. Maybe I'm broken."

The utter bravery it took for her to admit that she was scared crushed him.

"I want you to hear that you're getting it right," he said fiercely. "Safe space, Charli. I wouldn't lie to you. You're not broken."

If there was ever a moment in their history when he

wished he could call a time-out, it was this one. No one else existed in the world except her. A time-out would allow him to do exactly as he wished, and if he had that latitude, it would be to kiss her. To explore the way she made him feel, as if they were embarking on something new and wonderful together.

That wasn't what they were doing here, though. The romance part of their relationship didn't exist. But naming it and claiming it did nothing to lessen the tide of Charli in his blood.

Neither did the look on her face, as if she'd found something precious and could hardly believe her luck. He wanted it to mean something other than what it did.

"You heard me, didn't you?" he said, his voice huskier than it should be given the circumstances. "All this practice is not for nothing. You're this close to winning the bet."

He held up his finger and thumb with zero space between them and a smile curving his lips that he almost didn't have to fake.

Tipping her face up, she caught his gaze. "Does this mean you're finally going to take me on a date?"

Chapter Nineteen

Straightening things out with Charli should have worked to clear Heath's head. He shouldn't be so distracted. But the fact of the matter was that he couldn't concentrate on the security issues that should be his sole focus. Instead, the entire breadth of his mental capacity was going toward planning a perfect first date.

She deserved that. After learning to make his coffee and giving him a fair shot and a dozen other things that signified her commitment to their practice relationship, he needed to step up his game.

"Would it be totally cliché to just make reservations at a nice restaurant in Dallas?" he asked Pierce as they walked across the yard to debrief the new security guards their third-party company had sent.

Pierce rolled his eyes. "Yes, McKay. It would. Try again."

"A picnic?"

"Let's keep thinking," Pierce suggested, as if he could claim the title of Most Romantic Man Alive without breaking a sweat and Heath was merely a bothersome novice.

"If you're so smart, what would you do?" he shot back.

"I don't know Charli very well, so I can't tell you. That's for you to figure out. It's supposed to show her that she's worth the effort to take five minutes and plan something that is meaningful to *her*," he stressed. "What does she like?"

"To antagonize me," he muttered with a double take at Pierce's eyebrow lift. "What? It's her favorite hobby."

To be fair, he poked at her in kind pretty frequently. Maybe he even started it on occasion. But when she faced him down with that snap in her gaze—she was the most beautiful woman in the world.

The times they reeled it back…those were the best and came far too infrequently. Was it at all in the realm of possibility to call a time-out for an entire date?

Except that pretty much negated the experiment. Plus, he liked sparring with her as much as she seemed to. That's why this was such a strange, wonderful relationship—and yes, they had one. A friendship. Officially. It was new, and difficult to quantify, but real to him.

And so different in a good way than any relationship he'd ever had before. They were *friends*. It wasn't as terrible as it sounded. Plus, it was what he had to work with.

Pierce was right, but Heath had no plans to admit it out loud. Charli warranted whatever it took for him to find the perfect first date and he'd think on it until the idea unfolded naturally. It wasn't like he could spring for the time off tonight, not with all the additional security logistics.

The gun tucked into the holster at his hip was a part of that, a necessary one. That was the beauty of a place like Texas with open carry laws, and Heath had wasted no time getting the additional license to complement his concealed carry license the moment he'd arrived.

He just hadn't expected to use it in quite such an obvious way. Anyone in a half-mile radius—or further, pending their surveillance equipment—hopefully had zero question about his willingness to use his weapon to keep the peace.

Or destroy it if someone came after Charli. With or without his firearm.

He and Pierce got the new guys organized, showed them the extra beds in the bunkhouse where they would sleep during their off hours. They were running armed guards around the clock, three on the trailer where the jaguar heads lived in the safe bolted to the floor and two making rounds between the house and the woods, with unscheduled loops around both.

The hope was that this would be temporary, just until the university people rolled out with their treasure and took the chaos with them.

"If we're set here, I'm going to spend a few hours on my drone code," Pierce announced once they were able to leave the guards to their jobs. "The quality of the thermals is not where I'd like it to be given the circumstances. I got some new sensors that should solve the issue with the denser brush near the creek too."

Since all of that sounded like as much fun as learning Swahili, Heath waved him off to go do his geek things in solitude. That's why God made people like Paxton Pierce, so the Heaths of the world didn't have to think about the finer points of sensors and whatever nonsense went along with increasing the quality of thermal imaging.

All this tension and attention to the hardware of the surveillance *and* personal protection variety was making him antsy. They'd found the other head. Well, Charli had, by accident, but it still counted. This whole cuckoo environment should be easing up but he felt more on edge today than he ever had before.

But with Charli in the house and everything Madden had asked Heath to do completed, maybe he could spend some time googling date ideas. Nail something down. He wanted to show Charli that he was invested, that he could get this right too. In the name of practice, of course.

Internet reception was better closer to the house, so he headed in that direction, his phone already in his hand as he went with the "on the nose" option and googled "perfect first dates."

That's why he didn't notice the woman standing near the back door until she called out, "Hello, Heath," in that cultured voice that he used to hear in his dreams.

Margo's voice.

It was all wrong in this setting. Margo's voice didn't go with East Texas or the dirt in the yard. Neither did it sit right in his chest.

He glanced up, straight into Margo's stunning hazel eyes that could turn the color of molten silver or iced tea or a moss-covered log pending what she was wearing. Today, the armor of choice was a sleek black jumpsuit with wide legs and a crystal-encrusted belt around her minuscule waist. Barbie pink stilettos, of course, and a pink jacket thrown over her shoulder completed the look that he had no doubt she'd spent a fortune in time and money to pull together.

Her face had a flawless complexion thanks to the trifecta of genetics, expensive skincare routines and a deal with the devil, probably.

Good God, she was still an uncommonly beautiful woman, and he felt absolutely nothing when he looked at her. What was *happening*?

"What are you doing here?" he demanded, so floored that he couldn't have found his manners with a military-grade GPS receiver.

She laughed, the trilling, slightly amused one that used to make him smile, but now only confused his already beleaguered senses.

"No hug for someone who used to pick up your favorite Chinese food?" she asked sweetly, holding up her hands.

Heath's muscles jumped to do exactly as bid in some kind of Pavlovian response before he could check them. Shocking how easily she could *still* evoke a response in him. But then, she'd been doing that for a long time, and he'd always had zero resistance when it came to her.

She folded herself into his embrace, bringing with her a cloud of spicy perfume she regularly restocked from a store in Morocco, which he knew because he'd given her the first bottle for Christmas an eon ago.

Nothing had changed with Margo, apparently, even after she'd given him the boot.

It threw him off-kilter and he'd never quite been on-kilter with her in the first place.

He pulled away and crossed his arms, focusing his attention front and center on facts, not his own stupid hangups when it came to this woman. "I can't say a hug is how I thought you'd want to be greeted the first time we saw each other after...what happened."

It's not me, it's you.

That's what she'd said when she dumped him. It still stung, honestly. Not only the smug, sarcastic phrasing, but the whole concept.

What *was* wrong with him, exactly? That he liked being physical? That it made him feel good to protect people and make sure other people knew they couldn't threaten or bully their way through life?

That was Charli's voice in his head. He shouldn't be thinking about her or how much better he liked her narrative.

"Oh, Heath, let's leave the past in the past, shall we?" she murmured, her stilettos inching closer to him as she swept him with an appreciative once-over. "I'm a fan of how you're flourishing in this environment."

His eyebrows shot up so high that they nearly hit the brim of his Stetson. "You hate it when I don't shave, and I've never once heard you say a positive thing about boots."

It was so weird, but he'd sworn he would react differently the next time he came in contact with Margo. He'd planned it all out in his head, how he'd sweep her off her feet with his new, improved, much calmer persona. But here and now, with the real reunion happening, his temper had already started swirling twice in thirty seconds.

Was it possible that Margo *herself* had been the one to constantly provoke him into being such a hothead?

Margo folded her jacket over her arm, contemplating him. "Maybe I've come to appreciate things about you now that I've had time and distance to contemplate our relationship."

That was closer to the conversation he'd hoped to have, but very far from the one he'd expected. "So that's why you're here? You want to apologize to me and start over?"

"As happy as I am to see you again," she said, "I'm actually here on official business."

When Margo's smile gained a strange edge, every nerve in his body blipped into high alert. "JSOC is getting into the Maya treasure business?"

Margo lifted one shoulder delicately. "When the treasure in question is tied to the funding of a sleeper cell out of Iraq, I'm afraid the answer is yes."

His arms were crossed so tightly that his muscles started to ache. "And you naturally requested this assignment when you saw my name come across your desk."

The incredulity dripped from his voice but really, he shouldn't be so shocked. Word had gotten out all right. And brought with it a slew of new challenges that he couldn't have anticipated even with the aid of a crystal ball.

"Life has so few coincidences." She smiled and he didn't miss the glint in her gaze.

This wasn't just a job. Or just a drive-by reunion. It was both. And felt exceptionally mercenary all at once.

His knees actually went weak as he absorbed this blind-side. How like the universe to throw this enormous monkey wrench in his path the second he'd set up a practice run with Charli—which he wasn't done with, not by a long shot. He was supposed to be figuring out how to be in a relationship by spending time with her, not by shepherding Spec Ops representatives around who came with history that suddenly weighed more than an albatross.

The complications, they were legion.

If Margo wanted him back, great. He should *want* to spend time with her. He owed it to himself—and Charli— to try out his new husband material persona on his ex-girl-friend. It was what he'd been practicing for. Why was he being so weird about it?

Heath pinched the bridge of his nose. "How is this going to work, then?"

She smiled and it was the one she used when she wanted something. "I was hoping you'd be my ace in the hole. For old times' sake."

She *would* liken this to a poker match. Heath shook his head. "The jaguar heads are in a biometrically accessed safe and I'm not one of the people with the keys to the kingdom. You'll have to go through the bigwigs at Harvard for that, if they even decide to let you near them. And they don't have to listen to me on that, by the way."

Nor would he advise them to. He wouldn't get near that conversation with a ten-foot pole.

"Well, this is a dilemma," she said smoothly. "What can we do to facilitate my investigation? I don't want to pull in local law enforcement. I thought that by coming to you first, we could avoid all of that."

Yeah, dilemma was the word all right. As not-so-veiled threats went, this one landed a pretty hard punch. If he kept digging in his heels, she'd circumvent him and his partners, then blast onto the property with the blessing of Gun Barrel City's finest. He'd be completely cut out of the picture. That did not sit well, especially not when he still didn't understand what was happening here.

For the first time, he had the luxury of seeing Margo without blinders on. It was quite possible that she'd always used her connection to him in ways he'd never examined fully.

He'd have to play along. At least until he got a clearer picture what in the blazes this was all about. Because he didn't for a second believe JSOC cared about jaguar heads, nor that someone had magically unearthed a connection to terrorists half a world away.

He couldn't discount a sense of edginess since Charli had discovered the body of her father and there were too many other unknown elements in the mix. They didn't have a blessed clue about what kind of buddies David Lang might have picked up along the way. They didn't know how he'd died. The trailer break-in hadn't been resolved, not fully. And there were still too dang many people on this ranch coming and going as they pleased.

Margo was the last straw. How was he supposed to separate his win-back campaign from *his* job, especially when she insisted on combining the two? Funny how that had never been an issue with Charli.

"Fine, I'll be your liaison," he told her, painting a smile on his face that he hoped came across as genuine.

Margo practically purred as she sidled up next to him, heels boosting her into his space in a way that used to feel comfortable. Welcome, even. It was neither all at once.

"We should spend some time debriefing," she suggested silkily. "Maybe over a brandy."

His gag reflex nearly created a soundtrack of his opinion about that plan. Who actually drank brandy on purpose? She never had before. Oddly, that anomaly tripped his radar the hardest. "Sure. Give me an hour to take care of some things. I *am* working."

"Oh, right. Your new job." She said it as if naming a previously unknown virus and hooked her arm through his. "I'm sure I don't have to remind you that the brass at Fort Bragg don't like to be kept waiting. The sooner we can get this pesky terrorist funding issue dismissed, the better."

Was that her goal? To eliminate suspicion cast on this treasure? Somehow, he didn't believe that was her actual assignment. But the only mechanism to figure out what she wasn't telling him lay in playing her game for as long as it took to unwind all the layers of deception going on around here. Neither did he think she was the only one with an agenda.

"Thirty minutes," he amended, silently cursing the satisfied smile she flashed him.

"Great. We can catch up at the same time," she suggested with a heated once-over that had all the subtlety of a warhead.

"Great," he echoed.

Suddenly, he had a very bad feeling he'd been practicing all wrong.

Chapter Twenty

Charli felt really good about establishing the friendship boundary around her practice relationship with Heath. Sure, it smacked of self-preservation, but he didn't have to know that she'd thrown up as many walls as she could to keep herself on the straight and narrow.

It was far too easy for her to forget that when he took her hand, he was thinking about Margo, not Charli. Then she remembered and it burned through her as if she'd swallowed a quart of battery acid.

He deserved to be happy, to get what he'd been working so hard for without the additional burden of Charli's ridiculous and misplaced feelings.

She hadn't quite figured out what she deserved. To be alone for a while probably. Spend some time working on the Cowboy Experience and then see whether the Heath-shaped place in her heart had shrunk at all.

Ace had taken Sophia and Patricia into Gun Barrel City to talk to the sheriff. They needed to find out how long the autopsy and investigation would take, then drop by a couple of possible venues for a memorial service.

Charli had begged off with the excuse of sticking around the ranch so she could work on the guest menu for meals they'd serve once they were able to open. Sophia intended to hire a full-time chef who would probably have some ideas as well, but given their lack of income thus far, the pay range wouldn't attract top-tier talent at first, so Charli had volunteered to do some research.

That lasted all of fifteen minutes, the longest she'd ever sat in Sophia's desk chair, and it felt like fourteen minutes too long. How did her sister sit in this thing for hours on end?

Fresh air needed, stat. Charli pushed back from the desk and wandered outside. Maybe she could quiz some of the hands about their favorite dishes and call the menu Rustic Ranch Fare.

The moment she stepped outside, the entire ranch panorama fell off the face of the map. All Charli could see was a svelte blonde viper wrapped around Heath, a solid dose of possessiveness dripping from her fingers. There was practically a pop-up bubble above her head with *mine* in capital letters and flashing lights.

Heath's chin swiveled and he locked gazes with Charli. His expression flattened as if he'd snapped a cable supplying all his emotional energy. She barely recognized him, as if she'd stumbled over a doppelganger who definitely looked like Heath McKay but had actually been born in Argentina and didn't even speak English.

"Ms. Lang," he called, his voice a match for his expression.

Since she was the only Ms. Lang around thanks to her ill-timed bailout from the memorial service, she crossed her arms so neither he nor the viper could see how her hands shook to hear Heath address her so formally.

"What's up, McKay?" she said.

Heath walked toward her. Viper on the other hand, no. The woman strode across the yard as if she owned it and everything around her, including the town and possibly the whole state. If this woman had ever suffered from lack of confidence, Charli would eat Heath's hat.

"We were just coming to the door," Heath said flatly. "So I could introduce you."

"You must be Charlotte Lang," Viper said and even her voice had been specially crafted to be mesmerizing.

There was no reason to hate her. But Charli did. Instantly.

"It's Charli," she corrected. "No one calls me Charlotte."

Except Heath. But if he recalled their conversation about what it meant when he Charlotte-ed her, his expression sure didn't show it. His current one resembled granite.

Charli stuck out her hand, figuring it was her job to be civil to someone who was a guest on the property. Surely the practice would come in handy for when real guests came, because odds were high she wouldn't like everyone who paid to enjoy the Cowboy Experience.

"This is Margo," Heath added almost as an afterthought.

Charli's hand turned to lead and dropped to her side.

The name rocketed through Charli's soul like a throwing star ricocheting inside her, its cutting points drawing blood with each tender surface it hit. The viper was *Margo*. She had every right to wrap herself around Heath, and he had every right to enjoy it as much as he could.

"Oh," she croaked. "That's, um, nice. It's nice to meet you, I mean. Margo. Hello."

Margo ignored the fact that Charli stood there like a wax statue and extended her hand with enough grace to convince anyone that if her mother was a viper, her father had been a gazelle. "Margo Malloy. Intelligence analyst with JSOC. I'm happy to meet you. I'm here to investigate the recent discoveries on the ranch."

Woodenly, Charli clasped the viper—Margo's—hand and released it immediately.

"Investigate?" Apparently, Charli's ability to use her brain had been sucked out of her by the force of Margo's presence. "I don't understand. You're here to investigate something?"

Like, whether Heath still belonged to her? That was a quick one, requiring no intelligence whatsoever. There hadn't been a whole lot of pushing her away on Heath's part, after all, and the woman had practically been climbing him like a tree.

"Yes, the recent discoveries," Margo repeated without a drop of frustration, as if she had no clue she was speaking to an idiot who hadn't gotten her wits about her yet. "The Maya jaguar heads. JSOC has an interest in delving further into this situation."

Oh. *Those* recent discoveries. Charli blinked. Margo was here because of the stupid gold heads? If she didn't have an audience, Charli would scream. Actually, she might anyway. It wasn't like she could pale in comparison to Margo any further.

"Investigate away, then," she muttered. "Don't let me stop you."

Margo glanced between Charli and Heath, who'd turned into a mute bump on a log. Probably because he wished he could be done with his bodyguard duties so he could have a proper reunion with Vip—Margo.

"I'm told you're the best person to assist?" Margo said with a lilt on the end as if not sure her intel was correct.

Assist? Was that military speak for getting Margo coffee? "I own the ranch. Is that the skill set you're looking for?"

The joke fell flat. But it wasn't much of a joke.

Not only did Margo not laugh, she cocked her head, studying Charli curiously. "I just need someone in charge.

If that's you, great. I hope we can work together so I can get out of your hair as soon possible. My goal is to make this investigation fast and painless, especially for you since I've descended on you with no warning. The more you cooperate, the quicker I can leave."

Well, that sounded fantastic. Anything that would get the viper off the ranch and hopefully take Heath with her worked for Charli and then some.

The idea didn't relax her an iota. "Happy to help. What are you investigating exactly?"

Margo brightened, a feat since she'd walked into this conversation with a great deal of animation, as if she didn't have an off switch. "I'm so glad you asked. Most of the details are classified but the basics I can share. We intercepted some intelligence that suggests the jaguar heads you found might be linked to an organization we have eyes on. We think the treasure was intended to help fund their activities."

An organization? Like the government of a foreign country or the Boy Scouts? Charli had a feeling if she asked, Margo would say that information was classified, which was a handy way of never having to admit to anything. "What will you do if you can prove it?"

Margo smiled. "Shut them down. They can't operate without money."

But the treasure wasn't in their possession. It was in the hands of the Harvard people and heavily guarded besides. If Charli hadn't come into this conversation already intimidated, she might have a better handle on how to ask the right questions, but as it stood, she didn't want to stand here jabbering with Special Ops Barbie any longer than she had to, so she bit back her questions.

Probably she just didn't understand how any of this worked. Heath picked that moment to join the conversation.

"Margo will be here for a couple of days. She'll be combing through the sites where the two heads were found. I'll run point on security, to ensure she can come and go at will."

That made even less sense. After all this time, what possible clues did Margo expect to find?

"Great," Charli forced a smile. "Let me know what I can do to help."

"You can speak to the head of the dig," Margo suggested immediately as if she'd been waiting for that exact offer. "I'll need full access to the treasure so I can catalog it as evidence. Also, if this isn't too delicate of a request, I would really appreciate some assistance navigating your father's finances. We'd like to look for transactions that may tie him to the organization under investigation."

Follow the money. That part Charli got. But that didn't make it any easier to comply. "Sorry, I have no idea who could help with that. My father didn't live here or, like, communicate with us too much."

Or at all. Though it wouldn't shock Charli to find out her father had gotten killed by some nefarious "organization" out of the Middle East that he'd tried to sell his treasure to.

Margo nodded. "Okay, that's completely fine. We'll work with what we have."

That was not the first time she'd made reference to a *we*. "Do you have a team arriving?"

"Just me." The woman's smile hadn't slipped once, which was starting to grate on Charli. "Though I do plan to borrow Heath as frequently as I can."

"Heath?" His name on Margo's lips dumped a bucket of ice water on Charli's head. And she'd been off-balance in the first place.

Every scrap of Charli's spare energy funneled into pretending she hadn't just realized Margo's presence meant the end of practicing with Heath. Which didn't leave a lot left over to keep her on her feet. She might even be weaving.

This morning, Heath would have caught her. Not now. She was on her own.

Margo leaned in, tilting her head as if imparting a secret. "I'm sure I don't have to tell you how handy he is in the field. We used to work together. He was the kind of operative you could count on to get the job done."

The thread running through the other woman's voice carried more than a hint of longing. And familiarity. Neither did Charli think the phrasing was accidental—she'd totally meant it as a double entendre.

It put Charli's back up. "Yeah, he told me. Along with the rest of your history."

That got a rise out of the ice princess, who had thus far maintained a completely even keel. Challenge flittered through her hazel eyes as she evaluated Charli. "Then you know we were more than colleagues."

"That's not relevant, Margo," Heath interjected, his voice still oddly flat.

"I'm fairly certain that it is." Her gaze narrowed a flick. "I hope we can all be professional about working together, Ms. Lang. I've been looking forward to renewing my acquaintance with Heath."

Yeah, and Charli looked forward to acquainting Margo with a pile of horse dung, but she painted a smile on her face anyway, one that carried its own challenge. Whatever Margo thought she'd picked up on, it didn't exist. But Charli knew what a threatened woman looked like, and this was it.

Margo thought Charli represented some type of *competition*, here. Which was hilarious. But inexplicably put Charli in a much better mood.

She showed her teeth. "I can take you out to the site where

I found the second head. Hope you brought horseback riding clothes."

"Horseback?" Margo blinked. "Can we use the ATV I saw around the corner?"

"That belongs to the university people." Charli crossed her arms, leaving out the part where they let anyone use it who asked. She shot Heath a glance, but he didn't correct her.

"Oh, all right," Margo conceded with a faint voice. "Let me see what I have with me."

And like that, Charli was dismissed. "We'll be here when you're ready," she called after the rapidly disappearing Margo.

CHARLI DOUBLE-TIMED IT to the house so she could beat the viper back to the yard. And not be near Heath.

"Charli, stop walking away," Heath called and followed her up the stairs.

She liked it better when he called her Charlotte. At least then she knew nothing had changed. "I'm not walking. I'm stomping. There's a very clear difference."

She hit the last stair extra hard to prove her point.

The svelte viper was *Margo*. Of course she was. A living, breathing Barbie doll, with the perfect accessories and a sexy job, plus the preemptive claim on Heath's heart. No mystery any longer why Heath had framed the bet as practice. The real thing was leagues better than his practice field.

"Then stop stomping," he ground out as she strode into her room. "And talk to me."

"I have to change clothes to take your girlfriend out to the well."

She slammed the door in Heath's face, which helped her mood a little. It slid right back into a black place when he slung the door open, crashing it into the back wall, then stormed into her room as if he had every right to be there.

"Acting childish is not going to work," he said.

"Back at you. Go away."

This was her sanctuary and he'd invaded it. Of course, he'd done a thorough job of that the night they'd slept together. She could still smell him on her sheets, which she should have washed and hadn't, like a big Loser McLoser-pants who could only score the faint scent of a man. The real Heath belonged to the viper.

She made a big show of vanishing into her closet in search of riding jeans and her boots, so she didn't have to look at his stupid face, which was not disappearing into the hall as she'd instructed him.

"Stop pushing me away," he told her, and the door opened wider.

He crowded into the space that a real estate agent would have called a walk-in closet with plenty of room for clothes and two people, but really, really wasn't big enough for all of the stuff in her chest plus Heath.

"I'm not," she countered sweetly, clamping down the keening sound desperate to get out as every cell in her body sucked in Heath's essence, so close, but so far away. "Why would I do that? We're done practicing. The bet is over. Now we can move on. What's not to like?"

Heath stood there, his eyes the color of thunderclouds, hat in hand as he ran stiff fingers through his hair. "What is going on with you? I want to talk to you and you're being..."

"Hurricane Charlotte?" she supplied and shoved at his chest.

Big mistake. Huge. She'd only meant to get him out of her closet so she could switch her pants for jeans, but the wall of Heath didn't budge an inch. Her fingertips had amnesia and forgot that they weren't supposed to be enjoying the rock-hard feel of him.

"Yeah," he growled, smacking a hand over hers and lacing their fingers together. "I thought we were friends."

The tic at the corner of her eye picked that moment to flare up as she stared at him, all her ire leaking out of her pores, leaving her feeling deflated and like a crappy, jealous witch who couldn't get out of her own head long enough to see that Heath needed her to get this right.

"We are," she said with completely fake cheer. "So that's Margo."

"Yeah. That's her." His voice had lost none of its edge. "I didn't invite her here if that's what you're thinking."

No, that hadn't been what she'd thought at all. "Why didn't you? It's totally fine if you did. It's Margo. The pot of gold at the end of the rainbow. The prize in your Cracker Jack box. A—"

"I get it," Heath snarled. "What I don't get is why everything went sideways between us."

"Really? You don't?" Charli squeezed her eyes shut. "You were the one being weird. You could barely look at me out there. I felt like—"

My soul had been crushed.

She couldn't say that out loud. He hadn't done anything wrong. Just like he'd told her a long time ago, Heath had been nothing but honest with her.

Charli was the one who had fallen headfirst into their practice relationship and done the one thing she shouldn't have.

"Charli." She could hear him scrubbing at his beard in frustration. "Look at me. Please."

Ha, he'd like that, wouldn't he? Because then she'd start crying and she never cried. Except for the six or eight times he'd been so supportive and strong and beautiful that he wrenched that vulnerability right out of her, and she was not in the mood for a repeat, not under these circumstances.

She had to reel it back. Be the friend he expected.

She opened her eyes. The storm had passed in Heath's gaze, leaving behind a few choppy waves and darkness in the distance, but mostly calm. And a thread running through it all that she couldn't help but cling to.

This was the Heath she'd fallen in love with.

"This is so not what I planned," Heath murmured. "I was looking for perfect first date ideas when she showed up."

Well, this situation was not much better than when they were sniping at each other. "Good thing she did. It was time. You don't need any more practice."

Charli didn't either. She was done. There was no way she could step back into her role as his proving ground, knowing that's all she'd ever be. Knowing she was the other woman and Margo would be the one hurt by it. If she knew.

Charli wondered all at once if Heath would tell Margo that he'd practiced his skills with another woman. That it was Charli he'd spider-crawled down a well to rescue and cuddled later that night when she couldn't sleep. That he'd held Charli's hand while she navigated skinned animals and her father's death.

"Charli." He sucked in a breath and exhaled it on a broken note. "This is not—I'm having a hard time figuring out what to say."

She threw up a hand, stopping the flow of words that she already knew had the power to eviscerate her. "There's nothing to say. Margo is a lovely woman. Clearly gracious, and well, she's obviously not ever going to need rescuing. She probably spends her Saturdays volunteering at the animal shelter and befriending every person she's ever met."

"Yeah, no," Heath drawled with his eyes rolling heavenward. "If that's the impression you got from her, you need your eyes checked. She spends Saturdays eating navy SEALs for breakfast when they don't perform operations to her exacting standards."

"Then on Sunday, she'll spend it with you, marveling over how much you've changed." Forcing the words out of her mouth was getting a little easier the longer she did it. Practicing paid off. Who would have thought?

"That makes one of us who is sure."

Oh, man. He was adorably scared that his practicing *hadn't* paid off. That Margo wouldn't recognize the lengths he'd gone to in order to win her back. Her heart cracked.

"You've been working hard on yourself, Heath," she told him earnestly and squeezed his hands. "Safe space. I wouldn't lie to you. She'd going to be so wowed by you. You deserve to be happy. With Margo. Nothing else matters but that."

His expression flattened and he nodded. "You're right, of course. Nothing else matters."

Except the fact that Charli might possibly be in love with him herself. If Margo hadn't shown up, there'd been a lovely scenario running through her head where she told him and he smiled, his own heart in his eyes as he kissed her senseless and told her he'd been working up to a similar confession.

Obviously that wasn't happening.

"This is your chance," she said and bopped him on the arm. "You're one hundred percent grade A husband material now. Through and through. Margo showing up here now is the universe's way of rewarding you. The timing is too good to be a coincidence. Go get her and show her how much she means to you. She'll honor all the effort you went to."

I would.

Her chest caved in, and she struggled to breathe. Impossible when these tight bands had constricted so hard that it hurt to try to get a deep enough breath.

Heath's eyelids dropped as his mouth firmed into a line and he nodded once. "Yeah, okay. We've already jumped out of the helicopter. It would be ridiculous not to pull the parachute's rip cord now."

She gave him a watery smile. "I'm sure Margo would love to hear you compare her to a parachute. You should tell her that one."

Heath rolled his eyes. "She would love four dozen Dendrobium orchids in an heirloom vase."

"Then you should get her some," she insisted, refusing to think about how *she'd* have been thrilled to be presented a wildflower he'd picked in the fallow horse pasture.

"This is not how I thought this conversation was going to go," he muttered. "I thought you were mad about Margo."

Mad? No. Heartbroken might be closer to the truth, but she'd choke on it before she let even an inkling show. He didn't need her emotional crap piled on top of his reunion with Margo. It would make her seem pathetic and petty, especially since he'd always been very clear with Charli about the bet. And that this was practice.

"Oh, well." She ducked her head and warbled out a laugh that nearly made her wince. "I mean, she's beautiful and could give Blake Lively lessons on accessorizing. Who wouldn't be jealous, right?"

"She has nothing on you," he murmured, his eyes burning with intensity all at once.

She has you. "You don't have to say stuff like that to make me feel better. I have my own brand of awesomeness."

"That you do," Heath conceded and stepped back. "If you're sure there's not more to talk about?"

Like what? How it felt as if her insides had been scooped out with a shovel? Smiling brightly, she shooed him away so she could change. "We're totally good. I'm over my hissy fit about how unfair it is that she can prance around a horse ranch in heels and not trip. Do you think she'd tell me where she got those shoes?"

Chapter Twenty-One

"I hate her," Charli muttered as Sophia slid into the chair behind her desk, coffee in hand.

"Who, Margo Malloy?" her sister asked with an eye roll. "She is something all right."

Something Heath preferred. And as much as Charli would like to deny it, she could totally see how any red-blooded man would find himself slavering after her. The woman was gorgeous and cultured and orchestrated a lot of secret military stuff, particularly with Heath, once upon a time. Whom she clearly wasn't over.

His campaign to win her back was a cinch.

"Yeah." Charli sipped her own coffee glumly, her second cup on what was already a very long morning. "I thought I had her with the offer to take her out to the old well on horseback, but it turns out she can stay on a horse. And that she packed six-hundred-dollar jeans that she didn't mind getting dirty."

Plus a pair of riding boots of the English variety meant for fashion, not form, but Margo made it work with a laugh, telling Charli that she'd never expected to actually be on a horse in those boots. Joke was on Charli, then.

Plus, she'd had to watch Heath ride next to Margo, his stoic face back in place, uncharacteristically quiet.

No, that's how he'd been back at the beginning. All the time. They rarely spoke to each other after their one botched date, the only real one they'd ever been on. And then something had happened. Changed. They'd talked all the time after that.

She missed it. She missed *him*.

Heath had left early this morning to take Margo out to the site where they'd found the male head. They'd been gone for over an hour already. Not that she was watching the clock, but with each minute that ticked by, the jumpier she got.

Why, she didn't know.

It was the perfect opportunity for Heath to make a move. They were going to be alone in the woods. Why wouldn't he take advantage of it, spring a well-timed kiss on the woman he dreamed of getting back into his arms?

Good thing Charli hadn't eaten any breakfast, or it would be threatening to make a repeat appearance.

The doorbell chimed and Charli held up a hand to stop Sophia from standing. "I'll get it. I need the distraction."

She started to swing open the door and heard Heath's voice in her head warning her to be cautious, especially when he wasn't around. Good grief, the man had infiltrated even her conscience. But it wasn't bad advice, so she peeked through the peephole to spy her younger sister standing on the porch.

Veronica.

Oh, man. Not who she'd been expecting. Despite Sophia informing her that Veronica was coming down from Dallas for their father's memorial service, Charli hadn't realized she'd be here today. Or sporting a new haircut that put the *sever* in *severe*.

Charli flung the door open to admit her sister to the

house, meeting her at the threshold for an enthusiastic hug. It had been way too long since they'd seen each other.

"Hey, what's all this?" Charli called and riffled her fingers through the extremely short razor-cut ends of her sister's hair. "This is rocking."

Veronica touched her dark brown hair almost self-consciously. "Time for a change."

Oh, geez. Every woman on the planet knew that a man had to be at the root of that sentiment. "Did you and Jeremy break up?"

"Yeah, but right after Christmas," Veronica said vaguely and waved that off. "It's not a big deal."

Charli bit back the slew of questions that her sister clearly didn't want her to ask, meanwhile calculating how she was just now hearing about this. Hadn't she texted Veronica a couple of months ago to check in? Maybe it had been closer to three months. With everything that had been going on in her own life, she and her younger sister hadn't talked in far too long.

That was on Charli.

"Want some coffee?" Charli offered. "Sophia and I were just going over some business stuff. You can hang out with us if you want."

"Sure, that would be great."

Okay, now Veronica was scaring her. "I was expecting you to say no," she countered with a laugh. "You don't care about the ranch business. You were the one who was heavily in favor of selling, remember?"

"I remember."

Something was really off with her sister, and it wasn't just the breakup with her boyfriend of four years. There were fine stress lines around her brown eyes that aged her. Also, Veronica had never met a situation she didn't want to talk to death, usually with well-researched bullet points and a multimedia presentation.

"Everything okay at work?" Charli asked as her sister followed her into the kitchen.

Veronica laughed, a short brittle sound that didn't sound the slightest bit amused. "I have no idea. I quit."

Charli practically dropped the carafe in her left hand, which she'd been forced to use more often thanks to the cast on her other arm. "Oh. Are congrats in order? Did you get a better offer from a bigger law firm?"

There was a strange shadow in her sister's gaze, and it definitely didn't have a lot of better-job-more-pay type vibes. "No, I quit-quit. As in I'm not employed. It's still new and I'm still processing."

Carefully, Charli slid the carafe back into the coffee maker, wishing not for the first time that she had the money to spring for a Keurig. But all of the ranch's cash flow was tied up in renovations, and of course no guests meant no income.

No guests also meant Charli would have plenty of downtime to be there for Veronica. Something was clearly going on, but the fact that her sister hadn't immediately spilled all her secrets told her that it was more than a run-of-the-mill adulting dilemma.

She handed Veronica the coffee mug and tilted her head at the silver canisters full of creamer and sugar. "Help yourself. By the way, I know a little something about quitting your job and showing up at the ranch because you have no place else to go. So does Sophia. If you wanted to talk about it."

"I'm fine," Veronica said shortly and ran fingers through her hair with a jerky motion that maybe meant she still wasn't used to the new length. "I mean, I'm not here because I quit my job. I'm just here for the memorial service. Then I'm going to figure out the rest of my life."

She and Sophia knew a thing or two about that as well, but Charli kept that to herself since Veronica didn't seem to be in too much of a chatty mood. "Okay. I'm glad you came. It's going to be a little weird to have a memorial for someone who's been dead to us for years already."

Their mother had been the one to request that her daughters attend and insisted that everyone treat the service like a normal one, even though the forensic pathologist hadn't determined the cause of death yet, so the body hadn't been released to the family. Neither did Charli think she should point out that none of them had many fond memories of their father.

Veronica nodded, looking relieved at the subject change, and she followed Charli out of the kitchen, trailing her to Sophia's office. Sophia wasn't behind her desk, though. She was standing at the window, watching something out in the yard as she drank her coffee.

Curious, Charli joined her. Veronica took a second to give Sophia a hug and then did a double take as she caught sight of what had so thoroughly captured Sophia's attention. Not shockingly, her sister's boyfriend stood on the slope between the house and the barn, a small semicircle of ranch hands intently listening to whatever Ace was saying. Paxton stood directly to his right, listening with crossed arms.

"Who is *that*?" Veronica asked.

"That's Ace," Sophia said with a small smile. "Isn't he gorgeous?"

"Yes, I've seen nine hundred and forty-seven pictures of him on your Instagram," Veronica said dryly. "I meant the other one. The only one not wearing a hat."

"Paxton," Charli supplied helpfully. "He's cute, no?"

The three of them shifted their attention to the third partner in Heath's security firm, the one Charli had once thought might break her bad luck in the man department. Paxton was objectively handsome, but he couldn't hold a candle to Heath's sheer, rugged male beauty. Plus, it was entirely possible that she might be a little too much for someone with Paxton's mild demeanor. He kept to himself and caused zero waves, choosing to fade into the background when possible.

Heath was totally it for her. He'd ruined her for other men, and she couldn't even be mad at him over it.

Veronica on the other hand clearly appreciated the view. "He's definitely easy on the eyes. How do you get any work done around here if that's what's going on right outside your window?"

"Oh, it's easy," Charli replied with an eye roll. "We don't do any work. We sit around and wait for one of the *ologists* to show up with more bad news."

As if giving voice to that thought conjured the woman herself, Dr. Low exited the trailer perched at the edge of the wide space near the barn, closing the door behind her and locking it. One of the armed guards let her clear the short staircase and then took up a new position in front of the door, his semiautomatic rifle crossed over his chest. The scene was straight out of a movie full of special effects and actors with chiseled jaws, but this was Charli's real life and it kind of sucked.

Veronica watched with unveiled interest, the shadows Charli had seen in her eyes earlier completely banked. Maybe she'd imagined her sister's disquiet. But she didn't think so.

"Are we safe here?" Veronica asked, sounding more like her lawyer self than she had since she'd walked into the house. "When you said there were armed guards on the property, I guess I pictured it a little differently, like maybe they were doing rounds at the fence line and staying out of sight. But this is quite a bit more in your face than I was expecting."

Sophia sipped her coffee and nodded. "I'd trust Ace with my life and have, more than once. Heath is keeping up with Charli, no small feat, but I think he's the right man for that job."

"Hey," Charli protested without a lot of heat. But only because that wasn't wrong. "I have to do my share of keeping up with him too."

Ugh, she hadn't thought too much about what *that* would look like. On purpose. The bet had been designed to keep Heath entertained while he protected Charli, but at the end of the day, he still had a job—as Charli's bodyguard. Could her life get any worse?

The university people needed to clear out *soon*.

Veronica glanced at her with an eyebrow quirked, her gaze sharp as she took in Charli's expression, apparently seeing something there. "Sounds like a story there. Spill all the tea, Char."

A tight band snapped tight around her lungs all at once.

"There's no tea," she mumbled and drew in a breath. It didn't help.

Sophia bumped her with an elbow. "Oh, there's tea. It was a little hard to miss that he slept in your room the other night instead of the bunkhouse."

"Oooh," Veronica trilled and settled, her posture expectant, into the love seat Sophia had pushed against the far wall. "Tell, tell. This is a big development, yes?"

"Not even a little bit." It hit her all at once. Margo. The bet. How far she'd taken *practicing*. "It's not like that, not like you think. We're just friends."

Veronica and Sophia glanced at each other, but it was Sophia who spoke. "I've seen you two together. You could light firewood from ten paces. I know you said it wasn't working out after that one date you went on, but I thought...well, I mean, couples fight and make up all the time. I kind of assumed you were figuring it out."

"Yeah, we were," she responded glumly, slumping to the floor to lean against the wall under the window so her eyes would quit flicking to the horizon to see if Heath had come back from his jaunt with Margo yet. "Figuring out how to get him back together with Margo."

Sophia visibly flinched. "What? What is that supposed to mean?"

She told her sisters about the bet and how Heath had flipped it on its head by introducing the idea of practicing. It sounded ridiculous out loud. Even to her, and she'd been the one to blow it way out of proportion.

"That's..." Veronica blinked a bunch. "Fascinating. I didn't think people did stuff like that in real life."

Yeah, well, she didn't need her sister's hypercritical tone to feel stupid. And now she wished she'd kept her mouth shut.

"Judgmental much?" Charli shot back and set aside the coffee that had turned to mud in her mouth. "I just wanted to win. I wasn't expecting to fall—"

Abort, her brain screamed, and she clamped her mouth shut. Too late.

Sophia brightened and clapped like she'd just descended the stairs on Christmas morning to find Santa had dropped half of a Tiffany's store under the tree. "I knew it! I knew you guys were falling for each other. Ace owes me ten bucks."

Ace had bet against Heath falling in love with Charli?

The bands around her lungs became knives instantly. "That was a sucker's bet, Soph. He knows Heath is still in love with Margo. And it's fine. There's nothing between us."

Rubbing her forehead, Sophia sank into her desk chair, fiddling with her coffee mug, contemplating Charli with an unreadable expression. "If that's what you want to believe, okay. But I don't think that's even a little true. I've seen you together. There's a mirror on the wall behind the kitchen table, or did you forget? Every time y'all sit together, he's holding your hand on the down-low. You're constantly on his mind, whether it's to make sure you're being taken care of when he can't be around or talking about you to Ace."

This was news she hadn't heard. "He talks about me?"

Sophia rolled her eyes. "If I'd known any of this was in question, I'd have clued you in a long time ago, but yeah. Ace thinks it's entertaining, so of course he mentions it to me."

"Then why did Ace bet against me?" she couldn't help but ask. "Because he knows Heath is still in love with Margo. Like I said. They've been friends a long time."

The question was rhetorical, but Sophia treated the answer like she'd wagered everything on final Jeopardy. "I don't know why he took the bet. Ace never said anything of the sort, plus how would he know that? Men never talk about important stuff, just sports and firearms."

That didn't mean Ace hadn't figured it out. Her sister's boyfriend was sharp and intuitive, which made him good at his job, plus he'd worked with Margo too.

"I think the most important question is whether you've told Heath you're in love with him," Veronica said in her opposing counsel voice.

"What?" Charli croaked. "Why would I tell him that? It's not true. I would—"

"You're lying," Veronica interjected simply. "I have a very expensive degree in psychology and another one that says I can practice law, plus a dozen cases in my rearview mirror that every partner at my law firm said were unwinnable. I win because I pay attention to what people don't say. You're in love with him. It wasn't practice for you. Does he know?"

"No," she said flatly, figuring it was better to come clean instead of throwing even more kindling on the fire of her sister's argument. "And no one in this room is going to say a word. He's in love with Margo and that's that."

Honestly, his commitment to his ex-girlfriend spoke volumes about his character. Ironic that his most attractive feature meant that he'd never be hers. And that she'd lost the bet.

"Oh, honey." Sophia clucked. "Did he tell you that? He's a moron."

"He didn't have to say it," she insisted, letting her head thunk against the wall. "I saw them together. Plus, he's been really clear since always that he wanted to get back together with her."

"Sometimes people's feelings change," Veronica muttered, sounding as if she might have a lot more to say about that, but opted not to.

"And sometimes they don't," she countered.

"Sometimes they don't," Sophia agreed and pointed at herself. "And that's a good thing. I had to tell Ace how I really felt, or I might have lost him. Now we're talking about the kind of forever I didn't think was possible."

"Yeah, exactly," Charli said with her brows raised. "We don't have a lot of positive relationships to look at for inspiration. What if I do tell him and we ride off into the sunset? There's always a sunrise and those don't always bring good things. His feelings might change about *me* at some point. That's a running theme here."

Men *never* picked her. Not the way Sophia was talking about. It was too big a risk to lay it all out there, only to be left once again, either by cheating or abandonment. Same end. It was so much better to step back than to invest her entire soul in someone who would ultimately wind up shedding their relationship one way or another.

"Besides, it doesn't matter," she said and pushed away from the wall, done with this subject. Past done. "We have a lot of other things to worry about with everything going on around the ranch."

That's where her attention should be, with the treasure still on site, plus the unanswered questions about the trailer break-in and their father's cause of death.

Veronica seemed to realize it was time for a subject change and smiled slyly. "Does that mean I get my own personal bodyguard? Because I can do math and there's one left who doesn't seem to be otherwise occupied."

"Yeah," Sophia said, her mouth flattening out as she considered the point. "I wasn't thinking that would be necessary since you're only here temporarily. But it wouldn't be a bad idea to ask Paxton to keep an eye out for you and Mom while you're in town."

Veronica cleared her throat, her expression decidedly wry. "I was thinking more about the *personal* part of the equation, not the danger."

When Sophia gave her sister a strange look, Charli translated for her. "She and Jeremy broke up. I think we are witnessing a rebirth of her interest in jumping back into the dating pool. Perhaps we could ask one of the auxiliary guys to watch after Mom and arrange for Paxton to be directly assigned to Veronica."

"Oh." Sophia flashed a broad smile. "I will see what I can do as the employer of Madden, McKay and Pierce's services. No promises. Keep in mind that the danger is real, though. You can't treat him like his protection is optional, which some people seem to forget occasionally."

Charli shot Sophia a withering look. "Most of the bad stuff happened around the house or in the woods. Nothing exciting has ever happened in the horse pastures."

"Except for you falling in a well and breaking your arm," Sophia pointed out with a nod toward the cast on Charli's arm. "Fortunately, Heath has stellar tracking abilities, or you might still be down there."

"Wait, what bad stuff happened in the woods?" Veronica wanted to know.

"Charli and Heath ran across some dead animals that appeared to have been planted," Sophia supplied.

"Rather not relive that," Charli said with a shudder. "Let's just say I've never more strongly considered being a vegetarian than I did in that moment."

"So one of the trailers was broken into, someone planted dead animals, and Dad was found dead under mysterious circumstances." Veronica ticked off the points on her fingers. "Did I miss anything?"

Charli and Sophia glanced at each other and shook their heads, Sophia speaking for them both. "I don't think so. I mean, there was the incident when I was kidnapped and I guess before that, the same guy broke into the house. But Cortez is in jail. Why?"

Veronica stood and paced, looking every bit like a high-powered criminal defense attorney addressing the jury. "The animals and the trailer break-in are recent, and Dad's death is likely several years old, which means they're probably not related. It would be highly unusual for a murderer to return to the scene of the crime so much later and terrorize the victim's family."

"The statues alone are worth ten million dollars," Charli reminded her. "That means all bets are off. It's too much money to assume anyone is doing anything rationally. Plus, we already know that Karl Davenport is an associate of the guy who kidnapped Sophia."

And they knew that Karl was their father's treasure hunting partner. Anything their father may have been involved with, Karl would know about. The mystery of their father's death might be years old, but they'd just found his body recently. It didn't feel like a coincidence. Or unrelated.

"That's true," Veronica said and turned to pace in the other direction. "But why murder Dad and then leave the extremely valuable statue you killed him for with the body?"

No one had a response to that, least of all Charli, who had actually asked herself that same question during the hours she'd been alone with both her father's body and the statue. But if the recent threats weren't related to their father's murder, that meant they were dealing with two different people, not one.

And the danger quotient might be even higher than they'd assumed. That was the important thing to focus on right now, not all her confusing feelings for Heath.

Chapter Twenty-Two

The jaguar heads were gone. *Stolen.*

Heath stared at the open—empty—safe, his heart doing a tango and his stomach threatening to squeeze out through his throat. Outside the trailer, people shouted and milled about, crossing in front of the large picture window above the desk like panicked ants as their mound collapsed in around them.

"How are the statues gone?" he repeated for the fourth time as Dr. Low wrung her hands uselessly, the same thing she'd been doing since she'd reported that the safe had been broken into. One of the guards had grabbed him as he'd crossed the yard on his way to the house.

"I don't know," she mumbled, which was the petite academic's equivalent to a wail. She'd remained largely composed in the scant few minutes since chaos had erupted. "I came back from a meeting with Dr. McDaniel in her trailer and found this."

She gestured to the empty safe, her face etched with disbelief. The thief had carefully dismantled the silent alarm in a feat worthy of someone with Pierce's level of skill. They were dealing with a professional, obviously.

His eyes darted around the small, dimly lit space, taking in Dr. Low's undisturbed laptop, several labeled artifacts standing intact on a shelf near her desk, and her personal items, including a phone and an expensive-looking handbag. Nothing else had been so much as touched.

Just the safe.

Heath cursed as blue and red lights flashed against the far wall announcing the arrival of the local law enforcement. At this rate, they should get a room in the house and stick around. Save time on their commute out to the ranch.

Of course, there wasn't much left to protect.

The three guards who had been on duty at the time of the theft stood behind him, silently accepting their complete failure. They weren't the type to wear their emotions on their sleeves, but he could feel their nerves as they exchanged glances.

"Outside," he snapped to the guards, who immediately did as bid, likely aware that their employment contract with Madden, McKay and Pierce was not going to end with a favorable review.

He followed them so the police would have room to start cataloging the disaster, and then stopped where the three guards stood in a defensive clump. Nothing would save them from his wrath, but before he destroyed them, he needed answers. "What happened? How did the thief get past you?"

One of the guards, a burly man named Murray who had twenty years at the St. Louis PD in his rearview, shook his head. "You know as much as we do. Dr. Low went to her meeting. I saw her lock the door. Wilson took up position in front of the door like he usually does when she leaves, and Jones and I took perimeter. She came back and rushed out to announce the safe was open. I grabbed you. End of story."

Not end of story. This was not happening. Not on his watch. "There has to be something you can remember. Some detail. Thieves do not wave wands and magically appear inside a locked trailer."

The trailer was in view of the house and the barn, deliberately. The clearing had fifty feet of visibility from all sides. Only a ghost could have accomplished this feat.

Then there was the interesting timing, given that they'd only recently discovered the second head—and David Lang's body. Someone could have broken in and stolen the single head, especially since there was a period of time when the security hadn't been as strong, well before they'd found the second one.

Had someone been lurking in the wings, waiting for them to find the second head? Someone who knew there were two? Like Karl Davenport, David Lang's former partner, who topped the list as the likely suspect. And fit the profile of a ghost quite well since no one had actually seen him in the flesh.

Had he been one of the two people who had met at the fence line near the cigarette pile Heath had found?

Heath pinched the bridge of his nose as Murray, Jones and Wilson shifted restlessly. Finally, Jones offered, "That intelligence lady was asking questions yesterday. About the safe."

Of course. That was her job. "I'm sure she asked a lot of questions about everything."

Murray nodded. "That she did. For about an hour. I think she spent at least two with Dr. Low."

And two with Heath this morning. Margo was nothing if not thorough. He'd walked her to her car and as far as he knew, she'd left to fly home, since she'd finished the on-site investigation. She'd mentioned that she would be subpoenaing David Lang's financial records, but that would take weeks to be granted.

The rest of her investigation could take place at Fort Bragg. Such as it was. She'd invited him to stay at her place for an extended visit when he finished his assignment here, heavily alluding to an enthusiastic kiss-and-make-up session in the future. Until the theft had been reported, he'd thought of nothing else except why the idea of taking her up on it made his skin crawl.

Eventually, he'd have to let Margo know the statues had been stolen. But the trail was fresh at the moment and daylight would only last another four and a half hours. Madden was occupied with the local police, acting as their liaison while they did their initial pass on the crime scene, while Pierce had holed up with his surveillance footage looking for a shot of the thief.

That left Heath to do the legwork.

"You three," he said to the guards and pointed at the knot of locals who looked to be a mix of badges and possibly CSI, probably borrowed from a bigger city's department. "Give your statements to whoever is handling that, then park somewhere. Don't leave. You'll be dismissed when I say you are."

Satisfied that they would do as ordered, Heath set himself the task of looking for clues. With everyone else occupied, including the police who were good at taking statements and not much else, someone had to get the jaguar heads back.

The thief had entered the trailer some way and he wanted to know how. Pierce might turn up something in the recorded footage, but that would take hours, and Heath needed to be doing something now.

Preferably something that would burn off the adrenaline pumping through his blood and ease the black edges crowding his vision.

Except he'd taken no more than a half a step toward

the trailer when Charli burst from the woods behind him. Alarm flared in her eyes, widening them, and her hair fell around her face in a disarray that sent his pulse into the stratosphere.

"What's wrong?" he demanded.

She bent at the waist, breathless, but finally wheezed out, "Heath, someone's breaking into your truck! I saw him from the house and had to go out the front door, then double back—"

"Get behind me," he ordered, his brain already connecting dots. "Stay close."

It was the thief. Trying to escape with everyone's attention stuck on the crime scene. Clever.

But the filth hadn't counted on Charli still being in the house, likely with her gaze glued to the window since he'd explicitly told her to stay inside with her mother and sisters. He'd yell at her later for disobeying him.

Or maybe not, if her quick action helped him catch the thief.

He dashed toward the truck, his boots pounding on the ground. There was no time to ensure Charli could keep up, but he couldn't protect her if he opened a gap between them. Instinctively, he matched her pace, and automatically took her hand to pull her along.

The thief would not get away. Not from Heath.

But when he rounded the corner and his truck came into view, the figure crouched near the truck's wheel well was not stealing Heath's truck. He was vandalizing it.

And his name wasn't Karl.

"Harvard," Heath snarled as the kid jerked his head, dropping the can of spray paint in his hand.

It rolled under Heath's truck, right beneath the expletive marching across the door in three-foot letters.

The guy who had manhandled Charli leaped to his feet but didn't run like Heath had expected him to do. Instead, Harvard stood his ground in some misguided show of bravado. As if Heath wouldn't tear him apart in seconds with zero provocation.

Blackness edged through his vision, tempting him to act, pushing him to destroy.

"What do you think you're doing?" Heath barked and the kid had the audacity to sneer.

"Payback," he said with a cocky grin.

He'd gotten his nose fixed. It would look much better broken again and Heath's fist ached to repeat their first encounter. But there was so much more at stake here.

"Is that why you stole the jaguar heads?" It would explain a lot. Who else would have enough knowledge of the university's equipment and procedures to bypass security but an insider?

"Jaguar heads?" A glint of confusion flitted through Harvard's gaze as he glanced at Charli, who hovered at Heath's elbow, thankfully staying out of the line of fire. "Is that redneck slang for something, cowboy?"

Yeah, for the reason Heath was about to turn the kid into hamburger meat. He reeled it back. This was one of the times when he needed to use caution instead of letting his temper boil. Charli's trust in his ability to figure that out settled into his bones and he let that ride for a long minute.

"Where did you hide the heads?" Heath asked him, his voice evening out as the strangest sense of calm soothed his raised hackles.

Harvard edged back an inch, clearly confused by this new, less violent Heath. "Man, I don't know what you're talking about."

Sure. It was a total coincidence that this kid had showed

up at the exact time of the theft so he could deface Heath's truck. Maybe Harvard hadn't intended to steal the vehicle since he likely had another ride stashed somewhere. The vandalism represented an ultimate Screw You as Harvard rode off with his ten-million-dollar bounty.

"That's fine," Heath returned pleasantly. "The police can sort this out. Good thing they're already on site collecting evidence from your other crime. I'm sure they'll be quite thrilled I'm able to provide them a suspect to match the fingerprints taken from the scene. It'll cut down the investigation time exponentially."

"Wait. What?" Alarm flitted through Harvard's gaze as Heath watched calculations scroll through the kid's head. "You can't take fingerprints from skinned animals. You won't pin any of that on me."

Oh for the love of Pete. Heath bit back a curse. Pieces clicked into place instantly. The skinned animals had been *this* guy's calling card? Along with the vandalism, it fit. Random, petty acts of a desperately immature grad student who had suffered humiliation at the hands of someone twice his size with twice the intellect.

"Oh, we can and will," Heath promised him. "Plus the theft of the ancient, priceless artifacts that are currently missing. I'm sure everyone will appreciate it if you just return them."

Harvard sputtered. "I didn't take anything. I may have trashed some of the other students' research, but it's all garbage. They're analyzing bone fragments and sifting through beads like all that crap matters."

Bone fragments. A hint of a memory darted through Heath's head. That's what No-Logo had mentioned he was researching outside the ransacked trailer. Harvard wasn't confessing to have broken into the guarded trailer containing the safe, but the research trailer. Intending to cause havoc. Not to steal anything.

That would explain why the kid didn't seem to have a clue what Heath was trying to goad him into confessing. Was that really the case? Harvard wasn't the thief? Then who was?

The entire world had gone off its axis.

"All right," Heath said dismissively. "We'll let the cops straighten this out."

With no warning—and thus no chance for Harvard to make a break for it—Heath grabbed him by the arm and hustled him back the way he and Charli had come. Straight to Gun Barrel City's finest, where he deposited his protesting detainee. Given that Heath had a measure of authority at the ranch, none of the police officers batted an eye when he told them to arrest the kid and throw theft charges at him.

They wouldn't stick. Harvard had convinced Heath that he wasn't the mastermind of the statue theft, but that left so many open questions, it wouldn't help to mention them to the local authorities.

"You know he didn't take the jaguar heads. Right?" Charli suggested as she dogged Heath's steps away from the general chaos of the police taking statements and attempting to organize the scene.

Heath had plenty enough of that experience to want to avoid being the keeper of the peace at a crime scene on this ranch.

"Yeah, I know," he told her with an eye roll. "It was meant to keep everyone busy."

"You think it was Karl." Charli chewed her lip. "And that he killed my father too."

This was so not the conversation he wanted to be having with her right now. Or ever. She was wearing a T-shirt that was too large for her, so it sat off to one side, exposing a bit of shoulder that he couldn't peel his eyes from all at once.

What kind of dog was he that he couldn't think of her as a friend? Margo should be the woman on his mind, but he couldn't force that, even if he wanted to. There was no comparison between the two—and he couldn't envision starting things back up with Margo at this point. It felt...wrong.

And Charli didn't seem to be at all interested in his feelings on the matter. He'd even tried to broach the subject before Margo had showed up. And after, forget it. Charli couldn't have pushed him away fast enough.

He got it. Heath was fine for practice but not for real. It was never real, not on her side. Not even the times when it had seemed like they were so in sync that they were practically reading each other's thoughts.

Heath was just her bodyguard.

"Go back to the house and I'll be in later," he mumbled, aware that the situation was indeed an indictment on his abilities to do his job. After all, the name of the security company employed by the ranch had his name on it.

"Yes, sir, Mr. Babysitter, sir."

She saluted and wheeled to do his bidding, but not before he caught a glint in her eye that sat funny in his gut. As if her smart-aleck response might have more to it than just Charli giving him regular grief.

Great. Had he hurt her feelings? There was no scenario where he had the time to chase after her and yank an explanation out of her as to what was wrong. That part of their relationship was over.

Groaning, he rounded the trailer, avoiding everyone with a uniform, as well as Madden, who was still riding point with all the locals.

Heath needed to end this thing. Now, not later. Not by

sitting on his hands while less invested people took up the mantle. He still hadn't answered his own question about how the thief had gotten into the trailer, who was likely Karl, as Charli had surmised. Nothing Harvard had said pointed at him as the thief.

But Karl could be anywhere with those heads by now.

Careful not to disturb anything that might yield fingerprints, he checked the entire perimeter of the trailer for handholds that might allow someone with a bit of skill to scale the fiberglass siding and roll onto the roof.

There were a couple of spots that might be viable. The thief had surely worn gloves, but just in case, he opted not to press his own fingers into the crevices to check if they'd hold a man's weight.

Besides, going in through the roof would be like asking to be spotted. Especially in daylight. A niggle in his gut shifted his gaze. If he'd been doing this job, he'd never pick *up* over *down*.

He dropped to the ground and peered at the undercarriage. It took him a while to find what he was looking for, but eventually he spied the cleverly hidden square in the floor of the trailer. Just as he suspected. The thief had cut a hole in the floor. Just like Heath had done in an operation near Kandahar to extract a briefcase from a locked room.

Likely the thief had created the hole last night under cover of darkness, then accessed the brand-new entry point today. That's why none of the guards had seen the thief. Wouldn't shock him if the timing turned out to overlap with shift change.

The hole wasn't large either, which could explain Dr. Low not noticing the cut from the interior. He'd never seen a picture of Karl Davenport but if he measured in at an average male height and weight, Karl wouldn't fit through this hole. Neither would Heath, for that matter, a fact he knew for certain because the first time he'd practiced cutting a hole for Kandahar, it had been too small.

Margo had laughed at his poor judgment as she'd cataloged his progress on the mission, asking if he'd planned to invite her along to push *her* through the hole.

His pulse kicked up a notch due to the narrative forming in his head. The one where the thief wasn't Karl but someone with a much smaller stature. Someone who had established a perfectly legit reason to visit the trailer and spend as much time cataloging it as she wished to.

Margo.

She'd likely walked up and asked the guards when their shift change happened and they'd blithely told her, blinded by her smile and considerable charm as she stole the jaguar heads out from underneath them.

Heath let that wash over him as the truth burned a hole in his chest.

She'd played him. She hadn't taken this assignment to cozy up to him in hopes of rekindling something between them. She'd taken it to *distract* him.

And she had. He hadn't followed up on his suspicions about her orders from JSOC. Which likely didn't even exist. In retrospect, he should have asked a lot more questions about why Spec Ops would care about some Maya treasure.

What an idiot he was. Shame and not a little embarrassment coated his skin like shellac.

What he did not feel was heartbroken.

That told him everything he needed to know about why the whole scene with Margo had felt…off. He wasn't in love with her anymore. If he ever had been in the first place.

She'd reevaluated during their time apart—so had he. With distance, he could see their relationship was dysfunctional at best. At worst, toxic. And she wasn't as pretty as he'd remembered. She wore entirely too much makeup, and you could feed a small village for what her diamond earrings cost.

Now he knew what it was like to be with a woman who not only encouraged him to be himself, but seemed to *like* him, too. As if Heath McKay unfiltered and unaltered worked for her in a million different ways.

It was heady, especially in comparison. A relief. He should have realized all this a long time ago, saved everyone a lot of grief, especially Charli. What if instead of trying to give Margo the benefit of the doubt, he'd just told Charli how he felt about her? Would she have thought about it and realized how good they were together?

He had to find out. As soon as possible.

Unfortunately, that had to come *after* he fixed this other mess. If Margo was the thief, he was the only one with a prayer of finding her. He was the only one with the skill set. The score he had to settle with her for stealing from the Langs and making a mockery of him? That was just a bonus.

Chapter Twenty-Three

Heath texted Charli again at a rest stop and waited for a reply. Nada. Just like the last three times.

Her lack of response sat in his gut like a cocklebur, sharp and uncomfortable. And worrisome. Things between them were still strained, that much he knew, but come on. He'd gone out of his way to make sure they were okay, that Margo hadn't changed anything between them.

If nothing else, he and Charli were still friends.

Which he'd do everything in his power to change eventually. As soon as he could.

But no response could mean Charli had fallen down another well.

She better not have. He'd specifically instructed Pierce to stick to Charli like white on rice and he'd trusted his partner with his life on many occasions, so smart money said it was something else.

Was she ignoring him? He'd explained that he'd had to go in all three text messages, that he'd fill in the gaps as soon as he could. But he couldn't risk tipping off Margo, just in case she'd set up a tap on everything Lang-related. It would be her style.

With no time to waste, he pushed on, cranking the air conditioner in the SUV he'd rented. His truck was still at the body shop getting a new paint job to erase Harvard's art-work on the door panels. Too bad he couldn't have arranged a flight, or he'd have done it. His contacts in the military were suspect at this point, though—all the people he knew also knew Margo and there was no telling how many others had been turned.

Not to mention the fact that he wasn't 100 percent convinced he'd find Margo at her father's lake house in Austin. It was a gamble, but a good one given that she'd often spent time there when she'd had vacation from work.

If she wasn't there, he faced a long few days of trying to track her with a cold trail. He was trying not to think about that—but unfortunately his thoughts drifted to Charli the moment he let his guard down. The distraction alone made that a bad idea.

But he couldn't help it.

He missed her. Not for the first time, he wished he'd had the latitude to invite her along. She'd have made this trip a thousand times more interesting. It would have been a good chance to spend time together. Learn some things. Talk about their favorite movies. Whatever. He craved that kind of normalcy. He'd never had that before and wanted it desperately.

The roads in this area of Texas stretched for miles, long and winding and treacherous for someone who had been on the road for three hours already. He had to find Margo, had to confront her about the stolen jaguar heads and the lies.

The weight of her duplicity bore down on him. Who had turned her? And why? What was her end game?

When he finally reached the lake house after only one wrong turn, a chill washed over him. The structure itself stood up on a hill, a dark silhouette now that the sun had set. He parked the SUV a short distance from the house, rolling it into the heavy brush to avoid drawing attention.

As he exited the SUV, gravel crunched beneath his boots, ringing out in the still air. Heath froze. After a beat, he heel-toed it to the tree line, hoping there'd be enough ground cover to mask his steps.

The night air was heavy with humidity and the scent of sage from the bushes growing wild along the road. Hills rose behind the house, a majestic backdrop that he wished he had time to explore. It would be a lot more fun to have made this trip with the intent to hike. With Charli.

Was she thinking about him? Did she miss him?

That was one thing about being with someone like Margo. She was pretty self-sufficient, and she'd never once expressed a single personal thought about Heath being gone all the time when he'd been with the navy. She'd only cared whether he'd completed his missions or not and whether the team had been successful.

Honestly, sometimes he'd wondered if she'd have even missed him if he didn't come home. And not for the first time since he'd found the hole cut in the floor, he cross-examined himself on why he'd wanted her back so badly.

Pride. Probably. Which pretty much drove him now too.

With each step, his senses heightened. Crickets chirped, insects buzzed, and moonlight reflected off the giant picture windows overlooking the lake.

Slipping through the shadows, gratified that he hadn't lost his stealth skills, he crept through the row of hedges landscaped to the hilt, peering into the first window from a hidden vantage point. It was dark inside, but the front room led to a hallway and a single light shone from the back of the house.

Could be a security light programmed to switch on after dark. Or it could be Margo.

Heath circled the house, keeping to the darkest pockets as surely Mr. Malloy had cameras around this property and possibly pressure sensors to warn of intruders. But he couldn't take the time to study the security logistics. Especially given that he planned to get inside in a matter of seconds.

At a window approximately three-quarters of the distance to the back of the house, he surveyed what he could see from this vantage point. There were fewer shadows here thanks to the floodlight affixed to the highest peak of the roofline, but as he tilted his head, he saw her.

Margo. She moved through the room with purpose, clearly outlined by the overhead lights. It was a bathroom of enormous size, with an ocean of white tile. Fortunately, he had zero qualms about spying on his former girlfriend while she took a bath.

Not that he'd stick around to enjoy the show. It would simply be a good distraction for her while he figured out his entrance logistics.

She didn't stay in the bathroom, though. In typical Margo fashion, she checked out her appearance in the full-length cheval mirror, straightening the straps of the black tank top she wore. Then she exited the room, flicking off the lights with her index finger.

Heath waited a millisecond to ensure she didn't backtrack, then quickly scouted for a good way inside. A lucky break—several of the windows were open on the second floor to let in the cooler night air. Which also meant Margo wasn't expecting him.

He couldn't wait to see her face when she realized he'd figured out her game so quickly.

A trellis near the screened-in porch made an excellent ladder, though it wasn't so easy to push the ropy vines aside with his boots. He made it to the roof of the porch after a minor brush with a startled lizard. With agonizing caution, he crept across the porch roof to one of the open windows, an old-fashioned kind with a turn handle. Margo had cranked it just enough that he could get his arm up through the crack and lever it open wide enough for an entire former SEAL to slip through.

Glad he hadn't lost his touch, he toed off his boots and stowed them in a shadowy corner in case Margo passed by this room. The downside of being out of the Teams—he had boots, not stealth footwear, and had never envisioned a scenario where running security on a ranch in Texas would require anything different.

Granted, none of this had anything to do with the ranch. Charli and her sisters were just the unlucky owners caught in the middle of whatever game this was.

Heath slid across the threshold of the bedroom and into the hall. A light shone at the far end. Margo stood underneath it, hands clasped in front of her. Waiting for him.

The hall light glinted off a long kitchen knife between her palms.

"Hello, darling," she purred. "So nice of you to join me."

Adrenaline coursed through his veins, cutting off his self-congratulatory spiel. She'd set this up. It was a trap, and he'd fallen right into it, a blind lion scenting fresh meat, then limping his way right into the lair of the hunter.

"It was good of you to leave such an easy trail to follow," he returned, schooling the expression on his face, though it was likely a lost cause. She knew she'd bested him. This was her gloating face.

She lifted a manicured brow. "Honestly, I expected you much earlier. Couldn't find a ride?"

"Obviously I can trust no one," he said with a shrug. "Plus, there was a little matter of a vandal I had to ensure the police arrested. I can do two jobs at once. Can you?"

She had no reason to answer him, but she didn't hesitate. "Quite well, apparently. It's amazing how much information comes across my computer screen that presents interesting opportunities. Only a fool wouldn't see the potential to profit."

"That's what this was? A paycheck?"

Margo lifted her shoulders. "What isn't about a paycheck? That's what we work for, isn't it?"

Maybe *she* did. But he worked with Madden and Pierce because they meant something to him. Because they believed in each other. They all cared about their clients and about ensuring people who couldn't protect themselves had someone in their corner who could. At least that had always been the case before.

Charli had been different from the first. Who knew the perfect woman for him preferred jeans and horses over couture and superficiality?

But he couldn't think about her. Not now. This situation needed his full attention, particularly given the hardware involved.

Did Margo know he'd tucked his gun into the waistband of his jeans? Or did she truly intend to stab an unarmed man?

"I need the heads back, Margo," he told her with far more calm than he'd expected. Than the situation called for.

She clued in on it, too, cocking her head and surveying him with a puzzled sweep. "Who are you and what did you do with Heath McKay? Did you take a Valium in the car?"

There was nothing funny about this showdown, but he couldn't help laugh at her question anyway. "I didn't have to. I'm a reformed hothead. Sorry I didn't send you an announcement."

"That's an egregious oversight." She tsked and brandished the knife. "I'm overdressed for the occasion, then. I was expecting a knockdown, drag-out fight."

He lifted a brow. "You against me? I've never been *that* much of a hothead."

"Well, that's debatable," she said delicately and sniffed. "And I didn't want to find out what your limits were."

That stuck him in the gut far deeper than any piece of steel could. She thought he might lose control one day and… what? Actually hit her? The thought made him green all the way to his toes.

Thankfully, Charli hadn't flinched at being front and center with Heath. Present in a way that he'd never had before. Or realized he'd want so deeply.

"That's okay," he said with a tiny smile. "Someone else helped me figure out what my limits are."

Granted, a lot of that had come about because Charli had tested them. But it still counted.

"Oh, yes, your country bumpkin." Margo nodded sagely. "I could tell something was going on between you. That'll last about another two seconds, until you get bored and start spoiling for a fight. She does know that you're not overly fond of roots, right?"

"My relationship with Charli is none of your concern," he told her with zero heat and enjoyed every second of it. Holding out his hand, he flipped his fingers in a gimme motion. "The heads, Margo. They belong to the people of Mexico, not your highest bidder."

She laughed. "I'm not selling them on the open market,

are you insane? I'm the delivery girl. Half up-front, half upon transfer. You don't know the guy."

"Try me." He showed his teeth.

"Silver hair? About yay tall?" Margo made a shelf out of her hand at about the six-foot mark. "Name's George."

"George." Heath rolled his eyes. "Because that doesn't sound fake. We're not having a conversation here, Margo. This is my job and I'm not leaving without the statues. Don't get in my way or you will find out what I'm capable of."

She raised the knife, malice churning through her eyes. "Come and take them, Navy Boy. I've never been one to stay behind a desk. Might be a harder job than you anticipated."

Flashing her a smile that she didn't know what to do with—judging by the confusion floating around—he used the scant few seconds to catalog the hall, noting the window behind her, the staircase winding to the ground floor.

One second he was standing there, the next, he'd leaped forward, rolling into a crouch, then swept one leg in an arc to take out Margo's from underneath her.

She went down with a cry, but contorted midair and drove the knife downward. Straight into his leg.

White-hot agony lanced through his calf. He bit back a scream and rolled with the wave of nausea for a second. But he had to move. Couldn't just lie there and bleed.

Margo leaped to her feet, not the slightest bit dazed. They both glanced at the knife that had clattered to the wood floor near the wall. As she dove for it, Heath twisted and pulled the gun from his waistband, aiming it at her heart.

"Back away slowly," he rasped, and she threw up her hands. Good. She wasn't going to be stupid.

Fighting through the pain, Heath climbed to his feet, careful not to put weight on his sliced leg, and palmed the knife.

Blood seeped into the fabric of his jeans, but he didn't have time to check how deep the cut was.

"Take me to the heads," he ordered her and jerked the barrel of the gun to the left as he held the knife in her general direction. Hopefully she got the hint that he'd gladly use either on her.

"Not even if you shoot me," she said with a defiant toss of her hair and crossed her arms. "You can't fathom how much money I'm being paid to deliver these statues to my client."

"Is it worth the gamble that you might die in the process?" he asked her quietly, struck all at once that he'd imagined himself in love with this woman not that long ago. And she'd waltzed back into his life as an enemy—one who didn't seem that unhappy about the lot she'd chosen.

And she certainly didn't want him back. It was a relief to finally be shed of this woman forever.

She scoffed. "Please, you wouldn't kill me."

No, he wouldn't, not unless he had to defend Charli. Or himself. That was the thing she failed to realize. She'd meant something to him once, and still did, but not the way she seemed to assume. "I was talking about your client. Once he has the statues, there's no reason to keep you alive. And if you're dead, he doesn't have to pay you the second installment. You're dealing with criminals, Margo. They don't have to honor the rules of engagement."

Not that she was doing that either, but there was still a part of him who didn't want to see her suffer for the terrible choices she'd made.

"What would you have me do, darling?" she purred. "Hand them over to you in hopes my client will see the error of his ways? I don't think so."

Heath nodded. "Okay. We'll do this the hard way, then."

While they'd chatted about her descent into darkness, he'd

maneuvered close enough to the side table near the stairs to pull the long runner free. Before Margo could formulate an escape plan, he flung the knife to the other end of the hall, out of reach, then snagged her wrist, twisting it behind her with his free hand.

Shoving the gun against her ribs, he forced her to walk. "Move. Heads. Now. Or you will have a bullet wound through multiple internal organs. Your choice."

Margo hesitated for so long, he started formulating plan B. Then she spat out a curse, testing his strength with a surprisingly strong yank against his grip on her wrist.

He'd been braced for that since moment one. So it didn't work. He jammed the gun deeper into her ribs. "Try again. See where that gets you. Or cooperate. Then this is over faster."

Finally, her spine relaxed a fraction. Which in turn allowed him to breathe a tad easier.

He held the runner with his teeth as she stalked down the stairs. It was dicey trying to keep up with her and not let on that the pain piercing his leg with each step nearly stole his breath. The trail of blood he left on the floor should probably concern him more, but unless he passed out, it couldn't be a factor.

Once they hit the ground floor, he'd lost enough blood that he needed to make things easier on himself, so he tied her wrists together with the runner instead of using it as a tourniquet, which had been his first plan.

"Keep going," he advised her as she shot him a black look.

Snarling low-level threats that amounted to nothing more than grumbling, she led him to into a well-appointed office. Behind an oil painting of a ship, she revealed a safe.

"Good luck with that," she taunted. "I'm not going to tell you how to open it."

Heath's head swam from stress and blood loss. There was no guarantee that she'd even put the statues in the safe, but he had a feeling she'd wanted to see him sweat over this additional complexity or she wouldn't have led him to this room in the first place.

"You don't have to tell me," he informed her and un-plugged a lamp from a side table next to a leather chair, then force-sat her in the chair, tying the cord around her legs with a sailor's knot that she no doubt recognized.

She could still likely get loose if he gave her long enough, so he scuttled from the room as quickly as he could in search of towels and water to clean up his leg. Losing more blood wouldn't help this situation.

In seconds, he'd found a bathroom and cleaned up the worst of the wound. It wasn't as deep as he'd feared and the knife hadn't cut anything critical other than his skin, so he tied a fluffy guest towel with the monogram AAM around his calf.

As he exited the bathroom, he spied Margo's handbag sitting on the island in the kitchen. Not one to look a gift horse in the mouth, he took precious seconds to go through it. She'd slid her phone into the front pocket, which he didn't dare hope he could get into unless she'd enabled facial rec-ognition. No one in Special Ops would ever do that since an enemy could easily use it to gain access to important data, even if you were dead.

Something fluttered to the floor as he pulled out her phone. A slip of paper. Crouching, he picked it up, his eyes widening as he took in the sequence of numbers. They sure looked an awful lot like exactly what he was looking for.

But really? Surely Margo hadn't *written down* the combination to the safe.

But this was her father's house. Not hers. There was no reason for her to know the combination. And no reason for him not to try it. Worst-case scenario, it didn't work and he moved on to plan C.

"Found it," he said as he clomped back into the home office and flicked the paper up between two fingers to show her.

Something flashed across her face, informing him instantly that it *was* the combination. He shut his eyes in disbelief. If she hadn't stabbed him, he'd never have pulled his gun and none of this would have unfolded. She might have run, and he might have chased her, never realizing the statues were in the house all along.

Within seconds, the safe popped open. Gold gleamed from its dark interior. The jaguar heads.

He scooped them out and shut the safe. "Nice doing business with you, Ms. Malloy. I hope I never see you again."

Heath exited the room, Margo muttering slurs on his character that got more inventive the further he trudged. The trip to the second floor to retrieve his boots nearly killed him but an eternity later, he had everything he'd come for. Once he got out of the house, he called the local police to come pick up Margo, and explained—very patiently—that they needed to coordinate with the Texas Rangers and Gun Barrel City PD.

Not his problem any longer. He'd spent far too long thinking he wasn't good enough for Margo, that he needed to change to make her happy, but the truth was that she wasn't good enough for him. The missing element in his life wasn't the ability for him to manage his temper, but the acceptance of it. Of him. Wholly and unaltered. He only needed Charli to be happy.

And she still hadn't responded to any of his text messages.

Chapter Twenty-Four

Charli liked being babysat by Paxton even less than when Heath had been her shadow. Actually, it wasn't the same at all. With Heath, she'd felt like they were spending time together while he protected her from harm. Like they were connecting.

It was only when Paxton had materialized at her side and mumbled something about Heath asking him to fill in that she'd understood that Heath was gone. *He'd left.* As in flat out just walked out the door with Margo.

Well, of course he had. That's what she'd encouraged him to do. His commitment to Margo remained steadfast, ironically one of his best features.

But was it too much to have wished he'd said goodbye? That Charli had meant enough to him to take two minutes to call a time-out and pull her into his arms for the last time?

Clearly that wasn't a thing. Then he'd *texted* her.

Heath: I'm sorry, but I have to leave

Heath: Are you okay? I'm worried about you

Heath: I'll explain later. I just can't right now

Of course she'd ignored him. Oh, she'd read all the text messages, but what was there to say? To explain?

She'd known this was coming. What she hadn't anticipated was Heath still trying to maintain contact, like everything between them hadn't been torn up at the roots like a tree in a hurricane.

The missing jaguar heads provided an almost welcome distraction, tossing her into the middle of a mess that she and Sophia, along with Ace and Paxton, had to temper without Heath's help. Charli was just now coming to realize how much order he'd brought to the chaos. And not just on the ranch. He settled *her* in ways she hadn't honored nearly enough.

The local police had no leads but insisted on going over every inch of the ranch a second time. Keeping the dig nerds out of the way proved nearly impossible and Dr. Low kept trying to talk to Charli about insurance claims. By dinnertime, she just wanted Heath. And a bath. And to sleep for a million years.

None of those were going to happen.

Finally, she managed to roll into bed at midnight, exhausted but unable to sleep. Stupid cast. She couldn't get comfortable, and Heath wasn't here to soothe her with his heat and magical touch.

Fine. That was fine. She didn't need him.

The crunch of gravel outside made her bolt up and she dashed to the window to see a nondescript SUV rolling into the circular drive at the front of the house, then continue to the back. Just as she grabbed her phone to text Paxton that they had unwelcome company, Heath swung out of the driver's seat.

Heath.

Alone. Without Margo.

Oh, dear heavens. What was he doing here?

She watched him walk toward the kitchen door instead of the bunkhouse, hatless, his gait a funny one-two step. Was something wrong with one his boots?

More to the point, he had a lot of nerve showing back up here after not even bothering to say goodbye. Really, she should have realized that he'd come back to finish his assignment since his security company still had a contract with Sophia.

But still. She had a piece of her mind to give him.

She marched down the stairs without a single consideration for her Hello Kitty pajamas, meeting him at the door of the kitchen, arms crossed so she didn't reach out to touch him, just to assure herself that he was here and whole and real. This man didn't belong to her and for all she knew, Margo was waiting for him at a hotel somewhere while he picked up some of his things that he'd left behind.

"Look what the cat dragged in," she said.

The kitchen light threw his features in harsh relief, highlighting fatigue and stress. "I can't fight with you right now, Charli."

"I thought we were friends," she stressed, not because that's what she'd wanted them to be to each other, but she'd thought that part of their relationship was sacred.

He clomped past her into the room with that same one-two step. That's when she noticed the rust-colored stains caking the leg of his jeans, which had been sliced open to the knee. Her pulse shuddered to a halt in milliseconds.

"What's wrong with your leg?" she quavered as she forgot all the things she'd meant to lambast him with and rushed to his side to help maneuver him onto the bench seat at the table.

He didn't protest when she helped him ease off his boots.

When she saw the row of uneven stitches, the sound that came out of her mouth wasn't even human.

Not rust stains. Blood. *Heath's* blood and a lot of it.

"What happened?" she demanded and sucked in a hot breath, then asked a second time, but a little more calmly.

"I got the statues back."

Heath slumped without warning, nearly sliding to the floor, which left her with no choice but to slide over to him, cradling his head against her shoulder as best she could with the stupid cast.

"Of course you did," she murmured, smoothing his hair back from his forehead. Then what he'd said registered. "Wait. What?"

"The statues. I opened the safe. There they were."

He was slurring his words, which would have been alarming enough without his eyelashes sweeping up and down in exaggerated blinking motions, as if he couldn't quite focus on her.

"You went after the statues?" she repeated in the world's biggest duh moment. "Not Margo?"

"Both," Heath corrected, and his eyes closed for so long, she thought he'd gone to sleep, but then he pried his eyelids open with what appeared to be considerable effort. "Margo took them. Had to get them back. My leg hurts."

So many things crowded into Charli's chest she could scarcely breathe. "Margo took the statues. She stole them? From the safe?"

Heath nodded. "And then she stabbed me."

Charli's eyes widened so far that they started to ache. Nothing he was saying made any sense, but she did know one thing. He was scaring her. "I'm guessing you've lost a lot of blood."

"So much blood." His words slurred again.

Okay, two things. He needed to sleep for like twelve hours. And she needed to know that he was safe and that Margo couldn't touch him. There was a slight possibility that he'd mixed some things up, but she'd take Margo in the role of villain any day and twice on Sunday.

"We'll pick up this conversation later," she advised him and hefted one of his arms around her shoulders, trying to stand with Heath's dead weight leaning on her. "Okay, this is not going to work unless you help me. Let's get up, Heath. Come on now."

After three tries, he did it and then somehow, they managed to get up the stairs to her room with only one false start and a quick breather midway up. And they didn't wake anyone. A miracle.

As soon as he saw her bed, he whumped onto it and fell back crossways over the comforter.

"Not so fast." She crawled in after him and roused him enough to get him to scooch sideways so his head lay on the pillow. She'd sort out later what a colossally bad idea it was for him to be there.

Geez, he was so beautiful, even ashen-faced. The flutter low in her belly came hard and fast and she shoved it away. This was no time or place to be thinking like that, when Heath was practically catatonic. And still technically off-limits, at least until she heard the full story about Margo and the stitches. Probably not then either, dang it.

There was still too much unsaid between them.

It was harder to tear her gaze away from him than she'd like to admit, though.

What had happened? Never in five million years would she have guessed that Heath would be lying in her bed tonight. That was yet another miracle, one she didn't trust. At all.

The blanks in recent events were enough to get her moving—away from the temptation to forget all the questions and whatever unnamable things had started spreading through her chest, warm but confusing. Just as she started to roll from the bed, figuring it was better to let him sleep alone, he pulled her against his side, settling her in next to him with a soft sigh.

Oh, well, gee. Nothing she could do about it now. She snuggled into his body, careful of her cast and his stitches. The tide in her breastbone settled instantly and she might have melted into a puddle of Charli-goo.

Why had she done such a moronic thing as to fall in love with him?

"Missed you," Heath said into her hair, his breath stirring against her skin. "I texted you all those times. Is your phone broken?"

"Yep," she lied, figuring it was better to let him think that than to get into why she couldn't have responded. To make up for it, she drew little circles against his skin, wherever she could reach, hoping it would soothe him to sleep.

He shouldn't be talking. Not now, not ever. Especially if he was going to say sweet things that she immediately got busy misinterpreting.

"I'm not in love with Margo," he slurred and let that bombshell sit there between them as her fingers froze.

"Maybe we can talk about that in the morning too," she advised him. Man, he must have lost more blood than she'd realized. He was practically hallucinating now.

"Wanted to tell you as soon as possible. Drove very fast and far to get here."

With that pronouncement, he fell into the deepest slumber, leaving her to lie there replaying *not in love with Margo* over and over in her head until it lulled her to sleep.

IN THE MORNING, she opened her eyes to the sight of Heath's blue ones trained on her. They were much clearer than last night but still strained, with fine fatigue lines around them. Something else flitted through them that stole her breath.

And terrified her more than anything else ever had in her life.

"Hey," he murmured. "I don't know how I got here. Do I have a lot to apologize for or just a little?"

"You don't remember much of last night," she said. It wasn't a question because of course he didn't.

That would require him to recall the things he'd said without a reminder and her life didn't work like that.

"You don't have a single thing to apologize for. You basically passed out the second your head hit the pillow." She rolled from the bed despite it being the absolute last thing she wanted to do.

"Stop running away, Charli."

Heath's voice had gained a lot of strength too. That was the only reason she didn't flee to the bathroom after gathering up her clothes. Plus, she didn't like it when he read her mind. Or that he'd called it correctly.

She wasn't a coward and to prove it, she turned and stuck her non-cast hand on her hip. "For your information, you need a shower, and I was going to go downstairs to make you breakfast while you washed off all the blood and other… stuff."

Like Margo's fingerprints.

But saying that would require finishing their conversation from last night and she'd rather not. His presence here had so many land mines associated with it that she scarcely even knew how to talk to him.

If Margo had taken the statues and he wasn't in love with her any longer, what did that mean? That was the question she wanted to ask. Which was why making breakfast appealed so much more, because it was downstairs. Away from Heath. Who hadn't stopped watching her with that mixture of pure, unadulterated affection and slight exasperation.

"I can't take a shower with stitches," he informed her calmly. "Only a bath so I don't get them wet. And you're right, that's what I need, along with you in charge of the soap, washing the places I can't reach."

The implied intimacy in that nearly caught her hair on fire and she'd literally never wanted to do anything more in the history of time.

So instead, she made a face at him. "You'd like that, wouldn't you? To have me attending to your every need. Should I find a French maid uniform?"

Heath contemplated her. "What do you think is happening here, Charli?"

Oh, man, the million-dollar question. She sat on the very edge of the comforter, but only because her knees had buckled. "I don't know. You were here and then you left. Margo was gone too, so naturally I assumed you left together and that was that. I spent all day yesterday making my peace with that, and then...*this* happened."

She waved at the bed to encompass the enormity of his big body in it. The implications were clear. He'd come back to her once he didn't have any other options.

"Considering the fact that Margo's responsible for these stitches, I think it's safe to say she's no longer a factor in my life." The bed shrank as he locked her in his sights, his gaze heated and bubbling over. "I came home, which I should have realized much sooner was wherever you are."

"No." She sliced her hand at the air, blinking. "That's all wrong. You're in love with Margo and everything between us was just practice."

"It's not, Charli. It never felt like practice to me."

It had never felt like practice to her either. But hearing him say that, confirming that he'd been feeling the same way all along—it wrecked her. Last night, he'd said he wasn't in love with Margo. She desperately wanted to take that at face value.

But she couldn't. "And yet you still chose her. Not me."

The mournful last note made her sound pathetic. Heath reacted instantly, though, climbing to his knees and crawling to her. He was too close, and she didn't want him to sense how truly torn apart she felt inside. It was a lost cause, obviously, because he just tipped her chin up and drank in whatever he'd found in her expression.

"I'm sorry," he murmured. "It was a mistake from the first moment. I never should have put her between us."

Well, if there was anything sexier than a man who apologized and admitted he'd screwed up in the same breath, she'd never run across it. It weakened her and she didn't want to be weak. Not about this. "That's… I appreciate that, but it doesn't change the fact that whatever you think there is between us is only the result of the bet."

Heath shook his head, his mouth tightening. "We should have canceled the bet a long time ago."

"What?" She dragged out the word with exaggerated flourish to hide her genuine shock. "What is this thing you're saying to me?"

"There's no bet," he said with exaggerated enunciation, as if to make it perfectly clear he knew exactly what he was telling her. "Not anymore."

His thumbs came to rest on each side of her jaw and stars exploded against her skin where he touched her. Deeper down. Behind her eyes. In her heart. With no bet and no

Margo, what was she supposed to hide behind to ensure he didn't destroy her?

"You can't quit now. You're winning," she muttered, instantly sorry she'd blurted that out, but he'd beleaguered her senses from day one. Why should this be any different? "I don't know how to navigate all of this, Heath."

"What is there to know?" he asked, his thumb brushing across her cheek. "I'm here, you're here. Let's figure it out together."

She wanted that more than anything. Wanted to sink into him and know that it was real this time. But that would require her to take a step toward him too. To make herself vulnerable.

And she didn't know how to do that and survive if he left her again—if he didn't come back.

"Heath?" His thumb stilled. "It doesn't feel like practice to me either. I can't understand how that happened. How to trust this is real when it was never supposed to be."

"We came into this all wrong." He heaved a sigh. "But that doesn't seem to have made much of a difference in how I feel about you."

Her heart missed a few beats. "What way is that?"

"Like I stumbled into a wolverine–honey badger cage match honestly."

That almost made her smile. "Fair. I'm still mad at you."

Heath leaned into her, resting his forehead against hers. "Also fair. But I didn't know I had a choice, Charli. Be honest with me. With yourself. Did you give me one?"

"That's not the point," she protested and pushed back on his chest, a thread of panic chilling her. She wrapped her arms around herself for warmth. Protection. "It was always Margo for you. Until she turned out to be the bad guy. And then it was all Charli, all the way. I want to be picked first. I want to know that there's a man out there who sees my worth from the first and is like, *I want that*. No holds barred. No question."

To his credit, Heath didn't touch her again but the expression on his face sure did. It reached inside and squeezed her heart.

"Let me tell you what I thought was going to happen with Margo," he said, opting to slide off the bed in favor of pacing, though it was more of a one-two shuffle, as he ticked off his points. "I wanted to be different, the opposite of a man who is a self-confessed hothead. I thought if I did that, she'd see it and meet me in the middle. She'd be inspired to be different too. But I didn't know how to be that guy. I thought it was a failure on my part that I couldn't stop using my fists. Then you came along. You flipped that script on its head."

"Because it's stupid to want you to be someone different, Heath," she informed him crossly. "You're already perfect."

His quick grin faded. "That's exactly right. I'm perfect for you. Not Margo."

"But that's who you wanted the whole time," she countered, though his words were weaving a spell she feared she might not be able to break. "You never wanted it to be real. Every time things got a little intense, you threw down how it was practice."

"You jumped in to agree with that every time!" He sucked in a hot breath and exhaled, staring at her. "What in the blazes did you think the time-outs were for? Because I wanted it to be real, but I also didn't want you to accuse me of cheating. It's a fine line. One I wanted to honor and I did, but not solely because it was important to you, but it was important to me too. I needed to give my pride a chance with Margo, but that's all it ever was. Pride. A way to make myself feel better that she couldn't love me the way I am."

The sentiments winnowed underneath her skin, loosening her resolve. Dissolving her arguments.

He must have sensed he had the advantage, because he crossed back to the bed, halting directly in front of her so she couldn't look away, and pushed a finger to her chest. "You taught me that a relationship should make you better, not just different. You make me want to be the best version of myself. I'm only husband material when I'm with you."

Okay, that was going way, way too far. What was he saying, that he wanted to *marry* her? Panic licked through her blood as she slapped his finger away. "That's ridiculous. You're you, no matter what. What in the world could possibly be different with me that you can't—"

"Because I'm in love with you, Charli," he practically shouted.

Everything inside her exploded in a shower of confetti and fireworks as she stared at him. The moment shrank down, heavy with anticipation and meaning and a billion other things she couldn't sort fast enough. "Say that again."

"I'm in love with you." He squeezed his eyes shut for a blink. "Though this is not the way I would have liked to announce that."

Well, this was absolutely the way she would have liked to learn that. It changed everything.

Boosting herself up on her knees, she took his beautiful face between her palms, wholly unable to be anything other than honest in that moment. "I'm in love with you too. It's making me bananas."

Snorting, he pushed his cheek into her palm, his scraggly beard rough against her skin. "Obviously that's going around."

"Did I ruin this?" she asked in a small voice. "I don't

know if you know this about me, but I'm neurotic and I tend to pull the trigger first, then ask questions later."

Heath's lips tilted. "I thought I was the one ruining it with my late declarations and ridiculous temper. Though it is par for the course with us to get around to saying how we really feel during a fight."

"I like fighting with you," she murmured, gratified when he nodded his agreement. "You're my safe place. The only person I can trust when I'm Hurricane Charlotte."

And he hadn't given up, moving on to easier, greener pastures. Even when she pushed him away. He wasn't like Toby. Or her father, for that matter. *She* was the one like her father, running from the best thing that had ever happened to her.

This man was everything. So much more than husband material. So much more than a man tasked with keeping her safe.

He was her match.

The only man who could stick with her through everything she could throw at him. Whether he considered it practice or the cold, hard reality of being hit in the face with the brute force of Hurricane Charlotte, he took it all. And kept on ticking.

She couldn't fight this any longer.

"Heath," she murmured and nuzzled his face with hers, which turned into a kiss in the space of a heartbeat.

Their lips fused together, the sensation of finally, finally falling into this moment sliding through her with so much silk that she sighed. This wasn't the heightened, electric kiss she'd expected. It was far sweeter, far deeper, as if every thread in the universe coalesced into this meeting of souls. The way their bodies fit together felt like reuniting missing pieces.

His fingers threaded through her hair as he cupped the back of her head, tilting her neck to deepen the kiss and she let herself go, let herself open to the experience of being wholly consumed by Heath McKay.

This was not a kiss. It was a surrender. On both sides. He held nothing back, pouring himself into the kiss, stamping his signature over every cell in her body, and she accepted everything he was giving her eagerly.

He quite literally overwhelmed her. She loved him so much.

"There's no bet." He slid his lips into her palm, kissing it as he hooked her with his stormy gaze that was now full of something else, something hot and hungry. "No Margo. This is not practice. It's the real thing, no excuses. If you're scared, that's fine. There's a lot of that going around too. But talk to me instead of running. Or pushing. From now on."

She *was* scared. It was unreal how he could read her, how he continually made everything better by virtue of just being Heath. He had the power to destroy her, but she trusted that he wouldn't. That he'd be there for her always. "That's a deal. Now tell me again."

"That I'm questioning my sanity? Done." His smile lit her up inside. "But despite all of that, I love you, Charlotte."

"You know what this means, right?" She brushed a finger over his lips. "You won the bet."

"Oh no, my darling. We both won."

Epilogue

The day of the memorial service brought with it a cold front that required Charli to pull out her fall jacket to guard against the brisk wind. She buttoned up and joined Heath, gripping his hand tightly as they took their seats next to Sophia and Ace.

Veronica sat on Sophia's other side, Paxton next to her. Probably in his role as her newly appointed bodyguard, though—please God—there soon wouldn't be much to threaten any of the Lang sisters. The university people had their stupid jaguar heads back and as far as she knew, they'd found no evidence that Pakal had commissioned baby jaguar statues.

Their mother, Patricia, sat ramrod straight, dry-eyed, next to an empty seat. Symbolic? She'd lost her husband years ago when he'd abandoned them all in search of treasure. Thankfully, Charli had figured out that she didn't have nearly the same sense of wanderlust as her father. And that nothing could compare to the love of a good man.

Heath spread his arm behind her, his fingers warm on her shoulder.

The service began, a pastor Charli had never met walking up to speak about her father. The guy had never met David Lang either, opting to make benign comments about his work and the discoveries he'd made that contributed to the world's knowledge of Maya history and culture. But she knew there was so much more to him than that, layers upon layers she and her sisters had no opportunity to uncover now that he was dead.

She'd almost missed how like her father she was. She'd been so busy trying to paint Heath with the wrong brush that she'd never realized how David Lang's abandonment had shaped his family into people who could easily repeat his mistakes.

But she wasn't going to. Heath deserved 110 percent and she would give it to him as long as he would accept it.

As the pastor invited anyone who wished to share memories to come up, Veronica was the only one to stand. Ironic since she couldn't possibly remember their father too well. He'd left when she'd still been pretty young. Her bold, brilliant sister had the knack for words, though. That's how she'd won all those cases, not because of her fancy degrees.

Paxton watched her sister with careful attention, but he did that with everything. Charli hoped he would provide a lovely distraction for Veronica while she was in town, but the odds of lightning striking three times for the Lang sisters didn't seem very high. Especially not since Veronica still seemed to have unresolved feelings for Jeremy—otherwise, she would have blown off their breakup a long time ago.

The pastor closed the service soon after, leaving the family to receive the condolences of David's acquaintances from when he'd lived at the ranch and probably some people who had known Charli's grandpa.

Heath leaned down to kiss her temple, pulling her tighter into his side via the arm he'd kept slung around her waist the entire time. "You doing okay?"

She nodded. "I'll be a lot better when you can put your hat back on. It's weird to see you without it."

Grinning, he ran his free hand through the ridiculous curls at his neck. "You love my hair."

She did. It was her favorite thing to wake up with her fingers tangled up in his hair. He had a new scar on his leg, a near match to the one near his throat that he'd earned during an operation in Kandahar, but she got to fall asleep against his very lived-in body every night. She liked to think that the sheer force of her love had gone a long way toward healing all the hurts inside him.

He'd certainly made up for lost time loving her hurts away.

Some two hours later, Charli got sick of playing hostess. There were only so many times you could smile and nod when people talked about a man you'd never known. She retreated to Sophia's office, which was apparently her office too since her sister had bought her a desk and her own chair. Charli half sat, half fell into it, a different kind of chair than the one Sophia used, and it wasn't too bad. More comfortable for sure.

Veronica followed her into the office and Sophia poked her head in a moment later.

"Is this where we're hanging out to avoid all the mourners?" Sophia asked and slipped inside, shutting the door to lean against it. "Man, I love Mom, but she owes us for this."

"It's been interesting seeing how many people had good things to say about Dad after all this time," Charli allowed and jerked her chin in Veronica's direction. "At least we got to spend some quality time together. Have you decided what you're doing next?"

Her younger sister shrugged. "I don't know. I was thinking I might stick around for a little while, if you don't think I'll be in the way."

"No, not at all," Sophia said at the same time Charli said, "Yes, you'll absolutely be in the way."

But then she grinned. "I'm just kidding. We all know 'stick around' is code for 'I'd like to make kissy faces with Paxton.'"

Veronica didn't laugh. "I'm not sure that's going anywhere. I was thinking about writing a book, though. About the treasure and Dad's role in finding it. I was really inspired by what the pastor said at the service. And I don't remember him at all. It feels like a nice way to connect with him."

Biting back the negative comments instantly forming, Charli just raised her brows. "That sounds great."

Sophia's phone pinged and she glanced at it, then up at Charli, her expression puzzled. "Uh, Ace says you should go to the window."

What in the world? Charli jumped to her feet and strode over to the big picture window that overlooked the yard, Veronica and Sophia scarcely a half inch behind her. Heath stood there, obviously waiting for her. And wearing his battered Stetson, which he pointed to and flashed her a thumbs-up.

What an adorable goof. She nearly opened the window to yell out something about how it would be more of an improvement if he'd turn around so she could appreciate the rear view, when Paxton appeared with something wide and white in his hand. He handed it to Heath, who turned the card to the window.

It said:

This is my shame sign video.

Paxton pulled out his phone to start recording it, which felt silly when Charli was standing here watching the whole thing, but the fact that he'd held himself to the letter of their bet put a strange lump in her throat.

That alone propelled her toward the latch. She threw up the sash and called out, "We already established that we both won. What are you doing?"

He held his fingers to his lips and pulled the lead card away from the stack to shuffle it to the back. The second one read:

I made a bet with Charli Lang that I could change her mind about men. Except she changed my mind about everything.

The third one read:

The bet was never about winning but about Charli putting me through my paces so I could become husband material.

Oh, man, he was going to make her cry. She shoved a palm against her lips as Sophia grabbed her arm and held on. The fourth one read:

Charli told me I didn't need the practice, but that's only because she makes it easy to love her.

The fifth one read:

And honestly, I never dreamed about being anyone's husband but hers. Charlotte Lang, will you marry me?

Aw, dang it. That broke the dam, and she laughed through her tears as he got down on one knee and held up a ring box. She didn't bother to go around, just vaulted through the open window to the yard, and sprinted to the man she loved. Who caught her easily when she flung herself into his arms, despite being off-center.

"I like the way you do shame videos," she told him and held on to the brim of his hat as she kissed him with every ounce of the gale force winds inside her.

"Is that a yes?" he asked between kisses. "Because I have to send this video to my mom and she's going to want to know the answer."

"I don't know. Maybe we should practice some more so we can be sure I'm wife material."

"I already know," he growled. "You're everything I want and then some."

A few more tears fell to her cheeks as she nodded and held up her finger so he could slide on the ring. "You know a wedding counts as a date, right?"

And then they were both laughing, though Heath had a shiny glint in his eyes as well.

The Cowboy Experience represented a chance to change her fate, to find a place to belong, and that's exactly what had happened, just not the way she'd imagined it. Thank God. She'd found Heath. A cowboy who definitely had to be experienced to be believed. He was exactly what she'd needed but never dreamed would be possible.

* * * * *

LET'S TALK

Romance

For exclusive extracts, competitions and special offers, find us online:

f MillsandBoon

X @MillsandBoon

◉ @MillsandBoonUK

♪ @MillsandBoonUK

Get in touch on 01413 063 232